Betrayed in Blood

OF BLOOD AND DREAMS - BOOK SIX

KIM ALLRED

BETRAYED IN BLOOD
Of Blood and Dreams, Book 6
KIM ALLRED

Published by Storm Coast Publishing, LLC

Print edition October 2024
ISBN 978-1-953832-37-5

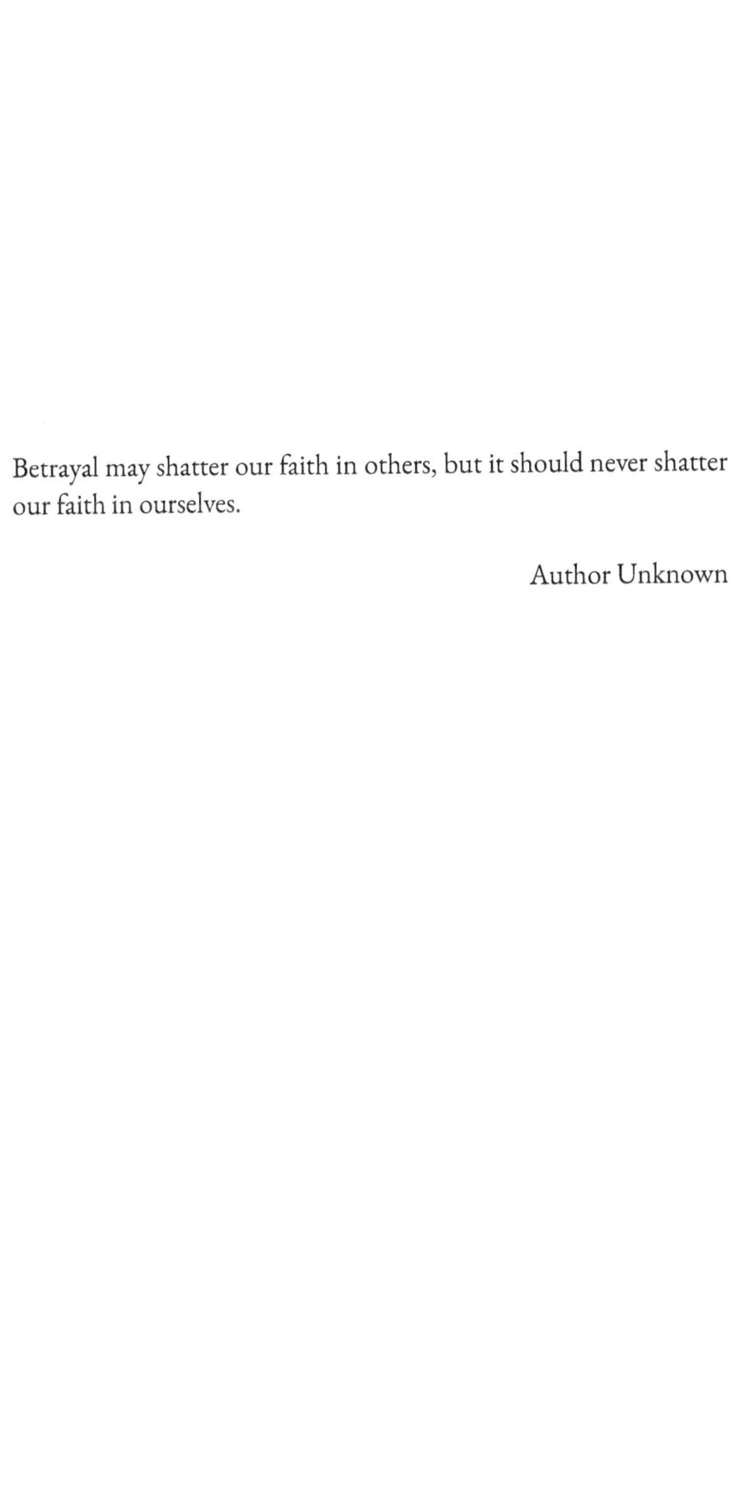

Betrayal may shatter our faith in others, but it should never shatter our faith in ourselves.

Author Unknown

Chapter One

MADRID, Spain - Present Day

BEADS OF SWEAT dampened my brow and the edges of my cream-colored sundress. The sangria worked its magic in cooling me down and contributed to my not giving a damn how wilted I looked. I glanced across the table of the sidewalk cafe where Devon Trelane lounged. He wore crisp linen pants and a long-sleeved shirt rolled up to mid-forearm and unbuttoned enough for me to get a decent look at his chest.

A new fact I'd learned was that a vamp's body temperature self-regulated in most climates. It had something to do with the magic of their blood. They would suffer the same as humans in extreme temps, but in this earlier-than-usual heat wave, he looked as fresh as a GQ model, his hair pristine and not one ounce of visible sweat.

"We could go back to the hotel and enjoy the refreshing view of the city from inside our air-conditioned suite." He wouldn't go for it without some encouragement, so I batted my eyes suggestively, but he just stared off into the distance, his mirrored sunglasses masking his thoughts.

He turned his aviator glasses on me. "I'd like to visit the National Archaeological Museum."

"Really? After all that time at the Renaud Library?"

"It has an impressive collection of ancient artifacts from the human royal families dating back centuries." When I didn't look persuaded, he added, "It's air-conditioned."

He knew me too well. I sucked down the rest of the sangria and stood. Perhaps a bit too fast; I swayed. "Let's go." I ignored the temporary double vision.

Devon was beside me in a nano-second, wrapping an arm around my waist. He felt my forehead. "You might have heat exhaustion."

"Maybe I just drank the sangria too fast."

"Your second sangria in extreme temperatures. You're used to life on the coast. I should have been more thoughtful."

I pulled him closer, my head falling back to stare up at him. "I might have miscalculated my ability to combine the two. But they were really tasty."

He grinned. "Maybe returning to the hotel isn't such a bad idea."

"Oh, no. You passed on that invitation, mister. Besides, the museum is closer." I ran a hand through his hair and pulled him down for a long, sensuous kiss, tongues colliding, promises made. "But, if you swear we'll only walk around the exhibits once, there might be a solid chance of spending the rest of the day in bed."

After setting a floppy hat back on my head, he led me down the street, holding hands. Who thought a vamp would hold hands in public? Well, maybe Lucas. Ginger had that vamp wrapped around her little finger.

"The first walk around the Renaud library was to rule out suspicious vampires, while the second was to peruse the collection."

"And confirm the *De første dage* was out for restoration like at all the other libraries."

"Exactly. Since you've been so good at allowing me a day of my favorite places, how about dinner with exquisite cuisine and a rooftop view? Candlelight, good wine—"

"Master Trelane."

Devon tensed, and all talk of a romantic dinner evaporated. We turned around, splitting apart for a more defensible position.

I smiled when I spotted the blond-haired vamp, who stood a few feet away, his hands held out to show he didn't have a weapon. Devon, on the other hand, was expressionless at the unexpected intrusion.

The vamp had an easy smile that could charm the pants off anyone—male or female. He glanced at the building behind us. "The Museo Arqueológico Nacional." Erik, who always seemed to take the lead over his brother in striking up a conversation, pointed at the building. "A fine selection for an afternoon of leisure. And to see La Dama de Elche is worth the trip to Madrid alone."

Devon didn't respond, and when he bent to the right to look beyond the Oslo twin, I followed his line of sight. If there was one, the other had to be close.

And there he was. Ulrik leaned against a midnight-blue Rolls Royce limo. His smile was broad, and he wasn't looking at Devon or his brother. His smile was for me, and I waved.

Devon glanced at me, and though this face was expressionless with those damn sunglasses still concealing his eyes, I could only assume that he was mentally shaking his head. I put my arm down, but it was difficult to hold back the grin.

These were friends. Weren't they?

Devon turned his attention back to Erik. "I have a feeling I won't be seeing La Dama de Elche today."

"Sad but true. It's unfortunate. Perhaps on your way out of town. But Aramburu is a busy man, which is why we were late in collecting you." He held an arm out toward the car. "If you would be so kind, we have a long drive to El Recinto."

"Will we be remaining there as his guest?" Devon asked.

I stepped closer to Devon. The fog from the sangria had cleared, and I no longer cared about the oppressive heat. The Oslo twins wouldn't harm us, but there were cryptic vamp non-verbals at play. Maybe they were just sizing each other up and not testing boundaries. I had to remember Devon hadn't met them before.

"For a day or two. Schedules have been rearranged, and a room prepared."

When we reached the car, Ulrik had the rear passenger door open and waved us inside.

"We'll need to stop at the hotel." Devon looked at the twins. He was firm on that point.

"Not necessary," Ulrik said. "We took the liberty of having the maid collect your things. Your bags are in the trunk."

When Devon's jaw clenched and his posture turned rigid, I expected the twins to take a step back. I was surprised when they held their ground.

"Don't worry. Your weapons are safely stored and will be returned to you once your visit is over."

When Devon stood at the open door but didn't get in, Erik shrugged and entered first. I glanced at Devon, and he nodded. This was apparently not the welcome reception he'd been expecting. And I had to admit, checking us out of the hotel seemed like they didn't trust us.

On the other hand, House Aramburu had survived for centuries outside vampire society. Perhaps Aramburu was itchy, even with allies. Though he tried to hide it from me, Devon had been a bundle of nerves since we landed in Madrid.

I climbed in, and Devon followed. We sat on the plush bench seat while the twins took seats across from us. The driver wasted no time in pulling away from the curb.

"I know these aren't standard procedures among allies, but

Aramburu is an extremely cautious vampire who wants his visitors safe. There has been a recent increase in interlopers." Erik continued his warm smile as if this were just another day at the office.

"Venizi?"

Ulrik shrugged. "Who's to say? They don't get much of a chance to speak."

Yikes. A take-no-prisoner defense.

Erik poured drinks as they settled into the drive. It would be more peaceful if Devon relaxed, but his tension was a palpable presence. Ulrik ignored us and focused on the rear window or—if I had to guess—searched for anyone who might be following us.

Thirty minutes rolled by as Erik provided a running commentary on the city and the local customs as we traveled into the countryside.

"Tell me, Erik." Devon lifted his empty glass, and the vamp refilled it. "What are the Oslo twins doing in Spain working for Aramburu?"

"Look outside. It's warm many months of the year. It might get cold during the evenings, but El Recinto is below snow levels most of the winter."

Ulrik glanced over. "And we travel a great deal."

"I'm dying to know. How did you get off Venizi's island?" I asked. If they were offended by my not-so-subtle question about whether they escaped on their own or if Lorenzo let them go, they didn't show it.

Erik laughed, and even Ulrik, still focused on the traffic behind us, grinned. "Fortunately, Venizi was more interested in the two of you than us. We were able to leave with the other guests. Then we thought it might be the best time to leave the country."

"But you were fighting his security teams," I pressed.

"In the mansion, yes. But so were others who felt the need to defend themselves in the confusion. Once we were outside, our weapons unseen, it was easy to blend into the crowd. We were delayed leaving the ship once we reached the mainland, but it wasn't our faces they were searching for."

Devon squeezed my hand, signaling he was satisfied with the response. For now.

An hour passed before the car slowed and turned into a small hamlet. The place appeared deserted.

"Are you armed?" Erik asked.

Devon nodded while Ulrik opened a concealed panel by his armrest and removed a sword, handing it to Erik before pulling out another.

"And the lovely Cressa?"

"I have my dagger." I glanced around but didn't see the threat Erik must have seen.

The car turned behind an old mission-style church and slowed to a stop.

"We have unwanted visitors following us," Erik said. "We had to wait to reach guarded territory before allowing them to get any closer to El Recinto. Normally, I wouldn't ask our guests to participate, but there are two cars, so this might be more than Ulrik and I can take care of before our chase car arrives. They typically remain a mile behind us." He opened the door and got out.

Devon followed, and I scurried out of the limo after him. Once Ulrik joined us, we turned to face the two cars that pulled into the dirt lot.

A sundress wasn't my choice to wear to a fight, but at least the flared skirt wasn't restrictive. The sandals might be cumbersome, and while not offering much protection for my feet, they fit comfortably enough.

There were four vamps in each car. Eight vamps to our five after the driver shut off the Rolls and stepped in line next to us. I'd seen Ulrik and Erik in action on several occasions, and they had impressive skills. But I had no idea of the opposing vamps' abilities and breathed a bit easier knowing a backup car wasn't far behind.

After a few minutes of staring at us, one of the vamps stepped in front of the others. "We can make this easy. We have no wish to anger Aramburu, but we need you to relinquish Trelane and his human whore to us. They have much to answer for back in the States."

The anger boiled off Devon. I guessed it might have been the whore comment. It irritated me, considering Lorenzo's plans for me while on his island, but I doubted these vamps would understand. And rather than me having to hold Devon back, he grabbed my wrist, keeping me at his side.

I slowly relaxed my grip on the dagger.

Erik took a step closer to me. "Aramburu will not allow interference with his business meetings. He has no care about House issues in the States. If your Master has business with House Trelane, he can wait until Trelane returns home. Your interference in Spain is neither wanted nor acceptable. I suggest you turn around and return to the airport."

The other vamp grinned and made a demonstration of counting how many vamps were on each side. "I think you're outnumbered."

I'd been so comfortable in the airconditioned Rolls, and though it was a touch cooler at the higher elevation, it was still miserably warm. And I was irritated by Venizi's gall. The twins might not be certain who sent these vamps, but no one else had a large enough beef with Devon to chase us to Spain. Add in the realization that my first meeting with Aramburu would be in a blood-streaked sundress, my emotions escalated to highly pissed off.

I pulled away from Devon and took a step forward. They want to mess with the human whore, then let's see if they had game.

"I've had enough of this bullshit. You want a piece of Trelane's whore—come and get me. It's a hell of a lot better than being Venizi's mesmerized slut."

The vamps' eyes bulged. I gave them my best demonic smile. I doubted it compared to Simone's fang-filled grin or Sergi's scary-as-hell leer, but the lead vamp glanced at the others standing next to me.

"What? Scared of a little human female?"

That did it. The vamp launched himself, and I didn't wait. I ran to meet him. Devon would be pissed, but he'd only be a step behind.

I couldn't use my favored surfboard maneuver where I leaped, kicked them in the chest, and followed them to the ground, standing on them as I slashed them with my dagger. Not in sandals. But I had other maneuvers to choose from, and as much as this was going to hurt, this vamp was going down.

When he was almost on me, I dropped and rolled, hitting him in the legs and taking him down like a bowling pin. I grimaced at the road rash on my arms and legs as I leaped up. The vamp was shaking his head, coming up on a knee, and I stabbed him in the back of the neck. While he leaned on his knee, I stabbed a kidney, this time twisting the knife. He dropped.

The first ones were always easy. It didn't matter whether any of them had been told not to mess around with Trelane's female—they never listened. One mark in my favor. But once they saw me in action, their doubts fled, and the next one wouldn't be as effortless.

I didn't waste time after I pulled my dagger, ready for the next one. When Devon yelled, "Duck," I wasn't sure he meant me, but I dropped like a stone. I felt a slice along my back as a vamp stumbled by. I leaped into a crouch. The sting on my back confirmed I'd been cut, but it must have only been skin deep because my legs and arms still worked.

The vamp who nicked me ran a few more steps before a sword took his head.

Erik gave me a quick salute before engaging another vamp.

I searched for Devon. He fought two vamps who were covered in blood. Crimson soaked one of Devon's sleeves. The Oslo twins and the driver were still engaged with a dwindling number of Venizi vamps, so I ran for Devon.

One vamp fell after a dicey stab to his middle before Devon twisted to block the second one who came at him. Rather than get in his way, I went after the first vamp. His wounds were sufficient to keep him immobile. When he saw me coming, he managed to get to his feet, if a bit wobbly.

I didn't slow down, and this time, I used my jumping round-house kick, twisting and leaping to clip his jaw. I landed on my feet and ducked as he swung his sword. The air whistled by. That was close. But I ignored it and came up with my blade, driving it into his chest.

Before I could twist the blade, arms pulled me back, and I struggled until a sword took the vamp's head.

I glanced up to see Ulrik smiling, his sword and shirt drenched in blood.

"It's over." Devon's words calmed me, and I leaned into him, breathing hard.

Erik strolled over and glared at the head. Then he grinned at me. "Your skills have improved."

I turned to take in the scene. Bodies and heads were strewn everywhere, and Aramburu's second car had arrived. Venizi never sent the right number of vamps when he went after his enemy. It wouldn't take long before he stopped making that mistake.

"Did we lose anyone?" I asked.

"No," Erik said.

"You didn't save anyone for questioning?" Devon asked.

"Aramburu doesn't take prisoners. He doesn't ask questions. If you come at him, he responds with deadly force."

"Will you return them?"

Erik spat on the dead vamp at his feet. "Whether it was Venizi or not, vamps not returning home are a strong enough message. The bodies will be burned in the pit." He took a moment to study Devon and then me. "You have no major injuries?"

When we both shook our heads, he nodded toward the church. "We typically use this spot for clearing away anyone foolish enough to follow us. The church appears abandoned, but it has running water and private rooms to clean up. We try to keep blood out of the Rolls. You have thirty minutes. Aramburu will be most angered by this." Then his smile returned. "But it will be tempered by stories of our fair Cressa and her battle cry as she engaged the enemy."

I stared at him, then at Devon. "I don't have a battle cry."

Devon just smiled.

Chapter Two

DEVON and I cleaned up quickly, and we were soon on our way. The limo cruised through low mountain ranges for another ten miles before reaching a plateau, green from spring rains and winter snow melt from the higher elevations.

Devon leaned forward. "What's that?"

I scooted farther in my seat to look through the front windshield. I squinted, not sure what I was seeing. It appeared to be a fortress, but all I could see—if what I was looking at was more than a mirage—were tall walls that seemed to stretch forever.

"We have reached El Recinto," Erik said. "The name of the compound is much longer, but over time it has become easier to just say El Recinto. Aramburu's land is vast. As I said earlier, we were well onto his land when we reached the old monastery. What you see before you is the main entrance. It sits in the middle of Aramburu territory and is well protected from outsiders."

I huddled next to Devon, our heads bent low to take in the scene as the limo approached the ten-foot-high walls. Two steel gates, browned with age, blocked the entrance.

"I can't see where the wall ends." I heard the awe in my voice, but no other emotion seemed appropriate. I'd never seen anything like it.

"This reminds me of the early fortresses in Asia." Devon sat back, pulling me with him, holding me close.

Erik and Ulrik both grinned. "You're in store for much more."

The gates opened on their approach. Two guard stations, one on each side, were constructed as an extension of the wall. A video monitor had been built into its own stone encasement and stood just outside the guard station. With all the security before we reached El Recinto, I wasn't sure when the video was ever used. Perhaps it was for when supplies were brought in.

The limo never slowed on its approach, and once we were past the wall, I turned to watch the gates close behind us. Devon squeezed my hand and the nerves that had been twitching settled. The landscape wasn't any different on this side, and it was another mile before the first outbuildings could be seen.

Devon tapped my shoulder and pointed to our right. I was pretty sure my mouth dropped open. There was an enormous hangar and a runway long enough for a private jet to take off and land. Cows and sheep roamed around it, grazing on what appeared to be prairie grass similar to the land around Oasis.

Most of the outbuildings were maintenance sheds based on the utility trucks parked near them, and it was another half mile before the outbuildings turned into homes with children playing outside and women tending gardens. After another quarter of a mile, another wall could be seen. This one appeared to be shorter, perhaps eight feet tall, and I could see the end of the wall, though it ran the length of a football field on each side of another gate. There were towers at the corners with at least one guard in each one. Along the top of the wall, I glimpsed another guard. The entire wall must have a walkway between each tower.

This time the gates were wrought iron, though tall wooden doors were mounted on each side that could be closed over the iron gates for additional defense. It was impressive.

The gates stood open, providing a more welcoming feel than the first gates we'd passed through. Inside was a floral masterpiece accented by olive and oak trees. The manor was as large as Oasis but built in the Spanish hacienda style with a tiled veranda and curved arches.

The limo drove around the fountain that sat in the middle of the circular drive and pulled to a stop in front of a wide but short set of stairs. The driver opened the door, and Erik got out first, followed by Devon, with me right behind him.

I pressed my sweaty palms along the folds of my sky-blue sundress and glanced around. It took a moment before the wooden front doors, each with a large lion sconce on them, opened as two vampires strode out. I was getting better at recognizing vampires by the tiny inflections they made and how they held themselves, but in this case, there was no question these two ruled El Recinto.

It was also obvious the two were related.

The only thing that gave away which one might be Gregor Aramburu, the House leader, was the touch of gray along his temples that quickly disappeared into thick black hair that touched the top of his collar and framed an arresting face. He had a broad forehead, a bent nose, and dark eyes that were currently dancing with pleasure, but I sensed they could easily change to anger. He wasn't tall, just under six feet, with a robust chest and a tan, weathered face. This was someone who spent a lot of time outdoors, not the typical ancient vamp partial to the dark.

The vampire next to him resembled Gregor, except he was a couple of inches taller. His midnight-colored hair was cut in a stylish manner with the top longer than the sides, and with his goatee, he gave off a roguish aura. He was handsome, but his eyes were similar to his father's—easily turning to displeasure—though they currently matched the smile on his face.

"Devon Trelane." The older man held out his hand. "This

meeting is a long time coming. I'm Gregor Aramburu, and this is my oldest, Alejandro."

"I appreciate the invitation to your home."

The men shook hands then Gregor's focused gaze turned on me. His smile was as warm as his hands. "So, this is the lovely Cressa that Erik and Ulrik talk so much about."

I blushed. What else could I do? Everyone was staring at me. "It's nice to meet you, but I'm sure they've exaggerated whatever tall tales they've shared."

"If my own guards didn't watch you eliminate the threat to my land upon your arrival..." He turned and spat, "Vermin." Then his smile returned. "Perhaps I could believe your self-deprecation. But let's not talk of that unpleasantness. I'm sure you would both like to get settled, though I prefer to give you a quick tour of El Recinto. By then your luggage will be taken to your suite. Your weapons will be stored down the hall from your room, though you won't need them here."

"I'm eager to hear more about your estate." Devon turned to scan the yard. "I do all of my business at my coastal manor, but I have a second discreet location that isn't nearly the size of yours. I'm working to make it as secure, though."

We followed Gregor down the steps with Alejandro bringing up the rear. A golf cart that accommodated six pulled up in front of the steps. The driver got out, and Gregor climbed into the driver's seat. Devon took the seat next to him while I climbed into the second row next to Alejandro.

Erik and Ulrik waved as the golf cart took off.

"I'm sorry my wife wasn't here to meet you, but she'll be back in time for an early dinner along with my other children. El Recinto is approximately nine hundred square miles—or five hundred thousand acres, give or take. The walls took four decades to complete."

"It encompasses the entirety of El Recinto?" Devon asked.

"About half. We'll discuss this more at dinner, but I'd seen firsthand the corruption building in the Council and decided the only way to protect my House was to build a fortress. Of course, this was many centuries ago, and no one questioned one more stronghold."

"You own an incredible amount of land. Have you never had problems with the government?"

Gregor laughed. A deep belly laugh that made me smile. "Oh, sí. But even the most incorruptible government doesn't say no to compensation. It's a simple matter of negotiation. It doesn't hurt to have a few vampires scattered within all levels of government to ensure we're left alone.

"We're fairly self-efficient here. This was a village several centuries ago. Then it grew to be the Family's sanctuary. We have several businesses within the tech industry. The corporate office is in Madrid, mostly to keep up appearances, but all the work is done here. Most of the people within our walls work for the company and make good money."

"Does no one leave here?" I asked.

"Most of the population are indigenous Spaniards who tend to stay close to home. For those who have the desire to leave, either for holiday or permanently, or those who travel for business, we have procedures in place to ensure the privacy of El Recinto." He glanced over his shoulder and gave me a warm smile. "Everyone here is a value to the community, and we have rigorous induction training for new members, though it's not often we welcome new vampires or humans."

Gregor drove through the village that boasted several businesses—a general market, a hardware store, two small restaurants, two bars, a movie theater playing a current movie, and a laundromat. On the other side of the village, Gregor pointed out the modern medical center and attached two-story hospital.

He drove on through pastures with more cattle and sheep and fields planted with various crops—some I recognized, others I didn't. Where there had been many houses surrounding the village, the farther we drove, the sparser the homes.

Gregor Aramburu and Devon fell into a discussion about business as my mind wandered. Alejandro contributed occasionally to the conversation while I focused my curiosity on what incident, or combination of them, had forced Gregor to isolate their family. They seemed a long way from the rulings of the Council, but I was never patient enough to listen to Anna's deep history lessons to understand how the Council worked centuries earlier before they moved to the States. From the information I'd read regarding House Aramburu, it had been a warrior House like so many others of those times. Now it seemed the Family had embraced technology.

Out of the blue, a stabbing pain pierced my head. I clutched the seat in front of me as I doubled over. Multiple voices slammed into me, most speaking Spanish, a few in English, not that I could make sense of any of it.

I wasn't in the golf cart anymore.

The table was in the middle of a quaint restaurant. My stomach grumbled at the scent of cooking fish and a savory dish, perhaps paella. I was wearing the same sundress and sandals. The other tables were filled with customers eating and those closest to me were speaking in Spanish. No one appeared to notice me.

I searched the room for the dreamwalker who'd brought me there. My first inclination was to force them into one of my own constructs, but my automatic defenses kicked in. This wasn't the time to show my hand.

Was someone testing me?

If it had been Colantha, she wouldn't be playing games. It was impossible to tell how strong the construct was without pushing back. I glanced around and realized the people looked similar to the locals in the village we'd just driven through.

Then it hit me.

Gregor had a dreamwalker.

They were somewhere close. I gave in to my curiosity and reached out to test the boundaries—but not too much. A Goldilocks approach to test how hot the porridge was.

Then I spotted him.

He was trying to ignore me. So was the woman he was sitting with. He was young—younger than me—with thin, straight dark hair that could use a comb, a flat nose, and a round face.

The woman was much older, based on the few wrinkles I could see from her profile. Her aquiline nose and sharp chin made me think the two weren't related, but it was only a guess. A long braid of silver hair trailed down her back to her hips. Her dress was similar to those around her—colorful and plain at the same time.

"Who are you?" I asked.

They seemed surprised that I spoke but continued to ignore me. I stood and stormed to their table.

"Tell me who you are."

They stared up at me, surprise flashing in their wide gazes. Then I realized my mistake. They had pulled me into their construct but hadn't expected me to take partial control. I'd been so busy wondering who the hell these people were that I hadn't paid attention to the momentary tug. The power in their attempt to control me was no stronger than a child grasping my arm to pull me back. I'd blown right through it without realizing they had been trying to hold me in place.

Then the voices came again. Dozens of them.

I pressed my hands to my head, trying to make them go away. I focused, remembering the candles Colantha used in her sessions. Within a blink, thin, tapered candles in tall, free-standing candelabras suddenly appeared in the middle of the restaurant. I held my attention on a single flame, closed my eyes, and—knowing this was going to hurt—ripped myself out of the construct.

The light was blinding before darkness descended.

～

I OPENED my eyes then slammed them shut against the harsh light. Muffled voices rose in anger and then quieted. I slowly opened one eye. I didn't recognize the room, and for a moment, I couldn't remember where I was.

Aramburu.

Dreamwalkers.

Now it made sense. Well, it didn't, but at least I understood what happened. A dull pain thumped from the back of my head.

The suite was richly decorated with all the standard features, yet the decor was minimalistic, with a single painting on each wall and a couple of knickknacks on the dressers.

I gingerly pulled myself into a sitting position and immediately noted the familiar colored vials on the nightstand. The bed was king-sized and comfortable. I was still in my sundress though the covers had been thrown over me.

I didn't know if they'd given me any drugs while I'd been passed out. The liquid in the pink vial wouldn't hurt me, so I drank half of it then leaned my head against the headboard, giving the liquid time to work its magic.

I took the opportunity to take a longer look around the room. The first thing I zeroed in on was our luggage, which had been unpacked. Clothes hung just beyond an arched doorway that must lead to a walk-in closet. Another door was opened to what I assumed was the bathroom.

I sat up and swung my legs to the floor, placing a hand on the bed as I waited for the dizziness to stop. The potion would need another five minutes to work, but I stood and made my way to a marble and glass bathroom.

Whatever voices I'd heard earlier were gone. I splashed cold water on my face and, keeping the water cold, wet a washcloth and placed it on the back of my neck. The headache was all but gone, but I was still unstable on my feet.

I was leaning against the doorjamb, holding the rag on my neck, when the door opened. Devon peeked his head in, his focus on the empty bed. When he spotted me, he rushed over and pulled me into his arms.

His hug was fierce as he laid his cheek on my head. "Are you alright?"

"A bit dizzy." My voice was muffled with my face pressed against his chest.

He took the rag from me and walked me to a chair by the window. It wasn't until then that I noticed the drapes had been closed, and the light that had bothered me earlier had been from a simple lamp.

"Is it alright if I open the drapes and let some fresh air in? You seem chilled, and the warmer air might feel better."

It couldn't hurt, and I nodded. "Gregor has dreamwalkers close by."

"That had been my guess, but he won't discuss it with me. I didn't think we were within Colantha's range."

"What happened? I remember pulling myself out of the construct, but then it was light's out."

"I'm not sure how long you were in the construct before I noticed. We'd been deep in conversation, and when I looked back, I immediately noticed you were in a construct."

I smiled. "I guess all those sessions with Colantha paid off."

He stood and walked to a cart that held a bar. He poured a glass of water from a clay pitcher and handed it to me before sitting in the chair across from me, a round table between us.

I drank half of it before setting it down.

"I yelled for Gregor to stop, terrified you'd fall out, until I noticed Alejandro was holding your wrist. At first, I thought he might have been the one who took you to a construct, then realized he was merely holding you in place."

"I don't remember seeing him in the construct. There were two dreamwalkers—a young man, maybe a year or two younger than me, and an older woman. They were surprised when I strode up to them before I pulled myself out." I reached across the table and grabbed his arm. "They must be close. I was in a restaurant that I swear had to be one of those in the village."

He nodded. "When Gregor refused to respond to whether he had dreamwalkers, he seemed amused. When you came out of it, you collapsed, and he rushed us back to the manor. He immediately called for his healer, who lives close by."

"I assumed a healer had been by when I saw the vials."

"Did you take one?"

"Half the pink one." I picked up the washrag Devon had placed on the table and folded it. "The headache is mostly gone. I don't know for sure, but my guess is that the two of them had to combine their powers to bring me to the construct."

"What does that mean?"

"I'm not sure, but if I had to guess, I'd say they aren't powerful enough to do it on their own. They were sitting at a table together, and I was a couple of tables away." I brushed back my hair and glanced out the window to a colorful garden. Spring blooms dotted the flower beds, and another fountain took center stage. The tinkling water was augmented by the twitter of birds that flocked to it. "They were attempting to hold me in place, but I didn't realize it until I felt the gentle tug when I stood." I snorted. "They seemed rather shocked when I walked to their table. When they ignored me, I pulled myself out."

"Why the headache? If they're not that strong, why did you pass out?"

That was an excellent question. I winced when I shook my head, but it was more an expectation of pain from a returning headache that never materialized. "I don't know." I reached for my neck, but I wasn't wearing my medallion. As far as I knew, it was still in my purse, locked in a tiny box Devon had made for it. "Maybe it was because I pulled on my powers without the medallion. How long was I out?"

"About two hours. But I think some of that might have been a combination of the heat, the fight with Lorenzo's vampires, and then the construct."

"Now what?"

"Gregor has some explaining to do, but we're guests here. He's quite aware of my dissatisfaction over the event. I don't think he's playing games, but—"

"It was a test."

Devon smiled. It wasn't his charming smile. The one that could make my panties wet in anticipation of him putting his intimate thoughts into action. It was his shark smile. The one that said he was letting things play out before calling on the beast. To be honest, that smile could also make my panties wet—as long as it wasn't in response to one of my stunts. There had certainly been more than a few times when it would have been justified.

"I agree." He glanced at his watch. "We have an hour before dinner. Feel up to a shower?" His smile said it would be more than a shower.

To prove I was back to normal, I jumped up and raced him to the bathroom, almost tripping as I pulled my dress over my head. He caught me and swept me up in his arms before slamming the bathroom door behind us with his foot.

Chapter Three

DEVON TUGGED at the sleeves of the light-gray linen jacket. Gregor had sent a note that dinner would be business casual on the back terrace. The anger he'd felt when Cressa had passed out from the surprise dream construct had been doused by their lovemaking and her words of counsel.

He hadn't needed them, but he appreciated her attempt at playing cadre when it was just the two of them. She could be as hot tempered as he, so he was surprised she didn't harbor more annoyance with being pulled into a construct.

He was a House leader, and after putting aside his concerns for Cressa, he reviewed the afternoon from Gregor's position. He didn't know Devon. They'd never met, so he could only go by what he'd heard, read, or learned from the Oslo twins.

If it had been Devon in the same position, he might have done something similar. It was one thing when two House leaders danced around each other, searching for common ground as well as possible deceit. These were dangerous times when two factions within the vampire world began taking sides while ruled by a fractured Council. Throw dreamwalkers into the mix, and everything got turned upside down.

The thought that Gregor might have his own dreamwalkers had been a shock, leaving Devon with a decision on how to play the next round. Cressa had suggested they do nothing and wait to see what Gregor did. Devon had made a mistake when he'd asked Gregor if he had a dreamwalker. Cressa could have passed out from the heat. But then why had she been in a trance with Alejandro holding her wrist?

When Devon had mentioned the word, Gregor had merely smiled. A test, to be sure, but Devon had been too worried about Cressa at the time to care. It could have been a fatal mistake if Gregor turned out to be an enemy after all. Though it was clear he had no love for Venizi, maybe he had no love for any vampire outside his House. His welcoming tour of El Recinto could have been a larger ploy.

Devon had seen little of his security other than a handful of guards and difficult-to-penetrate walls. With the manor located in the middle of thousands of privately owned acres, it was already formidable.

"Why is it you can take longer than a woman to get ready?"

He turned and devoured Cressa with his gaze. She wore a royal-blue sundress that looked delectable with her lightly tanned skin. Her sable-brown hair had been pulled back by diamond clips he'd bought at a store in Madrid. Her eyes sparkled with mischief.

Any side effects of her unexpected dreamwalk were gone. After slipping on sandals with a slight heel, she sauntered toward him. She gave him a long look, then traced her fingers down his cheeks to his shoulders before tugging on the lapels of his shirt.

"Have I told you how good you look in a suit?"

He grinned, and his cock stirred. If they only had more time. "Once or twice."

"Is that all?" Her words were nothing more than a purr.

He tugged her to him and gave her a hard, swift kiss before pushing her back a step. "You play a dangerous game."

Her laugh was throaty as she took a last look in a mirror. "I have to warn you. I'll be on my best behavior, but Pandora is itching to play."

She rarely mentioned her alter ego, her street name when she'd been a thief. Well, she was still a thief, and as she walked out the door, he remembered one other thing. Something they hadn't spoken of since her first days at the manor, which seemed longer ago than the several months it had been. She owed him a debt. A financial debt in which he'd released The Wolf in trade for a thief.

He pushed it aside. There wasn't time for that here. He caught up to her as they strode down the hallway, and he reached for her hand. "All I can ask is that Pandora remembers her decorum."

She patted his arm, and if she was going to respond, she held her tongue as they reached the Oslo twins, who waited for them at the end of the hall. Both vampires gave Cressa a long appraisal.

"I'm glad to see our Cressa looks well." Erik partially bowed as he held out an arm, directing them to the left. "I understand the heat might have been too much."

Before Devon could respond, Cressa laughed. "Don't worry. I can take the heat."

"There was never a doubt." Erik led them through the manor decorated with a combination of ancient weapons, fine sculptures, and superb artwork. Not overly masculine or feminine, it was a beautiful home.

The expansive sunroom opened on one side to a terrace where a long table overlooked the same garden visible from their room. Gregor waited for them, drink in hand as he leaned against a stone and wrought iron railing while he spoke to a vampire with his same features. Not Alejandro, but another son.

He turned when they approached, setting down his glass so he could take both of Cressa's hands. "I must apologize for my earlier deception, but you'll soon understand."

Cressa didn't waver from his gaze. "I'll expect nothing less." While the threat seemed to register with Gregor, Cressa's huge smile was difficult to ignore, and with an understanding nod, he returned her smile.

"The more time we spend together, the more I understand Erik and Ulrik's fascination with you. Come, meet the rest of my family."

The vampire he'd been speaking to was Miguel, his second oldest, who gave Cressa the European greeting of touching cheeks before shaking Devon's hand.

"I look forward to the time you'll be spending here. I don't believe Father has mentioned it yet, but I'll be giving you a tour of our offices. I believe we have some similar interests."

"I look forward to that as well." Devon turned when a young female vampire gave them the same warm greeting.

"I'm Mariah, the youngest."

"But the fiercest," said another male vampire. He had a fire in his gaze Devon had yet to see in the others, which was no doubt held just beneath the surface. "I'm Ernesto." He put an arm around his sister's shoulder. "Mariah leads our security teams."

Mariah elbowed him. "Don't embarrass me." She turned to Devon and Cressa. "Ernesto is a fine soldier, but he spends too much time chasing females."

If her brother took offense, it was hard to tell. Cressa seemed charmed by the young vampire.

"Don't let my children fool you." Gregor had retrieved his drink. "They are all well-trained fighters, but Mariah has a natural instinct for strategy as well as tactical defenses."

"I would love to hear more," Cressa said. "I have a few tricks of my own."

Mariah's laugh was musical. "So Erik and Ulrik have told me. Perhaps while my brothers bore Devon with our company business, we can spend time in the training room."

"It's a date."

"Don't let anyone fool you about Ernesto." A dark-haired beauty, who Devon would be hard-pressed to guess her age, entered the terrace and took a glass of what looked like sangria from Erik. "Alejandro is the leader of the cadre and the family business, Miguel runs the businesses, and Ernesto has technical skills unheard of in most circles."

"You mean he's a hacker." Cressa winked at Ernesto.

"The best I've seen," Alejandro wrapped an arm around the woman and gave her a gentle kiss on the cheek. "How are you, Mother?"

She patted his hand and gave him a return kiss. "I'm feeling much better."

"This is my wife, Sonja." Gregor's eyes caressed her as he said her name.

There was true admiration and love between these two, but as Sonja grasped Devon's hand, he was in for a shock. Sonja wasn't vampire.

I WASN'T sure what was happening, but I'd sensed a change in Devon the minute he shook Sonja's hand.

Sonja gave Devon a wicked smile. "We have much to discuss over dinner. Shall we be seated?"

I gave him a questioning look, but he shook his head as he placed a hand on the small of my back and led me to our seats at the table.

Dinner was mostly vegetarian dishes served alongside salmon and halibut. Wine was abundant as the servers kept the glasses filled, but I only sipped mine. While my mental faculties were back to normal after my nap, alcohol didn't mix well with the pink potion.

Devon was tense throughout the meal, though he didn't show it as Alejandro asked about our short time in Madrid. If they found our trip to the Renaud library strange, they didn't show it. Then Ernesto spoke of the village and shared his extensive knowledge of its early beginnings centuries before. He touched on some aspects of Gregor's tour but delved deeper into the connection between the townspeople and vampires.

I'd never heard of another place where vamps and humans knowingly lived simpatico. Though I wasn't a traveler, I had to wonder if the same relationship existed in enclaves distant from the larger cities.

"You know..." Gregor looked at me as he spoke. "Those not from vampire Houses don't realize how little we're spread around the world. Places like Santiga Bay have a denser population because of the Council, but in the rest of the world, we aren't as widespread. We tend to live in or around large cities like Madrid, New Orleans, Tokyo, and the like."

"Is that so you can blend easier among the populace?" I asked.

He shrugged. "Sí, we don't stand out as much. It's also easier for locating nutrient sources and to maintain relationships among our own."

It wasn't lost on me that nutrient sources meant humans, but I nodded.

"It's a behavior from centuries ago." Devon picked up his wineglass and leaned back as the server removed his plate. "Back when wars were our way of life and when allegiances swiftly changed with each new monarch or leader."

"And once a House is established, it's very difficult to move it." Gregor waved for a server to refill his glass. "At least for the aristocracy or those Houses that serve on the Council. It can be seen as an aggressive move when relocating to another city."

"But it's okay for the smaller Houses?" I asked. This didn't seem to be anything Anna taught, or perhaps it was in her advanced courses. I held my snicker at the thought.

"It's easier, but it requires a petition and agreement from the largest House in the city." Alejandro leaned back in his chair. He didn't speak often but paid close attention to the discussion, especially when Devon spoke.

"House Aramburu has remained behind closed gates for hundreds of years." Devon glanced around the table. "Yet you seem to be quite aware of how vampire society has grown over the decades."

Gregor laughed. "You know as well as I that nothing moves that fast in vampire society, and most keep to their own kind. Not many do business with humans, let alone shifters."

Devon grinned. "Only those with no concern for the old ways or those who have been ostracized by it."

"Or those hoping to take advantage of particular situations."

"You're speaking of Venizi."

Gregor shrugged. "He's not the only one pushing for traditional ways while taking a broader step into human affairs, but yes."

"So, why did you close your gates?" Devon asked.

The table grew deathly silent, and my first instinct was to scan the room for the largest threat—Simone's and Sergi's training never far from reach. When my gaze landed on Erik and Ulrik, they appeared amused by the conversation, and while that made me feel safer, it didn't completely settle me.

Sonja placed a hand on Gregor's arm. "We've danced around the topic all night. I think it's time we put Devon's mind at ease." Her gaze locked with mine. Volumes passed between us, yet I couldn't identify any emotion. The connection was strong on a level I didn't understand.

Sonja turned to Devon. "You're wondering why Gregor married a human."

I dropped my fork, and it clattered on the plate of my half-eaten cheesecake.

She smiled. "He didn't know until we shook hands. I've lived among vampires for a long time, and one's behavior sometimes changes to match those around us." Alejandro placed his hand on hers, and she gripped it before releasing it. "Mariah is my biological daughter with Gregor, and she's vampire."

"My first wife perished long ago after giving me three strong sons." Gregor's eyes misted for the briefest of seconds. "I didn't think I'd ever find love again. Marriage," he shrugged, "maybe. But love. It's a lucky man that finds it more than once."

"So, you were born within the gates?" Devon asked Sonja. "I mean, it's been centuries since Aramburu disassociated itself from vampire society."

"I closed off my House after the Council made a decision I couldn't agree nor live with." He pushed away from the table but kept his seat, as if he needed distance from everyone to share his story. He called again for his glass to be filled.

I really hated that vamps could drink alcohol all night when, after two or three glasses, Ginger had me singing lame songs from the eighties.

"This was almost a millennia ago," Gregor continued.

"When the Council gave the order to eliminate dreamwalkers." Devon's statement rocked me. Not just because he threw it out there like it was everyday news and not some decision the Council buried so deep that dreamwalkers became nothing more than a myth. No. It was that he boldly mentioned it with a House we barely knew.

Gregor nodded. "Dreamwalkers weren't as commonplace even then, and for the most part, they kept to themselves, preferring to live in communes or small villages. This was one reason the Council thought it would be easy to eliminate what they considered to be a threat to our race." He laughed, but it wasn't a nice one. And it was the first time I witnessed what a formidable man he could quickly become. "That was when dreamwalkers ran from their homes, scattering into the wind."

"Except for here," Devon said.

I glanced at Devon. My mouth had to be gaping open. I turned my attention to the Aramburus next, their focus completely on Devon and his reactions. It hadn't occurred to me how long dreamwalkers might have lived here. I'd assumed the two who'd pulled me into the construct were the only ones at El Recinto. That they somehow sensed me and, being curious, pulled me in.

"The village was a dreamwalker community before the purge." Sonja took up the conversation. "I only learned the story from my mother and grandmother. Once they heard about the Council's ruling, they were packing, preparing to run."

"It was my mother who talked them into staying." Alejandro sat straighter, his eyes shiny with memory. "She had developed a strong connection with the village and understood what the dreamwalkers brought to vampire society." His tone turned angry. "Things the Council knew but—to use a human euphemism—decided to roll the dice on our future."

"Alejandro, let's step back a bit." Gregor's rebuke was gentle. "My son is passionate. Sorry, all my sons are." He lifted his glass toward them. "All you need to understand is that I agreed with my wife. A deep resentment toward the Council had been building long before their fatal decision. But even as powerful as my House was, I could only save the dreamwalkers in the village. So, I sent my army to protect them while I built the walls."

"How did you know about Cressa?" Devon asked.

I don't know why he changed the subject to me, but I'd been wondering the same thing. Had the two dreamwalkers reached out to me by accident or on purpose?

"We suspected." Gregor's warm smile touched on me.

I turned to Erik and Ulrik, who were still savoring their dessert. I wasn't sure if they were even listening. When the conversation quieted, they glanced up, unsure why Devon and I were looking at them.

"It wasn't them." Sonja's words refocused our gaze on her. "They were sent to monitor Devon, Venizi, and the Council. But when they met Cressa, they knew she was special, they just didn't understand why."

"Then how did you know about me?"

"Are you familiar with the Nexus?" she asked.

I shrugged. "Not a lot, but my understanding is that our power to create constructs is through our connection to the Nexus that allows us to turn psychic energy into mass... Wait." Sonja's earlier words caught up with me. "You said your mother and grandmother were ready to run. That means they were dreamwalkers."

Sonja unbuttoned the top button on her silk blouse, revealing a silver medallion. "Just like me."

I PACED along the windows of our suite, too wired to settle down. Sonja, Aramburu's wife, was a dreamwalker. The wife of a House leader was a dreamwalker. If I said it a thousand times, I wasn't sure it would sink in.

Devon stopped me and pulled me into his arms. "How about an evening swim?"

"My brain won't stop racing through all the possibilities, all the questions of who these dreamwalkers are. Does Colantha know about them? If so, why didn't she say anything when she knew where we were going?"

He chuckled and tightened his grip, no doubt feeling my erratic energy. "I'm guessing this is why Gregor suggested we retire for the evening rather than allowing you to bombard Sonja with all your questions."

I snorted. "I guess that's why he's a powerful House leader, even hidden away in the Extremadura region of Spain."

"And we also know why he walked away and closed his House on vampire society."

I squeezed his waist and stepped away, though I didn't return to my pacing. "Can you imagine keeping this secret for centuries?"

"It explains his no-questions-asked policy and a quick dispatch of interlopers."

I shuddered. He was right. If even one word had gotten out.

"What do you think the Council would have done if they discovered this?"

Devon's features hardened. "It would have caused a war and possibly a divide among the vampires, depending on which century it was discovered. Questions would be asked, but by then, it might have been too late for Aramburu and the dreamwalkers."

That blew the steam out of me. I dropped into a chair and stared out at the garden. "I wonder if they've ever felt safe in their own home."

Strong hands kneaded my shoulders, and I leaned into them. "I don't think the Oslo twins are his only eyes and ears. And as the decades have gone by, I assume he's built quite the arsenal. From what I've heard of his tech businesses, he can probably do deeper monitoring from here."

"You think he has other hackers besides Ernesto?"

"Yes. The downside is that the Council keeps a closed network. They can download information, like what the Sentinels did when they accessed the drop box Roxie set up with Gheata's files that cleared me of Boretsky's death. But they would transfer the data to their internal network. It prevents hacking unless you had access to their network within Council headquarters."

"So how would Gregor know if the Council was planning anything?"

"He'd only know by what he could glean from other Houses. And while the Council itself uses an internal network, that doesn't mean the individual Council members do so within their own Houses. But my guess is that he simply uses spies across the globe to attend parties, like the Oslo twins."

I chuckled. "Where it's fairly simple to pick up the pulse of vampire society. Ginger always said the aristocrats were the gossip network." I glanced up at Devon. "Have you heard anything from Lucas?"

"Not much, but I wouldn't expect to unless there was trouble. Sergi's last report was that Lucas was on his way to Maryland."

I leaned back; my energy had dissipated under Devon's magic hands.

"How about that swim?" Devon asked.

"How about a bath and some private time?"

He pulled me up until I was snuggled in his arms. "A much better idea."

I giggled as I wrapped my arms around his neck while he strode to the bathroom. After lavender and cedar scented bath salts were added to the hot but still bearable water, I turned to Devon while the tub filled. I took my time undressing him, kissing his lips, then other parts of his body as they were revealed once I'd slowly stripped the clothes from him, tossing them toward a bench where some landed and others slid off.

Once Devon was naked, he used the same technique for undressing me, but he moved slower, spending time nibbling at my breasts and tracing feather-light kisses down my belly. Then he knelt and lifted one of my legs over his shoulder as he explored more intimate spots.

If I hadn't been close enough to brace a hand on a wall, I would have tipped over as his tongue released all the tension from my body. Just as I relaxed into the sensations, my skin overly sensitive to touch and tingles flowing through me, I gripped his hair. He pulled away and lifted me in one practiced motion, stepping into a tub that could fit four. His muscles were so controlled that he had no problem holding me as we sank into the water, my legs next to his as I faced him. He leaned me backward as he reached the faucet to shut off the water.

Then he kissed me. It was deep, his tongue playing with mine as his hands moved over my back. We kissed for a long time, stopping to focus on other spots still above the water line before moving back to lips plump with passion.

He was hard beneath me, and I raised up until I was over him. We were in no hurry as we rocked back and forth, holding each other. No one could touch us here. The only thing on our minds was each precious moment we were together.

We stared into each other's eyes. His beast came out through the shimmering brightness of an icy blue glow that warmed to a silvery blue. They were one, and we were one.

When the water cooled, he lifted us out of the bath, stopping a quick moment for us to towel dry before he tossed me on the bed. He stood over me, and his eyes lit up with the beast. This time it would be rougher, and hotter, and I couldn't wait.

I crawled over the bed to him and smiled as his hands gripped my hair.

Chapter Four

"WAKE UP, SLEEPY HEAD."

I groaned. The words hit my subconscious but didn't seem important. The bright light that hit me in the face did the trick. I opened an eye. Why did I always fall asleep facing the window? And why would the handsome vamp dressed in his charcoal-gray suit find it humorous to force me awake?

I threw an arm across my eyes. "Too bright."

"You have an appointment with Sonja this morning. If you get up now and run through a quick shower, you might make it."

I popped up. "What time is it?"

"Eight thirty."

"Why didn't you wake me?" I jumped up, and he caught me by the waist before I made it to the bathroom.

His kiss was warm and sweet. "You needed the sleep, and you're the fastest woman I've ever met, other than Simone and Bella, who can be ready in less than thirty minutes. There's coffee on the bar, Sonja is holding your breakfast, and I'm off to meet with Alejandro and Miguel for a deeper dive into their business operations."

I pulled away after giving him another kiss to grab a cup of coffee. "Where's Gregor?"

He paused before answering. "He asked to meet with you and Sonja."

I gulped the coffee and stared at him. "Are you serious?"

He picked up his cell phone and stuck it in his inside jacket pocket. "I told him it was up to you, but I think you should consider allowing him to participate." His blue eyes sparked with the beast for just an instant, reminding me of our passionate night. "He's very protective of the dreamwalkers. I don't know what they can do or what their power level is, but they could be instrumental in our mission. Though it will ultimately be up to Gregor on whether they participate. If he understands how powerful you are and that there are others with even more power, it could go a long way in gaining his support."

I sipped the coffee and stared out at the garden. "Shouldn't you be there too?"

He was behind me before I knew it, his strong hands rubbing my arms as he nuzzled my neck. "I don't want him to think I control or manipulate your dreamwalking. You and I know that while I might command what happens on a mission, your power is your own. This is the best way I know of convincing him that we're partners. You are not a Blood Ward."

I blinked, forcing my blurred vision to clear. "Thank you."

He released me. "Try to behave yourself. I'll see you for lunch."

I patted his ass as he turned. "You know me."

He chuckled. "Why is why I asked."

I was still grinning when I stepped into the shower. His trust meant the world to me. However, his words didn't quell the nerves jumping around in my belly like popcorn kernels on high heat.

I selected linen pants, a silk shirt, and kitten heels, then finished the last touch by pushing the diamond hair clips in my hair, smiling at the memory of Devon giving them to me one morning while still in bed at the hotel in Madrid. After a last look in the mirror, I searched my duffel for the small, locked box. I entered the combination, and the lid popped open, revealing my medallion. I slipped it around my neck, then left the suite and wandered around the first floor.

A maid dressed in a simple gray dress smiled as I strode toward her.

"Mistress Aramburu is waiting for you on the terrace. Do you need me to guide you?"

I smiled in return. "I remember the way, but thank you."

"Sí. Have a nice day."

"You too."

It was interesting she'd said Mistress Aramburu and not Master because they were both waiting for me at a table for four. Gregor stood when I entered and pulled out a chair for me.

"I'm sorry to be late." I took my seat, and my mouth watered at the fruit, scrambled eggs, and black beans.

"Nonsense," Sonja said. She picked up the bowl of eggs and passed them to me. "These just came out of the kitchen. Devon said this would be enough for you. Some days we eat light, other days it feels like a four-course meal."

"It's the boys." Gregor took the bowl from me once I'd taken a couple of scoops. "I understand it's the same in the human world. They reach a certain age, and their stomachs never seem to fill."

"I'll take your word for it. I only have a half-sister, and she always ate like a bird."

"Mariah won't admit it," Gregor continued, "but she eats as hearty as the boys."

Sonja nodded. "But she's very active, so it simply disappears." Once everyone had their food and they ate, she continued. "I thought it best if we had a neutral spot when meeting with the dreamwalkers. Only four will be joining us in addition to me, and I selected a windowless conference room. Would that meet your requirements?"

My requirements. I didn't have any of those and wasn't really sure what was expected of me. "I've been in a couple different environments when dreamwalking. My initial training took place in a dark room with just a single candle, but I've also been in a library, a study, and a rocky beach facing hostile vamps."

When Gregor's brows lifted, I said, "Sorry, vampires."

He waved his hand. "The term doesn't bother me. It was the hostile environment that surprised me."

"It was a rescue operation, and plan A didn't go as planned. Fortunately, we were prepared for that."

"I'm sorry, I'm not sure I understand." Sonja pushed her plate away. "Are you saying you went to a construct while facing an enemy?"

I nodded but wasn't sure how much to share. If this visit went well, Sonja and Gregor would need to be introduced to Colantha and maybe Hamilton. But I didn't want to share Colantha's name without her permission. It seemed I didn't need to worry.

"This was your raid of Venizi's island that Erik and Ulrik told us about." Gregor kept his focus on me, probably measuring the truth of my words.

I nodded. "We took the enemy force to a construct and held them in place until Devon could—" I searched for the right term. "Dispatch them."

Gregor grinned with delight, but Sonja paled. "You have that much power?"

I blushed. "No. There was another one helping. I'm sorry, but I'll need to ask her permission before sharing her name."

"We understand." He patted Sonja's hand. "This is a dangerous game we're playing. There's still a question as to whether this is the right time to show our hand. The best way to ensure victory in war is to plan your strategy closely. I knew Guildford Trelane before I walked away from that world, but everything the Oslo twins tell me, what I hear from other Houses, and what we know of Devon's partnership with the shifters, tells me we have the right man leading this. But still, there is much to plan."

"I agree, as does Devon. This was the reason we accepted your gracious invitation to visit your home. Devon is meeting with his allies and…" I gazed at the landscape of hills and grasses far beyond the gardens, not sure what I'd planned to say.

"You search for the *De første dage*."

That brought me around. "Who told you that?"

"If you remember, I was privy to the Council's discussions regarding the dreamwalkers. I knew about the book that was written after the Battle at Omar. It's the only document I'm aware of that can reveal the truth. But I'll leave that discussion for Devon." He checked his watch. "For now, let's go to the conference room. They'll be waiting for us."

THE CONFERENCE ROOM, painted a robin-egg blue, was large enough to fit a mahogany table that sat twelve with comfortable high-backed leather chairs and two side tables topped with vases of fresh-cut roses. Four people, who were already seated, had been conversing lightly and immediately stopped when the door opened, falling back in their seats.

I wasn't sure if that had to do with me or whether that was their typical reaction to Gregor entering a room.

"Good morning," Gregor said as he strode toward the head of the table. Instead of sitting, he pulled the chair out for Sonja, then took a seat in the corner where a few extra chairs lined the wall.

"Cressa, please take a seat at the other end of the table." Sonja pulled herself closer to the table and nodded at me.

I did as she asked and smiled at the two pairs of men and women who sat across from each other. They were dressed for success, with the men in tailored suits and the women in slacks and blouses, similar to me.

I couldn't see everyone's medallions, but a couple were prominently revealed, where the others, like my own, dipped below the shirts.

"Let's begin." Sonja pointed to the man and woman on her left. "I believe you remember Joseph and Nancy from your dreamwalk yesterday."

The two appeared embarrassed, but I smiled. "I do. I'm Cressa, and it's a pleasure to meet you." My tone seemed to relax them, and while Joseph nodded, Nancy managed a weak smile.

Sonja waved to her right. "This is Antonio and Genese. They have equal powers to Joseph and Nancy, and I thought it would be a good group to work with."

I nodded and gave them my same smile, but their expressions remained reserved, if not slightly hostile. I wasn't sure why. They must have heard about my encounter in the construct built by Joseph and Nancy. Were they concerned about my abilities, scared of them, or unbelieving?

My first thought was to coddle them and find a way to make them like me. But then Devon and Colantha invaded my head with how they would handle this type of situation. We were searching for allies, but it was more than that. We were building an army. An army of vamps, shifters, and dreamwalkers. This wasn't the time to grovel for acceptance or for making friends.

I was a member of House Trelane. I wasn't cadre. I was a thief. And I was sleeping with the House leader. Not sure that deserved a title, and I had to stifle a laugh that bubbled up. I wasn't a pushover. I might not be cadre, but I needed to act like one.

I turned my attention to Sonja and ignored Gregor, who silently watched. I gave her my most winning smile. "Show me what you've got."

Sonja nodded, her smile predatory. She closed her eyes, and the others followed her lead. I kept mine open, waiting to see if they could pull me into a construct.

It was an experience difficult to describe. It was like someone tapping at my consciousness, trying to get my attention. Then, without warning, I was snapped into a construct.

It reminded me of a time when April, my half-sister, and I were really close. It was the first year I'd been out on my own. She picked me up in her brand-new Audi that Christopher had given her. We'd taken a run down the coast, stopping at little stores and galleries. It was the best day I'd ever had with her, but on the way home, April wasn't paying attention. It might have been my fault, or that she tended to focus on who was riding with her than watching the road. Either way, she didn't notice the car in front of her slow to make a turn, and she smashed into them. The jerk of the hit gave me light whiplash and a headache that lasted a week.

That was what it felt like when I found myself in the same diner from the day before. I slowly rolled my neck from side to side, ensuring I was alright and satisfied there wasn't a headache. At least not yet.

We were sitting at a round table, the other five all staring at me. A light film of perspiration covered Joseph's brow, and Genese squinted as if she was using all her mental ability to remain in the construct.

I took slow breaths as I glanced around. The construct appeared complete. No half images of walls, the chair felt firm beneath me, and the people around us didn't seem to notice the six newcomers in their midst.

Everyone wore the same clothes as in the conference room. Certainly not the flare of Colantha's constructs.

"How do you feel?" Sonja asked.

"Like someone clubbed me in the head. It was a bit jarring." I took another look around. "I'm not familiar with this place. Is it one of the restaurants in the village?"

She nodded. "Everything is the same."

"Can you make modifications to it?"

She closed her eyes, and the colors on the wall changed from an off-white to a light coral color.

"Good. What about clothing?"

Her eyes opened, and the color on the wall faded back to white. Interesting.

"We haven't tried that."

"Are you somehow combining your powers to build this construct?"

"Yes."

"How do you do that?"

Sonja considered the question, but it was Antonio who spoke.

"Our first step is to think about the Nexus, then we reach out to each other. Then we focus on the same room."

"I noticed when Sonja refocused to answer my question the wall faded back to its original color. Did you do that on purpose?"

She shook her head. "I have to remain concentrated on that image in order to retain it."

"Hmm. Can you bring Gregor into the construct?"

The group glanced at each other.

"We would need a couple more dreamwalkers to assist with that." Sonja played with her medallion. "When we plan a construct, each of us brings a portion of it to make it complete."

"Can you make a construct on your own without the others?"

She shrugged. "Some can, others need more assistance."

"Maybe you could show us what you can do?" Antonio asked with a definite challenge.

I looked at Sonja. "With your permission?"

She nodded.

I considered the best approach without terrifying them. They had some power, but they were babies compared to what Colantha, Hamilton, and I could do on our own.

Without closing my eyes, Gregor appeared at the table. The others jumped, startled by his presence, and even Gregor's eyes widened in surprise as he glanced around.

"Welcome, Gregor," I said. "I thought it important for you to see what I can do with constructs. As my mentor likes to say, prepare yourselves."

I changed the environment first, settling us at a round table with comfortable rattan chairs overlooking a beach of white sand and soft waves. The air stirred with a light ocean breeze scented with salt and suntan lotion.

Mojitos appeared before everyone with tiny hot pink and lime green umbrellas.

I nodded at Gregor. "Give it a taste. This is a small resort in California that I once visited when I was flush with cash after a successful heist. I always thought they put too much rum in them, but my friend Ginger thought they were perfect."

Gregor tasted it and, after the shock faded, nodded. "I agree with Ginger."

I laughed and glanced at the others. "Feel free to drink but keep in mind the alcohol is the real deal."

They all took a sip. A few smiled and took another, but Nancy made a face and pushed it away. They were all still in their business attire, and giving it some thought, our clothing changed. The men wore faded pink linen shirts with board shorts and sandals. The women were in colorful sundresses.

Joseph stood and disappeared.

The others glanced around, and I shrugged. "I guess that last change was a bit too much for Joseph. He pulled himself out on his own. I'm not forcing anyone to stay."

Sonja studied me with a new appreciation. "Could you prevent us from leaving?"

I shrugged. "I've only attempted it with one person, but let's give it a go. This will test everyone's strength." I turned to Gregor. "If you don't mind, I'd prefer you stayed for a bit longer."

Either true to his nature or his role as House leader, he leaned back with his mojito, seeming to enjoy the show.

"Okay." I glanced around the table. "See if you can leave."

Sonja immediately disappeared. The others remained but

appeared nervous until they glanced at Gregor, seeming to gain confidence from him. Then Antonio disappeared, leaving Nancy and Genese.

"That's alright. I've stopped now." The two women lowered their heads. "There's no shame in this. It took me a few attempts before I could release myself from another dreamwalker's hold. And it comes down to who has more power and how much power they're using to hold you. It requires a great deal of energy to hold someone." I didn't want to mention that I'd pulled myself out of a construct built by Colantha, who seemed to have the power of a god. It was best they learned in baby steps.

I considered the dreamwalkers who'd pulled themselves out and decided to bring Sonja back.

She blinked when she returned, once again in the sundress I created. "Thank you for bringing me back. I didn't want to miss anything."

"Should I bring the others back?"

She shook her head and grinned. "I think they've seen enough for one day."

I returned her grin and glanced at Gregor, who'd finished his mojito. "Is there anything else you'd like to see?"

"I've heard it told a dreamwalker can move between constructs in one dreamwalk."

I nodded and glanced at the women. "Care to go for a ride? I promise to take it slow."

Their interest piqued, and while I was certain some of it was their innate curiosity, it wasn't lost on me that Gregor inspired their courage. "Remember, this is just a construct. You can either enjoy the ride or, if you put your mind to it, remove yourself at any time."

When everyone nodded, I took them on a short trip. Our first stop was Coney Island, where Devon said Colantha had taken him, then to the icy mountaintop Colantha had first taken me, then to the coffee shop in San Francisco, and finally to the made-up construct where I'd brought Devon when we'd been at odds after his addiction to the Magic Poppy and where we'd made mad love. I kept us there as I studied the group's faces.

The first stop had made them nervous, and the mountaintop frightened the women. I didn't keep us there long because it was too cold, and with my energy waning, I wasn't able to change their clothing. But then their faces turned to wonder as I made the last trips. They seemed to be enjoying themselves now, waiting for the next construct.

"This place doesn't exist as far as I know. It's made of bits of my favorite places."

"These are places from your memories?" Genese's tone was full of wonder.

"Yes. Have you ever tried this?"

The women shook their heads. I turned to Gregor. "If you've seen enough, I can take us back to the conference room."

He took a long look around the construct, then nodded.

We were back in the conference room, where the men who'd left the construct remained, and everyone stared at me. Antonio was the first to speak.

"I think I'm jealous I wasn't able to return. Tell us everything."

I didn't have to. Nancy and Genese explained it well, and it appeared those who had left the construct were disappointed in what they'd missed.

"Can we do it again?" Joseph asked.

I shook my head, a light headache was forming. "I need to rest and recharge. Maybe a short trip tomorrow?"

"Yes." Gregor stood and rubbed his hands together. "There is much to discuss, and I think Cressa could use the healer."

"I'm okay. I just need a nap." But when I rose, my legs shook, and I tilted to the left. Antonio reached out to steady me, and I smiled at him. "Well, maybe a potion wouldn't hurt."

Gregor led me out as the others remained with the men shouting out questions as to where the women had gone and what they'd seen. My head hurt the more we walked. I'd expended too much energy. What I needed was some of Colantha's special juice.

Gregor stopped in front of our suite. His brows furrowed. "The healer will be up shortly, but I have one question."

"Alright."

"In the construct, you mentioned a heist."

I shook my head, then was sorry for it. "I'm not sure I should have mentioned it, but since we're going to be allies." I glanced up and down the hall and held back a grin when Gregor copied my actions. "It's how I met Devon. Not during a heist, but he required a thief with special skills. Skills that I happen to possess."

Gregor studied me for a moment, possibly gauging whether I was lying. Then his head fell back and emitted a deep belly laugh. "This is a story I need to hear more about. For now, get your rest. I'll explain to Devon why you're not at lunch."

"Thank you."

When he was gone, I closed the door to my room and slipped off my shoes. I glanced at the purple vial I hadn't touched and took a small sip. It would put me to sleep, but I didn't want to be out the rest of the day.

I was debating whether to change my clothes but decided I was too tired. A second later, a knock came. I opened the door to find a slight woman barely older than me.

"I'm Jessica, the healer."

"Come in." Devon's healer was much older and, based on her age, I assumed wiser. It was hard to get my head wrapped around a healer who dressed like Ginger and was named Jessica. I expected something more exotic.

She did a quick exam, much like Madame Saldano, then brought out an orange-colored vial.

"I haven't seen an orange potion before." But it looked suspiciously the same color as Colantha's juice.

Her lips quirked into a quick grin. "I use the standard ones but add a special one when warranted." She brought out the standard pink vial. "You should finish the first one I gave you and this one as well. Gregor tells me you're going to dreamwalk again tomorrow. I'll ask that you keep it short. In order to mend the psychic strain from today, drink half of this vial." She held up the orange one but pulled it back when I reached for it. "Only half now and then the other half in the morning. Do you understand?"

I rolled my eyes, and she grinned. "Fine."

"Now, take a nap." She closed her bag and strode to the door. Before leaving, she gave me a mischievous grin. "I hear you're a strong one. I think you've breathed new life into Sonja and the others to continue their training."

Then she was gone.

I grinned. I'd never been anyone's inspiration before. I drank the remaining pink potion, then half the orange. Damn, if that didn't taste similar to Colantha's juice. I wanted to drink the whole vial but remembered Jessica's admonishment. I set the half-empty vial down then fell into bed.

Chapter Five

DEVON ENTERED their suite after lunch, concerned for Cressa after Gregor told him about the morning dreamwalking session and his sending for the healer. He'd been surprised by Gregor's and Sonja's excitement over the sessions.

It seemed Sonja had only heard stories of what dreamwalkers could do, never having achieved the mental levels required to modify constructs like Cressa could. Many of their leaders were persecuted and killed during the dreamwalker purge. And though she'd only lost her mother a couple of decades earlier, Sonja's mother had been extremely careful in what she shared with her daughter, even with Gregor's protection.

Devon wanted to get Cressa's feedback, assuming she was healthy enough to discuss it. Her mental stability and the toll it took on her body was his primary concern, regardless of how important she might be in the coming battle.

He expected to find her napping, but, instead, she was on the bench seat that overlooked the garden wearing her silk robe. She had a cup of coffee in her hands, and she turned to greet him with a smile.

"How did the tour of the Aramburus' empire go?" Her eyes

twinkled with mischief, and a knot released in his chest. She was fine.

"Empire is it?" He removed his jacket and then his tie, looking forward to wearing something more comfortable.

She shrugged and made room, patting the bench for him to sit. "From what little Gregor said at breakfast, it sounded like they control a good portion of the market in several areas."

"He does. And even though it's all based on technology, he appears fairly entrenched in multiple industries. From what Miguel says, they've recently reached out to the local shifters to discuss an opportunity."

"Really?" She grinned over the edge of her cup. "I wonder where he got that idea."

He kissed the tip of her nose as he sat and pulled her to him. "How are you feeling? Gregor and Sonja were quite excited about the dreamwalk." He glanced around the room, spotting the tray with several silver domes. "You didn't feel like coming down for lunch?"

"I feel great if just a touch of a headache. I thought it best to give it a little more time." She slapped his knee. "Stop staring at the tray. I ate every drop of food. I just put the lids back on so I didn't have to look at how much I scarfed down." She pulled away and sat cross-legged to face him. "The healer, Jessica..." She scrunched up her face. "What kind of name is that for a healer?" She chuckled, then got up to refill her cup before returning to her earlier position.

When he'd first walked in and saw her staring out the window, he'd assumed she was sedate, recuperating from spent psychic energy. He was wrong. She seemed more energized rather than tired.

"Anyway, she visited after the last session and gave me the normal pink potion for the headaches but also gave me an orange-colored vial. I swear it looks just like Colantha's juice, and it tasted like it, too." She nodded toward the dresser. "I still have half a vial I'm not supposed to take until tomorrow morning."

"That explains it."

"What?"

"You seem more animated than usual after a long session. From what Gregor shared of the dreamwalking, it sounds like you expended quite a lot of energy."

She took a couple gulps of coffee. "You're right. I slept for an hour, then Sonja had a tray sent up. I didn't think I was hungry, especially with the dregs of a headache, but I couldn't stop eating." She shook her head and stood, setting the cup on the tray. "I must have stared at the garden for an hour but now I want to just get up and move around. I could probably run five miles without a sweat." She gave him a wicked grin. "Or spend an hour on the mat with you. I can't believe I miss training."

"My point exactly."

"I think we need to have a chat with Colantha about what she puts in that juice."

"Not Jessica?"

"She didn't seem much on sharing, and I know healers like to keep their potions secret. I know, why don't I leave a bit in the vial? I'm feeling really good. I can keep the dreamwalk short tomorrow. Maybe Remus can analyze the potion."

"I'd prefer you take what the healer suggested. Your health is more important."

She sat on his lap and wrapped her arms around his neck. "You're too good to me and too cautious." She gave him a long sensual kiss that stirred his beast. "I'm fine. I'll be fine, and I want Remus to take a look. Aren't you just a wee bit curious?"

He chuckled. "Insatiably."

"Good. Now, what's on the plate for this afternoon?"

"Gregor said he had something he wanted to share with us. Something he hadn't been sure of until his experience this morning."

"That sounds intriguing."

"Hmm. Maybe. He wanted to make sure you were feeling well enough. If so, we need to meet him and Sonja at two." He glanced at his watch. "Which gives us a little over an hour to relax."

She jumped up and removed her robe, revealing a naked body beneath. "I need a shower." She lifted his chin with a slim finger and gave him another kiss. "How about working off some of my energy." She raced off before he could grab her, and he grinned at her giggles as she disappeared into the bathroom.

He began stripping off his clothes, leaving a trail behind him as he stalked to the bathroom, slamming the door behind him.

Devon peeked into the bathroom. "How much longer?"

Cressa smiled into the bathroom mirror as she dabbed on mascara. "I just need to grab my shoes. What's the hurry?"

He checked his watch. "We have five minutes to get to the foyer."

She dropped the mascara tube into her cosmetic bag and pinched his side as she pushed past him. "I don't think Gregor will be upset by us being one minute late." Before she took another step, she turned around and gave him a heated kiss and a wink. "I think it was worth the extra time in the shower."

He grinned. "This is turning out to be an excellent visit. Alejandro and Miguel are eager to meet with Simone and Sergi."

"You didn't mention that. When is that supposed to happen?"

He shrugged as he grabbed a linen sports coat. "I'll let Sergi set something up. It will be a video call since we're on lockdown."

"What's up with Ernesto? He seems to be a bit mysterious."

"We chatted for a few minutes this morning. Apparently, he rarely leaves his computer. Mariah forces him outside just to get fresh air, or so she says."

"I would expect someone like him to be out with the ladies, but I suppose there's not much of that here."

"From what I'm told, there are two nightclubs. A local band moves between the two during the week. And Ernesto already has a girlfriend, who is also tied to a computer."

She laughed. "Sounds like a match made in heaven." She slipped her arm through his. "If we walk fast, I think we'll be a minute early. Did Gregor give you any idea what this field trip is about?"

"No. It was strange. He doesn't seem to be a leader who gets nervous about anything, though I sensed some trepidation. But he insisted we couldn't leave until he took us on one more tour."

"Are we leaving soon?"

"Tomorrow. Gregor has another business guest arriving in the evening, and he said it was best I wasn't seen here."

"Interesting."

"Just cautious. Venizi somehow figured out we'd come here, or he simply keeps a few men here to keep an eye on Aramburu. He knows a House as large as this can sway other Houses that play both sides. He'd prefer Aramburu continue ignoring Council business."

"That makes sense. Gregor and Sonja appear to be vamps who look to the future."

They rounded a corner to find Gregor and Sonja waiting for them in addition to their three sons and Mariah. And for a split second, they all appeared nervous before they smiled. A practiced smile as if preparing for a family portrait.

A shiver of a warning played at the hairs on the back of Devon's neck. That slight shift in his stomach before a battle that said he hadn't prepared for every possibility but was unable to determine what he was missing. For a split second, he wished he'd stopped at the closet that held his weapons. A single dagger could go a long way in making a warrior feel confident.

He brushed it aside and returned their smile. "So, what do you have in store for us this afternoon?"

"I have two golf carts ready to take us to the community center." Gregor took Sonja's hand, and they turned for the door.

A tour of a community center didn't seem to warrant anxiety in vampires, but he set it aside as they exited the building. Gregor directed Devon and Cressa to the second row of the first cart. Then he and Sonja climbed into the front. The other four jumped into the second cart.

Cressa glanced at him as they approached another fortified wall with guards. From what Devon had observed of the other buildings and places he'd been taken, this appeared to be the most highly secured facility. A fort within a fort within a fort. Yet, the gates were open, and people walked in and out of them without paying attention to the guards, who appeared alert, yet they smiled and nodded to everyone.

"This is our art and music community center." Gregor waved to the guards as they passed through the gates.

"You must have some expensive art here." Devon nodded to the guards, who smiled in return.

"Our most precious treasures are here."

The main building was a two-story high Spanish adobe with large archways along the front porch. When the golf carts drove around the circular drive, Devon caught a glimpse of another three-story building in the back that looked like apartments.

Oak trees dotted the front and sides of the building, cooling the air, and Devon grasped Cressa's hand as they walked through the front door. Though the massive wood doors remained open, he noted the iron gates behind them, adding additional security.

They entered an open foyer that took up a quarter of the building. The ceiling was a glass dome that provided natural light for a pond and waterfall surrounded by potted plants and trees. The rest of the area was filled with pedestals and glass cases that, based on the signage he was able to glimpse, displayed statues and artifacts from various eras.

"This is beautiful. The artwork on the walls, are they from local artists?" Cressa asked.

"Sí," Sonja responded. "We have artwork from all over Spain, some from contemporary artists, some that have been collected through the centuries, and the rest from artists within our community." She stopped at a glass case. "These bracelets were created here. Ones similar to these are sold in galleries in Madrid, Barcelona, and Seville. The proceeds go directly to the artists."

Music could be heard from somewhere on the second floor. "You have musicians here?" Devon asked.

"Yes." Gregor turned them down a hall where the walls were filled with landscapes, portraits, and wall sculptures. "We have courses in most of the arts as well as several crafts. Anyone who is interested is encouraged to attend. We also organize several events throughout the year—concerts, plays, poetry readings, and such. The library is located on the far side of the building along with a bookstore."

Halfway down the hall, they exited the building into an interior courtyard. A breezeway with open arches extended around the entire four-sided perimeter, and glancing across the grassy field, Devon could see doors and windows along the other three sides of the building.

The first thing that appeared out of place were the casually dressed vampires positioned around the courtyard. Devon didn't see any weapons, not like at the gates, but he knew a security detail when he saw one. And he had no doubt they would be experts in martial arts and hand-to-hand combat.

Cressa nudged him and nodded toward one of them. He nodded in return, proud that she'd observed the security. But it was a rare moment when she wasn't fully aware of her surroundings. Her innate behavior, honed during her time as Pandora, had taught her to monitor security wherever she went.

Gregor led the group to a small seating area with several benches and tables. "Please, take a seat. The reason for our visit will become apparent in a few minutes."

Devon guided Cressa to a bench facing the courtyard near play gyms and swings. Something you'd see at any daycare, and he assumed they were for the worker's children. Then he noticed several picnic tables on the other side of the swing sets with boxes on them.

Gregor and Sonja took the bench to their left, Alejandro and Mariah the one to their right. Miguel and Ernesto leaned against the archways just behind them. Devon didn't pay them much attention, but it wasn't difficult to discern the increased tension.

What the devil was going on?

Cressa must have also sensed it because she scooted close until their shoulders and legs touched.

A moment later, a small chime sounded, and a minute after that, doors on the other side of the courtyard opened, and young children of various ages raced toward the gym sets and swings. The teenagers were more casual yet appeared just as eager as they strode to the tables with the boxes. They opened them, pulling out pads of paper, pens, brushes, paints, and what looked like jars of beads and other unidentifiable items.

Gregor leaned over. "This is recess for the school. The young ones love to climb on things. This seems to be normal behavior based on the school in the village. The older ones enjoy free time for arts and crafts." He nodded to their right. "We have a few bookworms." A mix of boys and girls, five in all, had either dropped onto the benches or the grass and already had their heads in their books.

"Do these children attend this school because of some instinctual love or passion for the arts?"

Gregor's expression became grave. "No. These children are here for another special reason."

Devon looked at Sonja, whose expression was locked down. He turned toward Alejandro and Mariah who sat silent as stones.

"What's going on here?"

Gregor sucked in a long breath and released it slowly. "These children are all vampires."

~

IT TOOK several minutes for Devon to register what he'd heard. Children. Vampires. They were so young.

"Let's say hello to them." Gregor strode out to the play gym and when the children spotted him, they all ran to him. He stroked their hair and laughed as the children shouted over each other to be heard.

Devon followed, knowing Cressa was a few steps behind him.

"Now, children, you must listen." Gregor waited for them to quiet. "This is my good friend Devon. He's the leader of a great vampire House in the United States. Let's make him feel welcome."

Two youngsters, a boy and a girl, each took Devon's hands and led him to the swings, where they pushed him toward one. He sat and gently swayed as the children surrounded him. They asked questions about the States, how large his House was, and whether he liked Spain and their home.

He glanced up to find Cressa standing off to one side, Sonja next to her as they watched. Once his welcome had worn off, the children returned to the gym, and Gregor walked with him to the tables where the teenagers were working on crafts.

Devon stopped by each one, asking what they were doing while watching them demonstrate the craft. He didn't want to disturb the readers, but he also didn't want to make them left out. He'd noticed them watching him over the tops of their books. So, he stopped to ask what they were reading and if they enjoyed their studies.

After a half hour, the chime rang again, and without hesitation, the children strode back to the building. Before they disappeared into the building, they all turned and waved, and he waved back.

Once they were alone again and seated at a table, Devon asked, "Are these orphans?"

"No. They were all born here within the last twenty years. We have several vampire females who are pregnant. The building in the back that you probably noted when we arrived are apartments, but also includes a state-of-the-art maternity ward, including a NICU, which, fortunately, is rarely needed."

"I don't understand." And he didn't. The vampire infertility problem was a known crisis and had been for decades. It was a rare moment that any female got pregnant. It was one of the reasons the Council sided with Venizi over a century ago that it was necessary to allow vampires to turn humans. There was a restriction on how many could be turned within a House over a given period of time, though a few of the Houses found ways around the restrictions.

"How can there be so many children?" Rage built as he glared at Gregor. "What are you doing here? Is this some sort of bioengineering?"

"No." Gregor must have sensed Devon's anger, but instead of matching his ire, he slowly shook his head. His demeanor appeared more sorrowful. "The Council has been lying to our society for generations." He shrugged. "I believe that many on the Council don't know the truth. But the ancients who still hold a seat know. Most ignore it. Others hide it."

Devon stood, and Cressa popped up beside him. "I don't believe it. This is too important to hide."

Gregor had stood in reaction to Devon. "No, my friend. This must remain a secret until you uncover the *De første dage*. It's the single document that can shed light on the dark and unite our society. And I trust you to be the beacon to our path forward."

Chapter Six

I GRIPPED Devon's hand as we walked through the manor toward our suite. The farther we walked, the more he leaned on me. I released his hand and grabbed him around the waist to provide more support.

I had no idea what was going through this head. The school had been a shock to me. A gaggle of baby vamps. Kids who would mature at a normal human rate until they reached puberty. At that time, their aging would begin to slow until they reached their late twenties to early thirties, when the process would decrease further, moving at a barely measurable rate.

From the first mention that the children were vampires and all through Devon's interactions with them, I'd kept an eye on him. His voice had shaken the first time he'd said hello to a young male. It grew stronger as he smiled and laughed with them. He maintained his cheerful attitude until their walk back to the golf carts, when his smile collapsed, and a tic formed along his jaw.

How he'd held it together for this long was beyond me. He'd always suspected more was going on with the vampire Council than just the purge—the attempted genocide of an entire race of people. Devon had always been concerned about the fertility issue within his race, but he'd never mentioned suspicions that the Council might be hiding something so crucial to their sustainability.

I opened the door and, once inside, immediately closed and locked it. We barely made two steps before Devon crumpled to the floor. I dropped next to him and wrapped my arms around him.

He leaned his head on my shoulder as his body shook. Then the sobs came. Never, not once through his addiction, or when he found the car carrying me to the manor nothing more than a burnt husk, or during my escape from Shadow Island, had I ever known him to cry. I'd never witnessed him broken.

No words were spoken as I held him until the crying stopped, and his arms came around me.

"Come on. Let's get you to bed." I kissed his cheek, but when he didn't move, I nudged him. "I can't properly hug you like this."

He lifted his head, and the air caught in my throat. A tortured soul stared back at me. He must have been thinking of his family and friends. All the vamps in his life who'd spent years—decades—trying in vain to have children, not knowing that somehow, the game had been rigged.

What else could it be? Somehow, the infertility problem within the vampire species didn't exist at El Recinto. Gregor hadn't elaborated on how this came to be. Maybe he didn't know. Maybe he understood how much this would impact a House leader—how much it would impact Devon.

I tugged on his arm, finally getting him to rise, and with my help, he removed his clothes before falling into bed. I threw the covers over him before I quickly undressed and crawled in next to him. His skin was ice cold, and I nestled next to him, sharing my warmth.

While I waited for his breathing to slow, I laid in the crook of his arm and stared at a spot on the ceiling. It was questionable how much Gregor knew of the fertility problem or, if he did know, how much he'd be willing to share. He'd allowed us to visit with dreamwalkers and baby vamps, but how much more was he willing to risk for his Family—his House?

It was time to leave, yet I wasn't convinced Devon was ready to go home. His discovery that El Recinto didn't have a fertility problem was something he'd need to come to terms with. The beast would rise, and it was only time before its rage would spark a light in Devon.

A soft tap on the door woke me, and I stole a quick glance at Devon. His eyes were open, and it was his turn to stare at the ceiling. I rose, grabbed a robe, and answered the door.

A maid stood outside with a tray. "Mistress Sonja thought you'd prefer a light meal in your room this evening. She wasn't sure if coffee or wine was preferred, so she asked me to add both."

"This is perfect." I took the tray from her. "Thank your mistress for me. I'll contact her later this evening."

The maid nodded and waited for me to back up before she grasped the door handle and shut the door.

I set the tray down. The coffee was in a thermos to keep it warm, and the bottle of wine had already been decanted. I lifted the dome lids to find huge roast beef sandwiches, what looked like homemade potato chips, a tossed salad with dressing on the side, and oatmeal cookies for dessert.

Then I noticed the vial between the linen napkins. It was purple. A sleep potion. I glanced at Devon, who was still staring at the ceiling, his face a blank slate.

I closed my eyes, thinking back to how many doses I'd given to my vamp guard during my escape from Shadow Island. I added two drops to a small glass of water, surprised at how easily Devon drank it down without question.

He was either really thirsty or trusted me to do what was best. Yeah, he was out of it.

I laid with him for another hour, finishing my thoughts around a plan. Once I'd made up my mind, I got out of bed and searched for my cell.

I punched the third number on my contact list and listened to the ring.

"What can I do for you, Cressa?"

When I couldn't get any words out, Simone asked, "Is everything all right?"

"There's no emergency." I paused. "But, no, we have a problem. Have Lucas and Ginger returned yet?"

"Sergi tells me it will be three or four more days."

I sighed. Perfect. "This needs to stay between you and me. Well, maybe the cadre, but I'll let you decide that. I need a huge favor, and I'm hoping you can help us."

I woke to icy blue eyes that warmed as I turned to face Devon. I ran a hand down his cheek and snuggled closer.

"You drugged me."

"How do you feel?"

"Amazed. Angry. Disillusioned."

"What time is it?"

"It's early."

"Did you just wake?"

He nodded. "No headache. Physically, I feel good."

I sat up and glanced out the window. Based on the soft rosy glow, the sun was just rising. I rubbed my face and stretched. "I spoke with Sonja last night, and they understood that we would miss dinner."

"I vaguely remember eating."

I grinned. "You woke for a short time. Ravenous, I might add. You ate a sandwich, potato chips, and an oatmeal cookie."

"The chips were homemade."

"You drank a cup of coffee—"

"Which you drugged."

"I did not drug your coffee." I smirked. "It was in the wine."

He rolled onto his back, rubbed his eyes, then pushed his hands through his hair. "I only remember bits of it."

I stood so I'd be out of his reach. "That's because you were still groggy from the portion I'd given you earlier."

He sat up then put his arm out to steady himself. "I guess I'm going to need time with this latest revelation."

"As Ginger would say—well, duh." I went to the bathroom to pee and brush my teeth. Devon came in as I was finishing to do the same.

I sat by the window, watching how the garden changed hues as the sun rose. It was a peaceful setting. I hoped one day we'd return when Devon didn't carry such burdens, and we could take the time to enjoy Aramburu's hospitality.

Devon strode out with a towel around his waist, his hair still wet. I hadn't even heard him turn on the shower.

"We need to leave today."

I nodded. "Sonja is expecting us for breakfast, then she'd like to take a dreamwalk one last time with the same group as yesterday. She said the healer would give me another vial of the orange potion to take with me."

"Do you think another dreamwalk is necessary?"

"Not everyone saw what I could do. This one will be shorter. It's important they understand the possibilities and not fear them. And Gregor wanted to spend more time with you. A car will be waiting after a quick lunch."

"You already worked it all out?"

I shrugged. "Based on what he'd heard about your temper, or at least the rumors of it, Gregor had prepared his Family for you to rage while at the community center. He was impressed by your, what did Sonja say?" I glanced at the ceiling, remembering the words. "Your resilience and even temper. They were both surprised by your interaction with the children. So was I."

He'd stepped next to me while I spoke and gave me an odd look. "You thought I would take it out on the children?"

"Never." My response was immediate, and I grabbed his hand. "I've just never seen you around children before. It never occurred to me you'd do them harm. I wasn't expecting how quickly they would take to you or your tenderness with them."

"My reputation could still use some work."

I pulled him down next to me and took both his hands. "Your reputation is solid. And with each House you interact with, when they see your compassion, your fight for the future of vampire society, and common ground with other races, it only strengthens how your allies perceive you." I gave him a cheeky grin. "I can't help it if I couldn't picture you with children."

He gave me another odd look. "I suppose it's something akin to watching Simone become closer with humans."

I laughed. "I think you're much further along than that, but I have to give Simone credit for trying." I stood, took his face in my hands, and gave him a slow kiss. "Let me take a quick shower, and then we can take a stroll through the garden before breakfast."

When he stood, I grabbed his towel, gave his ass a spank, and dashed for the bathroom before he knew what happened.

Once we were dressed in our traveling clothes—Devon in his linen pants and shirt and me in a sundress—we strolled hand in hand through the garden. We finished at the terrace and found Gregor's immediate family, along with Erik and Ulrik, already sitting at the table drinking coffee and chatting.

"Devon and Cressa, I hope you slept well." Gregor stood and held out his hand. "And I hope I'm forgiven for the shock you received yesterday."

Devon took the proffered hand and shook it. "Nothing to forgive. I'm honored you've entrusted your secret with me. I apologize for my reaction to it, but I'm afraid it's raised more questions than answers."

Gregor waved us to our seats. "And I'm afraid I can't tell you more than what I've already shared." He took his seat, passed the coffee pot around, and called out, "More coffee, please."

Within a minute, a young man scurried out with two fresh pots. "Are you ready for breakfast?"

"Sí, Louis. Thank you," Sonja answered. "I've arranged for a lighter breakfast before our morning plans, then another light lunch before your trip back to Madrid."

"We appreciate it." Devon laid a napkin over his lap. "I don't know about Cressa, but I'm starving, and all our meals here have been excellent."

"Can you share with us what your plans are with Venizi?" Gregor's quick change of subject didn't seem to bother Devon. But I was curious how much he was willing to share with Gregor, at least in front of his family. I surmised he'd share more when the two of them were alone.

Devon considered it as he sipped his coffee then waited when two servers came out with platters and bowls. Once the servers left and the food was passed around, he did what Devon always did with his allies. He'd already told his House that we were at war. This was the time to go all in with the other Houses and seek a firm commitment of support.

"I began my investigation some time ago with a specific mission in mind—to remove my censure with the Council so I could have a voice in the future of our race. My digging was also personal and involved my sister." He glanced at me. "Then fate, or however one chooses to look at it, brought me a thief to accomplish my mission. When I discovered...when we discovered Cressa was a dreamwalker, it was my first indication that the Council and the ones before it had been lying to us. Perhaps they all don't know, but Venizi knew. The Magic Poppy, the censure, even my parents' deaths were all lies to hide a horrible decision made a millennium ago."

He sipped his coffee, then glanced around the table, all eyes were on him as their food grew cold. "I've always suspected there was more to it, and after yesterday, the truth is darker than I thought possible. My plans are to expose it all." He cut a sausage in half and stabbed one with a fork. "I need to gather a few more documents to expose the Council's deception and officially declare war against House Venizi."

He bit into the sausage and grinned at the gasps of surprise and mumbled words.

"Hush," Gregor whispered, but it was enough as the table fell silent. "This is a dangerous game. I don't want the children exposed."

"I would never endanger the children, and their existence won't go beyond these walls without your express consent."

"You'll require many allies if you want to prevent a civil war."

"Which is one of the reasons I accepted your invitation." He swallowed a bite of eggs and grinned before picking up his cup again. "The allies I'm gathering aren't just vampire Houses, though I'm gaining support with many of them. The Wolf has given his pledge to stand with House Trelane, and while I won't mention her by name until she gives permission, we have a very powerful dreamwalker who is tired of their race living in the shadows." He sipped the coffee then set it down, glancing around the table before landing on Gregor. "I spent centuries as the general of my Father's army. I don't go to battle unless I'm prepared to win."

Gregor gave Devon a long look before he shifted his gaze to his family. I watched the interaction between him and Sonja and then his children. I didn't know them well, but I caught the fire in their eyes.

Gregor stood and walked to Devon, who rose as they met. Gregor held out his hand. "House Aramburu stands with House Trelane." The two shook hands. "While I won't sacrifice the knowledge of our children, I will devote what I can to the search for truth and your war against House Venizi."

LATER THAT AFTERNOON, Devon stretched back in the leather seat as the private jet rolled toward the runway. He turned his head to look at Cressa. Her eyes were closed but not in nervousness about the takeoff. She was sleeping off the vodka.

He glanced at the small cooler strapped into the seat across from them and closed his eyes. It had been a bold move to ask one more thing of Gregor, and it required the House leader to have faith in The Wolf. A shifter he'd never met.

The two of them had a good conversation while Cressa and Sonja met with the dreamwalkers. They'd discussed the old days like two old men sitting in rockers on a front porch, though they'd lounged on the balcony of Gregor's office that overlooked the front of the manor. Devon hadn't been sure of Gregor's response until after lunch when he and Cressa had reached the limo before leaving.

"I've thought about your request and spoke with Sonja and the healer." Gregor scanned his domain before turning his stern dark eyes on him. "I've heard many things about Remus over the decades since taking on the mantle of The Wolf. I only have your word that he can be trusted with this gift."

"You have my word."

Gregor's smile was wide, and his laugh deep. "And I believe the son of Guildford Trelane to be as trustworthy as his father. I hope it provides what you need to bolster your evidence for the Council." Then he'd shaken Devon's hand, kissed Cressa on the cheek, and walked up the steps to meet his wife and children as they watched them drive away.

When Devon slid into the limo after Cressa, he noticed the cooler next to Ulrik's feet. He couldn't imagine what Remus would think of another surprise. As if the Blood Poppy hadn't been enough.

He should have contacted Sergi on their way to Madrid, but Erik and Ulrik had engaged them in conversation the entire way. Surprising for Ulrik but not Erik. It might have had something to do with the vodka they kept pouring as they asked for their impressions about the Aramburus, El Recinto, the village, and the people.

Cressa laughed with them, and Devon couldn't help but smile. It took his mind off his problems, at least for a little while. He'd shaken hands with the twins when they were dropped off at Barajas airport in Madrid that catered to private jets.

"It will be good to continue working with you," Erik said as they shook hands.

"I wasn't aware we had been." Devon grinned at the twin. The vodka had mellowed him.

"Of course," Erik laughed. "But we couldn't let Venizi believe it was so."

"And is that what we can expect in the future?"

Erik shrugged. "Until you declare war against him, it's better if we continue our ruse and collect what information we can."

Devon looked to Ulrik, who simply smiled in return. "House Trelane can work with that. Thank you for watching over Cressa."

She elbowed him in the side before hugging both brothers. "See you on the other side."

They had watched the vampires return to the limo and waved as it pulled away.

He'd settled into his seat, planning on calling Sergi as soon as they reached altitude. The ding of the bell signaling they had leveled off woke him. Cressa was awake, munching on nuts, sipping ginger ale, and flipping through a magazine.

She glanced over. "Hey, you."

"How long have I been asleep?" Devon straightened and glanced out the closest window.

"About half an hour or so. I've only been awake fifteen minutes myself."

Something didn't seem right, and he glanced out the window on the other side of the plane. "That's strange."

"What's that?" She never looked up from the magazine.

The sun was moving toward the horizon to their right. "It seems that we're flying south. We should be flying toward the sun."

She didn't say anything for a moment, then set the magazine aside. "We're not going home. At least not immediately."

"What are you talking about?" He must have drunk more vodka than he thought.

She turned in her seat, bringing her legs up to sit cross-legged. "You were pretty out of it yesterday when you found out about the baby vamps."

His brow lifted. "Baby vamps?"

She shrugged with an infectious smile that tugged at his heart. "I checked in with Simone while you slept to see if Lucas and Ginger were home yet."

"You mean when you drugged me?"

She ignored his comment. "It will be another three or four days before they return, and you need time to consider everything we've learned at El Recinto. I thought it would be best if you did it someplace where you could relax and not worry over House business." She held up her hand. "Simone knows where we'll be and promised to call if anything important comes up. For now, all the orders you left with her are underway, and they've made excellent progress on the safe houses. Colantha and Hamilton returned to New Orleans, but she promised to come back once we're home."

A flare of irritation hit him at someone making all the decisions for him, but it dissipated as quickly as it came. He admitted to himself that the discovery of the children had thrown him. After his readdiction and recovery from the Poppy, the dreadful episode had taught him one thing. If he was going to survive the war, he had to pay attention to his health—both physical and mental.

Baby vamps. He held back a snort, wondering what Simone would think of that moniker. Or any of his cadre, for that matter.

He wanted to be home, but Cressa was right. It would be a distraction. The news of House Aramburu having no fertility problems was a major development and required time to reconsider his next move. He had gained Gregor's agreement that Devon could share the information with only his most trusted cadre and The Wolf.

"Where are we going?"

"Simone found us a private house in Cádiz. Sand, surf, an infinity pool, and plenty of wine." She smiled and reached for his hand, glancing over her shoulder before lowering her voice, apparently in case the flight attendant returned. "And hours and hours of sex."

He grinned. "You should have led with that."

Chapter Seven

I HEARD the squeal of Ginger's voice the minute I stepped into the manor.

"You're home!" Ginger raced down the stairs and practically flew across the foyer.

I dropped my bag to steady myself as she flung her arms around me. I laughed. "Apparently, so are you." I hugged her back and whispered, "I'm so glad you made it back. It must have been hard."

Ginger pulled back and wiped an eye. "It's all okay now."

She didn't fool me, but this wasn't the time or place. That would be later with a bottle of wine.

Devon put an arm around Ginger and kissed her cheek. "Thank you for a successful mission. I hear we have you to thank for House Bertrand's support."

She blushed and glanced down at the cooler he was holding. I was impressed by her blank expression when I knew she was dying to know what was inside. Devon wouldn't be carrying around a six-pack. She smiled at him. "That was all Lucas. It's his sister's House, after all."

"But it was Mason's decision as House leader, and you're the one who encouraged the visit. I know the intent was for Lucas to reunite with his sister, but that act was important to Lucas and, as such, to this House. So, thank you."

She blushed and played with the deep-lavender silk scarf wrapped around her neck, the only color in her black leggings and shirt ensemble. "Any time."

"I'll need both of you to join us in an hour. I'm sure the two of you have a lot to catch up on." He kissed my cheek then headed toward his office.

"You're late."

I twirled around to find Simone glaring at us with her hands fisted on her hips. Her signature Wonder Woman pose. "I missed you, too."

Her lips twitched. "We expected you yesterday."

"I know. But you said Lucas needed time to decipher the book, and Devon ran into an old friend who had some business deal he wanted to talk about. I should have found a more quaint village."

Sergi joined us and simply nodded at me. "Simone, Devon has asked to meet with you first. The rest of the cadre will join you in fifteen minutes."

Simone gave me another blistering look, though her lips were still twitching as she strode past us.

"So, did you miss us?" I asked Sergi.

Sergi's brow went up. "I forgot how peaceful the manor was with the two of you on missions. And I expect you in the training room this afternoon. You must be soft after two weeks away, schmoozing vampires and playing in the sand."

He strode away, and I called out, "You meant boring. The manor was boring before I arrived."

Ginger and I giggled as we climbed the stairs. The vamp wasn't wrong about the training, but I could tell he missed me. Somewhere. Deep down.

"Where's Lyra?" I asked.

"She's waiting for us in her room. She figured you didn't need a bunch of people crowding you."

"How is she?"

Ginger shrugged. "She hasn't heard from Hamilton since he left with Colantha, but she hasn't destroyed anything in a fit of rage, so that's something."

I wasn't so sure about that and was pleasantly surprised to find Lyra in an upbeat mood, painting a brightly colored landscape scene. She dropped her brush and all but raced to hug me when we entered.

"I hear your visit with Aramburu went well. I can't wait to hear all about it." She took off her apron and placed it over a chair before pointing to the couches that faced the west windows. A coffee and tea set was waiting on the coffee table next to two dishes covered with silver domes. "Cook sent something up for us to nibble on. He can hardly wait to see you."

"It was great to get away, but it's always good to be home." I thought about what I'd just said. It was such a normal response. Home. I teared up and blinked it away as Ginger poured the coffee, and Lyra lifted the silver domes, filling three plates with appetizers. Any way I looked at it, the sentiment was true. As strange as it was, the vamps in this House had embraced a human thief and her best friend. It really was her home.

"So, you have to tell us all about Aramburu. What's behind those walls?" Lyra took a bite of a tiny quiche.

"It's more amazing than mysterious." I told them of the drive to El Recinto, the vamps we encountered on the way, and Gregor's strict ask-no-questions policy with unwelcome vamps. Then, I lightened the discussion as I shared details about the manor, the Family, the local village, and their businesses. I left out the part about the dreamwalkers and the baby vamps. Devon wanted to talk with the cadre first.

Worried that I might slip and say something about the dreamwalkers, I changed the conversation to Ginger's mission.

"So, Philipe Renaud and Fiona really are a thing, and they have the book?"

Ginger nodded as she popped the last raspberry tart in her mouth and chased it with coffee. Once she swallowed everything down, she gave a quick recap of being overrun at the motel and the scary ride to The Retreat. Vamps do love naming their estates, but I had to admit, it made them easier to remember. One thing was the same between them all—the need for sustainability and secrecy.

"How far has Lucas gotten in deciphering the book?" I asked.

She glanced at Lyra before answering. "He's read it through once, but it will take another couple of days to transcribe the vampiric portion into English so everyone can read it."

"What do you mean the vampiric portion?" I looked at both of them since it was clear they knew something I didn't.

"Well, it seems that the last half, what Lucas considers the critical part of the book, is written in a language no one recognizes or can translate."

"What? Does Devon know?"

"I imagine the cadre is covering that with him now." Lyra glanced at an antique clock that sat on the mantel over the fireplace. "And we'll know his thoughts in another ten minutes."

"You can't leave me hanging with that." I squinted at them. Their furtive glances back and forth suggested they knew more than what they were sharing.

Ginger shrugged. "Philipe and Lucas believe the language might be a dreamwalker language."

I had no words. Dreamwalkers had their own language? "Has someone contacted Colantha?"

"Lucas was going to but decided to wait for Devon to review it. I guess we'll know soon."

～

DEVON STARED at Simone across the desk, and she stared back at him. She'd noticed him place the cooler on the corner of his desk but never gave it a second glance as she took her seat.

He'd wanted fifteen minutes with her before the rest of the cadre joined them, but she was being stubborn, and he could wait another five. He enjoyed the game, and it had been so long since they'd played.

Simone hadn't had an easy life, and now she was close to being the mistress of her own House. He had no idea where it would be. It didn't matter. They would always be close. She was a good friend, not just the administrator of his businesses and Oasis. She'd been battle-tested on many fronts, and it was critical that she remained integral to not only follow in their war against Venizi but also to lead.

War came in many shapes, and these days, it wasn't on horseback with thousands of warriors. It was executed with sophistication, technology, and power plays. But the basic tenets of any battle and whether you would win or lose never changed. And, in Devon's opinion, one of the most critical principles was to know your adversary.

She sighed and gave the cooler a curious look. "You win. What's in the cooler?"

He grinned and leaned over to open it.

She peered inside and blinked. Her first move was to sit back, then she leaned over again. "I was not expecting that." Then she considered where he might have gotten it and laughed. "Have you been carrying that around with you for the last five days?"

He nodded, and she threw back her head and gave a throaty laugh. He grinned. It had been a long time since she'd shown such joy. The next few weeks, possibly months, would see little of that.

She wiped her eyes. "The only thing missing is the handcuffs tying it to your wrist." Her tone was filled with mirth.

"Don't think I hadn't considered it." He closed the cooler and leaned back in his chair, then turned to open the blinds another quarter inch. He'd missed home and the cadre. Then images of Cressa, topless under the summer sun came to him, then the two of them splashing in the surf before things turned more intimate. Would they ever have time like that again? What would life look like on the other side of what was coming? Would he still be alive?

"Where did you go, Devon?"

"Sorry. Just thinking about our growing agenda."

"I told the cadre about the children."

He nodded. "Cressa said she'd given you the option."

Her brows knit together. "Was she testing me?"

He snorted. "Probably. But you made the right call, and it will save time when the cadre comes in. How's Lyra?"

"Better now that Ginger is back."

"Has there been any word from Hamilton?"

"No. Nor Colantha."

He picked up the white crystal he kept on his desk. It had been his father's, and it made him feel closer to him. "I wonder what my father would say if he knew we'd found the book."

"Damn time, I imagine."

He couldn't argue the response. "Does Lucas seem alright? I haven't seen him yet, but we both know what it's like to be close to death and have to depend on others to save you."

"He wasn't alone. That was the important part. I didn't give Ginger enough credit for what she did. He doesn't talk about that part of his mission. To be honest, as important as it was to him to find the *De første dage* and Philipe Renaud, I think reconciliation with his sister foreshadows everything else."

Devon understood. He had the same connection with Lyra and had made it his mission to save her from her mental prison. "Did you have anything for me?"

"I'd like to add more shifters to Oasis."

That surprised him. Simone had questioned the wisdom of adding them to their security detail but had been willing to test it out after reviewing the data Decker had provided on the rogues.

After seeing Aramburu's compound and the defenses he'd built over the centuries, Devon had immediately seen how difficult Oasis would be to defend in a massive attack. At the time that he'd built Oasis, the idea of war hadn't come to mind. How quickly the assumption of safety could change.

Oasis could have gone decades without anyone learning of it. At the time, he'd known it would be his weak point, but he'd never guessed how expansive his mission would become. How deep the deception had grown within the Council.

"The shifters have proposed additional options for guarding our borders," Simone continued. "And I agree with them. I'd like to discuss it with Decker but wanted your approval first."

"You have it. I'd like to see what you have so far and include Sergi. He'll be able to offer suggestions in battle logistics."

She nodded, and though she didn't grin, it was easy to see she was pleased. It was something in her posture or maybe the slight lift to her chin. He'd never been able to put his finger on how he could interpret her mood beyond her blank expressions. Maybe it was his own way of looking at her when her leadership skills shined. Maybe it was the growth in her weaker areas that made him proud of her.

The knock at the door told him their fifteen minutes were up, and she gave a quick glance at the cooler before her lips twisted into a smile. She wanted to know more.

Sergi and Bella strode in and took their usual seats. He watched Sergi open his tablet and immediately start reading. At times, it was odd to see Sergi in his suit, tied to his tablet as he stayed updated on the Family's security. It was a far cry from when they'd first met on a dirt field so long ago, dressed in armor, ready to battle each other. And now, Devon couldn't imagine how he would have gotten as far as he had without him.

"Where's Jacques?" Devon asked, turning his attention to Bella.

"We've picked up some interest at the new city safe house. I sent him over with two additional security details to check it out." Bella was already fidgeting, her leg bouncing.

"Venizi?"

She shrugged. "Most likely. Jacques will tail them if they show up again."

Lucas burst into the room. He'd taken a few steps before turning back to shut the door. "Sorry, I'm late. I wanted to finish the last of my report." He appeared tired as he dropped into his seat and must have been working around the clock since returning home.

"Your work is important, but not more than your health." Devon gave him a wry smile and set the crystal on his desk. "I heard you'd recovered well from your mission, but I think it's time for another blood donor."

"Ginger has already sent a request on my behalf." He shuffled papers, a book, and his tablet before settling down.

Devon immediately focused on the book, and a thrill of excitement ran through him. When he shifted in his seat and glanced at his cadre, he noticed them giving furtive glances to the cooler. Everything was coming together, but there were still loose ends. Ones he hoped the *De første dage* would wrap up.

Devon began the meeting with a review of his visit to Aramburu, including the vampire attack before reaching El Recinto, a brief overview of the extensive security, and a list of businesses the Family ran.

"Sergi, I'd like you to contact Miguel. He's the second son but runs the Family's businesses. I'd also like you to touch basis with Alejandro, the oldest, who leads the cadre and include Simone. Let's see what strengths we have in common and any weaknesses we might be able to shore up."

Sergi nodded as he made notes on his tablet. "There isn't anything major to report on security. We continue to make strides on final changes to both safe houses. They're serviceable as they stand, but the final changes expected to be in place by the end of the week will make them difficult to penetrate."

"Enough food, weapons, and ammo for a six-month siege will be in place by then as well," Simone added.

"Has there been any movement from Venizi?" Devon had expected an immediate attack, but Lorenzo had been unnaturally quiet.

"No." Sergi rubbed his forehead and glanced out the window. Not a normal reaction. "He's planning something, which is surprising. He prefers to act quickly."

"Our lockdown might have posed a problem to his typical hit-and-run attacks." Bella stood and began her pacing. "Our limited movement, except at the safe houses, doesn't give him much to work with."

"Which is why his vampires are watching us." Simone leaned back in her chair, her fingers strumming the armrest. "Have we had word of any other vampires patrolling our properties?"

Bella shook her head, her pacing never stopping. "No. But, if it's okay, I'd like to set up four teams of four to patrol."

Devon grinned. "Watchers to watch the watchers."

Bella returned his grin. "Something like that. But I know we're already stretched thin."

"We have several vampires who recently completed their work at the safe houses," Simone said. "They're at your disposal."

"Excellent. Let's move on to the cooler." Before Devon could do more than shift the cooler in front of him, Sergi had one last topic.

"I received a call from my contact with the Santiga Bay police about Christopher Underwood's murder investigation. We were able to obtain the non-secure files from the Gheata sting that were specific to Underwood. They were provided to the SBPD from an anonymous source, and after their own investigation, the police have closed the Underwood murder."

Devon hadn't known how important that was until he heard the words. Cressa hadn't given him any indication she'd been worried, but she'd wanted to contact her mother again. They had decided against it with her stepfather's murder still an open case.

"That's excellent news. Thank you for getting that closed."

Sergi gave a brief nod then looked at the cooler.

Devon didn't delay. He opened it and removed the dry ice pack that was attached to three vials of blood. He placed the bundle on his desk and noted all eyes pinned to it. Bella returned to her seat, most likely to get a better look.

"Simone told you about the vampire children at Aramburu." When they all nodded, he continued. "Gregor has been watching the decline in our fertility rates, but never experienced the same issue within El Recinto. He had his suspicions about why that was, and they relate directly to the *De første dage*. In pursuit of the truth and our coming challenge to the Council, he agreed to my request for three blood samples. These are from a female vampire, her three-year-old son, and the father."

Devon hadn't expected many questions, though the cadre was wide-eyed with interest. Since Simone shared the information before he'd returned, they would have already exhausted most of their comments. They understood the gravity of the situation, but they'd all been surprised by the blood samples. Even so, they understood the next steps. To prove his thoughts, Sergi spoke up first.

"You want me to set up a meeting with Remus?"

Devon nodded. "It has to be here. He needs to read the translation then he can take the samples with him. It has to be soon." He turned to Lucas. "Where are you with the translations?"

"The first half of the book is complete, but I need assistance with the second half."

Devon's brow quirked. "What's the problem?" Everyone glanced at each other. So, everyone knew but hadn't bothered to tell him. He had to remind himself that it had only been three days since Lucas received a copy of the book, while Devon had been on a beach with Cressa.

"The second half is written in a different language. Philipe Renaud and I both believe it to be written in an unknown dreamwalker language."

Devon sat back and turned his chair to look out the window. Their own language. It made sense. They were a different race, why wouldn't they have their own language? That meant the book wasn't written solely by vampires and required both species to translate it. "Have you reached out to Colantha about this?" He remained staring out his window, his thoughts racing through the possibilities and the best approach.

"I considered it," Lucas responded. "Then I thought it best if Cressa contacted her."

Yes. That was the best option. Cressa had wanted to contact her the minute they arrived home, but he'd asked her to wait until they met with the cadre. He swiveled back to the group but looked at Lucas.

"I'd like to read the master text you're working from. I'm not questioning your translation, but I'd prefer to read it in vampiric. I'll ask Cressa to contact Colantha this afternoon." He picked up the white crystal. "I want Remus to read the entire book, not just half of it, but I don't want to hold onto the blood any longer than required." He turned to Sergi. "Let's see what Colantha says, then I'll decide how soon to invite Remus."

When Sergi nodded, he turned back to Lucas. "Provide Cressa with a small sample from the book. Let's see if Colantha recognizes it. Is that the book Philipe gave you?" When Lucas nodded, he grinned. "Do you mind if I read it this afternoon?"

Before Lucas could answer, the phone on the desk rang. Simone answered it.

"House of Trelane." Her gaze flashed to Devon. "When?" After another minute, she nodded. "He'll be there."

"What?" Devon asked.

"The Council has requested a meeting. They expect you within the hour."

Chapter Eight

Simone immediately called for a motorcade, but Devon took his time. With the House on lockdown and the focus on securing their defenses, there wasn't any reason for the Council to request his presence. They shouldn't know anything about the case Devon was building against them and Venizi.

After the raid on Shadow Island, he'd expected an immediate attack from Lorenzo. The vampire either couldn't find a weak point, was planning a larger attack, which was unlike him, or would try to use the Council against him. Since no attack had come in the four weeks since rescuing Hamilton, it appeared the Council would try to rein Devon in.

Was it possible Venizi had changed his strategy, finally understanding his hit-and-run attacks didn't work against House Trelane? What was he up to?

Devon ran up the stairs to Lyra's room, where he found the women. He only took a few steps in before waving for Cressa to join him.

"What's up? We were getting ready to come down."

"A change in plans. The Council has requested my attendance."

Her brows drew together. "The timing seems suspect."

"I agree, but I don't have a choice. And it's better to know what they're up to."

"This is Venizi."

"Most likely." He lifted her chin so she'd meet his eyes. "Don't worry. I just wanted to tell you rather than you hearing it from Simone."

"She's not going with you?"

"No. I need her to remain in charge, just in case the Council does something stupid."

"Do you need me to go with you?"

"I need you to help with security should Venizi decide this is a good time to attack."

"Then who's going with you?"

"The motorcade is waiting for me. Lockdown procedures. Bella and Sergi will be coming along with twelve others. We'll be fine."

She hugged him, her cheek against his chest. "You give them hell and then come home."

He closed his eyes. What would he do without his thief? He kissed the top of her head. "That's my plan. I need to ask you one favor."

She pulled back and gave him a wry smile. "Stay out of trouble."

He grinned. "That should go without saying. I need you to call Colantha."

She nodded. "I was already planning on doing that. A second language." She stared off to some distant point before meeting his gaze. "But it makes sense, right?"

"It does."

"Consider it taken care of." She grabbed his hand and squeezed. "Watch your back."

"Always."

He was almost out the door when he turned back to her. "I

almost forgot. You've been cleared of Underwood's murder. They've closed the case and put out a warrant for Gheata."

"They'll never find him." Her words didn't hide the tension that seemed to roll off her. She'd never said a word about the investigation, but it had to have been bothering her, even if she refused to talk about it.

"No. But the important part is that you're cleared. Maybe you should call your mother."

She bit her lip then grinned. "I think I will. Come back soon."

He smiled as he walked down the stairs, not in any particular hurry. His agenda might be growing, but it had been a relief to know the SBPD had closed the case on Underwood. It was one item off his list.

He met his cadre in the foyer. "Simone, contact Decker and see what you can do to shore up defenses at Oasis as quickly as you can."

"He'll be here this afternoon."

Devon turned to Lucas. "Cressa will reach out to Colantha today. Can you share a couple passages from the book with her?"

"I have them ready."

He turned to Sergi and Bella. "Let's see what has the Council worried this time."

The motorcade, three vehicles total, included two SUVs and one limo. Sergi and Bella were in each of the SUVs, along with four other security personnel. Devon rode in the limo with four guards. He stared out the window for the entire drive, his mind on what the Council could possibly want. The only thing he could think of was the raid at Venizi's party. And that was none of the Council's business.

He pushed the meeting aside. Rather than review the long list of things still needing to be done, he returned to his days with Cressa and their time spent in the infinity pool. He was lost in the memories until Mateo cleared his throat.

"Sorry, sir, but we're here."

Devon refocused on the view outside his window and glimpsed the Council building as the limo drove up the circular drive and stopped at the front steps.

"Thank you, Mateo. I'd like your and Sergi's teams to join me. Bella's team will remain behind to give us cover if required."

"Very good, sir." Mateo exited first and scanned the area for threats before nodding to the rest of the team, who covered Devon's exit from the limo.

Sergi's team was already on the steps leading to the front door in a defensive posture. Devon nodded to Bella, who had her team spread around the entire motorcade. The drivers remained in their vehicles in case a quick escape was required.

Sergi followed him up the steps with the security force trailing behind and Mateo taking up the rear position. Once inside the building, they strode two abreast with Sergi at his side.

"I didn't see Venizi's limo." Sergi's gaze moved left to right as they marched toward Council Chambers.

"That's interesting."

A lone Council page stood at the doors to the Chambers. The page lifted his head when the sound of boots on stone reached his ears, and he turned to face Devon. There was no expression on the older vampire's face. Everyone in this place was excellent at retaining blank expressions.

"Master Trelane, your presence is requested in the solarium. If you would follow me."

This rang déjà vu bells from several months ago when he met Isabella Stanton under similar circumstances. That time had been a Council warning regarding his actions to clear his censure, which had been unsubstantiated rumors from Venizi.

Sergi and the security team followed Devon as the page led him to the solarium, taking positions on both sides of the door as he entered. The solarium, like so many other things with the Council, hadn't changed in centuries. The room was filled with giant ferns, various other potted plants, and a mass array of orchid species. The page had left him at the door, so he wandered down a path that curved through the lush garden and stopped at an eight-foot-tall palm tree.

Isabella stood next to a wicker chair with a high oval back that would give the impression of her sitting on a throne. It wasn't unwarranted for the most powerful vampire on the Council and, up to now, a friend.

She wore a gossamer emerald-green gown that flowed to an inch above the tips of her shoes. Her dark hair was drawn back in a single braid that hung over her shoulder and down to her waist. She was misting an orchid, her fingers softly brushing the tips of its leaves as if she were embracing it.

He waited for her, knowing she was quite aware of his presence. She set the mister down and picked up snippers to cut off a dead leaf. After she dropped it onto the side table, she placed the snippers next to the mister.

She turned to him. "You're late."

He bowed his head. "Apologies. I'd been in a meeting when they called, and it took a while to organize my motorcade."

She lifted a lip in disgust before settling into her chair. "Yes, I heard House Trelane was on lockdown."

It was his turn to sneer. "News travels fast."

Her mouth relaxed into a tentative smile, but with her sitting in the shadows of the sunlit room, it was difficult to see much more. She'd always been sensitive to light, preferring, like many of the ancients, the darkness. She wore light-colored shades, which made it difficult to read her true expression. But he knew her eyes were the color of soft caramel—an arresting color against her black hair and ivory skin.

"Perhaps if a House didn't raid another, such a dire action wouldn't have to be taken." She ran a hand down her gown and brushed off debris that might or might not have been there.

"And in these current times, a House shouldn't be driven to such actions to take back something stolen from them."

Her brow lifted just enough for him to know that whatever Venizi had been telling the Council wasn't the full story. What a surprise.

"This conflict between House Trelane and House Venizi has been going on for generations. Long before either you or Lorenzo were the House leaders. The Council, as you know, stays out of House conflicts, but actions on both sides are now becoming dangerously close to human notice. The other Houses are becoming distressed over the situation to the point it appears Houses are beginning to take sides. This is not the vampire society we have strived for."

He used to know what type of society the Council hoped to embrace, but now it was murky with deception. "I'm guessing the aristocracy was upset at the interruption of Lorenzo's fantasy ball."

Her eyes flashed with the yellow glow of her beast, dimmed behind her glasses, then it was gone. No one on the Council wanted the aristocracy upset. No one wanted to rock the boat. "The Council simply wants the tension within the Houses to ease. It would be to everyone's benefit if the two Houses would simply call a truce."

"A truce? You want House Trelane to forgive and forget everything House Venizi does to keep my censure in place? You want House Trelane to forgive and forget House Venizi's kidnapping of my Blood Ward? You want House Trelane to forgive and forget the imprisonment of a member of my Family for the last century? That is a difficult, and in my mind, an unreasonable request of the Council, who prides itself on remaining neutral in House conflicts."

Isabella gripped the arms of her chair, and for a moment, Devon thought she might crush the wicker. Then she took a deep breath and turned her focus on her orchids. The events he'd shared seemed to have surprised her, and he was curious about what other stories Venizi had been telling the Council.

He didn't envy Isabella. It didn't matter what she thought. There wasn't a specific leader in the Council. She presided over the meetings because she'd been on the Council longer than any other. She might have the last vote, but rarely was it the deciding one.

The Council had simply used her to deliver their message because they were aware of Devon's long friendship with her. One that might end up destroyed over the actions Devon was planning.

"Will you make peace with Venizi?"

"No."

She appeared weary. Whether it was with the Council, this never-ending topic, or the knowledge of how far this could still go, he didn't know. "You must see this can't continue to escalate. If tension between the Houses continues, the Council might have no other course of action than to add to your censure."

He snorted. "Add to my censure. What about Venizi? Will the Council simply take his word for our dispute without even listening to my side?"

Her gaze shifted away. "You know the word of a Council member tends to be taken more seriously than one who's been censured."

His laugh was cruel. "Oh, I'm quite aware that once a Council member has been censured, it's almost impossible to have it removed for that very reason. But I'm as weary as you. Tired of Venizi steering the Council to the old ways. Of conveniently doing one thing while telling the Council something different, never concerned about restrictions being placed on his House or Council seat."

"You have a successful House with profitable businesses. You're a leader in your community. Can't you leave well enough alone?"

He'd had enough of this cat-and-mouse game, and though his next words wouldn't help him, he could no longer hold them back.

She must know the truth, maybe not all of it, but she'd been on the Council for a long time. His tone was brusque.

"Don't you see, Isabella? This Council and those before them have betrayed us."

"Watch your words, Trelane."

"And what will you do? I've already been censured. I've broken no Vampiric Law. I've done no business with vampires, and there are no rules against doing business with humans or shifters. Will the Council bring me in without charge? If you're so concerned about civil unrest, what do you think would happen if I were arrested without formal charges?"

"Venizi claims there is evidence to support charges against you and House Trelane."

He laughed. "If he had proof of any wrongdoing, he'd be parading it in front of the Council, and I'd already be in chains."

Isabella glanced down, but he caught the twitch of her lips. She knew the Council had nothing on him. All they could do was intimidate him. But they were in a tight spot. After their swift move against House Trelane when Boretsky was murdered and the eventual dropping of all charges, the Council couldn't make another false move against him without starting the civil war they were attempting to avoid.

He felt like shouting out the list of lies and cover-ups, but he held his restraint. His Father had taught him better than that. After decades as the commander of Guildford's army, leading thousands of warriors in hundreds of successful battles, he understood patience. He'd studied Sun Tsu and lived by his tenants of war.

He had to bide his time and gather his evidence and allies. Then he'd face the Council and Venizi and shout to the entire vampire society the betrayal committed against them.

Then he'd see where the chips fell.

He gave Isabella a cold stare. "Take this back to the Council. I will not back down. I will not make peace with Venizi. If he comes at me, my House, or my Family, I will retaliate, as is my right under Vampiric Law. This is the time to take sides, Isabella."

Then he turned and stormed away. The polite thing would have been to wait for Isabella to dismiss him. But they weren't in Council, so it wasn't required.

And he was damned tired of being the only one playing nice.

Chapter Nine

ONCE DEVON HAD LEFT, I told the women about the Council summons. Then I went in search of Lucas, following Ginger's directions to a compact office down the hall that led to the theater.

I tapped lightly on the door, heard a muffled "enter," then pushed the door open and stuck my head in. "Do you have a minute?"

Lucas glanced up from the papers on his desk and grinned. "Sure."

He looked as tired as Ginger said he was, yet there was a fire in his gaze I'd never seen in him. Of all the cadre, he was the most relaxed. That didn't mean he wasn't fierce, just not as stiff as the rest.

I entered the room and took a moment to look around. It smelled of musty books and a touch of Ginger's perfume. The scent of books came from the three walls of bookcases, and I walked along them noting that most appeared to be vampire texts.

"This looks like a law library, but instead of books on the State of California or federal legislation, they appear to be on vampire law."

"That's right. Although I do keep a few books on state and federal legislation, specifically as it relates to commerce and trade. And one or two of shifter law."

That made me stop and take a deeper look at the room. The bookcase behind him had an open shelf with knickknacks and several picture frames. One was a black-and-white image of Ginger that appeared to be a candid shot of her. Her head was down, maybe reading, her face angelic. There was another of her and Lucas hugging each other, both laughing, and I was curious who'd taken the picture. A third photo was of a young female sitting in a garden. Her lips and eyes suggested it was his sister, Rosalyn, but it might have been his mother.

"So, this is your office." I must not have kept the awe out of my voice because Lucas laughed.

"I can't believe after all the time you've lived here, you've never visited."

"That's because I didn't realize you had an office. And, yes, I know how stupid that sounds now that I said it."

He was still smiling. "All the cadre have offices, Cressa. Even some of the other vampires in the Family, depending on their position."

I shook my head at my own idiocy. Of course, the cadre had offices. It just never occurred to me to visit them. "I know where Sergi's is, and Simone uses Devon's office at Oasis. Where's Bella's office?"

"It's down the hall from Sergi's."

I'd been through those rooms. They were all storage rooms, but now that she thought about it, there was one that held a desk. "Wait. You're not talking about the storage room with a desk with a monitor on it?"

He laughed. "That's the one. It's not really a storage room. Bella never unpacked when she came to House Trelane. On a good day, there's only a small mess of papers spread across her desk. Greta keeps it dusted, and Jacques uses it more than Bella."

I dropped into a chair in front of his desk. "I remember two chairs and a table now. The chairs looked comfy."

"When they're between shifts, Bella and Jacques use her office more like a lounge than an office."

"Devon collected an odd group for his cadre. Yet, you all seem to work well together."

"I'll take that as a compliment." Lucas moved a few pieces of paper around, didn't seem to find what he was looking for, then lifted a tome and pulled a sheet of paper out from under it. He pushed it toward her. "I think this is what you came for."

I leaned over and picked it up. The sheet was full of symbols that were broken into sections I assumed were paragraphs. I'd never seen anything like it. If they were words, they meant nothing to me, yet I couldn't take my eyes off of them. It was like I should know what they said, but it was just beyond my grasp.

"These look like some type of Asian language or maybe Middle Eastern."

"More like Ancient Egyptian or even Phoenician, but those languages are long dead. Though that would make sense if the dreamwalkers had been purged centuries ago. I emailed you an image of the same section of text so you can send it to Colantha."

"Thank you for this." I stood, still mesmerized by the symbols. "I'll keep you posted." I stopped at the doorway and turned back. "You really love this type of stuff."

"Yeah, I do. It drove my father crazy. He said I'd never be cadre because I didn't have the heart of a warrior."

I glanced around the room and rubbed my shoulder from the last training session. "If you don't mind me saying, your father is an ass. You have the heart and skill of a warrior and the brains of a scholar. Devon's lucky to have you."

When color suffused his cheeks, I winked and shut the door behind me. I'd just turned the corner, heading back to the stairs, and almost bumped into Ginger, who managed to save the tray she carried.

"Did you just see Lucas?" She repositioned the tray that held a coffee pot, a couple of mugs, and something savory hidden under silver domes.

I held up a page. "Yep. I'm on my way to contact Colantha. That vamp of yours needs a break."

She lifted the tray. "I can't get him to leave his office, but food usually does the trick."

"I thought he finished the translation already."

"It's a rough draft. He wants to clean it up before Remus comes."

"Will you have time for happy hour with Lyra?"

"Absolutely."

We parted ways, and I took the stairs two at a time. Ever since I'd heard there was a second language in the *De første dage*, there was no doubt it had to be a dreamwalker language. The only question was how to get the sample to her. Email was the most obvious, but how secure was that? I was probably being paranoid to think someone was hacking my email.

Devon had given me Colantha's cell number, and I stared at it on my phone. I could text her a copy of the image. But there was another option. I wasn't sure it would work, but no time like the present. I snorted. This could be better than a video call.

I went to the safe Devon had added after he'd seen my setup in the condo Ginger and I shared. And like that one, there was a secret panel built behind it where the real treasure lay. Yeah, I was paranoid. I grinned as I pulled out the tiny locked box that held my medallion.

Its instant warmth calmed me when it settled against my skin. I fingered it as I picked up the page of text and placed it on the table in front of the fireplace. I lit a candle on the mantel, then sat on the sofa, rolled my neck back and forth, took a deep breath, and focused on the candle's flame.

I spent the first five minutes clearing my mind, then created a construct that looked just like my bedroom. It required less energy and something told me I'd need a lot to attempt what I was doing. Colantha, Hamilton, and I were both able to create constructs between the manor and Shadow Island, but those two points were maybe twenty miles apart as the crow flies.

I was going to attempt to contact Colantha at her sanctuary outside New Orleans. In theory, since she and I had dreamwalked many times before, and there was a high probability she'd be wearing her medallion, this might work.

When my mind was as clear, I called out, "Colantha."

I stretched my mind, focusing on the room at the sanctuary where Colantha first tested my abilities. "Colantha?"

That was weak. I cleared my throat and gave a more authoritarian command. "Colantha. This is Cressa. I'm sorry for intruding."

"I would hope so."

I must have jumped a foot and turned around so fast that my feet tangled, and I fell off the couch. I pushed up, glancing around, unsure if this was still my construct or my real room. Maybe I should have built a different room, like the library.

"Behind you."

I twisted back around and dropped onto the couch. I was giving myself whiplash. I glared up into Colantha's smiling face. She was enjoying this.

"I take it this is now your construct."

"From the minute you jumped in surprise. When you call out to a dreamwalker who is not expecting it, you need to control where they will appear in the construct as well as maintain control of it." Her eyes narrowed. "Especially when they're more powerful than you."

I lowered my gaze and tugged my shirt down, trying to get my bearings. "Good to know."

"If you wanted to speak to me, why didn't you call? I left my number with Devon."

"He gave it to me. I was just having a hard time picturing you with one."

She snorted, and I glanced up in time to see her grin. "What's the emergency? You couldn't wait a couple of days?"

"Lucas found the book."

Her gaze lowered to the single sheet of paper on the table, but she made no move toward it. "Where was it?"

"The book itself is still with Philipe Renaud, but we have a copy of the original. Lucas translated the first half, which was written in ancient vampiric. It's the last half we're having a problem with. It's written in a different language."

A single brow arched, and Colantha circled the table, her gaze still on the page.

"Is there a dreamwalker language? We think there might be, and if so, is this familiar to you? Can you read this?"

Colantha sat in a chair but didn't say anything as she continued to stare at the page.

I glanced down at my hands, not realizing I'd been rubbing them. I stuck them under my legs and leaned toward Colantha. "Apparently, all the good stuff is in the second half of the book. Or we hope so, assuming we can find anyone to interpret it."

Colantha nodded at the page. "May I?"

"Yes. That's why I called for you."

Her lips twitched as she picked up the page. I couldn't find a drop of emotion as she read. Could she read it? Did it say anything important? I didn't have time to think any further.

It hadn't been more than a minute or two before she placed the page on the table and poured a cup of tea from a tea service that hadn't been there a second ago. She held up the teapot and looked at me. I nodded. Once the second cup was poured, we sat back and sipped. Then, Colantha shared what she knew.

"Dreamwalkers, like vampires or shifters, are their own species, so yes, we have our own language. Over time, there have been various versions. But at the time of this writing, our language had, what you might say, consolidated with only minor variations depending on which of the seven tribes you belonged to. Some of our elders still speak the language, but for most, the language has been lost."

"Because of the purge?"

She nodded. "It's much easier to blend when you speak the prevalent language of where you live. It was our language or evidence of it that made it easier for the vampires to find us."

"From my understanding, Philipe Renaud and his mate, Fiona, who is a custodian, have searched thousands of books in search of any with the same language. They believe they found one that's similar, but other than the *De første dage*, they have no—I think it's called a codex—that can be used for translation."

"No. I doubt many books in our language exist anymore, though I know where one or two might be."

She was being coy. There were probably a lot more than one or two, but I understood her reticence, even with me.

"Can you help us translate the second half of the *De første dage*? We would also need a second book in the same language, or as close as possible, so the Renaud custodians can confirm the authenticity of the text's words. Without it, we have nothing to take to the Council."

"Perhaps." She glanced at her watch.

"Before you go—" I had no idea when she would just disappear. "Are you aware of a dreamwalker community in Spain?"

Her eyes widened for an instant, but no other expression gave away her thoughts. But I didn't think she was surprised.

"There are small communities spread around the world. No more than thirty or so. Can I ask how you discovered them?"

"It was more like they discovered me." If she could be evasive, so could I. I trusted Colantha, but she held her secrets close, and there was a great deal about dreamwalkers she hadn't shared. "Do you know about the fertility problem in vampires?"

She nodded but didn't respond other than to finish her tea.

"Are you aware of a vamp compound where they don't have a fertility problem?"

She set down her cup and stood. "I'll see what I can find to assist you with the translations. Expect me soon."

Then she was gone.

The piece of paper was still there, but the tea service had disappeared with her. I was back in my room. On one hand, I was able to confirm that dreamwalkers had their own language, and Colantha could help. On the other, she was still keeping something from me.

Devon had tugged on a string when he began his search for dreamwalkers. Then he tugged another one when I came along. With every step he took, he tugged more strings. I stared at the paper. Everyone was worried about the impact the *De første dage* would have on vamp society. I thought it meant freedom for the dreamwalkers. Was it possible that once all the strings had been pulled, it would unravel both species? Not just a civil war within vamp society but a world war among vampires and dreamwalkers? Would the shifters join with the dreamwalkers?

Maybe I just needed a drink and someone to talk me off the ledge. I stood, my legs a bit shaky. Ginger was with Lucas. Lyra was probably still in her room. I picked up my cell and was halfway to the door when I remembered Devon's suggestion to call my mom.

I sat on the edge of my bed and made the call. It answered on the second ring.

"Cressa?"

"Hi, Mom."

A huge, breathy sigh. "I wasn't sure whether to call. Are you alright?" There was background noise, the sound of a door closing, and the voices faded. She must have people over.

"Can you talk?"

"Yes. Your sister has friends over." She barked out a nervous laugh. "There always seems to be people here now."

Christopher was a stickler on who we could invite to the

house. He might have just wanted to control the number of teenagers in the house, but still, now that he was gone, those rules no longer applied.

"I wanted to call before now, but Devon thought it wiser if I waited until the police cleared me."

"I understand."

"I know you're still grieving, but at least you can put some of this behind you now." My voice dropped. "How he died."

She laughed, and it was scornful. "Christopher was greedy and mixed up with the wrong people. He put all of us at risk. In some ways, he still is." She paused for a minute, and I didn't miss the importance of what she'd just said as my mom sucked in a deep breath. "His ending isn't a surprise, and what little grief I had for the man is long gone." She chuckled. "Maybe I'm just in my anger stage."

I laughed with her. "I could see that." I rubbed my leg and glanced out my window. "How's April?"

Silence.

"Mom?"

Her voice lowered to a whisper. "She's still very angry with you. She thinks whoever you're living with paid off the police."

I rolled my eyes. What had I ever done to April to make her like this?

There was a loud voice and a knock.

"They're looking for me, I need to run."

I stood. "Mom. Are you okay? Who are these friends of April's?"

"I love you, dear. Don't call me, I'll call you. Okay? Just until April calms down."

Then I heard the door open and voices.

"Who are you talking to?"

It wasn't April's voice. It was a male voice.

The line went dead.

What the hell?

Then Mom's words came back. "He put us all at risk. In some ways, he still is."

Mom was in trouble. I didn't know how, but it had to do with April. And if I was standing at a roulette wheel in Vegas right now, I'd put all my money on red.

Vamps.

Chapter Ten

DEVON STORMED out of the solarium and gave a quick nod to Sergi, who marched through the building just a couple of steps behind. He didn't need to look back to know his security detail monitored every door and hallway they passed.

Once he was inside the limo, he noted Lorenzo's flashy Rolls drive up. Venizi wouldn't be happy to hear about his discussion with Isabella. And maybe that was what the vampire was waiting for. With House Trelane on lockdown, it was more difficult to attack. Not impossible, but it wouldn't go unnoticed. And now Venizi could point to House Trelane as unwilling to make peace.

He would have preferred Sergi riding with him in the limo so he could discuss the meeting, but this wasn't the time to grow lax with his own orders. So, he took the time during the drive home to review the meeting. When that made him irritable, his thoughts turned to Cressa and whether she'd gotten a hold of Colantha. It was more important than ever to finish the translation of the *De første dage.*

When he arrived home, he pulled his tie off as he ran up the steps. "Get everyone in the office, and I want an update on our security teams. Fifteen minutes."

Sergi, who was still right behind him, responded with a "Yes, sir."

Devon almost chuckled. He rarely got a "yes, sir" from Sergi anymore, but it told him everything. Sergi might not know what the discussion with Isabella was about, but he understood it had pissed Devon off. He took the stairs to the second floor two at a time, stripping off his jacket and tossing it on the bed along with his tie. He changed into something more comfortable—a pair of black chinos and a black button-down shirt. Might as well keep his dark mood going.

He was back in his office in less than ten minutes and was surprised to find Simone and Decker already there.

"Decker. I wasn't expecting you today, or did I miss something on my calendar?" He dropped into his office chair and pulled the blinds shut.

Simone and Decker glanced at each other. Shutting out the sunshine was another sign of his temper.

"Simone and I've been discussing adding more rogues at Oasis. Maybe one or two at the safe houses."

He nodded, and a tightness around his chest relaxed a notch. "When can that be implemented?"

The two glanced at each other again, and this time Simone answered. "I have names of several that could start immediately at the safe houses. I interviewed them for Oasis, but they wanted to stay in the city. I think we can work out a schedule that would be acceptable on both sides."

"Get it done. What about for Oasis?"

"I have a few in mind." Decker pulled a bag of licorice from his pocket. "But we might want to talk with Remus. There's a small pack not far from Oasis that's struggling to find work. The Alpha's young, and he's slowly building a strong pack, but there's limited space."

"Why didn't he move farther out to a mid-sized city?"

"His mother lives in the local town and won't move away from her other pups. Her health isn't good, and he wants to stay close—at least for now. Remus gave his permission."

"Let's see what we can do to help them out."

Simone nodded as the rest of the cadre filed in, followed by Cressa, Ginger, and Lyra. He glanced at his watch. Two minutes to spare. No one said anything as they found their seats, and whether it was the tension already building in the room or Sergi had given them a heads up, it didn't matter. Most of them were used to his swift mood changes, and they knew he'd just returned from the Council.

"It appears the Council is getting nervous," Devon began. "I've been asked to back down from my conflict with Venizi and make peace." He explained the crux of the meeting. It was obvious by the immediate glowing eyes of the cadre's and Lyra's beasts, and the thinning lips and reddening faces of the others that they weren't any more pleased with the request than he'd been. Another notch loosened around his chest.

"What was your response?" Simone asked once she'd quieted her beast.

"I told Isabella that I wouldn't back off and I wouldn't make peace."

"Was Venizi in the building?" Lucas asked.

"No, but he arrived as we were driving out."

The room fell silent, and Devon let them organize their own thoughts.

"Venizi must have stirred up the Council after our raid at Shadow Island." Bella sat near the bar rather than her normal seat, and would probably start pacing soon.

"But why did it take so long?" Lucas asked.

"He's preparing something." Sergi was reviewing something on his tablet, his brows scrunching together. More bad news?

"Cressa," Devon turned to her. "Have you been able to contact Colantha?"

She startled, not expecting a quick topic change, but she

cleared her throat and grinned. Good news, then? "Yes, we dreamwalked, and I showed her a page from the book. It's definitely a dreamwalker language. She said to expect her soon, probably in the next day or two."

"That's fantastic news." Lucas couldn't help his grin, and Devon agreed with his assessment.

But that was as far as they got before Sergi stood. "We have a problem."

The desk phone rang, and Simone picked it up seconds before the alarms went off.

"Got it. We're on our way." She stood. "It's Oasis. We're under attack."

"I think we have visitors at the safe houses as well," Sergi added.

Devon was already up and heading for the door. "Level One emergency. Full defense mode. Lucas, I want you, Ginger, and Lyra to remain here to protect the manor. Who do we have at the safe houses?"

"Teams one and three are in place." Sergi reviewed notes on his tablet. "Our final security measures aren't in place yet, but they should be prepared."

"Bella and Jacques, I want you to monitor the situation and assist where you can. The rest of us are going to Oasis."

"The limo and motorcade are still out front. Emergency procedures are underway," Sergi called out as he fell in line.

"Five minutes to gather your weapons and armored vests," Devon called out. The message was more for Cressa than anyone. There were weapons in the limo, but he headed to the small armory next to the foyer and grabbed a sword, dagger, and a Sig Sauer 9mm.

He paced next to the limo as the team gathered. Bella and Jacques drove past on their way to the gate, a SUV following behind them. He pulled out his phone and called the gatehouse. "Do we have any visitors?"

"Not yet, sir. We called in more security."

"Very good. The limo and motorcade will be leaving in two minutes."

He turned around to find everyone jumping into the limo and the motorcade vehicles. When Simone nodded, he jumped into the limo where Cressa waited, her leg bouncing. Mateo was in one of the jump seats texting with the security teams. Simone and Sergi would be in the SUVs, complying with standard lockdown procedures. It was likely Venizi had a team on the way to the manor or could attempt an attack on their way to Oasis.

"We knew Venizi would eventually find out about Oasis." Cressa might have been trying to calm him or simply stating a fact as she prepared for battle.

When the limo drove south of town rather than east toward the hills and rural area beyond, Cressa's face scrunched. "Aren't we going the wrong way?"

He grabbed her hand. "You'll see." Five minutes later, they entered a private airport with a single airstrip and a handful of hangars.

A helicopter with the rotors already turning waited for them.

"You have a helicopter?" Cressa stared through the front window as they closed in on it.

"For emergencies."

When the limo came to a stop, they all piled out. Devon pulled Cressa with him, ducking low as Sergi, Simone, Mateo, and Roberta, raced for the copter and didn't slow down until they climbed in. The drivers of the motorcade remained behind with the rest of the security detail and the four vampires stationed at the airport for security.

Cressa grabbed Devon's hand as the copter lifted and banked sharply as it flew out of the city.

"You've prepared for this eventuality." Cressa stared at him with a bit of awe.

"And much more. We'd hoped it would be years before Venizi

discovered Oasis." He squeezed her hand as he monitored the landscape below them. "We have a few other surprises his team won't be expecting."

❧

I SLID the headset Devon gave me over my ears and stared out the window as the copter flew over the city. My stomach was in knots. Not for the battle that we might not be in time for but for the possible fatalities and the destruction of such a beautiful sanctuary.

It had been just a matter of time before someone discovered Oasis, no matter the safeguards that had been put in place to prevent that eventuality. Devon owned thousands of acres, and while some of it was fenced, it was a lot of land to secure. When things grew more heated with Venizi, Decker had suggested shifters, and after long consideration and a few interviews, Simone had agreed. The wolves had trained well with the vampires with only a few scuffles, but the two species working in defense of the same territory was breaking new ground.

Devon grasped my hand, and I squeezed back, giving him a half-hearted smile. His lips were firmly set, his jaw stiff, and his eyes shined with the glow of his beast. He was pissed. An attack barely an hour after Devon's return from the Council. Would Venizi have attacked regardless of what Devon's answer had been? Not that we knew this attack came from Lorenzo. But if not him, then who?

The headset crackled.

"They've breached the perimeter at the main entrance and two other points a quarter mile due north and south of the entrance." Simone's voice was calm and measured. "The shifters have retreated to the first checkpoints with the Alpha security team."

Devon nodded, his gaze moving to the window and the sky beyond. Ten minutes into the ride, Devon, Simone, and Sergi all moved closer to a window. We must be getting close. Devon put his arm around me, his cheek next to mine, as we watched more than a dozen vamps move from the perimeter inward. There were probably the same number, if not more, at the north and south breeches.

Several glanced up as the copter approached, and when one pointed something larger than a rifle at them, the copter banked hard to the right. I closed my eyes, waiting for the impending explosion, but nothing happened.

I opened one eye. Simone, who sat across from me, wore a wide grin. I stuck out my tongue, which was completely immature, but I didn't want to say anything over the mic. Her smile widened, and the tips of her fangs dropped.

I rolled my eyes, sticking with the immaturity. It worked so well for me. "Was that a rocket launcher?" I glanced at the others.

"A grenade launcher," Sergi replied.

Oh, great. So much better.

I caught the movement of a wolf racing behind scrub oak as we passed, then the first of the buildings coming up fast.

The sound of an explosion was muffled by the headsets.

I twisted around to see if I could see anything, but all I saw was the chaparral landscape.

Another explosion. Then another.

"What was that?" I asked.

"They just crossed the first checkpoint," Sergi answered.

When I looked at Devon, he shrugged. "C-4. It won't get them all, but it will slow them down."

"What about the wolves?" I asked.

"The explosives are remotely detonated. Alpha team would have waited for the wolves to join them before setting them off."

"What if they ran over them without knowing where they were?"

Devon shook his head. "The C-4 requires a shockwave to set them off."

I swallowed a lump in my throat. Devon meant business. He'd never mentioned using explosives as part of the security plan.

The copter made a slow circle as it landed several hundred yards from the manor. Everyone exited quickly, heads down, as we ran for the building. The rotors sounded as if they were slowing, but I couldn't be sure.

When we reached the manor, two vamps were waiting for us. I recognized one as Marta, who used to work at the coastal manor. Her smile was grim as she nodded at Simone and Devon.

"So far, the only activity has been along the main gate. We have three wolves watching our exit roads, and they're backed up by Delta team."

"Why wouldn't Lorenzo attack from more than one side?" It made sense to me.

"The north side of the property runs along a rocky gully, making it difficult for vehicles to approach," Simone answered. "There's a single road that runs along the gully before branching out on both ends. It would be easy to ambush trespassers on either end of the road. There's no road on the south side, but we've added fencing with razor wire for a mile to discourage anyone coming on foot."

"I don't remember any of this when we discussed Oasis as a fallback from our raid of Shadow Island."

"We installed it shortly after."

I wondered if that was when the C-4 was added, but decided this wasn't the time to ask. "So, what's the game plan? I assume everyone who isn't security has been moved to the manor, and the human staff is in the panic room."

Simone nodded. "All according to Level One security."

"So, do we wait to see how many make it here?"

"Hardly." Devon walked to a patio table where Sergi had set down a duffel bag. He removed several swords, a dozen daggers, and four handguns. Mateo placed a hard-sided case on the table and opened the lid.

Dozens of over-the-ear earbuds were displayed in a foam insert. Devon selected one, turned it on, and stuck it in his ear. He tapped it, said something, then nodded to Simone, who took one, and then Sergi and the rest of the security detail each picked up one.

"Where did you get these?" I took one and slipped it over my ear.

"Friends in all the right places." Devon already had a handgun in a side holster, a dagger on his belt, and his sword in a scabbard, but he picked up two more daggers and stuck them in his vest.

I had my dagger, but I picked up two more, refusing the sword. I'd started training with a short sword, but I wasn't comfortable enough to use it in the field. "You mean friends in the military?"

Devon had provided vests, hi-tech body cams, and earbuds for Harlow's team when they broke into Gheata's rented house, searching for evidence to clear Devon of Boretsky's murder. I'd never asked where he got them.

He smiled rather than answer my question. Instead, he pressed the earbud again. "Can everyone hear me?"

Multiple clicks came back. It sounded like more than the group standing on the patio. Devon turned to the group. "We move out in three teams. Central command, Charlie teams one, two, and three are ready to move out."

"Team Rogue is in place with Alpha and Beta teams one and two, waiting for the word to be given."

"Roger." Devon nodded, and Simone and Sergi immediately ran off in different directions, each with a four-man security detail. The others moved out in backup positions. Then Devon nodded at me and took off, with me on his six. I'd always wanted to say that.

I felt the presence of the security detail behind me, though they made no sound as we raced toward the main entrance. I had no idea where the checkpoints were, not that it would matter since

I knew little of the landscape and even less of the security updates. After today, that was going to change.

I stuck with Devon as we sprinted through the scrub oak and prairie grass. After a quarter of a mile, we slowed. The sun was behind us, and I questioned the wisdom of sending an invasion team that would be looking into the sun.

"Charlie Two has reached Beta One. Moving to the northern incursion group." Simone's voice was calm, low, and showed no signs of heavy breathing.

A couple minutes later, Sergi checked in. "Charlie Three has reached Beta Two. We're moving to the southern invasion group."

We ran several more yards when a wolf stepped out from behind a boulder. Devon stopped, holding up a fist. The shifter looked toward the west and made a chuffing sound. Devon nodded, and I assumed we met up with one of the teams.

"Charlie One has met up with Alpha team. All players are in position."

"Roger, Charlie team." I didn't recognize the voice but assumed it was someone from the command center. "The targets are a hundred yards out, moving slowly."

"How do they know that?" I whispered to Devon.

"Drones."

I looked up but didn't see anything, thought I knew they could be difficult to see. "I don't hear them."

"They're flying at a higher altitude."

I really needed to sit in on the security discussions.

"Let's try to keep one or two alive," Devon said over the comms. "Team Rogue, the word is given. Everyone move out."

The word given was something I understood. Team Rogue was the wolves, and Devon just gave them the okay to take down as many of the enemy as possible—no survivors required.

We moved quietly. Would these be the same halflings Venizi had been sending before, or would these vamps be his true bloods?

I scanned the area in front of us, watching for any movement.

Devon slowed as we reached a ridge. When I glanced to my right, I noticed the wolf working slowly several feet in front of Devon. He was using the wolves as scouts.

The wolf stopped, lifted its nose, then turned and nodded at Devon. I should have expected the human-like behaviors, having worked with them at the paper mill in my search for Devon when he'd been stuck in his beast form. It was still unsettling.

Devon nodded in return. "Charlie One has engaged the target."

We moved on, my hand reaching for my dagger.

The ridge wasn't much of one, and though the other side was filled with scrub oak, I caught movement. A shot rang out, and then another. Then we saw them. They'd brought rifles. An answering shot rang out from our side, and an enemy vamp fell. He wouldn't be down long, depending on where he was hit.

Sergi and Simone both confirmed they'd also engaged the target.

A movement to my left startled me. A vamp came at me from ten yards away, and without a second thought, I ran for him.

When he saw me coming, he raised his rifle, but he wasn't fast enough. I leaped up, hitting him with a kick in the chest. My foot clipped the rifle, the hard metal slamming into my ankle. I landed with a soft cry. That hurt.

The vamp was down, but he was rising. I pulled my dagger and shoved it into his side, giving it a good twist. I followed it up with another quick stab in his neck.

He pushed me off and struggled for his weapon. What was with firearms at a vamp fight? I kicked the rifle away and then kicked the vamp in the head. Then I was on my knees, stabbing at his neck until there wasn't anything left but bloody pulp. I really needed to reconsider the sword.

I turned when someone screamed. A vamp was only twenty feet away and looked like he'd been coming up from behind me. A wolf stood on his chest and proceeded to rip out the vamp's throat until his head rolled away. The wolf glanced at me, wiped his snout on the vamp's shirt, then trotted off for its next victim.

I surveyed the area, an occasional gunshot echoing through the ridge. Then my gaze landed on Devon and a security guard fighting off two vamps. I ran that way, keeping an eye out and staying low behind the oak. I tripped over a vamp who was on their stomach. His ankles and wrists were secured with zip ties. They managed to save one. I regained my feet when I heard someone behind me.

I twirled around in time to see a vamp running for me. He stopped and swung his sword over his head. I took the couple seconds before the sword came down to duck and roll. When I sprang up, I could only stare.

The vamp hadn't been aiming for me. He'd cut the head off the secured vamp.

What the hell?

He glanced up at me, smiled, then ran for me with his sword held high. On second thought, maybe I should have grabbed a handgun.

I held my ground and let him come. They always seemed to falter a bit when I didn't run, and when they saw I was a woman. I smiled back, and that always made them second-guess their actions. This vamp wasn't any different. I moved toward him as he came at me, my eyes focused on his arms rising and the position of the sword.

When his arm was two-thirds to its farthest point, apparently planning on putting all his power into his swing, I bent my head and turned my shoulder as I barreled into him. I felt the force of his arm and the side of the blade as it slammed into my back.

The breath rushed out of him. We were on the ground, rolling, and I stabbed him over and over in the side, searching for his kidneys until he dropped the blade. I hated the fact he'd killed one of his own. A vamp that couldn't defend themselves. This one needed to be saved for Devon, but I didn't have any zip ties.

I rolled him over and crossed his arms over his chest, kneeling on them to keep them in place. When I heard the rustle of brush, I twirled around as I stood. I stepped on the vamp's stomach and one of his arms that had fallen away from his chest.

One of the guards who'd traveled with us from the coastal manor held up a pair of zip ties.

I grinned and helped roll the vamp over, then waited while he bound the wrists.

"Alpha team and Rogue team clear."

"Beta One clear."

"Beta Two clear."

"Charlie Two clear."

"Charlie Three clear."

Then I heard Devon's voice, but I wasn't sure where he was. "Charlie One clear. Wait for the sweepers."

"Sweepers en route." I didn't recognize the voice of whoever was at central command. I really needed to spend more time here.

I wanted to meet up with Devon, but I waited for the sweepers as the partner of the guard reached us. She stared down at the headless vamp and then at me. It was Roberta, one of the lead guards at the coastal manor.

"Did you do this?"

I shook my head, wishing I had water, and nodded to the secured vamp. "I don't think they wanted anyone taken alive."

She gave the headless vamp a long look then walked to the other vamp and gave him a swift kick in the side. After giving it a second thought, she followed up with a kick in the head before moving to her partner. She didn't have to say anything to tell me how she felt about Venizi's orders.

Ten minutes later, I heard the sound of the jeeps. They picked up the dead, injured, and any vamps they were able to capture. Then Devon was beside me, surveying me from top to bottom until I pushed his arms away.

"I'm fine. I just need water."

He handed me a bottle that he must have gotten from one of the sweepers.

I dropped to the ground and took a long drink, wiping my mouth on a blood-stained sleeve. "Is the coastal manor safe? Did Venizi attack the safe houses?" I gave him the same perusal he'd given me. He appeared uninjured.

"The manor is fine, but there was an increase in traffic—there and at the safe houses."

I took another long drink and pointed to the secured vamp. "He killed the other vamp so he couldn't talk."

Devon nodded, then looked at Roberta, who stared at the secured vamp with a disgusted look on her face. "Perhaps I should let Roberta have the first crack at him."

"I don't think she'd say no." I sucked in a deep breath. "Did we lose anyone?"

"No, but we have a few injured, including a shifter. Mateo suffered the severest wounds, but he should be alright in a few days. Everyone else is accounted for."

"Why didn't Venizi attack at night? Wouldn't the advantage be on their side?"

He sat next to me. "Not really. The drones have thermal imaging, and we know the terrain better than an invading force. We also have night vision goggles."

"Who do you know to get all this hi-tech stuff?"

He chuckled. "We're not using anything you can't buy off the street, but I know a senator or two for when I require the newest technology."

I leaned my head on his shoulder. "Why am I not surprised." After a beat, I mentioned, "Venizi is getting bolder."

"And with every attack, he shows his hand and helps us shore up our weaknesses. He still has the numbers, but with the additional shifters added to our security, he won't gain any ground. He'll become frustrated and become careless. The Council will take note, and while they won't take any action, they'll put pressure on him. And that's exactly where I want him."

Chapter Eleven

THE CLEAN-UP AT Oasis didn't take long as dusk arrived. Once all the injured and dead had been removed, the security detail hauled away Venizi's lone surviving vamp for interrogation. Devon, Sergi, and Roberta had gone back to Oasis with him. I didn't feel the need to participate.

That left me with Simone, who had commandeered one of the jeeps so we could perform a quick assessment of the damage to the security perimeter and make note of anything that needed to be replaced, like the C-4.

We bumped over the terrain as she pointed to various landmarks so I could become oriented to the landscape.

"We try to use the natural features of the land to determine our security requirements." Simone pointed to a line of scrub oaks about a half mile in from the main entrance that stretched for several hundred yards on both sides. "The C-4 requires a detonation to set it off, which we can do remotely. The shifters know where all the explosives are located so, when necessary, as we learned today, they can lead the enemy to them."

She pointed to an oak tree. "We have surveillance cameras along the perimeter fencing, but we've also added them to trees at strategic points. The command center has a view of all the main entry points, as well as those areas that are easy to broach on foot, like the south border."

"This all sounds great and obviously worked, but they could have ignored the main entrance and selected spots far from the gates or taken a chance on the west entrance."

"Yes, and chances are that's what they'll do the next time."

"You think Venizi is still testing our security."

"Yes."

When we approached the areas where the explosives discharged, we got out and walked the line. One of the shifters joined us and helped point out where the C-4 hadn't been detonated. They must be able to smell it.

"Devon mentioned he knew a senator or two." I stared down at a hole created by the explosives. It was pretty deep. "Was he joking about where he got the C-4?"

"He's not joking about knowing a couple senators. He also knows congressmen and governors. It's mostly regarding human business, but also to ensure any cover we might need. Several people in government know about vampires and shifters and walk a line to keep the general public from knowing about us as best they can."

"It seems dangerous to be getting supplies from the government."

"We don't. There are other ways to get the supplies we need for defense. Devon knows people who know people."

I chuckled. "I see. The mercenary types."

"Everyone has something to trade for the right price or, as is the vampire and shifter way, for favors owed."

When we returned to the jeep, Simone glanced down at the shifter. "Are you ready for a break? We can take you back with us."

The shifter didn't need to be asked twice and jumped into the back of the jeep. When we returned to the main building, the shifter jumped out and trotted off down the road toward the bungalows.

"They seem to be working out." I rolled my shoulder, which had begun to ache after the adrenaline had worn off.

"Yes, which is why I'm adding more. We can't cover the entire property with our security teams, but we can set up enough defensive positions that once the enemy comes, we can funnel them into areas we want them."

"Makes sense." I was done with the security review. I needed a hot bath.

We parted ways in the foyer, and I headed for Devon's bedroom. After a long bath, I crawled into bed and fell asleep.

It was dark when something woke me. I found myself enveloped in strong arms and a warm chest. I burrowed into Devon. Fingers strummed along my back, and that must have been what woke me.

"How long have I been asleep?"

"I don't know. I've been asleep for a couple of hours myself. Based on when Simone last saw you, I'd guess you'd been asleep an hour or so before that."

"Should I ask about the interrogation?"

"We didn't learn much other than Venizi sent them. Another group of halflings."

"It seems he's saving his best."

"Agreed." He kissed my temple and then rolled away, laughing when I moaned and reached for him.

"We need dinner and more sleep. We'll return to the manor in the morning."

My stomach growled in agreement which made Devon give me an I-told-you-so look. We dressed, but before we left for the dining room, I pulled him to a chair and sat opposite him.

"There's something on my mind I wanted to talk to you about. I don't know if it's trouble or not, but I'm worried."

"Is this about Colantha? Is everything alright with Hamilton?"

I slapped my forehead. "I forgot about Hamilton. I should have asked Colantha. Lyra will be disappointed."

"She'll be here soon, and Lyra will be fine until then. If it's not that, what is it?"

I bit my bottom lip. "I called Mom."

"Is she alright?"

"That's just it. I don't know. She knew Christopher's case was closed, and she appears to have moved on, but April still thinks I had something to do with it." I snorted. "She thinks the cops are covering it up because of you." When Devon's brows lifted, I shook my head. "Not you specifically, but whoever I'm living with."

"Aah. I suppose that isn't unexpected."

I was a bit surprised by his response, but let it go. "There were people at the house. I heard them in the background. More than one."

"April's friends?"

"Maybe. Probably. But Mom acted like she didn't want anyone to know she was talking to me. She moved to another room and closed the door. I don't know. We'd barely spoken for more than a minute or two when someone pounded on the door looking for her. It was a male voice. Then she said not to call back, and that she'd call me once April calmed down."

"That does seem odd, but maybe she's just trying to keep the peace."

"Maybe." Something else had bothered me. "She made a comment about Christopher's death. That he kind of had it coming and that he'd put them all at risk."

Devon squeezed my hand. "If he was doing business with Venizi then it makes sense."

"Yes, but then she said, in some ways, they're still at risk. I don't know what that means."

Devon dropped my hand and leaned back in the chair. He

considered my words. "You think Venizi is still controlling them somehow."

I stayed on the edge of my seat, one knee bouncing. "All I keep thinking about is that night when you took me back to my apartment. April had been there with a vamp. What if she's messed up with Venizi?"

"A great deal has happened since then, especially with Underwood's murder. But I'll have Sergi look into it if it will make you feel better."

"It would." And I meant it.

When Devon pulled me up, he wrapped his arms around me and gave me a solid kiss. "Everything will work out. It always does. Now, let's get something for that stomach of yours. It sounds like a small volcano."

I punched him in his side, but he didn't fool me. A crease still marred his forehead. He didn't like what he'd heard. Instead of calming me, my worry ratcheted up. If Venizi had control over April, had he discovered who I was? If so, then Mom was in danger. Just what we needed with everything else going on.

As if he heard my inner thoughts, he squeezed my waist as we walked through the halls. "Don't worry. Let's wait and see what Sergi discovers before you create trouble where there isn't any."

I nodded. But that ship had already set sail.

THE NEXT MORNING, Devon, Cressa, and Sergi traveled back to Santiga Bay by helicopter, leaving Simone at Oasis to rebuild and enhance their security. On the return trip, Devon pointed out various landmarks to Cressa as they flew over the city, the ride more relaxing than the day before.

After the limo delivered them to the manor, Sergi and Devon went to his office while Cressa headed for the training room.

Devon dropped into his chair and stared out his window while Sergi grumbled as he reviewed updates on his tablet.

"The city safe house experienced a level two security threat this morning. One guard was injured."

"What happened?"

"There had been several drive-bys during the assault on Oasis. A couple of hours ago, two cars rammed the gate, and three vampires got over the fence. The vampires were eliminated, but a guard was shot. He's healing with the help of a blood donation."

"Venizi's attacks are like mosquitoes. Annoying but of little consequence." Devon swiveled back to face Sergi, feeling the need to pick up the white crystal, but he refrained. It was becoming something of an affectation whenever he was stressed.

Sergi laid down the tablet and stretched, rubbing his shoulder. "His testing of our defenses only helps us. With each weak point they discover, we have time to strengthen it."

Devon gave his friend a long look and a slow smile. "Did you injure yourself?"

Sergi growled. "An old ailment acting up."

Devon didn't respond. It was rare for previous injuries to bother vampires after receiving healing blood. But ancients had been increasingly susceptible to blood diseases, and he hoped this wasn't a sign of something worse. "Have you taken a blood donation since the attack?"

"No. But I'll see to it after training." Sergi glanced at his watch. "I called for Bella."

"She'll be here." The words were barely out of his mouth when a light tap on the door preceded the vampire.

"Sorry, I'm late." Bella strolled to the espresso machine and began making a cup. "I sent Jacques with several from our security detail to the city safe house to assist with repairs." She glanced over her shoulder. "Anyone want one?" When they both nodded, she continued on to the next cup. "I think we should stay on high alert for another day."

"I agree." Sergi ignored his tablet, which Devon found strange but didn't say anything.

Once Bella delivered the cups, she took a seat and leaned back with a crossed leg resting on her knee. "What's up?"

"Cress had a disturbing discussion with her mother."

"Is her mother upset that Cressa was cleared of her stepfather's death?"

"No. Their relationship seems solid. It's April, the stepsister. She believes the police are covering up Cressa's involvement due to her relationship to me." When Bella's brow rose, he added, "Not me specifically, but whoever the mystery man is that she's staying with."

Bella nodded. "And why is this our problem?"

"April had been seen with vampires when Underwood was searching for Cressa's medallion. From what Cressa could tell from her phone conversation yesterday, there were people at the house who might be controlling her mother. She admits there was little to go on, but it sounded like they might be watching who her mother speaks with."

"You think April is working with Venizi?" Sergi sipped his espresso, and though he glanced at his tablet, he didn't pick it up.

Devon wondered if Sergi was finding his attachment to his tablet as obsessive as Devon's attraction to the crystal. "It's a possibility. Maybe not with his House specifically, but perhaps one that owes him allegiance."

"Do you think Venizi has put it together that Cressa was Underwood's stepdaughter?" Bella asked.

"He didn't seem to think so when she was a captive at Shadow Island."

"Maybe he was holding that knowledge back as a weapon if Cressa wasn't controllable under the mesmerizing," Sergi suggested.

"Either way, it needs to be checked."

"You want me to monitor the situation?" Bella asked.

"Yes. But only the house. See who comes and goes, and who's in each vehicle."

"That might be difficult. If it's vampires, the windows will be tinted."

He nodded. "At least we'll have some idea of the activity level and maybe get a glimpse of the drivers. Don't trail anyone. This is a simple stakeout." He turned to Sergi. "Send Bella the address. I'd also like you to gather what you can on April. I know you have some preliminary background when you investigated Cressa. Dig deeper."

"Anything else?" Bella asked.

"Check the perimeter security. Sergi, see what images we can pick up on the property."

"What about inside?" Sergi asked.

"Cressa can give us that if needed."

Bella rose and picked up her and Sergi's empty cups, placing them on the counter. Before she left, Devon called out. "And take Jacques when he returns."

She waved as she exited and shut the door.

Sergi stood. "If there's nothing else for me, I'd like to review the security files from yesterday."

Devon nodded and turned toward the window, closing his eyes when he heard the door shut. His plans for war hadn't included Cressa's mother. But, it was a simple enough task, assuming they could reach her. Assuming there was, in fact, a problem and that vampires were involved. When Devon had met with Willa a month ago, she'd mentioned an escape plan. Was it sufficient for her current predicament? With any luck they'd know more in the next couple of days.

A knock at the door made him swivel his chair toward it. Lucas stuck his head in.

"Do you have a few minutes?"

"Of course, come in."

Lucas laid a folder on the desk before sitting. "This is the final translation of the vampiric portion of the *De første dage*. I've checked it twice."

Devon nodded. "I haven't had a chance to read the vampiric version yet with the raid on Oasis. I'll make a point to do that this afternoon." He glanced at the wall clock. "I'm hoping Colantha will arrive today. With luck, we should have a completed translation in the next couple of days."

"Have you spoken with Remus?"

"No. I want to see if Colantha can translate the second half first."

"That makes sense." Lucas stared at the pages, a frown appearing.

"Was there something else?"

Lucas fidgeted, and Devon waited for his young cadre to put his words together.

"It's something that came up when Ginger and I were searching for the book." He ran his hands through his hair, then didn't seem to know what to do with them. Unusual for any of his cadre.

"Go on." Devon kept his tone light and encouraging.

"Did Cressa ever tell you how she ended up with a debt to a loan shark?"

The question surprised Devon, especially when he'd recently been thinking about her debt. "I never asked, and she never shared."

"Ginger and I spoke a bit about our past during the mission." He laughed. "I guess it was brought on by the memories that came to me during my recovery. When I shared my past, she shared some of hers. I won't go into details, but someone saddled Ginger with the debt, and, for some reason I don't understand, Cressa took on the debt." He lowered his head, seeming to search his hands for something as they flexed into fists and then released. When he looked up, Devon was surprised by the sadness reflected in his gaze. "I don't know if Cressa thinks about the debt, but it weighs on

Ginger. She believes the reason for Cressa first coming here was her fault." He shrugged. "Or that's how she perceives it." He laughed again. "Though, I guess it worked out for us."

The comment tightened Devon's chest. The pain of Lucas's statement doubled Devon's own thoughts. His own worries. "I'll take care of it."

Lucas's laughter faded to lips thinning with some other emotion. "I didn't mean to interfere."

Devon smiled and shook his head. "I appreciate you reminding me of something I should have cared for long before now." When Lucas didn't appear any less concerned, Devon shook his head. "You're cadre. It's your job to remind me of my responsibilities, whether I like it or not. And truth should never be denied. Cressa being here has helped us. And if Lyra were here, she would tell you that all the events in Ginger's and Cressa's lives led them to us." He grinned. "And then you can try to tell her different."

Lucas released a breath, and though he didn't smile, the guilt appeared gone. "I think I'll leave those discussions between brother and sister."

Devon stood, walked around his desk, and squeezed his young cadre's shoulder. "That's probably a good idea. Take some time for yourself and Ginger. You've both worked hard to finish the translations. I'll need you rested when Colantha arrives."

After Lucas closed the door behind him, Devon returned to his chair and swiveled to the window. He stared at the sycamore tree and then at his parents' graves. "Soon, Father. Soon our House will be at peace—one way or another."

Chapter Twelve

I BARELY REACHED my bed before falling face-first into the soft covers—my limbs numb. I'm not sure if I passed out, but when I woke, I couldn't remember climbing the stairs. I do remember my legs feeling nothing more than melting, waxy imitations. Training had been going well. Ginger had thirty minutes to kill, and she was showing off some impressive new skills. Then Sergi showed up, and she begged off, claiming Anna would be waiting for her. I couldn't tell if she was lying or not, but I caught her grin before she shut the door behind her.

Sergi led me through several routines as if he had something to prove. Maybe he thought I'd spent too much time on the beach in Spain. Either way, he left me sweating on the floor, barely able to crawl to a water bottle. When my body cooled, and my legs showed signs of life, I finally dragged myself upstairs and didn't remember much after that.

"Wake up, Cressa."

The harsh command was like a gong going off in my head. I sat up, sputtering from the lint stuck to my lips. I brushed it off, realizing I must have drooled in my sleep. How embarrassing. I glanced up, searching for whoever woke me to find Colantha standing in front of the windows.

"Colantha. No one told me you were here."

"That's because I'm not."

Good grief.

"Did you wake me up in a construct?" I glanced around as I scooted to the edge of the bed. It looked like my bedroom. My sneakers were still on the floor at the bottom of the bed.

"I thought it was only fair."

I rubbed my head. Then her words hit me. "Really? This is revenge for calling you to my construct. You could have ignored me."

She smiled, but there was mischief dancing in her sparkling gaze. "Tell Devon we've left the airport and should arrive by two. If he could advise the guards at the gate, I'd appreciate it."

"Sure. How about calling next time?"

She winked and then disappeared. I felt a slight shift as I came out of the construct, which left me sitting on the bed as if nothing had happened. I really had to be more careful in dealing with that woman. Sometimes, she was just downright scary.

I sniffed my pits. Shower first. It was quick, and I was jogging down the stairs within fifteen minutes, my legs once again my own. It took me several more minutes before finding Devon in the library. I leaned against the doorframe. He sat in the chair I normally found him in. It was a well-cushioned, high-backed chair in a light floral print, and had been his mother's favorite, or so he told me. He was reading a book, his fingers softly brushing the pages as he read. The lamp behind him cast a yellow glow, softening his harder surfaces.

I loved watching him in his own silent world, a book in hand. If it was late evening, there would be a snifter of cognac within reach. At this time of day, the teapot wasn't a surprise.

"Are you just going to watch me or come in?"

His voice startled me, and I immediately straightened. Then, feeling foolish, I shuffled over. "Do you always know when I'm watching you?"

"Not always. But, as you know, we're expecting visitors, so I keep an ear open."

He took my hand and pulled me around to sit on his lap as he placed the book aside. I landed with a soft "oomph" and managed to catch a glimpse of the title before his mouth swooped down for a heartwarming kiss.

I waited for him, enjoying the moment, but the minute his head lifted, I blurted out, "Is that the translation?"

He chuckled. "I see I'm not going to get more than one kiss." He shifted me and laid the book on my lap. "I'd let you read it, but this is the copy Lucas brought back, and, as you know, the first half is in vampiric. Lucas has a transcribed copy available, though I'm not sure if you'll have time if Colantha arrives today."

"I won't. That's why I was searching for you. Colantha made a surprise visit to my room. She woke me from my nap."

"She didn't call?"

I snorted. "I guess she's still pissed that I pulled her into a construct when I needed to talk to her rather than just calling the number you gave me."

He chuckled. "Revenge. A woman after my own heart."

"I should have known I wouldn't get any sympathy from you." I flipped through the pages, stopping to review the tight script.

"What did Colantha say?"

After a minute, he nudged me. "What? Oh, she's on her way from the airport. She'll be here at two and would like the guards notified."

He glanced at his watch. "I would think by now they'd know not to question her, but I'll let them know. Did you tell Lyra?"

I popped up, and Devon winced when my elbow hit a sensitive spot. "Sorry. I can't believe I didn't think of that." Then I deflated.

"What?"

"I didn't ask about Hamilton."

"Aah. Well, I don't think he's coming, or Colantha would have said something."

"You think?"

He shrugged. "Not for sure, but something tells me he's not ready yet."

I nodded. "That won't be any easier for Lyra to hear."

"Maybe so, but she should still be told what we know so she can prepare."

I placed the book on the table and was getting up when he pulled me back down. The next kiss was more heated than the first, and his gaze glowed with the beast. Damn, if he didn't know how to turn me on.

Then he stood and placed me on my feet. He picked up the book, finished his cup of tea, then slapped me on the ass before striding for the door.

"And tell Ginger to be ready. I want everyone in my office when she arrives."

Then he was out the door. Relegated to messenger service, I considered where Ginger might be. Lyra was most likely in her room, but I preferred to have Ginger by my side. She had a knack for calming Lyra in difficult situations.

The problem was, I couldn't find Ginger. Since I was already on the first floor, I checked the solarium and the pool room, then squared my shoulders to track down Anna. I didn't want to have to face her so soon after our trip. I wasn't ready to restart the history classes, but I had a task and refused to be cowed by her. At least she was predictable. Anna, as I suspected, was in her office. I hated going in there. For some reason, it reminded me of my trips to the principal's office. I'd been an unruly student. Go figure.

"Hey, Anna. Do you have a minute? I thought you might know where Ginger is."

Anna was writing something on a pad. She was as old school as Devon when it came to her work, preferring pen and paper to computers whenever possible. I cleared my throat when it was apparent Anna either didn't hear me or was ignoring me. It was a fifty-fifty split most days.

On my second throat clearing, her head popped up. "Oh, hi, Cressa. I heard you were back, and then the Oasis attack happened." She sat back and rubbed her eyes, leaning her head against the chair. Dark circles made her look haunted, and a tick of concern hit me.

"I know. I should have come to see you sooner, but it's been one thing after another." I stepped in and sat in the chair across from her. "Are you alright?"

Her eyes were closed, and a soft smile eased my concerns. "Just tired. I didn't get much sleep last night."

"Was it because of the attack?"

Her eyes popped open, and she sat up. "Not at all." She shook her head. "Well, I mean, of course, the attack concerned me." She gave me a thoughtful stare. "I have to thank Ginger." That surprised me. "She talked me into defense training. She thought it would make me feel better if I had skills if we were ever attacked." She snorted a laugh. "She was right. When the alarms sounded yesterday, I was concerned, but the panic that usually comes with it didn't appear. Besides, I was too annoyed by the interruption."

I blinked. This was a different Anna. "Annoyed?"

She nodded, her eyes taking on a radical glaze. "When I was at Oasis, the library was a mess." She must have caught something in my confused expression. "Oh, not like the books were all over the place, they just weren't in any type of order. Fiction was mixed up with non-fiction. If you wanted to read something about the vampiric era during the human Victorian age, the books were spread all through the library." Her voice rose as the horror of it all took over.

All I'd wanted was a quick yes or no answer on whether she knew where Ginger was. Now, I wanted to curl up and take a nap until she stopped.

"Anyway," she blew out a breath. "It was Ginger again who

said I'd be the best one to fix it, and she was right. I spoke with Simone. She sent me the inventory for the entire library, and now I'm going through the list to organize the books. It's more daunting a task than I thought. I also have a schematic of the room and the layout of the bookcases so I can determine how and where the books should be shelved."

"Sounds like you have a handle on it."

"Yes, but there's still so much to do." She cocked her head to the side. "I'm glad you came. I had to handle other tasks while you and Ginger were away, so I haven't been able to get to the Oasis library problem until now. I was up until two last night working on it, then tossed and turned for a couple of hours before coming back down here." She chewed her lip. "I came to a decision this morning. I'll need a couple of weeks to complete this task. I'm afraid I'll need to push your and Ginger's lessons out until this is done. I know you wanted to get back to class."

Two weeks of no classes. I felt like the kid who left the principal's office with a two-week suspension. The principal thought he was punishing me, but to me—it was a two-week vacation. I forced a sorrowful tone.

"Wow, that's too bad. Ginger and I will do our best to keep ourselves occupied. I know how important it is to have a functioning library."

If she caught any innocent deception in my tone, she didn't show it.

"Oh, thank you, Cressa. Now, if you don't mind, I really need to get back to this." She picked up her pen and reviewed her notes.

Duly dismissed, I strode to the door and was shutting the door when I remembered why I'd come in the first place. "Have you seen Ginger recently?"

She didn't even look up. "A bit earlier, when she came for class, and I told her the same thing I just told you. She could be anywhere."

I shook my head and closed her door. That was fifteen minutes of my life I'd never get back and with nothing to show for it. I checked her room, then decided to go up and talk to Lyra without the benefit of Ginger.

Lyra wasn't in her room. Damn.

I snapped my fingers and ran down the stairs. I don't know why it hadn't been my first thought. There was only one other gossip magnet in the house besides Ginger. Cook. Fortunately, Cook was right where he was supposed to be—in the kitchen in the middle of making something, although I had no idea what it was.

"Hi, Cook."

He spun around, a teaspoon in one hand and a jar of herbs in the other. "Cressa, I can't tell you how wonderful it is to have you back. Come in." He turned back to his task. "I'm making sauces. I always like to have a supply available. Sit, sit."

I wandered over and plopped on a stool at the counter. "I don't have time to talk. Colantha will be here soon, and I can't seem to find Ginger or Lyra."

"Ah, it will be good to see Colantha. But to be honest, it's Frederick and Jamison I'm eager to see."

"Really?" As Colantha's bodyguards, the two vamps rarely spoke.

"Oh, yes. They're amazing chefs, and we often share recipes."

"Really?" I was repeating myself, but no other words came to me.

"Yes. While they haven't been officially trained like me, they learned from their mother and grandmother, or so they tell me. They have Creole recipes handed down from several generations, and several Cajun and French dishes as well. And, of course, I have an array of my own specialties."

I rubbed my stomach. "Don't I know it?"

He lifted his head. "I should show them my recipes for these sauces. What excellent timing."

I patted his shoulder. "I'll tell them as soon as they arrive. Do you know where Ginger and Lyra are?"

"Try the sycamore tree. They left about thirty minutes ago with a basket."

I kissed his cheek. "Thank you."

"Any time. Any time." But he was back to his sauces with as much enthusiasm as Anna and her books.

I took the route through the solarium to reach the backyard, my mind wandering to Anna and Cook. They had been so consumed by their projects. The only thing I had to look forward to every day was time in the training room and when the next meal was. I needed a project.

Ginger and Lyra were sitting on a blanket under the sycamore. Ginger was peering into the open basket then glanced up at my approach.

She looked chagrined. "I'm sorry. I should have asked you to lunch."

I shook my head. "I haven't been up long. Sergi kicked my ass in training." I plopped down and grinned at Lyra before stealing a pickle from Ginger's plate. Cook canned his own, and I'd be hard pressed to find a better tasting one. I munched the end. "Colantha will be here at two." I snapped my gaze to Lyra. After all that time searching for Ginger so she could help soften the news with Lyra, I just blurted it out.

Lyra nodded, and though her shoulders sagged, her smile was sweet. "Colantha told me. She said Hamilton is doing well but is working through a few issues, so he'll remain behind." Then she brightened. "He told her to tell me he was writing a letter. He's still not ready for the change in technology."

"Colantha called you?"

"She texted."

Who was that woman? I shouldn't be surprised. Everyone texted. But somehow, the image of Colantha using a cell phone or texting wouldn't solidify in my head. Weren't dreamwalkers supposed to be, I don't know, more mysterious?

Ginger changed the subject to the more critical topic of setting up a home shopping day. We'd gather around a big screen and watch the various shopping networks while we drank and shopped. Cook would keep the food coming. Since we were on lockdown, this was the closest to a girl's day out we could get.

Once we'd selected a date, we packed everything up, dropped the basket in the kitchen, and headed for Devon's office with five minutes to spare.

Simone met us at the door after arriving from Oasis. She wore her don't-mess-with-me face. It didn't have anything to do with us. She got that look whenever Colantha showed up, having never grown comfortable with the dreamwalker. They were both control freaks.

We were a boisterous group as we stormed into Devon's office. Lyra and Simone stopped, and Ginger and I plowed into them, not expecting the pause.

Colantha, Devon, Sergi, and Decker were sitting in chairs positioned into a tight square so they were all facing each other. Frederick and Jamison stood guard over them as the four stared into space.

They were dreamwalking.

What the fuck?

Chapter Thirteen

"WHAT'S GOING ON HERE?" Simone marched into Devon's office but stopped when Frederick and Jamison took a step toward her.

I tugged on Simone's caftan. Any other day, she'd spin around, fangs dropped, and if I was lucky, would only glare and not strike out. Today, she took it for the warning it was. Don't mess with the dreamwalking. It was obvious by the way the chairs had been placed so the occupants faced each other that this was voluntary.

"Hey, there you are." Lucas walked in with Bella at his side, each carrying a tray of food and a glass pitcher of what looked like sangria.

They set the trays on the table in the sitting area. Lucas had a book under his arm, and he dropped it next to the tray.

Simone turned on them, repeating her earlier question. "What's going on here?"

Lucas glanced around the room and recognition blossomed in his gaze. "Oh, Colantha arrived early, just after Decker. Remus was becoming anxious waiting for news about the book. He wanted to talk to Devon, but since we want communication between them limited, Colantha suggested a dreamwalk. Decker texted Remus, and he agreed." He glanced at the wall clock. "They shouldn't be much longer. Colantha said ten minutes at the most."

Simone glared at me.

"Don't give me that look. I'm as surprised as you."

"You knew nothing about this?" Simone asked.

"All I know is that Colantha scared the shit out of me when she woke me up in a construct, telling me to inform Devon she'd be arriving at two." I replayed the memory. I'd still been a bit drowsy at the time.

"What?" Simone must have seen something change in my expression that made her hackles rise, and the tip of her fangs became visible.

"She winked at me." I glanced to where Colantha sat. "She couldn't have known that she'd need to dreamwalk right away. I'm sure the wink was just her way of teaching me another lesson."

"And what lesson might that be."

"Nothing that has anything to do with what's going on here."

"Simone. Everything is fine." Devon's voice silenced our conversation, and Simone spun toward him.

Every time she twirled, her bold red caftan—her power color— flowed around her like gossamer silk. I would have liked to watch her on a catwalk. She denied my every attempt to catch her admitting that she'd modeled. She'd lived in all the fashion capitals of the world, and not always as cadre. How could she not have walked one at least once? Of course, then she'd end up on the front page of every magazine in the world. That would have been too much human intervention for her.

"Perhaps some warning ahead of time." Simone's tone had mellowed to one of reverence, though she gave Colantha a glare or two.

"Didn't Lucas tell you?" Devon glanced his way.

"Completely my fault." Lucas didn't sound apologetic. "Bella and I went to the kitchen to save Letty a trip and missed Simone's arrival."

"There you have it." Devon stood and took Colantha's hand to help her rise. "Let's move to the sofa, and we can bring everyone up to speed." He waved me to his side, taking the two chairs closest to the unlit fireplace. "Colantha arrived early. It provided an opportunity to bring her and Remus up to speed on our success with retrieving the *De første dage* and Lucas's translation of the first half of the document. Colantha agreed to review the second half and provide a translation."

"I would like to get started with the review as soon as possible." Colantha poured a glass of what I could now confirm, glancing at my already half empty glass, was sangria. It tasted almost as good as what I'd had in Madrid. "I understand Lucas, with Ginger's assistance, completed the translations on the first half of the book. It would be helpful, for possible continuity issues, if they could assist with my work."

If Lucas were a puppy, I think he'd be sitting at her knee with his tongue hanging out, adoration in his gaze. Hard to picture his enthusiasm for books in conjunction with the instinctual killer he could be. Ginger had told me every detail of their mission, and, after chastising her for not calling when Lucas had been gravely injured, followed by a long, breath-stealing hug, I'd listened with rapt attention as she described the endless stream of vamps who'd tried to stop them. Lucas was no light weight, and I had a scar or two from training that proved it. But I still grinned at the expression on his face while he waited for Devon's response.

Devon held back a smile and gave a short nod.

"Excellent." Colantha placed an empanada on a plate and used her fork to cut it into small pieces before taking a bite. "Tell us about your trip to Spain."

Devon provided a high-level recap, and I wondered if he purposely left out the dreamwalkers and baby vamps. The cadre didn't bat an eye at the omission. He wove the tale with equal measure of humor and stoicism, and while I didn't sense any deception from Devon, Colantha kept a close eye on him.

She knew he was leaving something out, but decided not to call him on it. I'd forgotten to mention to Devon that I'd asked her in our dreamwalk the day before whether she knew about dreamwalkers in Spain and of a compound where vamps didn't have a fertility problem. The two of them were playing a game I wanted no part in. I wasn't stupid enough to get caught in the middle, but, after a quick rethink of my actions, I might have inadvertently stepped in it this time.

The group soon disbanded once the food and drink were gone. Lucas handed Colantha the book he'd brought with him. It was the original copy of the *De første dage*. For some reason, I didn't doubt that she'd be able to read both languages. She left with her two vamps, explaining that she wanted to read the book once before starting the translations the following day. Before she left, she grabbed my hand.

"I think it would be wise for you to join us."

She wasn't wrong. I wanted to be there. This was my ancestry. I hadn't been raised in the culture, and it was time to learn more about my heritage. Maybe I'd learn a word or two of the language. At the same time, the idea of sitting through the painstaking effort of translations made me queasy. On second thought, perhaps it would be best to wait until the translations were complete. Then, I could read them and discuss my interpretation with Colantha. Rather than make a decision now, I simply nodded.

Devon squeezed my shoulder after she left. "Come with me. I've made plans."

DEVON PULLED me down the hallways, his hand warm and tender as he tugged me along.

"Where are we going?"

"It's a surprise."

"With everything else going on?" The manor was filled with

vamps and guests. This didn't seem the right time for whatever he'd planned.

"We have a spare evening. Colantha is reading the book, and everyone else has been given time off to rest. I don't know when we'll have another moment together once activities heat up tomorrow, and Remus will be arriving the following day.

He turned down a dead-end hall, and I knew exactly where we were going, though it surprised me. He opened the door to the home theater. It wasn't completely dark. Images were already playing across the huge silver screen—forest landscapes, tropical beaches, and glittering city nights.

"What's all this?"

He led me halfway down the row of seats before guiding me into one, pushing me toward the center section where the armrest had been removed from between two seats. Blankets and several pillows had been piled on the seats. A tabletop covered the next seat, where a huge tub of popcorn and an ice bucket filled with bottles of hard cider waited. The scent of Cook's famous mixed-type popcorn made my stomach stir.

My first thought was to ask how he did this, but that was stupid. When Devon had the will, he always found a way. So, I went with, "Movies?"

He pulled back a blanket and took off his shoes before sitting down next to the seat with the food and drinks. "I know we just got back from vacation, but after the attack on Oasis and a full agenda for the next few days that will undoubtedly modify our mission to something even more dangerous, I thought we needed a small break."

When he nodded to the seat, I slipped off my shoes and curled up next to him, tugging the blanket over us. It was useless to argue with him when he was in a mood, and I had to admit, I wasn't willing to destroy the moment. We wouldn't get many times like this once war was officially declared.

"When I commanded large armies, the hardest task wasn't

marching on the enemy, it was keeping the men stimulated before battle."

"Don't tell me—more battle training."

He laughed. "In a sense. A makeshift arena was formed to allow the warriors to test each other. Most relished the opportunity to match their strength against their fellow warriors. Others preferred the peace of solitude. Even in those days, vampires understood the benefits of meditation. At nights, there were endless feasts."

"And women?"

He didn't respond, but a huge grin flickered in the light from the screen.

"I should have known."

He opened two ciders and handed me one, which I put in the drink holder to my right. Then he picked up a remote control. "I've preselected three movies, so get comfortable."

Ginger and I always made time for movie nights when we could, but it was rare for Devon to agree to one. And when it happened, he only had the patience for one movie. The fact he'd selected three made me curious, but after snuggling up to him under the blankets, I decided not to question my good fortune. Live for the day.

He started with *Nosferatu,* an old black-and-white silent movie that was Sergi's favorite. Then he followed it up with *The Lost Boys,* a cult classic, and finished with *Fright Night,* which had us both in tears from laughing so hard.

When the last movie ended, he took me to the widow's walk, where a thermos of coffee waited for us. We spoke of nothing important—memories of our time in Madrid, the coast of Spain, and a new studio he wanted to build for Lyra on the far side of the yard. It would be built to provide several views, including the gardens, the sycamore, and the coastline. He'd had preliminary plans drawn up to present to her on her birthday, but he wanted her to modify it to her heart's content to make the place her own.

Afterward, we strode hand-in-hand to his room, where a table for two had been brought in, dressed with a linen tablecloth and two place settings. Three candles burned in the centerpiece. Two silver-domed plates waited for us, along with a bottle of champagne. It was a light meal of salmon, fresh green beans, and mashed sweet potatoes.

"No dessert?" I asked as I finished my glass of bubbly.

His brows wriggled.

My laugh was throaty, and his gaze glowed. The beast was still hungry, but I didn't think it had anything to do with food. I'd barely set my glass down when he lifted me into his arms and dumped me on the bed.

Once we'd stripped to our underwear, I thought he'd make love to me. I was wrong. We cuddled, fingers entwined as talk turned to business. He wanted me to review and provide suggestions for Sergi's latest security plans, Lyra needed more stimulation, and I expressed my desire for some type of project.

Somewhere in all of that, we fell asleep.

Until Devon woke me with warm hands that roamed my body, stopping every few inches as strong fingers massaged my muscles. I moaned with delight as he worked each leg and then my arms before his hands ran up and down my back, working the knots in my neck and shoulders. Had I died and gone to heaven? Were angels restoring me? I needed more dreams like this.

I groaned again as a hard body lay next to mine, and I managed a smile. His hot breath against my ear sent shivers down my neck and spine. This was no angel giving aid, and I rolled over as his arms wrapped around me.

Devon.

His kisses were as soft as butterfly wings on my temple and then my nose. Then he ravaged my mouth with a passion that could raise the dead.

"Don't move."

As if I could.

He removed what little clothing I had on, leaving me naked and starving for more. His kiss might have been molten, but his hands were gentle as they once again traversed my body. This time was more an exploration, soft swirls of his fingertips sending ripples of pleasure over me. Through me.

This was the tender Devon—the seducer, the dark nights and secret hideaway lover. The one who made making love a living art form. There was the hot sex in the back of a jeep Devon. The vamp who held me against a shower wall as his thrusts made me scream. There was the missionary Devon when neither of us had any energy left after a hard day, yet we couldn't sleep without our joining. But this Devon was the slow and methodical lover. The vamp who slowly torched every inch of me, growing the ripples into gentle waves, building until a tsunami of pleasure washed over me.

I'd seen all the versions of Devon while at the resort in Spain. Simone had arranged for a seaside bungalow the farthest away from neighbors. We had a private beach and spent days making love on a blanket spread across the sand. The evenings were best after our passions were spent when we lay entangled under the stars and spoke of silly things. A small respite in our preparations for war.

Regardless of which of his lover personas came to me, it all ended the same. A sweet release and a knowledge that no other vamp, human, or shifter could ever give me the love and safety that this vamp provided. And when he released his beast, his eyes glowing their icy blue hue that faded to a warm pool of moonlight, I knew he felt the same.

We were one.

After Devon found his own release, he carried me to the shower, where we washed each other with soft strokes. We dried each other off, giving light kisses over still-damp skin before tossing the towels on the floor and finding our way back to bed.

With our legs entwined, we stared at the ceiling as if we could see the stars until we fell asleep, our hearts beating as one.

Then, without thinking, I mumbled, "Love you." I was asleep before hearing a response.

~

DEVON WATCHED HER SLEEP. Her slow breathing and the rapid movement of her lids told him she was dreaming. Was it of him? He hadn't realized how much Cressa's debt had weighed on him until Lucas mentioned it.

In the beginning, it tied her to him. A way to force her to work for him. To steal what he needed to remove his censure. After the first few days, and she'd stolen her first item for him, which had been a rash decision on her part, she didn't seem to want to leave. She put her entire being into their missions.

If someone asked when she'd taken possession of his heart, he wouldn't have an answer. It wasn't one moment. It was a gradual entrapment. A slow burn that only made the journey more enticing. More stimulating. She'd changed during her time at the manor. She'd become a warrior and discovered her true nature even without having full control of it. However, that was rapidly changing.

She had to spread her wings. He hated that saying even more than before. Whether she realized it or not, she'd been tied to House Trelane not by choice but through a business arrangement. Something he'd been blind to as well. Not anymore.

He sat on the bed and pushed her hair back to regard her face. Her eyelids had quieted, and she began to stir. Her legs stretched, and then her arm. When it met resistance, her eyes popped open.

She blinked, and her gaze focused on him, followed by an instant smile. "Morning." Her voice was still groggy from sleep. Her morning smile disappeared. "Is everything alright?"

He gripped her arm and gave it a gentle squeeze. "Everything's fine. I have a meeting I need to run to, but I wanted to discuss something before I left."

She rubbed her eyes, then pushed herself up to a sitting position, wrapping her arms around her knees. "Okay."

Her hair was a mess. The shower hadn't been enough to remove her mascara, and now it left sultry black smudges. She was beautiful.

He cleared his throat. "It's time to release you from your debt. I should have done it long before now."

"What?" She rubbed her eyes again, and his heart did a little flip.

"I've opened a bank account in your name with the agreed-upon figures from our updated contract. The money has been deposited, and I'll provide you with all the required details and paperwork."

Instead of relief for an unwanted burden, her eyes narrowed. "Is this payment for last night?"

"What?" Devon stood up. "What are you talking about?"

She shrugged. "It's not that I'm not grateful to be out of your debt, but why the sudden decision?" She glanced away before softly asking, "Is it because of what I said last night?"

He thought back to their evening. At some point after their lovemaking, she'd said she loved him. Hadn't she told him that before? Those damn dreams confused him. Their nights together blended between real events and dream constructs to the point he couldn't remember past realities from future events.

"No, of course not." He didn't know what else to say and turned her back to the topic at hand. "The days before us will be more dangerous than I'd originally considered, and I don't know how long this war will last. I can't ask you to be part of it when you're tied to this House not by your own choosing." He sat back down but didn't touch her. "I understand you have skin in the game, but you need to decide whether you want any part of this war, and if you do, will it be next to Colantha or me? I realize we're fighting the same battle, but that choice does make a difference."

Did he have to tell her that her desire to stand with him was more important than the war itself? Should he tell her? He didn't know. He didn't want to sway her decision.

"You also have Ginger to think about. I know she has a strong relationship with Lucas, but you both have to consider why you're here. You and Ginger will always have a home here, but it has to be on your terms, and you need the freedom to make that choice."

When she didn't respond nor reach for him, he ignored the twist in his chest. She appeared dazed, and he'd been foolish to dump this on her upon waking. Maybe it was his cowardice—his fear of what her decision would be.

He stood. "We can talk more after my meeting when you've had time to consider what I've said. And if you need time away to consider what you want for your future, I can send you and Ginger to Oasis. There are bungalows on the far side of the manor where you can almost forget you're at a vampire estate." He quirked his lips. "It's the best I can do with the lockdown."

He bent down to kiss her, hesitated at her bewildered expression, then tugged her to him, telling her with action, if not with his stumbling words, how much she meant to him. The kiss was deep, persuasive, and promising. He stroked her cheek before standing.

Then he left, feeling like an asshole. Maybe he should have told her during their dinner the night before. Yes. Where his heart was concerned—he was a coward.

Chapter Fourteen

I WATCHED Devon walk out the door, unsure what to do. I rubbed my eyes, still waking and not sure if that was a remnant of a dream or the real crazy deal. Did he say he wanted to send me away to Oasis? I dropped back on the bed. My brain was fuzzy at best from too much champagne the night before.

He released me from my debt.

Shit.

I'd forgotten all about it. Sorrento was long dead.

He'd set up a bank account for me?

I threw off the covers, scrounged for my clothes, dressed, and stormed down the hall to my room. I slammed the door, surprised by my building anger.

Should I be angry? God, I needed coffee.

I went to the bathroom and grabbed my toothbrush, then dropped it and leaned over the counter. A tear fell in the basin. I wiped my eyes. Why was I crying?

The outer bedroom door opened. Devon?

"Cressa? Are you there?"

Ginger.

"Here." My voice cracked. The stomping of feet across the

floor was the only indication she might have heard me. She stuck her head in the door.

"Oh, my god, what's wrong? Has someone died?"

I glanced up, caught her grimace, then dared a peek in the mirror. Black smudges from my mascara made me look like the Joker, and the fresh tears had created streaks through it. I turned on the water and waited for it to get hot.

"Devon released me from my debt. Something about sending me away to Oasis. Setting up an account."

"What?" If I'd been more awake, I might have heard something more in that single word, but I was pretty much in my own head at that moment.

Ginger entered the bathroom, pulled a wash rag from the rack, and tossed it to me. "Clean up and meet me in the bedroom. I'll call for coffee."

I washed my face, brushed my teeth, and peed. More awake than I'd been several minutes earlier, my head was still fuzzy from a hangover. It had to be the champagne. Damn vamps. The champagne wouldn't have affected Devon.

I shuffled out of the bathroom as Ginger was closing the door holding a tray of coffee and a plate with a silver dome.

"Come sit by the fireplace. We'll talk after you've finished a full cup of coffee."

My face must have reflected some form of petulance because she gave me that mama bear look.

"Don't argue with me. We've been through this rodeo before. Sit."

Yep. Not the first time she'd nursed me through a bender. But all I remembered from last night was Devon's hands. A shiver ran through me at the memories of the sensations those touches created.

I was halfway through my first cup when it hit me. "Aren't you supposed to be with Colantha and Lucas?"

"Well, you're part way to recovery. Keep drinking." Ginger

opened the silver dome to reveal scrambled eggs and bacon. "Bacon first. You need the grease."

I did as she asked, mostly because the heavenly smell was too good to resist. And she knew me better than anyone when it came to hangovers. Bacon and coffee usually did the trick. Once the bacon was gone and half the eggs, I was well into my second cup of coffee.

I fell back against the couch, definitely feeling better. "Thank you. Now, shouldn't you be with Colantha and Lucas?"

"They don't need me to translate. I'll catch up." She bit her lower lip, then shook her head. "So, tell me what happened."

I ran a hand through my hair and sipped the coffee. "It's all a bit vague, to be honest. He woke me up and said he released me from my debt." I replayed in my head what I could remember, but there were gaps. "Something about setting up a bank account and sending me to Oasis." I glanced at her. "I think he said you should go, too."

Ginger tidied up the tray, her eyes not meeting mine. Then she bit her bottom lip again.

"What?" When she didn't say anything but kept rearranging the tray, I leaned over and grabbed her arm. "Just tell me. No secrets. Right?"

She blew out a breath and fell back on the sofa. "I think this is all my fault."

"What do you mean?"

She picked at her scarf. This was one of the knitted ones her mother had sent her. It was lime green and somehow fit with her ensemble of a rose-pink, short-sleeved T-shirt and black print leggings. "When Lucas was on the mend from the vamp attack, we shared some personal stories."

I sighed. That was enough for me to know where this was going. "You told him about the debt."

She nodded. "I didn't think he'd tell Devon." She didn't look at me.

"It's alright. Go on."

She gave a single-shoulder shrug. "There's nothing more to tell. Lucas knows you covered my debt with Sorrento. He must have said something to Devon."

I leaned my head back against the couch. Now, it made sense. Well, not really, but it was a start.

We sat in silence for a while. Not a sound pervaded the room. Not even the sound of a ticking clock, which would have been appropriate.

"But this is a good thing, right?" Ginger got a second wind. "I mean, I'm guessing you and Devon haven't spoken about the debt. So much has happened since then. But now, he's settled it. You said he renegotiated with you. If you helped him, he'd clear your debt and pay half back. That explains why he set up an account."

"I suppose."

"That's why it's a good thing. It puts your relationship on even ground." She took my hand. "This means no contract is holding you here. I'm not sure I understand what he really said about sending you away to Oasis. Maybe he just wants to make sure you're here because you want to be and not because you owe him something."

More of his words slipped into my fractured memory. "He said something about the war. Making a decision if I'll be at his side or Colantha's." I shook my head. "Something about it not being my war or yours."

"That makes sense."

I glowered at her. "So, explain it to me."

She scooted to the edge of the sofa, sipped her coffee, then turned to me. "Your contract was to help him get his censure removed. We're way beyond that now. This has turned from a seat on the Council to something that could upturn the entire vamp society. He's going after Lorenzo. This is bigger than either of us. He wants you to make a decision on your own. Do you want to be in this fight? If so, would it be by his side?" She took my hand again. "Now, you have Colantha. You're both dreamwalkers. Would you prefer to stand with her during the war instead of Devon?"

"Why can't I do both?"

She shook her head. "You're being obstinate. It's not about that. Dreamwalkers are going to be part of this one way or another. Standing by Devon doesn't mean you're not standing with the dreamwalkers. It just means you want to be with him. Not as a boss or a House leader but as a vampire."

"I told him I loved him."

"For the first time?"

I shrugged and rubbed my face. "I only vaguely remember saying it. Sometimes, I can't remember what was a shared dream or the real deal."

"Maybe that's why he suggested Oasis. We're on lockdown. He's not going to let you just take off to figure out what you want to do for the rest of your life. Oasis provides a buffer between you."

"And why bring you into it?"

She rolled her eyes. "I think you need another cup of coffee. Or maybe the hair of the dog."

I was still confused, so I finished the second cup and poured a third.

"The only reason I'm here is because of you. Everything has changed now that I'm with Lucas, but maybe he's concerned about whether both of us are here because of the debt. We could take that bank account and find a place to hide until the war is over."

Everything was starting to click. I touched my lips. He'd given me a passionate kiss before he left. He wasn't sending me away. He was giving me the freedom to choose.

"I don't want to leave." The words seemed strange, but the more I repeated them in my head they seemed to be true.

"Well, good. I don't want to leave, either." This time, she took both my hands. "I love Lucas, and I don't want to leave him, especially if he's going into battle. Whatever that looks like. But if you need to go, I'll go with you. You're not leaving here alone."

I nodded. Tears welling up again. This time, because of how much I owed this woman. When had she become the adult in the room? I snorted out a laugh. "I'm okay now."

She gave me a long look, squeezed my hands, then stood. "I think that's still open for debate, but I'll leave you to your thoughts. I need to run." She gave me a look before leaving, and I just waved with what I hoped was a convincing smile.

I turned back to my coffee, curled my legs underneath me, and pulled a blanket from the back of the couch to wrap over my shoulders.

I was free.

I had no idea how to face that reality. I had my own account with a shitload of money. Ginger and I could disappear until Devon's war was over. Did he want me to go? Did I want to go?

Some days, it seemed better not to have the freedom to make my own choices.

AFTER MY TALK WITH GINGER, I worked out in the training room for a couple of hours. Nothing too physically demanding as I ran through a mini obstacle course using the climbing walls and ropes before cooling down with a couple martial arts routines. They were exercises I could perform by rote, which was good since my head wasn't in the game.

The idea that I no longer owed a debt, that both Ginger and I were free, was slow to accept. It seemed we'd lived with it over our heads for so long it had become as natural as breathing. Even though my last job before Sorrento had captured me all those months ago would have only scraped a portion of what I owed, it kept me focused on finding larger jobs with bigger payoffs. Then, I landed in the world of vamps.

My entire life had changed, and I'd forgotten all about the debt.

Was that because of Devon or because I discovered a part of myself that I'd been sheltered from my entire life? I was a dreamwalker. When I tried to separate Devon, his mission, and my knowledge of my heritage, I couldn't. They seemed irrevocably connected.

After training, my mind calmer, if still not accepting of the fact I was debt free with a sizeable bank account, I hit the pool. By the time I took a shower and dressed, I went in search of Devon to have a deeper conversation, only to discover he wasn't at the manor. No one could tell me where he went. At first, all my insecurities returned with Devon's whispered words about sending me to Oasis.

I shook it off. It didn't surprise me that the vamps I'd asked wouldn't know Devon's schedule, and other than Lucas, who was locked down with Colantha, the rest of the cadre couldn't be found. Colantha had wanted me to join them, but Ginger would give me an out. Then I cringed at how much she might share with Lucas and Colantha and decided to hide away with Lyra. My plan was destroyed when I found a vamp stationed at her door. She was resting and wasn't to be disturbed.

I somewhat expected that. She was no doubt depressed over Hamilton and needed time alone. It made sense, but it left me with absolutely nothing else to do.

Cook was my last resort. It was after the lunch hour, and I could use something to eat since I'd missed lunch. The kitchen smelled of savory meats, and Cook was at his counter, making small pie shells.

"Hey, Cook. Is this a bad time for a visit?" I poured a cup of coffee from the urn he always kept filled.

"Ah, Cressa. I have a few minutes to talk before we start dinner preparations. It will be a full house tonight."

"Really? It seems pretty empty right now." I plucked a biscuit from a basket and found half a platter of sliced cheese in the fridge. "Is it safe to take some of this cheese?"

"It's left over from lunch. There should be another one with sliced meats, and there's some fresh marmalade for those biscuits."

I made a small plate of leftovers and sat at the corner of the counter to watch him work.

"What are you making?"

"Meat pies. They're The Wolf's favorite. It took some doing, but Decker got me in touch with The Wolf's personal chef, and he gave me a few ideas.

A slice of cheese fell out of my biscuit. "The Wolf? Is he coming here today?"

Cook nodded and ran a sleeve under his nose. "Argh. My nose always itches when I have my hands filled with dough." He placed the shells in tiny pie pans then pulled over a mixing bowl that had been covered with a towel. Each tiny pie was filled with a spoonful of an herb-scented mixture. "In fact, he should be here soon, but I heard Devon was running late from his meeting at Oasis."

So that was where he went. "He must be checking on the security since the attack."

"From what I hear, everyone else has gone to one of the safe houses. Although they weren't part of the Oasis attack, Sergi wanted to add some additional features since Venizi's men have been doing drive-bys."

I picked at my food. I could have helped with that if anyone had bothered to ask. "I'm starting to feel useless around here."

Cook's brow lifted. "I heard you were in the thick of it at Oasis."

"Yeah. But what do I do between the attacks?" I worked up a grin. "A girl can only train for so long."

"Ah. Yes." He pointed a spoon filled with meat mixture at me. "You need a project."

I slammed my fist on the counter. "Exactly. I've been thinking the same thing. I just can't figure out what it might be."

Cook finished filling the pie shells then placed little pie crusts on top. He began fluting the edges. "What skills or knowledge do you have that you could share? Maybe Sergi has something you could help with."

"My specialty is stealing things."

Cook grinned. "And I hear you're very good at that."

I laughed. "But it's not a skill anyone needs on a regular basis."

"What about your defense skills?"

"I'm pretty sure the vamps don't require my assistance in that area."

"What about the humans?"

"Ginger was doing that."

"Then she went on a mission and has been busy with Lucas and the translations since she returned."

"Sergi was filling in for her."

"Somewhat. His schedule was impacted while everyone was on missions and the training was canceled."

My gaze flickered to the far window that looked out at the sycamore tree. "I wasn't aware."

"Maybe you could get that running again."

"I don't know. That's Ginger's project."

"Can't you have more than one instructor? You have different skill sets. Don't you train with different members of the cadre?" He finished the last pie and pushed the cookie sheet aside, wiping his hands on a towel he wore over his shoulder. "Think of it this way. With two instructors, there's a better chance classes won't have to be delayed or canceled if one of you is sent on a mission."

I nodded. "Ginger was teaching defensive moves during an attack. Maybe that could be augmented by what to do if you're captured. I could teach skills like picking locks or scaling walls that could help with an escape. Not everyone will be interested, but there are always a few who don't like feeling helpless. We could call it a how to survive an invasion course."

"Now you have it."

And once Cook filled my head with ideas, I was itching for a pad and pen to start jotting them down. I shoved the last piece of cheese in my mouth and was picking up my dishes when a vamp I'd seen a number of times but never knew his name raced in.

"Cook."

Cook turned as he moved the cookie sheet to the top of the stove. "Walter. What's wrong?"

I grinned. Not so much at the panic on his face. My heart jumped at what could be wrong, but Walter? What kind of name was that for a vamp? For some reason, it hit my funny sensor. But I bit my lip when the vamp noticed me.

"Miss Langtry. Thank the stars. The Wolf is at the gate and there's no one to receive him."

I really struggled. The Wolf is at the gate. Maybe part of my day could be spent in psychotherapy. I couldn't stop myself. I laughed. Loud. Wake the dead loud.

I was aware that no one else laughed. Even Cook appeared concerned—his mouth open with no words coming out, his brows meeting his hairline, his hands rubbing together as if he was dry washing them.

This was all Devon's fault.

He'd given serious news to a woman who'd just woken up with a hangover. Then he stormed out, leaving me with gaps in what he said. Then Ginger laid it all out like it made perfect sense. The manor was close to a ghost town, and now we had a vamp called Walter worried about a wolf at the gate.

I bent over, hands on knees, to catch my breath. The action made my head spin, and when I straightened, I grabbed the counter from falling over. I wiped a hand over my eyes and cheeks, drying the tears. But when I glanced at Walter and Cook, the giggles erupted all over again.

But now, whether in solidarity or simply to make it look like I hadn't blown a fuse, Cook joined in the laughter. Walter, his head swiveling left and right trying to understand, began to smile and nod like he had a clue what the hell was going on.

I heaved out a huge breath and picked up my dish and glass, leaving them in the sink. Then I wiped my hands and clapped them once. "Let's welcome our visitor."

I winked at Cook on my way out. He smiled, his brows still lifted, and I stifled more giggles that were eager to erupt. I had to get a hold of myself. When I stopped at Devon's office, I gave Walter his instructions. "Bring The Wolf to the office as soon as he arrives."

As soon as I closed the door behind me, the rest of my pent-up laughter rushed out of me. Good grief. I needed to get a hold of myself. This was the worst time to lose it. But honestly, sometimes humor was just lost on these vamps.

I strode to the bar, figuring I had maybe five minutes before The Wolf made it to the front steps. I poured a double shot of vodka, swallowed it down in one gulp, closed my eyes for a minute, then faced the desk.

I couldn't. The desk wasn't mine to command or greet from. Besides, this was just a welcome until Devon arrived. It had been some time since I'd spoken to Remus without an audience. That had been the day I walked into the paper mill to save Devon from his beast.

The desk might be off limits to greet an ally, but I searched the drawers and swiped a pad of paper and pen. I plopped into a chair near the fireplace and scratched down the ideas Cook had given me for a training course. I'd just listed the sixth item when the knock came.

Walter stuck his head in, and I bit my lip. *Remain calm. You're the ambassador for House Trelane.* That did it. My stifled giggles turned to nausea.

"The Wolf is here."

I set the pad and pen down and rose. "Send him in."

Remus strode in, noticed I was the only one in the room, and asked his two bodyguards to remain in the hall.

His smile was warm, and he held out his arms in greeting. "Cressa. It's been too long." He gave me a hug, and when he stepped back, he grabbed my shoulders. "I see a bit of sun on your skin. From Madrid?"

"We took a detour to the southern coast."

"Aah, the beaches of Spain. Some of the best in the world." He glanced around the office. "I was expecting others."

I laughed and guided him to the chair opposite me. "I was as well when I came down after training. But I'm sure they'll arrive soon. Can I get you a drink? Maybe an espresso?"

"An espresso would be wonderful. Tell me of Spain."

I gave him a recap of our visit to Aramburu, leaving most of the important stuff out, unsure how much Devon wanted to share, as I made our drinks.

Remus played along, the consummate guest, and didn't ask any important questions. "How did Venizi know you'd be in Spain?"

"Gregor believes they were on assignment to watch his House, and we might have been a surprise."

"Do you think they told Venizi?"

"If they did, it would have been before they followed the limo. House Aramburu has a rather deadly policy about strangers on his land."

He shrugged. "Not so different from shifters. Not nearly as much as in the old days, but you'll still find that behavior in less populous areas." When I lifted a brow, he explained, "In the old days, we were hunted. If a vampire found their way onto our land, they didn't leave."

"Makes sense when you put it that way."

"So, what's new other than that."

I don't know why I said it, but the topic was still fresh, and he'd been there from the beginning. "Devon just released me from my debt."

He sipped his espresso. "I would have expected him to have done it after you saved him from his beast."

"He might have if I hadn't been kidnapped the day after he was cleared of the Council's charges."

"It did get complicated after that."

I grinned. "And here I thought it was just another day in the life of vamps and shifters."

He chuckled. "Now that it's done, what will you do?"

"And that's the million-dollar question, isn't it?"

"I imagine you have many options open to you."

That made me pause. How many did I really have? Before I could answer, which was a blessing since I had no idea what I would have said, multiple voices came from the hall, and the door opened to a string of people. It was like they were coming back to work after a long lunch.

Devon, looking like the House leader he was in a three-piece dark charcoal gray suit, made my heart thump. "Remus, I'm sorry I'm late. I trust Cressa has kept you occupied."

"As only she can do." Remus stood, and they met in the middle of the office to shake hands. "I wasn't sure this day would ever come."

Colantha had been behind Devon, and she bowed her head to the shifter. "Only the first step in our journey."

Chapter Fifteen

COLANTHA. Our little Debbie Downer.

Remus frowned. "I hope it won't be a long journey."

I was thinking the same thing. It already seemed like we'd been dealing with the book for months.

"That's why we're here." Devon unbuttoned his suit jacket and took a seat at the bar. He waved to the others filing in to find a seat near the fireplace. "We have a solid team to close the gaps before we take our information to the Council."

The cadre, Ginger, Lyra, and Decker found seats. Colantha's vamps, always on guard, stood at the door. I assumed Remus's guards were still outside the door. Once everyone was settled, Devon nodded to Sergi, who turned on the LCD display mounted over the fireplace.

"Other than Colantha, who's now read the complete *De første dage* and was able to put a draft translation together, there are a few of you who have read the first half. As we discovered when Lucas and Ginger brought a copy of it home, the book was written in two languages. The first is old vampiric, and Colantha has confirmed the second half of the book was Drakrotian, an ancient dreamwalker language that hasn't been used since the purging of their race.

"The complete translation is still being finalized and should be available later this evening. Due to its sensitive nature and a promise made to Philipe Renaud, only one copy will be retained here in the manor. It will be made available to Remus first. In the meantime, Colantha has provided a few notes for us to discuss."

He nodded at Colantha as Sergi tapped a key that brought up a large image of the dreamwalker medallion, which clearly displayed three images—the Blood Poppy, an ibis, and a dagger.

Colantha, who chose to sit in one of the armchairs near Devon rather than her typical spot on the sofa next to Lyra, smiled at the group. "The medallion that dreamwalkers wear was originally created to channel the power of our constructs. In the days before the Battle of Omar, the medallion reflected the sigils of the various tribes, of which there were seven main ones, with smaller tribes aligned with the larger ones. Not too dissimilar to vampire Houses. When a truce between species was created after the battle, these three images became symbols that reflected the symmetry and connection between our races."

She nodded at Sergi, who moved to the next slide, which was a closeup of a flower. "The Blood Poppy has become so rare most vampires believe it to be a myth. It's not." She smiled at Remus. "I believe the one I gave to Devon is now in one of your labs."

"We've been carefully studying it," Remus answered. "At first, we ended up with more questions than answers. After Cressa was kind enough to supply a blood sample, we haven't resolved those questions, but we've narrowed them down."

Colantha nodded. "You should have more information to take back to your lab when you leave, but let's move on for now. The Blood Poppy used to grow wild several millennia ago. As the earth warmed, the flower began its decline. It requires a cooler environment, and over time, human's continuing damage to the ecosystem hasn't been kind to it. As far as I know, there's only one last remaining location where the Poppy grows wild, and it's behind very secure borders. Over the centuries, both vampires and dreamwalkers worked toward finding a way to grow it in an artificial environment with slow progress. Today, that process has been well documented by dreamwalkers. The evidence was in the Blood Poppy I left for Devon."

The few mumbles were a combination of disbelief and curiosity. The first word I thought of was hope. If the Blood Poppy was important enough to put on a medallion, then it made sense it was critical to both races. The ability to cultivate it had to be a good sign, regardless of the current animosity between the races.

Once the voices quieted, Colantha continued.

"The Poppy, like many other plants, has various uses. The roots themselves aren't of much worth other than propagation. The leaves, small as they are, have some medicinal value and can be used in cooking, but the bulk of the possibilities come from the flower itself. We'll come back to this again, but for now, I need you all to understand that for both races, the Blood Poppy was considered the 'bringer of life.'"

"This is beginning to make sense based on our first lab results." Remus sat forward in his chair, completely focused on the screen.

Colantha merely smiled. It was one of her looks that said we hadn't gotten to the good stuff yet. "Let's move on to the ibis." The display changed to show the outline of the bird. "Some consider it a symbol of knowledge and wisdom. Some see it as a bridge between life and death, while others see it as a sign of rebirth. For our species, I, like many of our leaders, believed it to be a sign of fertility and the continuance of our species. This idea of fertility ties in with the properties of the Blood Poppy."

"Are you saying the Blood Poppy has something to do with vampire fertility rates?" Bella had, as usual, left her seat some time ago to pace in front of the coffee bar.

This time, Colantha's smile was all-knowing. "Not just something. It means everything to the life forces of both races."

My mind instantly returned to Spain. Dreamwalkers living at Aramburu. A young generation of vampires being born with no fertility issues. Gregor had shuttered his House behind walls when the purge began. Had he held the single key to the future of vampires as well as the knowledge of it the entire time?

The mumblings in the room grew loud, and Devon let it run for a minute before yelling over it. "Quiet. We'll delve into this more after Colantha finishes with the last image."

When the group became silent, Sergi flipped the display to the dagger.

"This is the Dagger of Omar," Colantha said.

Simone gasped. When I glanced over, her face had paled. "This is nothing more than a myth." Her tone was one I'd never heard from her before. There was something surreal about it, like someone had explained the mysteries of the universe to her, and as much as she wanted to believe, her mind denied every word.

"No myth, but lost through the ages." Colantha nodded to Sergi, who overlayed the image with a circle around the carving on the handle. "At first, it's not readily recognizable, but on further inspection, you can see the outline of the letters V and D, which symbolizes the synchronicity between the two races. The dagger was forged after the battle to symbolize our new beginning, but there was no record as to when the blade disappeared."

"And this is one of the most critical pieces to find." Devon turned in his seat to face the room. "I don't think it will prevent us from approaching the Council, but it would put, as the humans say, a bow on it. As Simone said, most believe it to be nothing more than a vampire fairy tale. Most don't believe the Battle at Omar ever happened. But all of this is written in the *De første dage*. Unfortunately, that piece is written in Drakrotian."

"That seems convenient," Remus said. "Why would they have written this book in two languages where each side has to trust the other in its meaning?"

"At the time the *De første dage* was written," Colantha

answered first, "vampires and dreamwalkers understood both languages. No different than someone understanding both English and Spanish. Over the centuries, and specifically during the purge, the dreamwalker language began to disappear, mostly because it wasn't used."

"Like Latin?" I asked.

She nodded. "I have access to other ancient texts that are written in Drakrotian." She turned to Lucas. "I believe you mentioned that Philipe and Fiona could develop a codex if they had other source material to work from."

"Absolutely. They would be ecstatic to learn the language," Lucas agreed.

"More like the culmination of their entire life's work," Ginger added.

"We can discuss how to make that happen." Colantha turned to Devon. "In the meantime, everything I've covered is in the translation."

"Let's go back to the Blood Poppy." Devon stood and leaned an elbow on the bar. "We've assumed that the Magic Poppy was created from the Blood Poppy, and if that's true, then we know the Blood Poppy could be used to our detriment. However, as Colantha referenced, it also has properties that impact our race's fertility. We need more testing to prove our claims. Remus currently has my blood, my blood in beast form, Cressa's dreamwalker blood, and a Blood Poppy. With that and some additional testing, we can derive certain hypotheses. But we need more."

He walked behind the bar to the mini-fridge and brought out a small package. It was the dry ice pack with the vials of blood we'd brought back from Aramburu. "I've already shared this information with the cadre and Colantha. I'm now sharing this with all of you under strict secrecy. Do I have your word this information won't go any further than this room?"

Devon accepted everyone's nod but seemed more concerned

about Remus, who was one of the last to agree. He was probably running statistics through his head on how anything could be more secret than what had already been shared.

"Aramburu owns a great deal of land in Spain and, over a long span of time, has completely enclosed the majority of it behind walls. Within those walls is a thriving community of vampires and indigenous people. In addition, there's also a surviving group of dreamwalkers." Slight murmurs rippled through the group. "In addition, Gregor shared a more heavily guarded secret with me and Cressa. Their children. A group of vampire children of various ages. Young ones that were born well after the problems with our fertility issues. No one who has tried for a child has had any problems conceiving."

"How is this possible?" Remus asked.

"Gregor never said, but based on a small incident with Cressa and the dreamwalkers, she was given a vial from the healer. The potion tasted like Colantha's special juice used to increase the vitality of the dreamwalker psyche, specifically when creating constructs. After a quick discussion with her, we believe Gregor has access to Blood Poppies. We now have the ability to test that theory. Gregory was willing to provide us with three blood samples." Devon tapped the package. "One vial is from the mother of a young vampire. The second sample is from her three-year-old son, and the third is from the vampire father." He returned the package to the fridge. When he turned back to the group, his focus landed on Remus. "I'm giving the samples to Remus for his lab's use in comparing these with the other tests they've already completed. Let's put Colantha's translation of the book to the test."

Remus's eyes glittered. "Yes. We have enough blood from the previous donations to perform additional testing."

"Then let's give you time with the translation. I've arranged a room for you. We'll meet again for dinner. Lucas has created a schedule for the rest of you, and he'll notify you once the translation is available. That's all I have for now, but I'd like the cadre to meet back here after lunch."

Everyone stood and mingled. Lucas handed what must be the full translation to Remus, who tucked it under his arm. The only one who didn't stay to chat and made an exit as soon as the last words left Devon's mouth was Simone.

Something Colantha said had bothered her. She never liked the dreamwalker hocus-pocus as she once referred to it. But she'd paled during Colantha's overview of the symbols. The one thing I knew to be true of Simone was that she wouldn't speak a word of what spooked her until she needed help. And help was something I'd never once heard her ask for.

Chapter Sixteen

DEVON CALLED a morning meeting with his cadre, minus Simone, who'd returned to Oasis the previous morning, to review general House business that had been ignored since his return from Spain.

His planned meeting from the day before had been interrupted when Colantha requested Lucas's assistance to review the *De første dage* a second time. Dinner had been boisterous, with Remus and Sergi competing with who had the best battle story. Cressa had joined in by sharing some of her heists gone bad that had everyone laughing. Rather than adjourning for brandy, the group decided to make it an early evening, but Devon knew Remus would be reviewing the updates Colantha had made to the translations.

Ginger was given time off from her duties with Colantha to spend the rest of the evening with Cressa and Lyra while Devon prepared for the morning's meeting. He wanted to spend the evening with Cressa but was relieved for the reprieve. They hadn't had time to discuss his poor timing in releasing her from her debt, and it was best they stayed focused on their guests.

Devon stared at his dwindling list of agenda items, pleased that most of them had already been cared for by the cadre.

"Lucas, is there any update on the latest business projections with our interests back east?"

Lucas was just bringing up the information when the phone rang.

Sergi answered it. He glanced at Devon as he thanked the caller and told them to wait further instructions.

"That was Levi at the city safe house. They're experiencing higher than normal traffic, and they believe most of the vehicles belong to vampires."

Devon turned to look out the window in a vain attempt to curb his anger. Venizi continued to test him and their defenses. How long before he tired of losing vampires? Or was he busy making more halflings? What they lacked in skill, they made up for in volume.

He swiveled back, his anger still stewing. "Give me a plan to deal with this."

"You don't want to wait for an attack?" Sergi asked.

"If the Council was concerned about our growing battles with Venizi, they should know by now that he drew first blood by attacking Oasis."

"But everyone has a right to the road." Sergi countered.

"So, we make it look like something else," Bella interjected. "The neighborhood is mostly humans, so we'll need to stay low-key."

"What do you suggest?" Devon asked.

"Provide enough distractions and irritations to make them angry enough to either make them do something stupid or grow tired of the game and leave. If these vampires are anything like what Venizi has thrown at us before, they're either young vampires or halflings.

"Like shooting fish in a barrel," Sergi replied. "Without the shooting, of course."

Devon grinned. "Of course not." He turned to Bella. "How many do you need?"

"I'll need to contact the safe house and get their estimate of the opposing force. Six cars at a minimum, maybe more."

"Contact Levi and set it up. Lucas, advise Colantha and Remus we'll be leaving. Sergi, see how many you can pull from security. Decker, can you stay here and lead the security team?"

He didn't look happy about it, but he nodded.

"I'll grab Cressa and Ginger." Devon stood. "I think they're in the training room. Let's meet in the foyer in fifteen minutes."

Devon arrived in the foyer five minutes early with Cressa and Ginger in tow, who'd made fast work of changing clothes.

Remus stood in the foyer with Decker and Mateo, who'd healed from the Oasis attack but appeared to need another blood donation.

"I take it Lucas briefed you." Devon had also taken time to change, and he patted his armored vest to ensure his dagger was in place.

"I'd like to come with," Remus said.

Devon shook his head. "I'd love to have you. We've yet to go to battle side by side, but this isn't the time, my friend. It's conceivable Lorenzo knows you're here, and the safe house might be his way of getting us both out in the open."

Remus glanced up at the ceiling, a slow grin on his face. "I've always loved this ceiling. The artwork is truly amazing. And, of course, you're right, but it didn't hurt to ask. However, I will insist you take Decker."

Devon shook his head again. "We don't need Lorenzo's vampires seeing a shifter with us."

Remus chuckled. "Lorenzo knows how far you and Decker go back and that he's on your payroll. It's also possible someone escaped the attack on Oasis and reported the shifters. But after the raid on Shadow Island, Lorenzo is no fool. He knows I provided resources to assist you. He just doesn't know the extent of my involvement."

Devon glanced at Decker. "I assume you're satisfied with that call?"

He grinned. "Who do you think suggested it?"

Devon shouldn't have been surprised. Decker had been aching for a chance to strike at Venizi. He wouldn't disappoint his old friend. "Alright. Remus, can I ask you to lead the defense of the manor?" In all rights, it should be Mateo or Lyra. Remus wasn't a House leader or a vampire—he was more than that. He ruled all shifter wolves. It would be unseemly not to ask.

"I'd be honored." He gave Devon a slight nod.

"Mateo will bring you up to speed on our defenses." Devon glanced around and noted that the cadre, plus Jacques, were ready.

"Absolutely, sir." Mateo didn't seem to take offense at Remus taking charge. In fact, he seemed pleased to be working with him.

"Let's roll." Devon led the group out the door and down the steps to where eight various types of vehicles waited for them including SUVs, sedans, and two older model compact cars used for surveillance.

It was a twenty-minute drive to the city safe house that was located in one of the poorer neighborhoods. The motorcade split into four groups of two cars each and parked two blocks away on the streets that surrounded the safe house.

Devon got out of the SUV and met Bella on the sidewalk. "What's the plan?"

"The situation has changed from our last contact. The vampires are still here, but apparently, the local street gang has gotten involved."

Devon scratched his jaw. "Is this the same gang Levi has been developing a relationship with?" Much like the coastal safe house where Devon had made special accommodations, primarily with money, to keep the neighbors happy while ensuring them extra security.

Bella nodded. "And it seems to be growing into a decent one. The gang has a street party every Friday, and anyone not working security is invited. We usually supply the beer, burgers, and dogs. My understanding is that they're clear that we don't support their drug activity, but our presence tends to deter police activity."

"What are our new friends doing to assist?"

She shrugged. "Basically, what we were going to do. They're harassing the drivers, blocking the streets, preventing them from leaving, or letting one car go but holding the others. I'm not sure it's having much effect, other than irritating the drivers and one vampire in particular who's parked his car directly in front of the safe house. Seems he just sits on the hood and stares at the security detail."

"So, we know the leader." Devon glanced at the SUV, but he wasn't able to see Cressa beyond the glass. "Block two streets with two vehicles each. No one passes. Make it close to the safe house."

He waved at the second SUV, and Sergi joined them. Devon replayed the situation with him and his order for Bella.

"Let's have a few vampires walk the streets and reach out to the gang. I'd like our detail to join them and be the spokesperson with Venizi's vampires. I want the heat off the gang, but let's use their forces."

Devon nodded at them both. "You have a go."

He returned to the SUV while Sergi and Bella returned to their vehicles and drove off. Cressa gave him a questioning look, and he just grinned as he took out his phone and texted Decker.

"Ready to go wolf?"

"I thought you'd never ask."

"Nips and bites only. Unless it's survival."

Decker responded with a happy face and a dog emoji.

Devon could only shake his head. "Let's go to the safe house. I'd like a front-row seat to this."

Lucas drove slowly and stopped every few feet to wait in a line of vehicles the gang had stopped. When one of the gang members discovered who they were, they immediately opened a lane, keeping the other vehicles from moving as they let the SUV pass until they drove into the gated safe house facility.

Levi met them at the gate and directed Lucas to park a couple spots over facing the fence.

"All we're missing is the popcorn." Ginger leaned forward to look through the front windshield. "Is the guy sitting on the hood of that muscle car the leader of the vamp squad?"

Devon chuckled. "I assume so."

"I know him." Cressa scooted next to Ginger to get a closer look. "He's on Venizi's security detail, but I don't remember his name."

"Not a halfling?" Devon asked.

"I doubt it."

"I agree," Lucas added. "If he's part of Venizi's security on the island, he won't be a halfling."

"Interesting." Devon considered this. "So, he wants to gather information to take back to Lorenzo."

Lucas's phone buzzed. "Yes." He listened and grinned. "Excellent. Nothing here yet." He was still grinning when he looked at Devon. "Bella's in place. The gang's motorcycle members just arrived. They're driving in and around the vampire cars, their guns prominently displayed."

"We're not parked on the best part of the parade route." Ginger sat back, arms folded across her chest, a pout on her face.

Lucas gave her some hope. "They're working their way toward the safe house."

"Why aren't the vamps just leaving?" Cressa asked.

Lucas chuckled. "It seems while we've blocked two streets, the gangs have blocked the other two. They're not being allowed to leave."

"The intimidation is increasing." While Devon liked it, he was concerned the vampires would retaliate. Venizi's security man was on the phone, most likely reporting the situation and getting new instructions. "We need to make a bigger presence. I don't want this to be Venizi against the gangs. They might have guns, but this could get messy. We need to show we're working together, not hiding behind our fences."

Devon got out and waved for Levi. He knew Lucas would be on the phone to release their security teams from the cars, except for those blocking the streets. From the safe house, a dozen security ran to the front gate, meeting Devon, Lucas, Cressa, and Ginger. "Mingle with the gang. Keep them safe."

When the gate opened, as if choreographed for the situation, the motorcycles arrived. House Trelane vampires walked into the crowd of gang members, nodding and shaking hands. Cressa and Ginger remained but held a hand on their sheathed daggers.

Devon stood in front of the gates, which had closed behind him. He stared at Venizi's guard, who slowly shook his head and slid off the hood of his vehicle to stand in front of it. He was muscle-bound with close-cropped hair and a nose that had been broken several times

"Do you need the help of a filthy street gang to come to your aid, Trelane?"

"I think it's more they don't like your type wandering their streets. It's not that they don't like vampires, they just prefer those from a more powerful House."

Devon knew that would hit a soft spot, and he wasn't disappointed when the vampire's face darkened, and his hands formed fists. Before he could say or do more, barking, followed by a scream, interrupted the moment.

The gang members and Venizi's vampires looked toward the sound but didn't move from their positions.

Out of nowhere, a huge, if not a bit ragged-looking, red wolf jumped to the top of the flashy muscle car. He snarled as blood dripped from his muzzle. He'd bit someone hard enough to draw blood. That would have been the screaming.

Devon glanced at a nearby gang member, who appeared to be

the leader based on the number of men receiving orders from him. Instead of being nervous about the changing events, he threw his head back and laughed. Then he glanced around and yelled out two words that riled the gang into a frenzy.

Soon, they were all chanting, "El Lobo! El Lobo!"

That was when Devon noticed the name of the gang emblazoned across the back vest of one of the members. The gang's name was El Lobo. The Wolf. Devon laughed as Venizi's henchman stared up at the wolf, who appeared ready to spring.

"Call it off. Call it off now. You don't want to escalate this." The vampire was clearly scared of Decker.

Devon couldn't blame him, and when the gang members began the mantra of El Lobo that could be heard blocks away, the vampire glared at Devon, his gaze glowing with the beast.

Devon waved Decker off. The wolf barked three times and then lifted its head and howled. Devon knew the wolf, yet the eerie sound still raised hairs on the back of his neck. The wolf jumped down to the hood, and Devon cringed at the sound of nails scratching paint as Decker came to a stop. When he was eye-to-eye with the vampire, he stood his ground.

Devon took out his dagger, prepared for a fight. When the vampire backed up two steps and turned to glare at Devon, he noticed the dagger. Since he couldn't get in his car without getting close to the wolf, he walked to the nearest car with his own vampires and got in.

With another cringe worthy scrape of nails on the hood, the wolf jumped to the ground. Devon had to smile. The wolf stood proud as the El Lobos cheered. Decker gave them one long, powerful howl.

Devon nodded to the gang leader, who whistled into the crowd as they began to break up, giving Venizi's vampires a single access lane out of the neighborhood.

Decker trotted up to Devon, and they strode back to the security gate. Devon didn't look down, but he wanted to. He had no doubt Decker was trotting with his head tall and his tail waving back and forth. His one strike at Venizi. May he have many more.

Chapter Seventeen

I STRIPPED out of my gear and took a shower. If I'd known teasing Venizi's vamps would be that much fun, I'd have offered suggestions to Bella weeks ago. I hadn't expected the local gang to be so helpful, but then Levi mentioned El Lobo held Friday street parties, hauling out the coolers of beer and the grill mid-afternoon and dragging everything back to the clubhouse well after midnight. The gang was responsible for the carne asada street tacos while the vamps grilled organic hamburgers and brats.

I laughed when Levi said the vamps went completely vegan all week in preparation for the party. Since it lasted so long into the evening, all the vamps were able to attend either before or after their guard duty. The weekly event had built camaraderie in the neighborhood, and then Bella mentioned that much of the contract work on the safe house was performed by various El Lobo members. It was a win-win that Venizi would never understand since he considered humans only one step above shifters in his species ranking.

Devon wanted to meet with the cadre after the incident at the safe house to discuss more security changes to ensure El Lobos and the rest of the neighborhood were notified of future issues.

Whether the gang wanted to get involved or not was up to them at that point. When I'd heard Sergi had several options he wanted to review, I begged off with the excuse I didn't want to let Lyra down by missing our planned happy hour, especially with her missing Hamilton so much. Devon saw right through my ruse, but he simply kissed my cheek before disappearing into his office.

I towel-dried my hair, leaving it to dry on its own, and put on leggings and one of Devon's shirts I'd pilfered from his closet. I cycled through them, changing them out when his scent faded. If he noticed, he never said anything. I wore them when I was alone in my room, the smell of cinnamon and cloves reminding me of the first time I'd seen him, and the memory always comforted me. It was strange I felt the need to wear one now.

I grabbed my phone and sat on the bed, my back against the headboard as I checked messages while waiting for Ginger. I wasn't expecting any, but sometimes Harlow or Trudy checked in. What I was hoping for was a message from my mother.

There was one from Harlow, and I laughed out loud when he mentioned working a job with Calypso. That was always a train-wreck. Calypso ran a small crew on the north side of town. She was never prepared, usually had bad intel, yet somehow never got caught. Harlow typically ran a job with her about once a year and always swore never again. But a job would come along that was too good to pass up, and he'd give in.

It was surprising he risked it, considering how much money they'd accumulated from the few jobs he'd worked with House Trelane, but Harlow was always saving for that island getaway. They'd also moved to a nicer neighborhood, so rent was steeper. Based on his cryptic message and foul language, nothing had changed with Calypso, and they'd barely gotten away. Sounded about right. At least they were safe.

I was considering trying Mom, even though she told me not to, when my phone pinged. A text from an unknown number. Worried it might be my mother contacting me, I opened it.

Rasmussen is in trouble and needs your help.

I stared at it. *What the fuck?*

I was still staring at the phone, my brain frozen seeing my father's name on the screen, when the door popped open.

"I hope you're in the mood for margaritas," Ginger called out in a sing-song voice as she strode through the door. "I just made a pitcher in Lyra's kitchen. She should be down in a minute, and Cook is sending up some food." Ginger stopped when she caught my frozen stare. "Cressa? What's wrong?" She set down the tray and raced over.

I stared up at her, but I couldn't seem to get any words out.

She glanced at the phone I gripped in my hands. "You're worrying me. Is it your mother?"

I managed to shake my head and finally spit out, "My father."

Ginger pried the phone from my hand, but I didn't put up much resistance. She scanned the message. "It's from an unknown number."

I nodded and stared out the window. What kind of trouble would he be in? Had someone discovered he was a dreamwalker?

"I didn't think anyone knew about your father." Ginger sat on the bed. "Cressa, do you hear me?"

"Here I am. I brought another glass in case Anna finishes her work early." Lyra waltzed in, and somehow, through the haze of neurons bursting in my head, I noted her good mood. "What's wrong?" She set down the glass and rushed over. "Did she get hurt on the raid?"

"No." Ginger handed her the phone. "I think we have a problem."

GINGER HANDED me a glass of her specialty margarita, and it cleared the daze. Now the three of us sat around the fireplace where I'd curled up on one end of the sofa, thankful for whatever possessed me to wear Devon's shirt.

The soft scent of Devon calmed me while Ginger and Lyra set out plates from the tray Cook had sent up. The aroma of something spicy snapped me into the present.

"That smells great." I sat up and glanced around, rubbing my head, my hair still damp. "I'm sorry. I think I lost it there for a moment."

Ginger glanced at Lyra. "It was more than a moment, but as long as you're with us now." She pushed a plate of mini burritos and street tacos toward me. Cook must have heard about El Lobo. "Eat something, or that margarita will drop you back to Oz or wherever you went."

"Who's Rasmussen?" Lyra asked.

I glanced up. "Didn't Ginger tell you?"

"No. She wanted to wait until you could participate in the conversation. I take it this person is someone important to you."

"He's my father."

If Lyra was surprised, she didn't show it. That vamp stoicism ran strong in her. "When was the last time you heard from him?"

I laughed then took a gulp of my drink. "Never. He left my mother when I was very young." I ran a hand through my hair then played with the ends as I dredged up long-dead memories. "He had eyes the color of brandy, and they crinkled at the edges when he flashed his wide grin. He always seemed to be smiling." I stared at my drink. "It's weird. I can't remember his voice, but a strange melody plays in my head whenever I think of him, which is rarely, and surprisingly, even with discovering I'm a dreamwalker like him, I haven't thought of him in months." But I remembered the melody. Something from my dreams.

"That's odd that you would receive a text from him after all this time." Lyra picked up my phone. "It's an unknown number. Could it be from your mother?"

I shrugged. "I have her number programmed in the phone. It's possible she called from another one, but why not tell me it's her?"

"Who else knows about Rasmussen?" Ginger asked. "I thought it was just your mother."

"Devon and Sergi, maybe all the cadre. Sergi ran a background check on me when I first came to the manor. He ran into a dead end when he tracked my father." I considered Colantha, trying to remember what she'd told me when we'd first met. "Colantha knew of him. At least, she knew my family name was Rasmussen. I didn't get the sense she knew his whereabouts."

"What about April?" Ginger swallowed a big gulp and sputtered a cough. "Wow, I made this batch rather strong."

I snorted. "They're always this strong." I took another sip. The bite of the tequila was working its magic. "April would only have known if my mother said something." I shot them both a worried glance. "There's something going on in that house that my mother won't talk about. I think April might be working with Venizi."

This brought more worried glances between the two. I couldn't blame them. It troubled me, too. The thought of my father being out there—still alive—was more than I could bear. But it was most likely a sham, and it was best not to get my hopes up.

"They're trying to lure you out." Lyra finished her glass and poured more. Damn vamps and their ability to drink alcohol like it was water. "If April is working for Venizi, maybe this is another way to get to Devon."

"We might be getting ahead of ourselves." Ginger bit into the mini burrito and talked around it. "April and your mother might have nothing to do with this."

Lyra and I both stared at her like what else could be going on. Ginger was all about conspiracies and gossip. She gave us a rueful smile.

"Sorry. It's possible that Lucas's need to consider all the angles seems to be wearing off on me."

"Well, that's not a bad thing, but there's not many other options that I can think of." I took a long slow sip of the tangy drink. "Did you put chili in this?"

"A bit. I like the extra spice."

"We need my brother." Lyra, still holding my phone, typed into it. "Is he still in a meeting with the cadre?"

"Did you just send him a text?" I wasn't sure whether to be appalled, nervous, or grateful. Did I want to share this with the cadre? That was stupid. We were on lockdown, at war with Venizi, and I get this message about my deadbeat dad. Yeah, the cadre had to get involved.

Lyra placed the phone on the coffee table and picked up a crab roll. "He's almost finished and told us to wait for him."

Ginger snorted. "As if we're going anywhere before we finish the pitcher."

We all laughed at the notion and the last of the tension the margaritas hadn't been able to remove finally released. Then a different thought came to me. I gave Lyra a closer look. There was concern in her expression, but there was a soft glow. And it wasn't her beast.

"You seem rather cheerful."

Her melodic laugh proved my point. "It's nothing and certainly not as important as the text you received."

"Don't bullshit a bullshitter. You have good news."

Ginger scooted up in her seat. "You're right. I noticed it when she walked in, but I was focused on the text. Well, and the fact you'd turned into a zombie."

I laughed. "Not a zombie, but yeah, I might have zoned out a bit." I turned my attention back to Lyra, who was obviously dying to tell us something. "Is it Hamilton?" I was almost too nervous to ask. Lyra had a mercurial mood that one never wanted to push to the dark side.

She nodded, her joy radiating from her. "He dreamwalked with me. We talked for almost an hour." She reached out and gripped our hands. "He had a breakthrough and hopes to return here in the next few weeks."

"That's wonderful news." Ginger refilled our glasses, emptying the last of the pitcher. "Did he mention what the breakthrough was, or is that too personal?"

"He didn't say it in so many words, but I believe he's come to accept that the decades he's lost isn't anything he can change." She shrugged and sipped her drink, then stretched like a cat, her arms rising above her head as she burrowed into her seat. "Acceptance. He meditates a lot and dreamwalks with others, learning to gain his power back." She gave us one of those looks that said she was holding something back, unsure whether to share.

"Go ahead," I encouraged. "You're among friends here."

"He said I was his inspiration." She stared at her lap, her fingers interlacing. When she looked up, her eyes glowed with unshed tears. "Why would he say that?"

"Oh, honey,. Ginger moved to sit on the arm of Lyra's chair and put an arm around her. "Is it because of your own struggles during that time?"

She nodded, but words appeared difficult for her.

I ran for the bathroom and came out with a box of tissues, dropping it in her lap. "You don't give yourself enough credit. You've had your own demons to battle, and just when you were getting to a place where you felt normal, you were handed a huge burden becoming the House leader. And you faced it with grace, courage, and loyalty. Who wouldn't look to you for inspiration?"

Lyra shrugged. "You make it sound so honorable. I was terrified the whole time."

Ginger laughed and hugged her. "That's what makes you so amazing. A lot of people push their fear aside to do amazing things. I think Hamilton is right to look to you for his recovery. Not just as his lover but as the strong female that you are."

"Devon's never afraid."

I snorted. "He's been leading men into battles for centuries." I considered my next words, not wanting to share Devon's perceived weaknesses with his sister, but there was one thing she'd understand. Something I could only sympathize with when I remembered the first time I wore my medallion, and someone took control of me during a dreamwalk.

"He was terrified when the beast took over while he'd been addicted to the Poppy, and he thought he might never regain his physical form or mental acuity. You know this."

"When Lucas was severely injured," Ginger stopped and swallowed two gulps of her drink. We were officially on the path to Wasted Land. "I was terrified he was going to die. It's not nearly the same as your struggles after such a great loss of your parents and Hamilton, but we have to give ourselves time to heal. All I know is that when our loved ones are on the line, and the road is dark, we always find a way to pull ourselves up. We do what we have to do for those around us. Be Hamilton's inspiration, because that's what you are."

Lyra pulled more tissues and wiped at her eyes. Then she gulped two swallows of her drink. "Sometimes I wish I could get drunk."

I glanced at Ginger, and we both busted up as I handed her the empty pitcher. She knew what to do. Then I gave Lyra my sternest look, which might have been some funky leer. "That's only because you're not trying hard enough."

Chapter Eighteen

DEVON CLIMBED the stairs to the second floor with Sergi close behind. Lyra's message had been cryptic.

"We have trouble."

His concern had increased when he noted Lyra had used Cressa's phone rather than her own. Had that meant Cressa was in trouble, or the women were talking and discovered a problem?

They'd just reached the landing when Letty rushed down the hall from the direction of Cressa's room, holding a tray of empty platters and dishes. She stopped short when she saw Devon.

"Oh, sorry, sir. I wasn't watching where I was going."

"That's alright, Letty. We were moving rather fast." His brow lifted when he confirmed there wasn't a drop of food remaining on the tray. "Are they still in Cressa's room?" His initial worry drained away at the evidence of a happy hour in full swing.

She rolled her eyes while grinning. "Yes. I just brought them another tray, though they tried to convince me it was for you." She moved past them then stopped. "I believe they started a second pitcher of margaritas." She didn't get far when Devon called out, "Bring a carafe of coffee, please."

"Yes, sir." She had a grin on her face before she turned to scurry down the stairs.

Devon glanced at Sergi, who only shook his head with a look of irritation. Did this mean the women drank too much and had created a problem where there wasn't one? One pitcher of margaritas between three females, and one of them a vampire, shouldn't create a false crisis. Lyra wouldn't have been intoxicated, yet whatever was going on, she felt it was worth involving him.

When they reached Cressa's door, the laughter inside was boisterous.

"Are you positive they're not drunk?" Sergi asked. "Maybe this is their third or fourth pitcher."

"I was before, but now I'm not so sure." He grinned at Sergi. "Maybe you should go first."

Sergi grunted. "A House leader standing behind his cadre? Not very commanding. You've ridden into battles facing hundreds of enemies. Are you scared of three females?"

"As a House leader who's not at war with the females inside, I could quite easily assign this task to you."

Sergi growled, but he paled, and that was good enough.

"Alright then. Strength in numbers." He knocked on the door.

This time, Sergi snickered. "Then perhaps we should have brought Lucas and a couple from the security detail."

Devon forced his expression to go blank as he entered the room. The women hadn't responded but were too loud to have heard the knock. When he entered, all three went silent in what had obviously been a full-blown discussion, though he doubted it had been a serious one.

"Brother," Lyra called. "You must save me from these women. They're making me drink most of this pitcher by myself." She giggled. "I think Ginger made this one even stronger than the last."

Was she drunk? He strode toward the group, giving Cressa and Ginger a quick glance, but they were busy trying to hold in their laughter. His sister's eyes were clear, so not drunk, just pleasantly relaxed. Considering her mercurial emotions after Hamilton left, this seemed a positive direction.

"You mentioned trouble in your text. This doesn't seem like trouble." Devon placed his fists on his hips as he looked down on them.

"That's because Lyra said to wait for you, so we moved on to other issues." Ginger hiccupped, which created a new round of laughter from the women.

Sergi picked up a nearby pitcher of water and filled three empty glasses. "Drink up and eat. We don't have time for your games."

Devon had to give him credit. It was good advice, but he'd learned that giving orders to women when not on a mission didn't typically work. And it proved to be the case this time.

In defiance, and only something Cressa would have the nerve to do in Sergi's face, she pushed the glass of water aside and refilled their margarita glasses. Then she took a long swallow. Her gaze was a bit glassy, but she set the glass down without a pause and gave him and Sergi stern looks.

"We're in our scheduled happy hour. It's not my fault or theirs —" she waved an unsteady arm at Ginger and Lyra, "—that I got a strange text." She searched the coffee table, then between the cushions on the couch, before finding her phone in her lap. "Oh, here it is." She held out her phone. "Go ahead, read it." She turned her focus on Sergi while Devon read the text.

"It says Rasmussen is in trouble and needs my help." She leaned back, both arms outstretched on the back of the couch as if she didn't have a care in the world.

Sergi took the phone to read the short text that matched Cressa's words. His brows scrunched. "I'll get Cressa a new phone for her contacts. We'll keep this one to work from."

Cressa sat up. "What does that mean?"

Devon answered the question. "It means your phone is compromised. We don't know who sent this message, and while

Sergi will try to get the information, it's quite likely it was sent from a burner phone. But we might get lucky. Either way, your phone is no longer safe. No one should be able to track it, but it would best if you let your contacts know you have a new number." Devon hated what he had to say next, but Cressa had to know it was for the best. "Everyone except your mother. If she contacts you, it needs to be on this phone. At least until we know what's going on."

"Does anyone know about Rasmussen other than your mother, Devon, or the cadre?" Sergi asked.

Cressa gave it a second before she shook her head. "No, we already considered that."

Devon sat next to Cressa on the sofa while Sergi leaned against the fireplace mantel. "Sergi hasn't had time to check on April, but this is now a high priority. Have you tried contacting your mother?"

Cressa shook her head. "I wanted to wait for your guidance on this. I really don't know what could be happening."

"Could it be another dreamwalker?" Ginger asked.

"How would they get her number?" Lyra asked.

"Let's ask Colantha anyway," Devon answered. "Perhaps she might have some insight into this." Devon would have expected Colantha to have said something if she'd heard news of Rasmussen, but the woman wasn't always forthcoming.

"Should she answer the message?" Ginger asked.

"It's been a couple of hours since they sent it." Sergi handed Cressa the phone then returned to lean on the mantel. "It's not inconceivable that she might not have read the message yet."

"Or they think she's called in the troops like we've done," Ginger responded.

Sergi shrugged. "If they know anything about Cressa, they should know she'd find this suspicious. Or perhaps it's someone who believes she'd do something rash."

"If it's April, she might believe that." Cressa nibbled on a strawberry tart. "We haven't spoken since I first moved to the manor, and whenever the topic was Christopher, I did tend to react before thinking." She gave Sergi a wink. "I'd like to think I've learned some patience."

Sergi grunted but didn't respond.

"We might as well see what they want," Devon said. "We don't have enough to go on. It won't take Sergi long to see if he can trace the number. When can you have a detailed background on April completed?"

"I have the preliminary information from Cressa's original background check and when April was seen at her apartment, but there's not much there. I'll dig deeper, but if I don't discover anything interesting by the end of tomorrow, there's nothing to find. At this point, any additional information can only help. I agree she should respond." Sergi scratched his chin. "I find it interesting that Cressa recently reached out to her mother, was worried about the call, and a couple of days later received this message."

Devon had found the timing curious as well. "Get an update from Bella on what's happening at the house."

Cressa leaned forward. "Is she monitoring Christopher's house?"

He gave her a long look. She didn't consider it her mother's house. But Underwood's murder wasn't that long ago. "I put her on the detail as soon as you mentioned your concern."

"Oh." She glanced down at her hands then gave him and Sergi a nod. "Thank you for taking me seriously."

He studied her. Her gaze was still glassy, but she'd put away her sass. "Go ahead and respond. Let's see how quickly they answer."

"Okay." She stared at the phone. "I think the first message should be to ask who they are, right?"

Ginger nodded. "Absolutely. It's what we all immediately wanted to know. It only makes sense."

When Sergi nodded, Cressa spoke as she typed. "Who is this?"

It wasn't more than thirty seconds when a ping came back.

"It says 'a friend'." She snorted. "That narrows it down." She typed a response. "I need more than that."

This time the return message took a full minute. Cressa read, "We'll get back to you."

"That's interesting," Sergi said.

"How so?" Cressa asked.

"For two reasons. They seem to be testing you or their plan. Perhaps they were expecting you to respond a different way. Their first response said they were a friend. Their next response was that we would get back to you. Emphasis on the we. There's more than one person involved."

Devon rubbed Cressa's arm. "We've got it started. Now, I'm going to ask you to do something with your newfound patience." He gave her a warm smile, and the defiant expression she'd been building up faded. She nodded. "Keep the phone. Sergi has what needs from it." He glanced at Sergi, who nodded. "But you need to contact either me or Sergi the minute you get another text. No responding, regardless of the message, until we have a chance to see it and discuss options. Okay?"

She nodded. "Should I call my mother?"

"No. If this is April, she might become suspicious that you immediately reached out to her."

"But this is about my father. Wouldn't that be natural?"

"Perhaps. But your mother also said she would contact you. We have to make the assumption that she's being heavily monitored." When her face fell into disappointment, another thought occurred to him.

"When you first reached out to your mother a few months ago before Underwood was killed, you said she was strict about her appointments."

She sat up. "Yes, her spa and her salon appointments. We could see if she's still going to those."

"That would be a start. What days were those?"

"Hair on Wednesdays, followed by lunch with her friends. The spa is on Thursdays."

"Hair day is tomorrow." Devon took a moment to consider their options. "There's been enough time for mourning that she should be back to her normal activities. Bella and Jacques will know if anyone leaves the house, but they probably won't know who's in the vehicles. Either way, let's see if Willa is getting out of the house. Sergi, I'd like you and a full security detail to take Cressa to see if Willa shows up for her appointments."

He turned back to Cressa. "Absolutely no contact with your mother. This is critical. Surveillance only at this point."

Cressa nodded vigorously. "I promise. I'll play by the rules."

"Alright." Devon breathed out a sigh. While this was an added problem they didn't need, at least Cressa was being agreeable. "Is there anything else?"

"Yeah," Cressa said. "The two of you can leave. We have a happy hour to get back to."

DEVON RETURNED to his office while Sergi made a quick stop in his to set up a trace on the phone number from the mysterious text. When he dropped into his office chair and turned to look out the window, he considered Cressa. He wasn't sure how to read her responses. While she was intoxicated, she was still respectful and had thought things through, most likely with guidance from Ginger and Lyra.

Once she had time to come down from the adrenaline rush from the incident at the safe house and the alcohol was flushed from her system, how would she really feel about the text message? It wasn't lost on him that they'd both been dancing around his untimely release of her debt. He'd played that all wrong. But it was done. Should he attempt to fix it or wait for Cressa to work through it?

He wasn't sure there was anything more for him to say, and he needed to be patient. Give her time. If he pestered her, it wasn't really giving her a choice, and she had to come to him with her heart. Maybe that was asking too much.

The slight rap broke his musing as Bella strode in with Jacques two steps behind her.

"I wasn't expecting you. How did the clean-up go at the safe house?" Devon asked.

Bella dropped into a chair. Her hair stuck up in places, probably from running her hands through it. Her eyes were sallow. "I was surprised to hear Venizi sent one of his own security detail to stir things up. I know Levi has made friends with El Lobo, but having humans involved in our business could be a problem down the road."

"Levi has been instructed to have another talk with the group. If the gang understands the rules and still wants to play, there isn't much we can do about it. They consider it their neighborhood, and if Venizi stirs up trouble in a human neighborhood, that's something the Council can't ignore."

"I've tried telling her that." Jacques glanced at his fingernails, then slowly lifted his eyes to meet Devon.

He couldn't remember the last time Jacques said a word in their meetings, though he was always fully engaged. Perhaps he didn't think he was supposed to speak, since he wasn't cadre, but he wasn't just Bella's partner. He was an intelligent and loyal vampire. Maybe a one-on-one discussion with him was in order.

"I'm going to ask one thing of you." Devon's gaze locked with his. "See to it after this meeting that Bella gets a full feeding."

Jacques's grin was predatory as he glanced at his partner, who had enough energy to scowl at both of them. "Not a problem, sir."

"Excellent. Ah. Here's Sergi."

Sergi closed the door behind him and sat in his usual seat, his tablet on his lap. "Have you brought them up to speed?"

"I was just getting to that." Devon spent ten minutes

reviewing the text Cressa received and the return reply when Cressa asked who was texting her. He also added that it was possible that it tied back to the recent phone conversation with her mother. "Sergi, do you have anything to add?"

"Not much. I wasn't able to start a deeper dive into April's background or access information on the Underwood estate. I just forwarded what limited information I have to all of you. I just made a couple of calls, which is why I was late. One was to my friend at the SBPD. I'm curious about what they might have dug up on April during the Underwood investigation. I'm also checking to see what Underwood's will stated."

"Why is the will important?" Bella asked.

"If April is working for Venizi, it would be interesting to know how much she got from Underwood's estate. It might mean something, and it might mean nothing. Either way, it helps paint the picture along with other bank records I'm gathering. In the human world, money is the most valuable commodity."

Bella nodded. "You mentioned that outside of the cadre, only Cressa's mother knew about Rasmussen and that April might have learned of him from Willa. That's her name, right?"

Devon nodded.

She continued. "Why are we thinking Venizi?"

"April was seen going to Cressa's old apartment with a vampire when Underwood was searching for the medallion. We don't know who the vampire was working for, but we know Underwood had connections with Venizi."

She considered it for a moment. "Cressa isn't a common name. Is it possible Venizi has connected the dots?"

"If so," Jacques interjected, "I would think he would have kept Cressa locked up rather than give her an opportunity to escape."

Sergi glanced over, as surprised as Devon had been by the vampire's participation. Bella didn't seem fazed by Jacques's comments. Maybe she spoke with him about his ability to participate.

"He has an ego," Sergi replied. "He probably thought the mesmerizing was working."

"If Venizi has discovered that Cressa is April's sister—" Bella leaned forward as she worked through a theory. "Maybe this was recent news to him. Something he didn't discover until after Cressa escaped from Shadow Island." Her leg began bouncing, her energy returning. "Let's say when Underwood was searching for the medallion, he didn't tell Venizi who had it."

"Which was one of our theories as to why the drawing of the necklace was left next to Underwood's body in the limo." Sergi nodded, seeming to know where Bella was headed. "It was meant as a lure for the person who had it."

Bella stood to pace. "He probably thought the medallion was lost to him until April said something. Cressa told you April was still upset with her. If April is working for Venizi or one of his underlings, perhaps her disgruntled words floated up to him."

Devon didn't like where this was going. "Now that he's lost Hamilton, his dreamwalker, he might believe Cressa is another dreamwalker. That was something I didn't want him to discover."

"If any of this is true," Sergi picked up the trail, "with the lockdown, it's almost impossible for him to gain access to anyone in the Family. But with a lure of one's missing father, someone she barely remembers, it might be enough to get her out in the open."

"Maybe April considers Cressa rash enough to jump at the opportunity and leave the nest." Bella stopped and leaned against the coffee bar. "I've only run a couple of drive-bys in different cars to get a look at the neighborhood and the house before the problem at the safe house. But we can get back to the surveillance tonight. We found a couple of places where we can watch the front drive without notice."

"I was able to get a couple of images of the property and neighboring houses. It's in the information I sent." Sergi went back to his tablet. "I have the name of the estate's security company from your earlier request, but not the specifics. I'll have something for you later this evening."

"Let's meet back in the morning. I'd like Cressa to join us. I don't want her left out of this. I'll speak with Colantha and see if she can track down Rasmussen. This might not be Venizi at all. Maybe it's another dreamwalker who's just being careful."

When the group gave him patronizing nods, he chuckled. "We need to consider all angles. I know we all want to blame Venizi. Maybe this time we're wrong."

Chapter Nineteen

DEVON LEFT Cook with his last-minute instructions then met Letty in the solarium, where she was preparing a dining table for five. His mother's favorite china and crystal set had been placed on the red table linen and sparkled in the light of the setting sun. His mother had served special meals in this room for her friends, usually after one of her successful garden parties. It was a way to thank everyone for their efforts.

"Oh, sir." Letty scurried over. "I didn't see you there. Everything has been arranged and the invitations delivered."

"Thank you, Letty." He walked to the table and noted the flower arrangement. The flowers were fresh, and while he typically didn't take note of the embellishments Letty and Greta spread through the manor, this particular arrangement of hydrangea and cosmos brought back strong memories. Memories cut short by a ruthless House leader.

"I hope you don't mind." Letty stood next to him. "I think your mother would have approved."

"They were her favorite flowers. I think that's why she loved summer more than any other season. I remember when she had dozens of them trucked in from a greenhouse in San Diego. Father thought her eccentric, but I think that was what made her so endearing."

"Your mother was a strong-willed female. If you don't mind me saying, your sister is just like her. Kind yet with a backbone not to be trifled with." She dabbed at the corner of her eyes with the edge of her apron. "It's so good to have her back to her old self."

He squeezed Letty's shoulder. "It is indeed. You've outdone yourself. Our Family and guests will be touched by your efforts."

"Oh, thank you, sir." She ran a hand down her apron, setting it back in place. "Now, I must find those dessert dishes."

He laughed. "You mean those little plates with fairies painted on them?"

"Of course. Your mother always used those for these occasions. And Cook will serve his famous custard in those special demitasse cups. They'll look wonderful on the plates."

"If you say so. I trust you and Cook have this well in hand." He turned to leave as Letty called out.

"Please be safe on your travel."

He stopped to smile over his shoulder. "All precautions will be in place. And if you need anything, Sergi and Lucas will be here."

He left Letty to her work and climbed the steps to the third floor. Lyra typically served daily tea in her room, even on days when they had happy hour. He suspected today was no different with Colantha in residence. The dreamwalker had been quiet since her arrival, locking herself in her room with a computer, only allowing Lucas and Ginger to enter. He shook his head, understanding Cressa's disbelief that Colantha would have a cell phone. It surprised him how tech-savvy she was when he'd seen the workstation she'd arranged in her room.

She'd given Lucas specific requirements for a computer, which he'd delivered the day after her arrival. When she wasn't in Lucas's office, reviewing and modifying minor points in the *De første dage* translations, she was in her room, apparently on her computer. She said little to Devon, but she did make a point to tell him she was assisting Philipe and Fiona on the codex over an encrypted link. The plan was to complete the codex so Philipe and Fiona could attempt a translation of a secondary text written in a similar language. It would take several more days to finalize that work.

But one thing Colantha observed was her daily schedule of meals and that included late-afternoon tea in Lyra's room.

He heard the voices through the door before he entered. He gave a light tap in deference to Lyra but didn't wait for a response. Even with her vampiric hearing, he'd probably have to pound on the door to be heard above the women's chatter.

When he entered, Lyra must have heard because she had turned in her seat, her gaze locked with his the moment he moved beyond the screened wall.

"Hello, brother." Her tone was cheery, and she held one of the invitations, tapping it on her chin.

The room grew quiet as the women turned to look at him. He nodded at Frederick and Jamison, who nodded in return. Over their time at the manor, they'd grown more relaxed, now sitting in chairs by the window rather than standing, their faces expression-less, ever the diligent guards.

His eyes flicked to Cressa, who tilted her head, a question in her now-sober gaze, a light smile on her face. He couldn't fathom what she was thinking. His actions over the last two days must have her head spinning. He gave her a warm smile then took in the rest of the group.

Colantha was on the couch with Lyra, and Ginger and Cressa sat on chairs across from them. They usually sat at the seating area near the hearth, but today they were close to the window that overlooked the ocean. The windows were open, and the fresh sea air ruffled the drapes.

When he drew closer, he noted the round silver tray with opened invitations spread across it.

"Thank you for the invitation." Lyra nodded to another chair, but he shook his head.

"I have a car waiting, but I wanted to ensure you had everything you need for this evening."

"Mother would be pleased by this. I told everyone about her planning parties and the special dinner she held for them afterward. And before you ask, Anna received hers. She's still working on the library inventory for Oasis."

He chuckled. "She is single-minded when she has a project."

"Where are you going?" Cressa's tone wasn't quite accusatory, but there was a touch of worry.

He strode to her and, placing a hand on her shoulder, bent to give her a light kiss on her cheek. Her hand covered his as she glanced up at him. "I need to make a quick trip to Oasis." He straightened and squeezed her hand before letting it go. "I need to review the security with Simone and go over some business matters that have been delayed with our other activities."

"You're not going alone, are you?" Cressa's worry for him spread a delicious warmth through him.

"Standard lockdown protocols, and while I don't like using the copter any more than necessary, I'm taking advantage this time. I don't know if I'll return tonight or tomorrow morning. I'll call you once I know my plans. Until then—" He glanced at the others. "Sergi and Lucas are in residence should you need anything. Dinner should keep you busy the rest of the night."

He turned back to Cressa. "I assume there's been no response to your text."

She shook her head. "Do you want me to call if I get one?"

He considered it. "Show it to Sergi first, then call me. Until then, let's not worry. This evening is a break from your hard work and to replenish your energy."

Before leaving, he stopped next to Colantha. "I feel as if I've not been the best host."

"Nonsense, vampire. I've been too busy to give you a thought." Her smile was the same predatory one she'd given him the first time he'd met her in New Orleans, waiting in his hotel room with her magic red powder.

He chuckled, seeing the humor dancing in her bright gaze. "Then I'll take my leave. Have a good evening."

He was halfway to the stairs when Cressa caught up to him.

"Don't you want me to go with you?"

Her question tugged at his heart. He turned, and when she got close enough, he wrapped an arm around her waist and pulled her close. "Of course. But you need to be here until we know more about the text. I won't take a chance of you leaving the manor unless it's for a mission or in response to a raid. Even then, I worry."

"Then why are you going?"

"I can't monitor the security updates from here. Besides, I need to speak with Simone."

Cressa bit her lip as she considered that. Then she nodded. "There's something up with her."

"You noticed it, too?"

"I assumed it was just being too close to Colantha, but now I'm not so sure."

"That's what I hope to find out, but it will be difficult enough to get her to talk to me. As close as the two of you have become, I don't think she'll open up to anyone but me."

"Better you than me. But I want you to be careful."

"Don't worry. I have a six-vampire security detail going with me, and once we're in the air, it will be fine."

She put a hand on his neck and pulled him down for a kiss. It was tender, and he matched it until a fire built that he couldn't control. When he finally pulled away, her lips were swollen from his passion. She gave him a quick hug, then walked away, glancing over her shoulder once before entering Lyra's room and shutting the door.

～

DEVON CONSIDERED the last glance Cressa had given him during the entire ride to the private airport. They hadn't spoken about her debt or his release of it. And as much as he wanted to ask, he'd left it to her. He'd always been known as a patient, if easy to anger, vampire who considered his options thoroughly before taking action. That notion seldom applied to his interactions with Cressa.

Once he was in the copter and flying to Oasis, he relaxed against the seat and closed his eyes, the sound of the propellers muffled by the headset. Familiar with the light vibration of the engines and occasional chatter from the pilot, he let his mind wander, not stopping for any length of time on any one subject. He'd tried meditation, and while he had enough control to close out all his thoughts, it never provided the relaxation or mental clarity it gave Simone and Lyra.

For him, freeing his mind and allowing his thoughts to wander provided a clear image of all the current missions, tasks, and Family concerns on House Trelane's agenda. From that vantage point, he mentally organized and prioritized them, determining a clear path on how the items fit together and what steps were needed to complete each one. There was only one area that remained murky because the necessary steps continually changed. When one piece was placed in the puzzle, the entire image shifted, leaving openings for new pieces.

Was the text Cressa received about Rasmussen part of Venizi's campaign against House Trelane? Or was there some new threat? If Rasmussen was alive and in trouble, why all the subterfuge? The only explanation would be that another dreamwalker was seeking help and wasn't sure how much Cressa knew about dreamwalking. If that was the case, how did they get Cressa's number? He'd meant to speak to Colantha about it, but the time got away from him.

If he knew Cressa, she would speak to her. Maybe that was enough.

"We're five minutes out, sir."

The pilot's announcement shifted his thoughts. He straightened and stared down at the landscape.

"Can you take a low run around the perimeter before landing?" Devon asked.

"Yes, sir."

Devon oriented himself to where they were in relation to Oasis and soon the landscape became familiar. The copter flew over the main gate and followed an approximate line around the estate's boundary. A fence stretched north and south from the main gate for a quarter mile on each side, which was why Venizi's vampires broached the perimeter at those points as well as the main gate. Two wolves stepped out from under scrub oak and glanced up at them.

His sharp eyes found a security monitor, but most of them weren't visible from this angle. When they reached the back entrances to the property he was pleased to see the fencing was farther along than he thought. The longest gully ran along the north side of the property but there were more gullies on the east end and three different roads available as emergency exits. With the additional fencing and difficult terrain, intruders would be forced onto the roads, leaving them vulnerable to ambush.

If Venizi attacked from the west, and Family members required an exit, Venizi could block the east side exits. With security monitors and drones, the opposing force would easily be spotted. In a worst-case scenario, a fleet of off-road vehicles could transfer the humans off the property on the south perimeter. Nothing was foolproof, but it was a lot of territory for an invading army to cover.

He grinned. That's why they'd added C-4. Decker's suggestion to include wolves had been an excellent idea, and Devon wasn't sure why he hadn't thought of it himself. Soon, having received Remus's and the local pack Alpha's approval, they would gain another dozen wolves to rotate through security.

"Is that good, sir?"

The copter was approaching the main gate.

"Yes, you can take us down."

Simone waited on the far side of the copter pad. Her midnight-blue caftan fluttered in the wind from the chopper's blades. She smiled as he ran over to her, but her gaze was hard. There was no question something troubled her.

"Simone." Devon kissed both her cheeks and put an arm around her as they moved away from the noise of the copter's slowing blades.

On the short walk to the manor, he noticed the increased security patrols loitering at the security building. If he'd driven by car, there was a small road that veered off to the right of the main drive. It led to a grouping of outer cabins and housing units, but not before passing by the security building.

The building was two thousand square feet. There were two spacious rooms with bunks similar to a fire station, a full kitchen and dining area, the command center, and a lounge with an entertainment center for breaks between assignments.

The fact there were so many outside the building could be explained by a shift change or, as he suspected, a build-up of their defenses. The Trelane Family was small compared to Venizi's but had the advantage of being full-blooded vampires—all trained in various martial arts and military-style combat. They'd also been through black ops and navy SEAL-type training. Every one of them was deadly with a variety of weapons.

Several hundred yards from the security building was the medical facility. Each safe house had small medical facilities, but with Oasis located so far away from the city, the building also included a surgical unit. With vampires, most injuries could be healed with donor blood, but surgery could reduce the amount of blood required for healing.

From what Cressa told him of Shadow Island, Venizi kept his humans in their own apartment building, separate from the manor. Devon didn't believe in species separation. The blood donors that serviced the Trelane House weren't there just for their blood. They each had jobs to perform and were paid for their service. They lived among the vampires, which built a seamless structure within the Family. One recent change, similar to what Ginger encouraged at the coastal manor, was that the humans were undergoing defensive training. Those with the right skills and desire were also provided with offensive training.

And it didn't go without notice that with the addition of the shifters, his dream for Oasis was coming together. A place where all species could co-exist. And to think it required a coming war to make it happen.

"I'm glad you told me you were coming by copter." Simone stepped into the manor first then led Devon to her office.

For a long time, she'd used his office since he rarely found time to visit Oasis. But when he'd been recovering from his addiction to the Poppy, she'd stopped using his and had hers remodeled to fit her style.

"I had someone drive the perimeter and inform the shifters." She dropped into her seat behind the desk. Now that they were out of the sun, Devon could see the shadows under her eyes. Another cadre member not getting enough blood.

"That explains their calmness when we flew over." Devon took a seat across the desk from her. "Thank you for taking the time on such short notice. I see the fencing on the back property is moving faster than planned."

She chuckled. "Apparently, shifters get bored easily when not on assignment. They asked for more work. I gave them several options, and most wanted to work on the defenses. They offered a few ideas that made their job easier, and the security chief agreed."

Devon's focus shifted to the window. Simone's office faced the front of the property, preferring to see who drove up rather than have a view of the garden in the back. "Can you imagine how our society could have evolved had shifters and vampires worked together through the centuries?"

"Perhaps House Trelane will lead others in the preservation of both our species."

"Assuming we prevail in our war."

"Are you having doubts?"

It was Devon's turn to chuckle. "No. But sometimes, it feels as if the battlefield is a blanket of sand. With each step, the landscape shifts beneath our feet."

"Everything is connected. We simply have to wait for the pieces to align."

"I was thinking along the same lines on the flight over. It's not the pieces I'm worried about but the final image. Did Sergi tell you about our latest wrinkle?"

"About?"

"Cressa received a text after our raid on Venizi's vampires plaguing the city safe house. The message said Rasmussen was in trouble and needed help."

Simone's brows lifted. "Isn't that Cressa's father?"

He nodded. "We believe it to be a ruse, possibly created by her sister April, who might or might not be working for Venizi."

Devon explained the situation with Cressa's mother and the assignment Sergi and Bella were running to gather more information on April and the estate.

"What can I do?"

"Nothing at this point. Perhaps something once we hear back from the mystery person and I decide on a plan." He rubbed his hands together. "Shall we take a drive?"

"I have a jeep waiting." She checked her watch. "We just had a shift change; the shifters should be in place by the time we arrive. We'll start with the back of the property."

They drove the perimeter, stopping occasionally for Simone to point out security cameras and perimeter sensors. Devon had to give her and their security chief credit for their creativity in the camouflage. Unless you knew they were there, physically ran into them, or had equipment to identify their energy output, most would walk past them.

When they arrived on a knoll overlooking the north side of the property, Simone stopped the jeep.

"We don't expect an invasion from this side because of the gully. It's not impossible, but it's a hard run to the manor. We've increased the number of monitors and have two shifters that patrol this area at any given time. We'll increase to three or four once the new pack joins us.

"You've done a marvelous job. Credit to both you and Decker on integrating the shifters, and the security chief as well for the additional tech."

"The teams deserve most of the credit."

"Of course, but I assume you've already cared for bonuses."

"Yes."

Devon scanned the landscape and breathed in the air, the scent thick with sage. It was a peaceful setting. The only sounds came from birds and Simone grinding her teeth.

He sucked in a sigh and kept an eye on a slow-circling hawk, searching for its next meal. "When are you going to tell me what's wrong?"

She jerked at the question but didn't look at him. "As you said, everything is coming along well."

"And you know I'm not asking about Oasis."

When she turned to him, the tips of her fangs showed. She began to say something, then closed her mouth and gazed into the distance.

He waited. It was important to take things slow with Simone when the topic became personal. It was a fifty-fifty chance she'd speak now. Otherwise, he'd have to try again after dinner.

They sat together for almost thirty minutes before Simone relaxed.

"I've been trying to reach a friend, but I haven't heard back."

"How long has it been?"

"Since I returned to Oasis."

"Not very long. Not all vampires monitor their emails or texts often."

She shook her head. "Not this vampire. He might be an ancient, but he stays on top of world news. An old habit."

"So, a close friend." If he was an ancient, it was most likely she'd known him for a long time.

"No. When I walked away centuries ago, it wasn't on good terms. But I had a reason to contact him recently."

She turned to him. "He's the one that gave us Gheata." When Devon nodded, she returned to gazing at the landscape. "He'd changed from the last time I'd seen him. This time we separated on good terms, or at least better than how it had been before."

"Is there anyone you could contact that would know where he is?"

She gripped the steering wheel, her gaze unfocused. "No."

"Give it some more time."

"There's not much else I can do with the lockdown."

"Keep me posted if you don't hear from him after a few more days." He laid a hand on her shoulder. "Let's go back, have a nice dinner, and watch the sunset."

She growled. "You're spending too much time with humans."

Chapter Twenty

I STEPPED out of the evening gown and hung it in the closet before pulling on sweats and my favorite sweatshirt. The cool ocean air blew through the opened window, circulating through the room and clearing the wine from dinner.

The knock came as expected, and Ginger popped her head in before pushing her way through the door.

"Did you turn on the air conditioning?" Ginger shivered and pulled open drawers until she found a sweatshirt to pull over her head.

"Sorry. Would you prefer your room?"

"No. But let's sit by the fireplace so I can pretend there's a toasty fire. I'll just grab a blanket." She pulled the one from the back of the sofa and stretched out, tucking it around her. "You must be in one of your thinking modes."

Another knock came, and Ginger said, "Do you mind getting it? I just got settled."

I snorted and shuffled to the door, then backed up as Letty entered with a tray. "You didn't need to do that. We could have come down for it."

"Nonsense. It's no trouble. One urn is coffee, and the other hot chocolate. The bottle is one of the manor's finest brandies." She set it down then hurried out of the room with a final good night.

"I'm not sure I can handle any more alcohol after that dinner." I poured a cup of hot chocolate for both of us and added a touch of brandy anyway.

"Did Lyra say her mother hosted one of those dinners every week?" Ginger asked.

"Yeah. But those were different times back then. It was kind of nice dressing up in our finest. I'm not sure a dinner table adorned as it was deserved anything less." I sipped the cocoa and melted into my corner of the sofa. "How did Colantha know to bring an evening gown? Or do you think she borrowed it from Lyra?"

"Nothing that woman does surprises me. Did she seem tired to you?"

I considered the shadows under Colantha's eyes. "From what Lyra told me, Frederick has been reducing the amount of juice she's been drinking."

"I thought it was the translations taking a toll, but I hear she's been dreamwalking several times a day."

"What? I hadn't heard that."

Ginger nodded as she licked cocoa from her upper lip. "Lyra thought she was dreamwalking with Hamilton, but he said no. He told Lyra that she'd been reaching out to dreamwalkers all over the world."

"About what? Did he know?"

"Not really, but he thinks it might have something to do with the translations and the codex Colantha's helping to create." She pulled the blanket away so she could sit cross-legged on the couch, somehow not spilling a drop of cocoa. She leaned in. "He also thinks she found something in the translation that stirred some old memories. The rumor is that she's looking for another book that was hidden away."

I stared at her. That's just what they needed—another secret book. "What could that be?"

"Lyra thinks it might have something to do with the Seven Tribes."

I thought back to the first time Colantha had mentioned her being the daughter of Adelice and Heiress of the Seven Tribes. "Does she think they still exist?"

Ginger shrugged and pulled her blanket up. "That might explain the dreamwalking around the world." She fell back against the armrest, slapping her forehead with the palm of her hand. "Oh my god!" She leaned forward again, and my first thought was maybe I shouldn't have added the brandy. "Do you think she's calling them together? You know, like preparing them for war?"

Well, maybe the brandy was a good idea after all. I'm not sure I would have ever considered the notion. "There's so much we don't know. And I think Colantha has only shared five percent of what I should know about dreamwalkers. I know she mentioned there were Seven Tribes, but I have no idea how they worked together. Did they act similar to the vampire Council?" I shrugged. "I just don't know. Colantha isn't going to share anything until she's ready. I think we need to focus on what we do know. Or, hopefully, what we'll know when we get the report from Remus's lab on the new blood samples. My belief is that we don't know everything we need to know about the Blood Poppy. And I think it's something Venizi knows about and has been taking advantage of."

"Well, that sounds dark and mysterious and a bit dangerous."

A ping sounded, and we glanced around.

"Is that your phone?" I asked as I set down the cocoa and searched the room.

"I didn't bring mine."

I found my phone in the bathroom after the third ping and dropped onto the couch, pulling up my knees as I opened the text message.

"What is it? Is it about your father?"

I snorted. "Yeah. They don't want to divulge their name over the phone. They want to meet." I rolled my eyes. "Alone. The only thing missing is their request not to call the cops."

"Do they say where?"

I dropped the phone on the coffee table, topped off the cocoa, and added more brandy. "Newberry Park. Tomorrow at midnight."

Ginger barked out a laugh. "Why don't they just say walk into my web so we can kidnap you?"

"Right?"

"This can't be Venizi. He couldn't possibly believe you'd be that gullible."

"No. But I think April might believe it."

"What are you thinking?"

"April was never business savvy. At least not when we were still speaking. She was more interested in fashion and going to parties. It was only recently that she seemed to be following in Christopher's shadow." I stared into my cocoa. No one changed that quickly. Why did April? Devon said her mom had an escape plan. I'd always thought Christopher was rolling in cash, but what if it was all for appearance? What if his estate wasn't a boon but a pile of mounting debt? Sergi should be able to check that out.

"I think it might be possible that April is working for Venizi but at a much lower level than she likes. Maybe she thinks it would make for a nice payday and a shot up the power ladder if she was able to pull me in along with the medallion."

"But she doesn't know you're a dreamwalker. Does she even know you're living with vamps?"

That was the problem. "I don't know how much Christopher knew and how much he might have shared with April. Maybe it's just about the medallion, and April doesn't know about anything else. I need to talk to my mother."

"Is it safe to call her?"

"No. But Devon is sending me on a surveillance mission to see if she shows up for her hair and spa appointments." I rubbed a hand over my face. "All we have at this point are assumptions. We need hard facts."

Ginger nodded toward the phone. "Are you going to answer it or wait to talk to Devon?"

"He won't be back until tomorrow."

"What about Sergi? Maybe his investigation has turned up something."

The phone pinged again.

"What the hell?" I leaned over and grabbed the phone. "It's them again." After a quick read, I wished I had the vamp strength to crush the damn thing. "Unbelievable. It took them hours to come up with their stupid plan, and now they're harping at me for an answer."

"You can't tell them you're on lockdown. Or do you think they know?"

I hadn't even considered that. "It's probably best not to mention it either way, but tomorrow night is too soon." I tapped the phone against my chin, considering my options. The sane thing to do would be to ignore it. But I wasn't in the mood. This was pissing me off. If Rasmussen was alive and in trouble, why all the mystery? Tell me where he was and tell me how I can help. I typed a reply, ignoring Ginger's pleading look to not do anything rash. But if this was April, I knew how to deal with her.

I lifted a finger at Ginger. "I haven't sent it. How does this sound? I'm out of town on a job and won't be back until Thursday. And unless you want to tell me who this is, I prefer a public spot to meet." I reread my message again. "That gives us two days to come up with something."

"Why don't you wait until you talk to Sergi?"

Another ping came in. I laughed. "They seem to be desperate for my response. If this is April, I think it's best to answer with something she'd believe. If it's someone else, they need to know I'm not going to do something so obviously stupid."

Ginger tilted her head, giving it some thought. "Read your answer again." When I did, she nodded. "They can't refute whether you're out of town without giving away how they know that. And you're right. Anyone who's watched at least one horror movie knows meeting a stranger alone in a place with no other people is stupid. I mean, you're not even blonde."

We both chuckled.

"I'm going to send it. Just because I'm getting home on Thursday doesn't mean I'll drop everything to meet them, right?"

"Right."

I should be contacting Devon or at least Sergi. Then I got my dander up. Why did I have to pass everything through them? This was about my father. Yes, there was the whole lockdown thing. And yes, this could be Venizi or some other vamp yanking my chain. But if it was April, my mother was unwittingly in the middle of whatever this was. If anything, we needed time, and my response would give us that.

I looked at Ginger.

She nodded. "Go ahead. I have your back."

Then we both snorted as if that would matter one iota to either Devon or Sergi.

I pushed the send button.

Ginger pushed her blanket off and slid over to sit next to me, shoulder to shoulder, as we watched the phone.

After a couple of minutes, she asked, "How long are we going to stare at the screen?"

Then we got the giggles. Maybe I should have considered this when I was more sober. I finished the cocoa in one large gulp. Too late to worry about it now.

We both jumped when the ping came.

I rolled my eyes again as I read the text.

"We'll be in touch."

~

DEVON ARRIVED BACK at the coastal manor later than he'd planned. At breakfast, Simone mentioned a rumor she'd received in the previous evening's reports.

She had picked at her spinach and egg-white omelet but looked better than when he'd first arrived. The shadows under her eyes told him she'd taken blood. At least he didn't have to remind her.

"I don't know how accurate this information is, but word has it that Venizi is holding a Family-only party on the island."

"Who's the information from?" Devon always asked even though he knew Simone might not answer. She was cautious about her informants.

She shrugged a shoulder and nibbled on a scone. "I should ask Lucia to get Cook's recipe for scones. These are good but not as good as his." She swallowed another bite. "All I can say is that she's connected to a House faithful to Venizi. She has considered requesting a transfer to another House or going rogue, but she realizes she's in an opportune position to help us. And before you ask if she could be providing false information, that, of course, is always possible. However, I knew this vampire before she was traded to her current House. Her previous reports, while rare, have always been accurate."

"Alright. Did she give you a date?"

"Friday."

"Interesting. You think this might help us with what April might be up to?"

Simone leaned back with her cup of coffee and stared at him. "That would best be answered by Bella and Cressa. But I think it gives you an option."

"I agree."

Before he left the manor for the helicopter, Simone stood next to him, watching the rotors spin up.

"Do you need me to assist with this Rasmussen problem?"

"No. At least, not yet. If we plan something where we need

you, I'll let you know. Otherwise, I think you have your hands full completing the security precautions."

"Alright."

Before he stepped out the door, Simone touched his arm to stop him. She appeared uncomfortable. "Tell Cressa that I'll be there if she needs me."

He wasn't sure how to respond to that. Her request wasn't a platitude. She didn't believe in those. He placed a hand over hers. "I'll tell her. And keep me posted on your friend. I'm serious when I say if you don't hear from him soon, I'll help you locate him."

She kissed his cheek, then turned and walked away. A sign that the discussion had become too emotional for her.

Devon smiled as he ran for the copter. She'd changed over the last year and was almost ready for her own House. He had Cressa and Ginger to thank for that, though he'd never tell Simone that. Although she probably already figured it out, which no doubt irritated the hell out of her.

He watched the estate as the copter lifted and flew toward the coast. Oasis was in safe hands and ready for anything Venizi might throw at them next.

He sent a text to Sergi to prepare for a meeting upon his arrival. The drive to the manor from the airstrip took longer than expected due to an accident. When he arrived at the manor and strode directly to his office, the cacophony of voices, some raised in heated discussion loud enough to be heard through the closed door, made him grind his teeth.

Now what?

He stormed through the door, which provided the results he'd hoped for. Everyone shut up, and a few seemed chagrined, which surprised him. The cadre was positioned around his desk as usual. Decker was at the bar, smiling as if he'd been enjoying the fray. Jacques sat in a corner as if wanting to separate himself from whatever disagreement had been in full throttle.

Cressa, Ginger, Lyra, and Colantha were grouped together by

the fireplace. It only took a second to scan the women, whose defiant look told Devon where the battle lines had been drawn.

He sighed, wanting nothing more than to drop onto the sofa next to Cressa, give her a warm kiss, and let someone else finish whatever discussion had created such an uproar. But he couldn't show sides, and more's the pity for that.

He took his obligatory seat at his desk and turned to readjust the shades to let in more light. Then he turned and picked up the white crystal from his desk. This time there was no question he was using it as a security blanket, shielding him from whatever news he was about to hear. After some consideration, he decided to take another approach, hoping to calm the emotions still stirring tension in the room.

"I have excellent news to report from Oasis." He was satisfied when some appeared relieved by the change in topic while he received irritated glances from others. Sergi was the only one who seemed to be interested in Oasis, which undoubtedly had to do with his role as head of security.

His shoulders relaxed as he reviewed the updates Simone had made since the attack.

"I've vetted twelve of the shifters from the local pack to add to your security." Decker had been pleased to hear about the shifters' willingness to help with the fences. "I think Simone has begun her interviews."

Devon nodded. "She's approved four, and they'll be incorporated into the patrol schedule by the end of the week after a day of training. The rest of the interviews should be completed by the end of next week."

"May I ask a question, vampire?" Colantha hadn't seemed interested in the report, so her request surprised him.

"Of course."

"Where are these shifters housed at Oasis? Do they have a single house? A building of their own?"

He wasn't sure why she asked or what she hoped to learn. If he had to guess, it was a test of how his House treated shifters. He gave her the truth as he knew it.

"Actually, it's an interesting topic." He returned the crystal to his desk and, leaning back, looked at Lucas. "I could use an espresso if you don't mind."

"Absolutely." He jumped up, receiving a couple of requests from others.

"As you know from your brief visit to Oasis, there are several houses and bungalows spread around the manor. The houses are meant to house several vampires or shifters. The bungalows are smaller, some grouped together, while others are spread out for privacy. We also house many within the manor itself.

"From what Simone has reported, the first ten shifters selected a house not far from the security building, but of those, one has recently moved into the manor, taking a room close to the kitchen. Turns out, he's a rather good cook, and when he's not on shift, he's been working in the kitchen with Lucia. Another one, well, he wasn't comfortable in a house full of other shifters."

"That must be Laslo," Decker added. "I wasn't sure he'd make the cut. He's got some issues and needs his space."

"Yes, Simone wasn't sure, either, and had given him a short probationary time. Once he confided he required more space, she assigned him one of the private bungalows closer to the lake. That seems to have resolved the issue, and he's been removed from his probation period. I believe the others are happy with their assigned housing." He gave Colantha a smile. "Does that answer your question?"

Instead of answering, her next question was to Decker. "And do you believe the shifters to be happy with this new arrangement?"

Decker didn't hesitate. "If they're offering to assist with building the fences in addition to their patrol shifts, that's answer enough for me. But I've spoken with a few. They're well-housed, well-fed, and given plenty of room to run. There was a brief period of wariness with the vampires, but now that they're training together, they seem comfortable with their assignment."

"I know we've begun to add shifters to the safe houses, but we should add a couple here at the coastal manor," Sergi suggested. "They bring a different form of security and build up our numbers."

Devon nodded. "That's an excellent idea. Can you work with Remus or Braden, his beta?"

When Sergi agreed, Devon looked to Colantha and waited for her to answer his question. Her grin was predatory, but he was used to it. She'd been testing him. To what end, he didn't know.

"Yes. Thank you."

"Okay, so that brings us to what the uproar was about when I walked in."

Chapter Twenty-One

I WATCHED Devon from the moment he walked into his office. A tic played along his jaw. He was either bothered by his trip to Oasis or by the loud voices coming from his office. He'd given me a glance, testing the waters, and I smiled. I couldn't help it.

He'd texted the night before to tell me he'd be home in the morning. Then texted again when his motorcade had been held up by a legitimate accident. He was trying to keep me included, and I had to give him points. We still had so much to talk about.

It didn't surprise me, and it certainly didn't surprise the cadre, that he would run his own meeting and not play into the heated discussion we'd been in before his arrival. The question was, once we got to the topic, would he be as irritated with me as Sergi had been?

Now, we'd find out. But when he asked the question about the uproar, I wasn't going to go first. I wasn't cadre, and it was times like this, I was happy I wasn't. So, I crossed my arms across my chest—defensive much—and put on a smile, knowing Ginger had my back and, surprisingly, Bella's and Lucas's.

Who knew?

It was a control issue, and Sergi was all about control, especially where security was concerned. I couldn't blame him. At least, I'd considered contacting him before replying to the mysterious text. If I'd considered it rationally at the time, and not after I don't know how many drinks, I might have realized I'd been searching for my own control. It was my father, my history, my family.

But what done was done, and now I'd face the repercussions.

When silence was Devon's only answer, I was surprised when Sergi glanced at me. Was he expecting me to explain it?

Devon was an astute vamp, and it didn't take him long to see the glares between his head of security and me. He turned his chair to look out the window. Great. He was going to wait us out.

Sergi smiled. God, he knew how much that irritated me. Like he'd won or something.

"I received a return text last night, and I responded without asking Sergi," I blurted out. "So, now he's pissed at me."

Devon let a few minutes slip by before asking. "Sergi, do you have the transcript of the text exchange?"

"Yes."

"Please read it back for everyone."

Sergi glanced down at his tablet. Apparently, he'd been ready for the request. I hated to admit it, but the vamp was good at his job.

Once the conversation had been shared, Devon, the back of his chair still facing us, said, "So we have a couple of days before they expect another response."

I didn't think it was a question, and the cadre didn't respond. I glanced at Lyra, who had on her serene "I'm just here because it's expected, but I'd rather be painting" face on. No help there.

Colantha was reading something on a tablet. Was she still reviewing texts? I still couldn't get used to her working with technology. For some reason, I was still expecting her to roll out sheets of papyrus.

I didn't and wouldn't look at Ginger. It was impossible to ignore her silent snickers at the entire situation.

"Remind me again," Devon said. "When's the next time Willa goes for her hair or spa appointment? And which one is it that she has lunch with her friends afterward?"

I was surprised by the question since we'd talked about it yesterday, and Sergi had already prepared a surveillance team to monitor both locations. Was his discussion with Simone bothering him, or something else? "Her hair appointment is tomorrow, followed by lunch with her friends. Her spa day is on Thursday."

"Bella, what do you have regarding the estate?" Devon leaned over and moved a clay sculpture, then relaxed in his chair, putting his feet on the shelf.

"The estate sits too far back to see from the road. There's limited activity and, as we expected, when someone leaves or arrives, it's impossible to know who's inside the vehicle. The driver sometimes has their window down. I've only seen it happen twice, and it's been the same white male. If I had to guess, I'd say vampire, but that's only speculation.

"We drove down the alley that runs behind the back of the estate. There are two gates. One rolls back, allowing a vehicle or truck to enter, and there's a single man-sized gate a few feet from that. There are security cameras on both."

"Sergi, anything on the security system?"

"The aerial view matches Bella's report with security cameras at all gates. According to the security records, there's a security system in the house for the windows and doors. Cameras are located outside the house at each door in addition to the ones at the gates. They send a patrol car through the neighborhood four times a day, two of those during the evening."

"We haven't been watching long enough to know if the security patrols are consistent in the timing of their drive through the neighborhood or if they change it up," Bella added.

"Any men stationed outside?" Devon asked.

"Not according to the aerial footage," Sergi said. "But that doesn't tell us anything."

I would have added something, but Sergi and Bella seemed to have it covered. Of course, it had been almost a year since I'd been there, and if someone else was controlling the estate other than my mother, it was anyone's guess what changes had been made.

"Cressa, you used to meet April when Underwood was out of town. I believe you met her at the pool house."

His statement shocked me. I told him that months ago. Who was I kidding? He was a vamp. Solid memory recall when it suited him, which only made me wonder why he didn't seem to remember which days my mother went to her appointments.

"I went over the wall. There are a couple places where the trees grow close, and they're easy enough to climb. I'm obviously out of touch with any security updates, but Christopher was lax in his security, always depending on the tech. From what Sergi shared, it doesn't sound like anything has changed, but I'd need to see the report. If there aren't guards walking the property, then it's not any more secure than places I've robbed."

Devon remained quiet, and when the cadre shifted to get more comfortable in their seats, it was a sign that Devon was considering the information he received, and we'd have to wait for him to mull it over. The silence was deafening, and my rebellious nature got the better of me.

I went to the coffee bar and made an espresso, not taking Lucas up on his offer when he'd made the earlier ones. The sound of the machine was jarring. I smiled to myself, knowing without looking that Ginger was having a hard time holding in her laughter. Yeah. There were days when we were still twelve.

I was just picking up my cup of espresso when Devon swiveled back to face the room.

"Cressa, do you mind refilling my cup?"

I took the one I was holding, set it on his desk, and picked up his first cup. His smile was breathtaking, and I think my heart might have stopped for a moment.

"Thank you."

I went back to the machine and made another one. He waited until I returned to my seat, and I felt his gaze on me the entire way.

Devon wasted no time from that moment on.

"Sergi, I haven't had a chance to review your surveillance plan, but I want two motorcades for tomorrow. You'll take Cressa in one, and I want Bella and Jacques in the other in case we need a distraction. Let's see if Willa shows up for her appointment." He paused and glanced at me. "Cressa, do you know any of the women your mother has lunch with?"

Again, he surprised me. "I know them all from the time I lived at the house."

"If Willa shows up for her appointment, I want Cressa to find a way into the salon for a chat. If she doesn't show up, the teams will move to the restaurant. Again, if Willa shows up, Cressa will determine the best way to approach her. If she doesn't show up, then Cressa, I want you to meet with the women. See if they know what's going on. Play the worried daughter, and I apologize, I know you're worried, but you need to play the part in a way that the women will be willing to divulge what they know."

Surprised by the plan, I had to admit I liked it. "Understood." I glared at Sergi, who gave me his predatory smile. Devon wasn't going to get in the middle of our argument. He wasn't going to say which of us had been right in our earlier disagreement. He was going to make us work it out in the confines of a vehicle as if we were fighting teenagers.

Damn. It was so adult of him.

"Cressa, I have one last request. Can you contact Harlow and see if he can meet us tomorrow evening, assuming he doesn't have a job? Actually, if they're both available, have him bring Trudy for dinner."

I stared at him, and he gave me a look that said I had no idea what he was planning, but he'd wait to see if I figured it out. I was so turned on at that moment.

I just nodded, since I had no idea what might come out of my mouth. He was right. My head was spinning with possibilities.

"Great. Keep me updated on his response so Cook can plan ahead." He glanced around the room. "That's all I have. I'd like to meet again once Cressa and Sergi return from their surveillance tomorrow. Colantha, if you have time this afternoon, I'd like to catch up. How about lunch on the back patio?"

"That will be perfect." Colantha's response came with one of her sweet smiles that left you wondering what she was really thinking.

"Excellent, thank you." He turned to the others. "I trust you all have your work to get back to. Decker, if you could stay for a few minutes. And Lucas, you too."

The group got up to leave. I wanted to talk to Devon, but I didn't know how long he'd be with Decker and Lucas. Training wasn't scheduled until after lunch, so I went up to my room.

Ginger followed me. "That was crazy, right? I didn't just imagine how strange the meeting was."

"You mean because he didn't chastise me or Sergi?"

"Yeah. I was expecting a smackdown." She snapped her fingers. "He's playing nice while you work out what to do with your new stash of money and the open door he offered you."

"Huh?" Then it hit. "You think he's being nice to me because he's worried I'll leave?"

"Sure. Why else?"

It was a good question until I considered everything I knew about Devon—the vamp, the beast, the lover, and the House leader. A laugh burst out of me.

"What's so funny?"

"One thing I can honestly say I know about Devon Trelane— never underestimate him. He's learning and adapting." I couldn't hold in the grin. "He's got a plan, and he's daring me to figure it out." I shook my head. "God, I love that vamp."

Chapter Twenty-Two

AFTER HIS MORNING MEETING, Devon read security reports regarding the safe houses from his private office in his bedroom. It was the easiest way to ensure privacy from the dozens of calls and requests he received each day. And it gave him time to continue his plans for dealing with whoever was sending Cressa text messages.

He laid down the tablet and leaned back to stare at the ceiling. A grin touched his lips as he thought about Cressa and the surprise on her face with his request that she attempt a meeting with Willa or, if necessary, her friends. The dinner invitation for Harlow and Trudy had put a spark in her eyes, and she met his unspoken challenge. There was no doubt she was somewhere in the manor working through various scenarios as to why he wanted Harlow to come to a meeting.

He could have given her, and the rest of the cadre, a hint about Venizi's party, but that would have made it too easy. Was he giving her what she wanted before she knew she wanted it? His smile widened. Yes, he was. And if that made her want to stay with him after giving her her freedom, well, as they say—all is fair in love and war.

He chuckled when he realized he was currently playing at both.

He glanced at the clock on his desk, closed his tablet, and pulled on his jacket.

He jogged down the stairs and strode to the solarium, whistling a tune. It was a haunting melody, though he didn't know the words. He grabbed a doorjamb, almost stumbling when he realized where he remembered it from.

It had been in one of Cressa's earliest dreamwalks. They were by the lake at Oasis, and there had been a party under a large tent on the other side of the lake. The music had traveled across the water, where they watched and danced. Other than the melody coming easily to him, he'd never heard it before. It must have been a song that meant something to Cressa. He shook it off but continued to whistle it as he strode through the solarium and out the French doors.

Colantha was already seated at the table, staring at the garden or perhaps the ocean beyond. Her fingers began to tap the table as he drew near, still whistling the song. She startled when he pulled out a chair and sat.

"Vampire." She gave him an odd look. "Was that you whistling?"

He grinned sheepishly. "I'm not very good at it. I didn't mean to surprise you." He scanned the table, ensuring everything was in place. Condensation was forming on the pitcher of black peppermint tea, Colantha's favorite, and he filled their glasses.

"I haven't heard that song in a long time."

"You know of it?"

"Yes, most dreamwalkers do. It's an old song, what humans might call a lullaby, though there's more meaning behind it than a simple song to sing a child to sleep. How do you know it?"

He shrugged as he lifted the lids from the platters revealing a light lunch of finger sandwiches, potato salad, and fruit. "I heard it in one of Cressa's dreamwalks, either the first or second one. To be honest, I don't think I've heard it since." He chuckled as he pushed the plate of sandwiches toward her. "I'm not sure why it came to me now."

Her only response was a light grunt, but she gave him a look of interest. There was more to the song, but he set it aside for now.

They spoke of generalities until they poked at their fruit.

"You've either been locked away in your room or with Lyra these last couple of days," Devon started. "Is the codex giving you a problem?"

"No. The codex was completed a day ago, and Lucas sent an encrypted version to Philipe Renaud. Didn't he tell you?"

"I admit to being behind on some of my reports, but it pleases me that you've made such excellent progress."

She didn't appear convinced. "That will depend on whether they can find more than the one text with dreamwalker language. Without that, it will be difficult to sway the Council."

"From what I know of the Renauds and Lucas's reports on his visit with Philipe, he's a stubborn vampire where ancient texts are involved. I wouldn't be surprised if he doesn't send someone to the home library to search."

"The one in France?"

Devon nodded as he chewed a chunk of pineapple. "I'm sure they already have someone combing the one in New Orleans. I'll ask Lucas to provide an update on the search."

He refilled their glasses and let silence take over, hoping Colantha would share what else she was up to without him asking. They sipped the tea for several minutes as they appreciated the view. Colantha was the first to speak.

"I've been dreamwalking with others around the country and overseas. At least those I can reach. I've had to contact many by conventional means. I never realized how many were out there and how little of their powers they understood, let alone controlled."

She tapped her fingers on the table again, then gave him a side glance. "Do I have your permission to take us to a construct?"

The request surprised him, and he couldn't help the smile that accompanied the nod. "I'm honored you asked this time."

Before he could take another breath, he found himself in an old pub with comfortable leather chairs. A glass of dark beer was in front of him, and Colantha sat across from him, gripping a martini glass.

"I recognize this place. You brought me here when I met you in New Orleans." He glanced around, turning in his chair to check behind him. "Dublin, right?"

She nodded as she sipped her martini, a light sigh escaping after her first swallow. "I thought for the next part of our conversation, we could use something a bit stronger."

"I could have asked Letty to bring us something."

Her predatory smile was similar to Simone's. "It doesn't carry the same flair."

"I would agree with that." He tasted the beer. It was excellent. "So why the secrecy? While I appreciate the fine beer and comfortable atmosphere, it doesn't explain the need for a construct."

She took another drink and tapped her nails on the base of the glass. "After reading the *De første dage*, and specifically the dreamwalker portion, it reminded me of how much we've lost over the centuries. Loss of our abilities, loss of rights, loss of life, all due to unwarranted fears. I've always known about the dreamwalkers who were accused of controlling the minds of others. But I'm no longer convinced that they were the extremists the Council believed them to be."

"Over time, stories change, especially if only told by word of mouth. A story can expand to great exaggeration or become anemic and eventually die. I assume you believe the first to be true in your example."

She nodded. "I believe someone saw an opportunity for great

power and wealth, and to the detriment of their race, forced events to their benefit."

Devon hadn't been expecting that, and he swallowed a quarter of his mug, anticipating he might need a scotch or two after this discussion. "Are you saying a vampire made a power play knowing it would not be in our best interest?"

"Who's to say for sure? But based on what I see as the outcome of the decision to purge dreamwalkers, it's hard to believe otherwise. Consider everything occurring within vampire society over what, to us, is a rather short period of time: the creation of Magic Poppy, the decline in vampire fertility, the increased cases of vampire blood disease, and the growing numbers of halfling creations."

If he'd been standing, he'd be on the floor by now. "Are you saying all of these events are linked?"

"What I'm saying, as The Wolf will soon discover, is that the Blood Poppy is vital to both vampire and dreamwalker. That without it, both species will eventually die out." She gave a tired laugh. "It would take hundreds of centuries, of course. But here's another secret hidden by time and ignorance. Each species needs the blood of the other. This is the foundation of unity between vampire and dreamwalker. Not ideological but biological. And it's only been proven to me now by how weak the dreamwalkers have become."

"I feel as if my mental fugue has returned. What do you mean we have a biological connection? I've never taken dreamwalker blood that I know of. And the only time I've had association with Blood Poppy, or at least it's our working theory, is through Magic Poppy, and I can assure you, that was not a positive effect."

"That depends on your point of view."

"What do you mean?"

"For you and your Family, the beast taking control was of great negative consequence. You were losing control." She leaned closer.

"Think of it from the perspective of war. If you had the ability to force the beast out, possibly permanently, and then direct them…"

"You'd have an almost unstoppable army." Devon sat back. He'd always considered himself a leader who thought big and understood the stakes. He'd been so wrong.

"Don't beat yourself up, vampire. You couldn't know all of this because you didn't have all the information."

He stared at his beer. Then blinked. A glass of what he presumed to be scotch appeared next to the beer.

"I thought you could use something stronger."

He swallowed the two fingers and reveled in the burn. When he sat back, he noted the glass had been refilled. "I'll need some time to consider all of this. What's next?"

"I once mentioned the Seven Tribes while bringing Hamilton back to us. I need to reform the tribal structure, assuming there's at least one member of each tribe still alive. From what my mother told me, each of the Seven Tribes used their dreamwalking powers in different ways. Most for forms of healing, others to stay in communication with members who lived in distant lands, and so on. Each tribe had enough power to ensure one wouldn't become more powerful than the other. But if all Seven Tribes came together in the Nexus, our combined powers could be a rather formidable force. I believe this, more than the rogue dreamwalkers, was the reason for the purge."

"But you don't have access to all Seven Tribes."

Her face lost all emotion except for the sadness in her gaze. "The leaders of the Seven Tribes were the first purged, including my mother. Though I was very young, she had passed on many of the old ways, which have guided me through the years. Now, I must call upon all I can remember. Three tribes are easy enough to find. My own of course, Hamilton's, and then Cressa's."

"How do you know one tribe from another?"

"It's not something outsiders would know. The only reason the vampire Council knew who they were was because we never hid them. Each dreamwalker gives off a different essence within their link to the Nexus. Most dreamwalkers today have no understanding of it. The closest way I can describe it is that it's similar to a person's aura. I felt it immediately when I dreamwalked with Hamilton and Cressa." She gave him a wry grin. "Last names can also be used to identify a tribe, but typically only through the family of the leaders. Rasmussen isn't a common name. I wouldn't mention it to her, but I believe Cressa might be an heiress in her tribe."

He barked a laugh. "I'm not sure that would do anything more than make her give up her dreamwalking."

"Exactly. And that would be detrimental to our plans. I will continue my search for the other four tribes. You need to find out what The Wolf's lab results show, but I suspect they'll prove my theory."

He took a sip of the scotch then pushed it aside. "There's no question as to what this information would do to the vampire community. There would be outrage, denials, and, most likely, the complete eradication of the entire Council. There might even be a move by the Houses to greatly curtail its power. But a civil war is now more likely than ever."

"That would depend on how the Houses divide themselves if they do."

"Agreed."

The bright sunlight forced Devon's hand up to shield his eyes. He blinked several times to acclimate to being home.

"I wish you'd give more warning when you do that," he grumbled.

Colantha laughed. "I can't help myself with parlor tricks. It's a good way to stay in practice."

"I'll contact Remus and see where they're at with the lab work."

"Yes, but first, you must take care of this issue with

Rasmussen. Someone is after Cressa. It's critical you find out who and put a stop to it."

"Do you know this for certain because you know where Rasmussen is?"

"No. I wish I did. He would be instrumental in reforming the Seven Tribes. I don't know whether he's alive or dead. What I do know is that whatever is happening now, it's not safe for her."

"We're in agreement. And I already have a plan to take care of it."

I RAN at the rock wall, attempting to hit it three feet higher than I normally do. In perspective, three feet doesn't seem like much, but considering I was already hitting the wall at four feet off the ground, I was asking a lot of myself. I wasn't expecting to achieve it, but sometimes it's good to have something to constantly strive for. Besides, I was bored to tears.

The lockdown was having an impact. After days of working with Lucas and Colantha on the translations, Ginger was basking in the pool, reading her women's magazines, and catching up on the shopping channel, enjoying a couple days of doing nothing.

The only relief was Devon's surprise announcement that instead of surveillance, I was going out to not only find my mother but also talk to her. The question was why.

The answer was obvious. She didn't want me to call her, and I assumed it was fear of whatever April was up to. My suspicions were based on that single call, Mom's whispered voice, and the man's voice in the background. When I had more time to think about it, maybe she merely wanted time for April to cool off, and if Mom remained in contact with me, it could make the situation worse. The man's voice might have been one of April's boyfriends, who just happened to be an overbearing asshole.

The bottom line was I didn't know what was happening in

that house, and the only way to know for sure would be to talk to her outside of the house. I had done it before when I surprised her at the spa. What if she had vamps escorting her everywhere? What if they were actually going into the salon with her? How creepy for the stylist and the other customers. But that was where Bella and Jacques came in for diversionary tactics.

After the third failed attempt at the rock wall, I studied it from a different perspective. Maybe if I hit it at my usual four feet, then used the first rock as a springboard while I grabbed for a higher hold. I ran, jumped, hit the first rock, but my foot slipped, and I slammed into the wall face-first before landing on my ass.

Damn. That hurt. I touched my nose. It hurt but wasn't broken. That was something.

"I'd ask what you were attempting, but I'm not sure I want to hear the answer."

I twisted around from my seated position and glared at Devon. He'd changed from his suit but wasn't wearing his normal spandex gym shorts. The loose-fitting, sleeveless shirt was normal, and my gaze locked on his lean muscled arms for a second too long. The board shorts were a surprise. He looked like he was ready to strip off his shirt and go surfing.

My gaze drifted down to his legs, and my attempts not to imagine those strong legs tangling with mine under the sheets failed.

He held out a bottle of water and nodded to the single bench in the room.

I dragged myself off the floor and took the bottle as I sat, drinking a quarter of it.

"How was lunch with Colantha?" I was a little hurt at not being asked to join them, but Devon had been in House leader mode the last couple of days. A sure sign he was up to something.

He gave a half-shrug and a deprecating smile. "To be fair, I came here hoping to run aimlessly at the wall myself."

"Wow, that bad?"

Then he told me about his discussion with Colantha, and by the end, I stared at the wall, wanting to slam into it over and over again.

"Are you sure you heard her right? She's saying all the issues with vamps over the centuries—the declining fertility, the increase in vamps with the rare blood disease, and the Magic Poppy production are all tied together?"

"We should know if she's right or not once Remus has the lab results back."

"How long is that going to take?"

"Decker is checking with him. He was going to drive over to discuss it rather than use a phone."

"You must be feeling sick."

He ran a hand over his head and leaned against the wall. He looked tired—almost beaten. But every leader needed time to regenerate. Right? Maybe a change of topic.

"I get why I'm going out tomorrow to find my mother, but what are you up to with Harlow?"

He'd closed his eyes, and a slim smile appeared on his face. "Still trying to figure it out?"

I huffed and slumped next to him. "I knew you were playing with me."

When the silence continued, I considered for the umpteenth time what he was up to. It must have something to do with Rasmussen and my mother. He must think she was being kept in the house against her will. My task tomorrow would confirm that. So, if she was being held hostage, why would he want Harlow? A vamp strike team would be better suited for pulling her out.

"You don't want Harlow, you want Roxie to deal with the house security, but you have to go to Harlow for that. But if there are vamps, wouldn't there be more than a couple? I don't want my mother getting hurt."

"I haven't told the cadre everything yet. I'll do that with

Harlow present, but Simone already knows because she's the one who gave me the information."

"You've been holding out on me?" I said it jokingly, but I was a bit hurt until he told me the rest.

"I only found out while I was at Oasis. The rumor is that Venizi is holding a Family-only party on Friday."

I let the news sink in, and everything made sense—for the most part. "So, if April is working for Venizi, she should be attending and probably taking most of the vamps, however many there are, to the party with her."

"It would only take one vampire to contain your mother. Or they might just lock her in a room where she can't get out until they return."

My blood boiled at how they might be treating her. Though April, regardless of how far off the ledge she might have gone, wouldn't take it out on their mother. Would she?

"So, you need Roxie to handle the security while you send in a strike team."

"I'll have a strike team, yes, but they won't go in first."

When he didn't finish, I sat up. "You're going to let me go in first?"

He gave me that wicked beast grin with a light glow in his eyes. "You know the house, and though we're waiting for Sergi to get the latest security details, you know the security."

I laughed. I had to do something to release my excitement. Not at my mother being held and us having to go in, but that Devon was trusting me to do what I did best. And to be honest, I'd always wanted to break into Christopher's house and prove that I could. Too bad the asshole was dead.

Then my laughter died. "Are you expecting my mother to leave? Because I'm not sure she will if April is committed to her path. Regardless of April's beliefs, Mom won't abandon her."

"Of course, not. That's while we'll give you time to discuss things with your mother and see if she knows if April is behind the

Rasmussen texts. Perhaps she'll know who April is working for. Once we have those answers, I'll send in our strike force and a full security detail. When April and her escorts arrive home, we'll be waiting."

"Waiting to do what?"

He pushed a strand of hair out of my face and tucked it behind my ear, taking the time to run a finger down my cheek. "We're taking over the house, unless your mother wants to leave. Then I'll be sure she has a safe location with all the luxuries she's used to in addition to a security detail. If she prefers to stay, then the security detail will remain until our war with Venizi is over."

"What about April?"

He sighed. "That's a more difficult resolution. I'm hoping your mother can tell us how involved April might be. Maybe she's lashing out because of her father's death and now finds herself in a position she can't get out of on her own. If that's the case, this is her chance to break free. She doesn't have to like you to make that decision."

"And if she's fallen for Venizi's lies?" A thought struck. "What if she's been mesmerized?"

"It's a possibility. There are ways to deal with that, depending on how deep the mesmerizing. The best course would be to remove her, then see what we can do for her."

"You've worked it all out."

"I always like to think so, but after many battles, I've learned that something can always go wrong, so we need to be prepared as best we can. April and your mother are the gambles here. The plan might need to be modified once you get in and make contact."

I nodded. "And what if the texts didn't come from April?"

"One worry at a time." He placed a hand on my shoulder. "I hate to have to say this, but Colantha believes this is all about you, not your father. She doesn't know whether Rasmussen is alive or dead. She's never met him, but she is searching. What she does know, and she had no hesitation in telling me this, is that whoever is sending texts about Rasmussen is lying to you."

I didn't want to admit it. It was foolish to think my father might be out there somewhere and needed my help. I didn't doubt Colantha. Not where other dreamwalkers were concerned. But hearing it out loud. Well, that crushed that tiny ball of hope.

I leaned against Devon's shoulder, and he wrapped an arm around me. We didn't move for a very long time.

Chapter Twenty-Three

I scowled at Sergi when I climbed into the SUV with four other vamps from the security detail. It was all to push his buttons. Of course, it apparently had no impact because the damn vamp just grinned.

I'd been grinning too when I woke that morning in Devon's arms. I was ready for this day, needing a face-to-face with my mother to know that she was okay.

But deep down in those places we share with no one, well, I just refused to go there, allowing Devon to erase those dark thoughts with his passionate kisses and soft strokes. And when I cried for no apparent reason, he held me and promised everything would be alright. Because what else does one's boyfriend do when you cry after he's made such sweet love to you.

But once I'd kissed him and jumped in the shower, I put on my game face. I didn't eat breakfast, too jacked up on nerves and buckets of caffeine. Ginger, wanting to do her part to show support, picked out my designer-labeled ensemble of pants, blouse, and jacket, all in silk, and topped it off with three-inch heels, a gold bracelet, and a diamond pendant necklace. I would have preferred my jeans and sweatshirt, but that wouldn't have been acceptable in the neighborhood I'd be visiting.

Devon gave me another passionate kiss on the front steps of the manor, not caring who saw. Then he patted my ass and told me once again that everything would be alright. This was nothing more than a fact-finding mission.

My leg bounced all the way to the hair salon. Sergi watched me. Not out of the corner of his eye, but with one of those damn vamp stares. I ignored him most of the way to Castle Street, the ritzy part of Santiga Bay. Bella and Jacques were in the SUV behind us. They stayed close until we got into the middle of town, where they backed off, giving us space in case they needed to run a diversion.

We drove past the salon, and even with the large windows, it was impossible to see who was inside. Like the day spa my mother went to, the front of the store was all retail space with the stylists behind a wall in the back where no one could see the clients with curlers or tinfoil in their hair.

Mateo turned the SUV around and parked on the opposite side of the street, a block away. The other SUV was parked facing the way we'd just come but found a spot a block before the salon. I waited for Bella and Jacques to get out. They walked the street hand-in-hand, each with a cup of coffee. Where had they gotten those? The cups probably held nothing more than water or might even have been empty. I had to admit, they were excellent at their job. They walked past the salon, eventually turning and coming down our side of the street. Bella gave the slightest of nods before continuing on.

"You have a go," Sergi said. "We'll wait here. If we suspect trouble, prepare for something loud and remain in the salon until one of the SUVs pulls up for you to jump in. Understand?"

"Yes." I checked my pockets. My dagger was in my inside jacket pocket, and I touched it, feeling calmer by the action. When I reached for the door handle, Sergi laid a hand on my arm.

"You already know what you'll find. Don't let it deter you from the mission. It only confirms what we already suspect and what we're preparing for."

I stared at him. I should be angry, but I wasn't. How did this stoic, seemingly uncaring vamp do it? A calm swept through me. Somehow, I knew he had his own dark places he shared with no one.

I took a deep breath. "Thank you."

Then I was out the door, glancing around as if I was getting my bearings and deciding which way to my destination. I crossed the street in the middle of the road, not bothering with a crosswalk, and strolled the half block to the salon. Bella and Jacques had stopped at a boutique bookstore across the street. How perfect was that?

I ducked into the salon, five minutes past my mother's salon appointment. I glanced around the retail area, not seeing her. No surprise so far.

I'd spent most of the previous night trying to remember her stylist's name, but it wasn't until I was in the shower that morning that it came to me. Louise. There was a receptionist station for the stylists, and I waited behind a woman who was changing her appointment. I wanted to tap my foot with impatience, but there was plenty of time before Mom's lunch date. Her hair appointments were an hour long—a quick color touch-up, a trim, and off she went.

Finally, the woman moved on, and it was game time.

"Hi, I was wondering if Louise was in?"

The receptionist with frizzy brown hair pulled back in a headband, perfectly applied makeup, and bright red lipstick, clucked her tongue and reviewed her display screen. "She usually has an appointment at this time, but it looks like she's on a break."

My heart sank at the news, then remembered what Sergi said, and I leaned in. "Then maybe she has a couple of minutes. It's about my mom, who usually has an appointment at this time."

The woman blinked. "You mean Willa?"

I nodded and blinked rapidly. I hadn't expected the burning tears, but they came unbidden, and I had to admit was the perfect touch.

"Oh my, yes, let me just check." She turned away and tapped an earbud.

I didn't bother trying to listen in. They were worried about my mom. I stared at a display of lip balms, not seeing them as their image blurred. I blinked faster and channeled Sergi, Simone, and Ginger. Wow, that was a strange combination.

"Miss? Are you alright?"

"Hmm. Oh, yes, I'm sorry."

"Louise will meet you by the wash station."

"Oh, thank you so much."

"It's no problem, sweetie."

Louise was short, thin as a rail, with long red curls that reached the middle of her back. Like the receptionist, her makeup was perfectly applied. Everything had to be flawless for their uber-rich clientele. And while she wore a smile, there was worry in her gaze when her eyes met mine.

"Come this way." Her cheery voice gave nothing away.

She stepped into a mini solarium. The room was small, but there were dozens of windows, a tile floor covered in Persian rugs, several comfortable chairs, a long couch, and a kitchenette. Their breakroom was pretty sweet.

Louise sat in a corner chair and tapped the one next to it, a Mediterranean-blue table between us.

"Is your mother alright? I mean, she didn't—"

Did the woman think I came to tell her my mom was dead? Good lord, I needed to work on my delivery.

"No, no. She's fine, but I am worried about her."

Louise placed a hand over her chest. "Oh, thank god. When Ella said her daughter wanted to talk to me, I'm afraid I thought the worst." She chuckled—one of those hysterical ones. "I know she was upset about Christopher's death." The woman eyed me, probably wondering how much I knew about their relationship. "But, I don't think it was a surprise."

"Really?" I decided to use Devon's suggestion. "I know I've been out of town for some time, and our communication hasn't been the best. I'd had my problems with Christopher..." I let the rest hang because Louise was nodding. I shook my head as if pushing Christopher to the netherworld where he belonged. "How long has it been since she's been in?"

Louise sat back, her eyes rolling toward the ceiling as she considered the question. "About three weeks now."

"How did she seem the last time you saw her?"

She huffed out a breath. "Don't take this the wrong way. She talked about you every once in a while, more so the last few months. I guess she hadn't seen you for some time, but then she mentioned she'd recently seen you." She gave me a weak smile. "She seemed to think you were in a good place and, I don't know, appeared proud of you."

Damn. Those fucking tears. I blinked and stared out the window before turning back with her next comment.

"It was strange because it was the first time I ever heard her say one negative word about April."

"April?" The statement startled me because I wouldn't have thought Mom would ever say anything bad about her in front of others.

"It was the last time I saw her. She was quite angry with your sister. Oh, she didn't go into details—she never would. All I know is she mentioned her getaway stash. Then, two days later, April called and canceled her mother's appointments. She said her mother wasn't feeling well and had a small breakdown about Christopher. I thought it odd, but what could I do? I thought of calling her but decided against it."

I reached out and took Louise's hand. "Don't worry. I'll be

seeing her tomorrow. I'll let her know you've been worried about her."

"It's funny, you know."

"How's that?"

"Even though I knew she worried about you, she always said you were her strongest daughter. She always knew you'd be just fine."

I STARED out the window as we drove to Chantel's, an upscale restaurant with a lovely garden patio, my mind still on Louise's last comment. Mom knew I'd be okay. She actually told someone else that she was proud of me. It bolstered me. Even though I knew Mom wouldn't be there, perhaps I could get more out of her friends than the hairstylist.

"This meeting could be more emotional for you than the last."

I turned to find Sergi watching me, but not with his usual placid stare. His brows were furrowed with concern. Was it for me or the mission?

"I'll be fine." I forced my leg to stop bouncing. Then I sighed. "What does it matter, anyway?"

"I might be an ancient, but I remember my mother."

That got me.

"I'm sorry. I take it she's not around anymore."

"She, like my sister, was a casualty of war." He grunted. "More like bait to start a war, but in the end, it's all the same."

I glanced down, disturbed by the flash of grief I'd seen in his gaze. I didn't have to ask how long ago. The fact it happened during a war told me it had been a long time, yet he still carried it.

"Sometimes our family problems are so personal, so painful, that we forget others have faced the same thing. Maybe not in how it played out, but the emotions that stick with us. If April is truly mesmerized, can she be saved? Or my mother?"

"As Devon would say, let's not get ahead of ourselves. We're gathering information to help us decide how to move forward."

I nodded. "Right. Eyes on the prize."

The SUV pulled up to the front entrance, and Mateo waved off the valet. I tugged my jacket into place and dusted off my silk pants. The driver opened the door, but before I got out, Sergi grabbed my elbow as he had at the last stop.

"Devon will do whatever he can to ensure your family's safety. Not just your mother, but April as well. We all will."

I turned and blinked away the tears that seemed to be a stream of waterworks today and placed a hand on his. With a shaky breath, I gave him a weak smile. "Who would have thought meeting with my mom's friends would be scarier than escaping Shadow Island?"

Sergi's laughter bolstered me as I exited the SUV and strode to the door with my head high and shoulders back. I wasn't that woman from the Hollows anymore. I might not live in the same neighborhood as these rich bitches, but I was from House Trelane. A new thought came to me. Once we were out of lockdown, I was going to make a reservation for the females of House Trelane and have one hell of a party right here.

The hostess, a petite dark-skinned woman with huge amber-colored eyes and a bulldog expression like most in her profession when dealing with the rich, blocked my entrance.

"Can I help you?"

"Yes, I'm meeting Veronica Stevenson and her party."

She gave me the once over, and I silently thanked Ginger for dressing me. While I might have passed the first inspection, I didn't pass the second.

"We only have her down for a party of three, and everyone else has already arrived."

"I know. I didn't think I was going to be able to make it, but my other appointment was canceled." I hadn't grown up in Christopher's house without learning a thing or two, and I hated having to use his name now. "Would you be a love and let her know Cressa Underwood is here."

I didn't have to look down my nose since she was shorter than me, but I did lift it a bit. She would have expected it. After she scurried off, I prayed the women would be too curious to say no to me joining them. If mom hadn't been to the hairstylist for three weeks, had she been able to stay in contact with her friends?

The hostess was all smiles when she returned. "I'm so sorry to have to check. You know how it can be."

I wasn't sure, but I could guess. The rich didn't like to be disturbed by riffraff.

I put on my best smile. "Of course."

"Just this way." The hostess led me onto the patio to a far corner made more private by the potted ferns and roses that were in full bloom. The light scent energized me as I strolled by to find three wide-eyed, curious faces.

I almost laughed out loud. The last time they saw me, I was a feral high school girl in ripped jeans and a cropped T-shirt. They'd probably written me off as a sad example of how things could go so wrong.

Veronica, Agnes, and Monique continued to stare as the hostess pulled out a chair for me. They were all perfectly quaffed, their fingernails expertly polished and kept at the perfect length with the same boring, sedate colors. They were of varying heights, but they were all thin, perhaps too thin, and were impeccably dressed in their Dior, Gucci, and Chanel and wearing the latest Jimmy Choo shoes.

All three were long-time friends of my mother's and married to rich businessmen who'd been friends of Christopher. For a hot minute, I wondered if any of them had gotten mixed up with Venizi, but I doubted it. However, I decided to tread lightly and see where the women took the conversation.

"Cressa, my dear, it's been ages since we saw you." Veronica, as the ringleader, spoke first.

I gave her a huge smile. "I imagine I looked a bit different back then. But we all grow up."

"I'd say," Agnes blurted out, then covered her mouth as she glanced around before taking a sip of her wine. Chances were good she'd probably had a martini or two before leaving the house. "That was so rude, but you look marvelous."

"Thank you. You all look exactly as I last remember you." I nodded when Monique held up the bottle of wine once another place setting was put in front of me, but I waved off the server when he handed me a menu.

"Please, give her a plate so she can enjoy the appetizers. They're still quite fresh." Veronica waited for the plate, which was in front of me in a blink of an eye.

I dutifully placed a crab tart and a mini quiche on my plate and sipped what tasted like a very expensive bottle of Pinot Gris.

Once the server left and we were left alone, Veronica got right to the point. "Why are you here?"

Monique gasped then sipped her wine while Agnes rearranged her plate. Veronica was not only their leader, and she'd never pulled punches. That was fine with me. Neither did I, and I wasn't here for a friendly lunch. I wanted out of there and out of these heels.

"When was the last time you saw my mother?"

That took a bite out of Veronica's sails. She glanced at the others, but before she could speak, Monique did.

"She's missed the last three lunches. I've tried calling, but she doesn't answer anymore."

"When she missed the first lunch, we all called her and got the same answer," Agnes added. "She wanted to spend time with April."

"When was the last time you spoke to her?" Veronica asked, her eyes narrowed as if I had some ulterior motive.

"About three days ago." That got everyone's attention since Mom had answered my call but not theirs. At the same time, I didn't see a reason to play games and gave them most of how it went down. "You know how moms worry about their kids. At first, she seemed okay, but there were several people at the house. I heard them in the background. Then she made some comment about how it would be better if she called the next time and not to worry." I shrugged. "You know what a rebel I am. I worried."

All three of them tittered at that, almost seeming relieved I was still the little troublemaker. It somehow put their world back on the correct rotation.

"I have to say we're worried, too." Veronica sipped her wine and tapped her light-pink nail against the glass. "But we're not sure what to do about it. We considered driving over."

"It's April," Agnes spat out. "There's something wrong with her." She leaned in, her voice lowering. "I think she might be dangerous, and I know how that must sound, we're not really sure it's even her fault."

Before I could get a word in, Monique broke in. "It's that boyfriend of hers. We all thought you'd be the one to break Willa." She shrugged her shoulders. "Sorry, but you were a bit wild. But Willa never said a bad word. She always knew you'd be okay. She said you were the strongest of her daughters and that you'd find your way."

My heart almost cracked hearing that for a second time in one day.

"Several months ago, Willa said April brought home a new boyfriend." Veronica refilled the wineglasses as she took up the tale. "He was handsome and had just gotten a high-paying job at one of Christopher's businesses. He was what Willa called a fast riser in the company. But after a month or so, Willa was worried. April wasn't acting like herself, and..." Veronica gave the other women a glance, and when they all nodded, she continued, "Willa had been having problems with Christopher. He was keeping long hours, going away on business trips that she didn't think were business trips."

"Christopher was cheating on my mother," I cut in, wanting to get to the chase. "I know. Mom knew and, from my understanding, had an escape plan."

Veronica sat back, and though she'd been shocked for an instant, a knowing smile lit her face. "You've been keeping tabs on her."

I sighed. "It wasn't a secret I hated Christopher. And from what I understand, even though the police cleared me as a suspect in his gruesome murder, April still believes I was somehow responsible."

Agnes snorted. "Christopher had been known to be wheeling and dealing with unscrupulous men and women for months. And what? They thought you waited how many years to show up out of the blue to slice and dice him?" As soon as the last words were out of her mouth, her eyes almost popped out of her head.

The table went deathly silent until I erupted in laughter. It took a second for the rest to join in.

"I know it's not nice to speak ill of the dead." I gave the women a conspiratorial wink. "But let's face it, the asshole got what was coming to him. But this boyfriend, I assume he was close to Christopher."

"Like peas in a pod, from what Willa said." Monique fluffed her hair and checked her fingernails.

"Do you happen to know his name?"

The women glanced at each other, their foreheads scrunched in thought, which was a surprising feat based on how much Botox they were probably pumping into it.

"Henry?" Veronica said.

Monique shook her head. "Peter."

Agnes rolled her eyes, which was what I'd been about to do. "Jasper Hunnicutt."

We all stared at her.

"How can you possibly remember that?" Veronica asked.

"Richard has a cousin named Jasper. He's a crazy old drunk

but a kick at parties. And our neighbors at Martha's Vineyards are the Hunnicutts. At first, I thought there might be a connection, you know, since Christopher and Willa have come to the island with us several times. But I don't think that was the case this time."

Monique shook her head and glanced at me. "Agnes always plays a memory game with names. You know, trying to remember by associating something with them." She tittered. "I obviously need to try the same thing."

I glanced at the watch Ginger made me wear at the last minute. Devon had given it to me one of the first days I'd been at the manor, but I've never worn it because I don't wear watches. I touched the small diamonds around the face. He must have paid a fortune for it, and it didn't escape my notice that the others took note, their eyes growing wide.

"You can afford that?" Veronica leaned over. "That's a limited-edition Rolex."

I grinned. "If it makes you feel any better, I didn't steal it." I flipped my hair back and almost cringed at the automatic response. Then decided to go with it and leaned in. "My boyfriend bought it for me the first week we were together."

I made my excuses, knowing they were dying to start the gossip once I was gone, but left them with one promise.

"I don't know what's going on with my mom, April, and whoever this Jasper Hunnicutt is, but I can assure you I'll get to the bottom of this."

"And you think there's something you can do?" Veronica sounded doubtful.

"Not me alone, no. But my boyfriend will see it done, and he's never gone back on his promises." I stood. "I can't say it will be next week or even a month from now, but soon, there will be four place settings at your weekly lunch again."

They all stared at me with a mixture of hope and downright terror at this new Cressa. If they only knew the truth, as I walked out feeling my dagger snug in my pocket, they'd all piss their pants.

When I strode out of the restaurant, feeling more confident than when I went in, the SUV pulled up as if it had been sitting outside the door all that time. The valet opened my door, I got in, and we were out of the lot and on our way home. The second SUV, which had been waiting down the street, pulled in behind us.

"Well?" Sergi asked.

"I need you to find a Jasper Hunnicutt. Also, I want you to check the video you have from when April and a vamp went into my old apartment. Let's find out if that vamp is our mysterious Jasper. I think April and my mom have been mesmerized."

Chapter Twenty-Four

I PACED BACK and forth in Devon's office, staring at the clock then at the door. It was five minutes to four. When Sergi and I returned from our afternoon excursion, Devon was nowhere to be found. From what Sergi said, the only message that had been left was the time of the meeting.

On the way home, I'd explained to Sergi everything Veronica, Agnes, and Monique had shared with me. Afterward, all I wanted to do was punch something.

Mesmerized.

Venizi had my family mesmerized. Okay. There wasn't proof—yet. But that would explain so much. They probably started with April. The question was whether it began before or after Christopher's death.

Had they mesmerized Christopher? It was a reasonable question, but I didn't think so. He'd been running with bad crowds since I could remember. Didn't want to remember. At some point, after my services had been traded to Devon for a debt and Christopher began searching for my medallion, April had stopped talking to me. That could have been Christopher's influence winning her over, or one of his new vamp buddies had gotten April in line. Hell, Christopher might not have known, too ecstatic that she found an interest in the family business to look any further.

I glanced at the door and clock again. Three minutes until four. Where was everyone?

Ginger had been locked in a meeting with Lucas and Colantha when I'd gotten home. I found Lyra in her room painting a bold floral landscape.

"Hey, what's going on? I can't seem to find anyone in the manor." I'd plopped onto a nearby sofa and watched her mix paint with her brush before she dabbed a few spots on the canvas.

Her musical laughter filled the room. "You found me."

"Does that mean you know where everyone else is?"

She was too cheerful, and when she turned around to glance at me, I could tell she'd taken blood, and for the first time, I noticed she wasn't as rail thin as she had been. But there was more to her glow than that.

She mixed black in with her paint mixture as she spoke. "Colantha has completed her final version of the codex, though she claims there could be a second edition after Philipe and Fiona use it to transcribe another document they have. They've recently discovered two other books that might have been written by dreamwalkers, and they're being flown over from the old country."

"Wow, that's great news."

She nodded. "She's asked Lucas and Ginger to help her with updating the *De første dage* based on the latest version of the codex. They'll be busy until Devon's meeting."

"And where is Devon?"

She had returned to her painting, and I had to ask a second time. "Hmm." She glanced upward as if the ceiling held the answer. "I don't think I've seen him since this morning. I have to admit, I just finished a dreamwalk with Hamilton, and I can't seem to think of anything else." She added a few more dabs to a flower, the color a bare shade darker than what was already there, before turning to mix more paint on her palette.

She'd just dreamwalked with Hamilton. That explained her inability to focus on the conversation. And by her glow, they did more than talk. I snorted. It was none of my business, and they had a lot of time to make up for. I doubt she heard me leave.

My next search focused on Bella and Jacques, who had returned with us in the motorcade. I even checked her sparse office, remembering Lucas's insight that the two vamps used it as a lounge. Bella never seemed to be in one spot. She appeared and disappeared as if she could magically transport herself to wherever she needed to be. She'd always been the most elusive of Devon's cadre.

Cook didn't know where Devon had gone, and after checking every room in the manor and the widow's walk, I finally pulled out my phone and texted him. No response.

Sergi was in his office, and when I tried to enter found the door locked. Before I walked away, he called out through the door, "Go train, Cressa. I need to prepare for the meeting."

That was always his answer. If he wasn't worried about his missing House leader, then I wouldn't be, either. I had two hours to kill, and after an hour in the training room, a soak in the pool, and then a shower, I was ready for the meeting. Yet, here I was pacing the office—alone.

At four o'clock on the dot, Sergi popped his head in. He had one of his shit-eating grins on. "Devon's guests have arrived. He's changed the location of the meeting to the solarium. You might want to join us there."

I stared at him, and his grin widened.

"You knew all along the meeting would be in the solarium." I planted my hands on my hips and gave him my best evil glare.

As usual, it had no impact on the vamp. "Yes." Then he turned and disappeared.

I raced after him as he marched down the hall. "What guests? I didn't hear anyone arrive."

"Lyra met them and took them around through the garden. Trudy wanted to see the flowers."

"Trudy? You mean Trudy and Harlow are here."

"Yes."

Him and his damn one-word answers.

"I thought they were coming for dinner."

"And the meeting."

I was ready to leap on his back and attempt a new maneuver Simone had taught me, but we'd reached the solarium, and multiple voices shattered my dream of taking him down.

Devon met me at the door—a huge smile for me and a glance at Sergi I couldn't read. Sergi smirked and walked to a computer station Lucas was setting up.

"I'm sorry Sergi didn't inform you of my afternoon plans." He gave me a light kiss and rubbed my arm. "I take it the two of you haven't worked out your issues."

"Evidently not."

He chuckled. "I've been at the coastal safe house reviewing our final security upgrades. When Sergi contacted me after your lunch meeting, I called Harlow and asked if they could come early for the meeting. He was supposed to tell you all of this."

"I suppose you're not going to have him drawn and quartered."

His smile was more than charming, and all I wanted to do was melt into him and forget the room full of people. "I think that might be a rather harsh punishment. Perhaps the two of you locked in the training room for a day might be a better resolution."

"I could work with that." I was already thinking of how that would go, another one of my evil smiles forming.

"Pandora," a familiar voice called out. "Get your sweet ass over here and give Trudy and me a hug."

I laughed as Devon shook his head. We both knew Harlow just

wanted to squeeze my ass. But he did more than that. He wrapped me in a huge bear hug then dragged Trudy in so the three of us looked like idiots in the middle of the room.

"I always pictured a three-way with us." Then Harlow grabbed my ass.

I pushed him off, unable to stop grinning. "You're still a pig."

"I think it gets worse the older he gets." Trudy gave me her own hug. "So, what trouble are you in these days?"

"When are we not in some type of trouble?" Then my smile faded. "I'm afraid this one hits close to home."

"Yes, Devon mentioned that." Harlow pulled his serious face together for a slim moment, then his face lit up. "But don't worry about that. We'll save your mum and sister."

"If everyone could take a seat. Let's get this meeting started." Devon stood next to the computer station where Lucas typed a few last keystrokes before finding a seat with Ginger, a tablet firmly in his grasp.

The cadre were all accounted for, including Jacques and Decker, who I was beginning to think of as Devon's extended cadre. Colantha, Ginger, and Lyra—the triple threat as I called them—had filled a sofa. When I glanced around for a seat, I found Simone leaning against a wall, which wasn't a normal position for her to take. She gave me a smile, the tips of her fangs showing, and nodded toward Devon.

He was motioning me to a chair next to where he stood. I took it, feeling like everyone was up to something. Or maybe it was my own doubts and concern for my family and having no one to talk to about it before the meeting.

"As most of you know, Cressa received an anonymous message from someone who claims her father is in trouble and needs her help. Their responses to her most basic questions, like who are you, have been slow in coming. Their last request was for a meeting tonight at midnight in a secluded spot, and, of course, she was to come alone. She responded that she was out of town and wouldn't return until tomorrow." He glanced down at me. "I believe we're still waiting for a reply."

I nodded.

"We have come to the conclusion that this is a ruse to lure Cressa out of the lockdown. We assume the threat comes from Venizi, but we hadn't been able to confirm that until Cressa met with her mother's friends earlier today. That meeting provided us with a valuable lead."

Devon nodded to Lucas, who turned on the LCD monitor that had been rolled in on a stand. A black-and-white freeze frame image appeared on the screen. It was from the video feed the evening that April and, at the time, an unknown vamp, had gone into my old apartment. The video I'd asked Sergi to pull.

"Cressa was able to get the name of her sister's boyfriend—Jasper Hunnicutt. Sergi has spent the last couple of hours searching to see if Hunnicutt is a vamp by putting the name and this face out to our entire Family. Based on a hunch, Sergi also checked the list of rogue vampires. Now, we know not all rogues will declare themselves for the records, but this one has." He nodded to Lucas.

This time, a color photo popped up with a very clear view of Jasper. It was the same vamp. Now we were getting somewhere.

"Being a rogue wouldn't tie him to Venizi," Decker said.

"No," Devon agreed. "However, two of our security detail know this vampire. Though he retains his rogue status, he's been known to work on the payroll for three Houses—Pearson, Larkin, and Wakefield."

"They're all Houses under the protection of Venizi." Bella began to pace. "And we know Venizi tends to use other Houses for his dirty work."

"That still doesn't tie him directly to Venizi," Sergi added. "These particular Houses have been known to perform tasks they expect will please Venizi, but not necessarily with his approval. It's a fine line, but nothing they've done in the past would be of interest to the Council based on speculation that Venizi is pulling the strings."

Devon waved a hand at Lucas, who moved to the next picture. "In this case, it's not the Council we're worried about. This is a House matter. But Sergi is correct. While we might suspect Venizi of being behind this, the only concern we have at this moment is the safety of this woman—April Underwood. She's the daughter of Christopher and Willa Underwood and Cressa's half-sister.

"We believe that Christopher brought April into his business arrangement with Venizi. Either on purpose or by accident. The question now is whether April has been mesmerized to continue working for Venizi through this rogue. Also at stake is this woman."

The photo shifted to my mother. It was a photo from the day I'd surprised her in the spa, back when Christopher had been frantic about finding my medallion. We'd spent five uncomfortable minutes talking in a coffee shop, and though she'd confirmed Rasmussen was my dad, it hadn't been a friendly meeting. Someone must have taken a photo of her leaving the shop after me. Had she been crying? My heart clenched.

"This is Willa Underwood, Cressa's mother," Devon continued. "Her closest friends haven't heard from her in the last three weeks, and, in that same time, she's missed her weekly appointments. We have no reason to believe anything has happened to her and assume she's being sequestered in her home."

Another picture came up. A sprawling mansion in the Woodbridge estates northwest of the city.

This time, Bella took over. "We've been monitoring the Underwood estate for the last couple of days. There's plenty of activity with SUVs, all with heavily tinted windows. We've been able to obtain visuals of two drivers who we believe belong to House Venizi. Whatever is happening in that house, it's under vampire control. And while Jasper might be rogue, we've been able to confirm the drivers belong to House Venizi and not the other Houses."

The next photo was an aerial view of the estate. The manor sat toward the back of the three-acre estate, heavily landscaped with trees. Bella continued, "A six-foot wall runs the entire perimeter. There are two vampires stationed at the front gate. There's a back gate that leads to an ally, and there's at least one vampire there. It's impossible to tell how many others are at the house. We're working on getting updated satellite images, but we're not sure it matters at this point."

The next picture was the layout inside the manor. It was the typical floorplan one would find in a sales brochure for a newly built house and reflected the various rooms, including all entry points. The screen was split in two. One picture showed the ground floor and the other the upstairs.

"Cressa needs to review the floorplan and revise for any inaccuracies in addition to adding any details pertinent to our mission." Bella nodded to Devon then went back to her corner where she'd be free to pace.

"This is all great information." Decker pulled out a bag of licorice bits and chewed one as he glanced around the room. "What exactly is the mission here?"

I knew what his plan was, but it seemed he hadn't shared it with many others.

"We're going to extract both women." When the room went silent, Devon added, "And if we're lucky, we'll take Jasper Hunnicutt as well. All other vampires are expendable."

Someone gasped, and I assumed it was Ginger. He'd modified the plan. Was that based on my earlier lunch meeting?

"We need to move quickly on this." Devon scanned the room, stopping to meet everyone's eyes. "We're going in on Friday night for one specific reason. Venizi is holding a party on his island— Family only. He might have been hoping to show off his new acquisition," Devon glanced down at me. "But I imagine even without luring Cressa out, he won't cancel the party."

"Of course not," Sergi sneered. "It would only show weakness."

Devon's smile was predatory. "Exactly." He glanced around the room. "I've invited all of you here in support of this mission. Each of you will have a role to play, assuming those outside the House Trelane Family wish to participate."

There were a few head nods, but no one walked out or said no.

"A table has been set up on the back patio for dinner. There's also a bar for drinks. Dinner is in an hour. Afterward, I'd like to regroup here to work through a high-level plan and determine tentative assignments. From this point forward, Cressa will be the mission leader." He smiled at me as the impact of his statement rolled over me. "We have a lot to do to prepare. Until then, let's adjourn to the patio."

The crowd quickly dispersed, leaving only Devon and me in the solarium.

I was still sitting, not sure what to do. I was thrilled I was being given the lead, but how was I supposed to tackle this in less than forty-eight hours?

Devon pulled me up and wrapped his arms around me. His kiss was tender, then he whispered in my ear, "You've got this. We're all here to support you. I know that head of yours is already spinning with possibilities. Remember to listen to the experts before making a final decision. You know this. No one is better suited for this mission."

I hugged him so tightly I thought I might have cut off his oxygen, but he let me stay that way for a while. Then I stepped back. "What if they're not the ones behind the texts?"

"Then we'll know who isn't involved, but we might discover that it is Venizi, and he'll continue to try. Either way, your mother and sister will be out of his reach. And there's really nothing more important than keeping you safe."

My heart swelled at his concern for my family. "Does being the team lead mean I have to stay outside while others go in?"

He chuckled. "To use a human vernacular, you mean benching the most valuable part of our strike team? No, Cressa. You won't just be the team lead. You'll lead the strike team as well."

I was grinning so widely as Devon led me out to the patio that I thought my cheeks would crack. I finally had a project.

Hold on, Mom. We're coming for you.

Chapter Twenty-Five

Myriad shades of pink signaled the first signs of sunset and played off the blue-gray lining of clouds as they built along the horizon. An unexpected light rain was forecasted for that evening, marshaling in cooler temperatures. Odd for this late-summer evening, but not a showstopper for my plans.

I glanced down at the sycamore tree from my vantage point on the window seat in my bedroom, already dressed in my favorite black cargo pants and a light, long-sleeve T-shirt. My armored security vest and utility belt lay across the back of a chair, waiting for the call to go.

I'd given Sergi the assignment of coordinating the six teams. Two nights ago, after dinner, Devon arranged for after-dinner brandy in the library, where he opened the discussion for everyone to share their ideas. They ranged from worry over the number of rooms in the house, not knowing how many vamps were in the manor, how many would remain behind rather than go to the party, to how to extract my mom and April.

Harlow and Trudy had been offered a room for the night but preferred going home with a promise to return in the morning for the planning session. Remus sent Elijah and Rachel to assist upon

Decker's request and my approval. It had been a long day, with a few squabbles, but everyone had worked well together before.

The one thing Devon's cadre had taught me was that there was a time for guerilla tactics and a time for an all-out invasion.

I decided to use both. Everyone had a role to play, including several members of the security detail, which meant current lock-down security protocols had to be modified for the evening. Fortunately, Simone was happy to make the changes—as much as Simone could appear happy.

Once the training session was over, which lasted well into the evening, everyone either went home or to a room at the manor. We met one last time for a late lunch and a review of the plan before everyone went to temporary rooms to rest and change for the evening.

I was going over the plan for the umpteenth time when a light knock was followed by a question that pushed everything aside.

"Are you as jacked as I am right now?" Ginger's soft voice was incongruous for the question.

I laughed out loud, grateful for the company. My response was provided with a boisterous, marine-style response of "Hell, yes, soldier."

She all but bounced over to the window seat, plopping down to stare out the window. "It's going to be a spectacular night. Do you know what we need? Lightning. And a touch of thunder to let them know we're coming."

We giggled like schoolgirls, and my pent-up nervous energy rushed out of me. It would be back before the mission started, but I needed the release of the roiling pressure. I gave Ginger a long look as she continued to stare out the window. She dressed in similar clothes to mine, but rather than cargo pants, she wore thick spandex pants and would add a thigh holster and utility belt once she was fully geared up. She was in the second invasion team with Lucas.

The two had fought side-by-side during their hunt for Philipe

Renaud and the *De første dage*. They knew each other's moves, and I'd be an idiot to break up the team.

"Have you slept at all?" she asked, finally giving me her own perusal.

"Not much last night, but I got a couple of hours earlier. I nodded off in our last meeting." I snorted. "Devon carried me to bed, and I slept like a toddler." I grinned at her. "I think he mentioned something about drooling."

She laughed and grabbed my hand. "This is a tight plan. Lucas was impressed by how quickly everything came together. Even Bella mentioned it when we went over our run-through this afternoon. We'll get them out."

"Assuming they're even there."

She gripped my arm and squeezed—hard.

"Ow." I pulled away and rubbed my arm.

"Stop it. Right now. No doubts."

"I'll take care of that."

We both turned as Devon strolled in. And while I scowled, Ginger perked up.

"Excellent. The calvary has arrived." She stood. "You know she gets this way when she has too much time on her hands before a job. Harlow always had to piss her off to keep her focused."

"Not an easy task, but knowing Harlow as I do now, he'll get his opportunity. Until then, I'll see what I can do."

Ginger squeezed his shoulder as she all but bounced to the door. "I'll see you at the checkpoint. Lucas and I are heading over to the safe house for last-minute drills."

The door shut behind her, and I turned back to the window. I didn't have to look to know Devon was checking my utility belt and vest. It wasn't that he didn't trust me to have everything I needed. Between my days as Pandora and the various missions I'd been on for House Trelane, preparing for a job was never a problem. It was Devon's way of working off his own tension and nervous energy.

Strong fingers scraped along my back then massaged my shoulders and neck. I leaned into it, wincing as he pressed the knots that had built up in the last hour. After ten minutes and before I became completely limp, he tugged me off the bench seat and led me to the sofa.

He sat sideways on the couch, leaning back against the armrest as he pulled me down, twisting me so I was wedged between his legs, my back to his chest. I stretched out my legs, letting my body relax into his, and closed my eyes.

"Did I ever tell you the story about the time Sergi and I hid in a harem while on the run from the sultan's guards?"

My eyes popped open. "I'm pretty sure I'd remember that."

His chest rumbled with humor. "My father had received a request from a House in the Ottoman Empire to broker peace between two sultans. Their skirmishes were creating a problem for the trade route. I took Sergi and a small contingent of guards to meet with both sultans. One agreed to host a dinner to talk peace.

"It was a ruse by both sultans. The one hosting had prepared an ambush. The other one suspected it and brought an army who waited close by. Sergi and I were at the meal, caught between the two forces. Fortunately, Sergi had caught the eye of one of the sultan's concubines. She was aware of the duplicity and led us toward what she claimed was a safe place."

Devon played with my hair as he shared his tale, and my body relaxed further into his, fitting together like puzzle pieces.

He chuckled. "Sergi balked when she handed us silk wraps to cover our heads and armor. She knew of a secret passage that led us around the harem guards, who were more focused on fighting off the opposing army. We were hidden behind women and children, dressed in their same colorful cloth, waiting for a chance to escape out the balcony."

"I think I've seen this movie." I smiled as I tugged his arm closer.

"When the young concubine told us to go, Sergi and I refused.

The battle was at the door to their harem, and neither of us was willing to leave the women and children if the sultan's guards were unable to hold the door."

I pictured them in ancient armor draped in silk with their swords drawn. It should have been a funny story as Devon meant it to be, but all I saw was honor among two friends, unwilling to leave those weaker than themselves. I wouldn't have expected any less from either of them.

"After what sounded like a contentious battle, the door burst open. Without a second thought, and only seconds before me, Sergi jumped out in front of the huddled women, who held their children close, his sword raised. The palace guards had won the day, but they weren't quite sure what to make of us. The concubine, a brave young female, stepped in front of us, shouting to the guards that we were there to protect them should they have fallen."

He sighed. "It had been a tense moment as the guards stared us down. Then their leader told us it was time to go, but to take care —the battle still raged outside. We didn't have to be asked twice. With our silk wraps still hanging from our heads and shoulders, we jumped from the balcony. Fortunately, our men were waiting not far from the battle with our horses.

"Once we were far away, the silk wraps ragged and filthy, my army couldn't stop the jeers. Of course, they weren't meant for me. They wouldn't dare. Sergi took it all in good jest until he'd had enough and challenged them all to a fight."

"How many was that?"

"Oh, about thirty men in all. He fought them one by one and quickly beat nine of them before the rest backed off and took a knee." He chuckled. "I can still see Sergi's face when he finally ripped the last of the silk wraps from his shoulders and draped it over the last vampire, still recovering before his feet. Sergi walked off that field with his head high. But later that night, while we were in my private tent drinking raki, Sergi swore if I ever allowed him to be dressed in silk again, he'd personally take my head."

I could feel his grin against my temple.

"What I never told him was that I caught him stuffing one of the silk wraps, freshly washed and folded, into his knapsack. Whether it was for the concubine or her act of kindness—perhaps both—I never forgot his simple deed to hold on to that memory."

"I wonder whatever happened to it." Devon's story touched me, my worries about the mission temporarily stuffed away. But what stuck, maybe because Sergi and I had developed an ongoing and unexplained challenge between us, was a glimpse of his rarely seen soft side. And I suddenly questioned who he had loved through the centuries. Had there ever been a woman who'd captured his warrior's heart?

"I never saw the silk again," he answered. "Though I'm sure he kept it for a long time."

We laid quietly for some time, and we might have dozed.

When I opened my eyes, the sky had an orange cast to it. It was almost time.

Devon kissed my temple. "We should go down. I imagine Sergi will have the transports in place for the teams."

He helped push me up, and I slung on my vest and utility belt. Then he pulled me in for a kiss that made my knees weak. "The plan is solid, and the teams are prepared. You've got this."

I nodded. My energy was restored and not with nerves but with steely determination. This was my family we were saving. There would be no mistakes.

We strode down the hall shoulder to shoulder. Maybe Devon's story wasn't to relax me after all. Perhaps it was to remind me of what was at stake, and no matter what, we didn't leave the defenseless behind.

THE TRANSPORT VEHICLES were waiting for us in the front drive. Four black SUVs and two black vans waited with doors open and vamps stationed next to them. Everyone was dressed in black with vests and belts. Some had their scabbards hanging from their hips, while others wore their daggers in thigh holsters.

Devon had bought me a short sword because he got tired of watching me stab vamps in the neck until their heads were barely attached. It was a long and tedious process until one day, he finally said, "You're taking too much time to kill. It puts your team at risk."

That hit home. I didn't always want to kill, just maim long enough to keep them down, but he was right. There were times when there wasn't a choice. But tonight wasn't that night. I didn't want my mother to see that—at least not from me.

We had no idea what we were walking into, and I wouldn't put the team at risk by telling them what they could or couldn't use in completing the mission and coming out alive. Devon and I stopped next to Sergi, who stood on the top step, reviewing his tablet and ensuring final measures were in place.

Simone walked along the vehicles, speaking with each detail, probably going over last-minute assignments. Lucas and Ginger stood next to the second SUV, and as usual, Ginger was chatting up the other two vamps that would be going with them. Each of the SUVs would have a team consisting of four vamps and one driver.

The vans held the majority of our second wave. There would be eight vamps in each van, plus their driver and team lead. Decker stood next to Elijah and Rachel in addition to Rafael, a vamp that had worked with the shifters before. And bringing up the last SUV would be Simone and three of her guards from Oasis.

Bella and Jacques had left an hour ago with Harlow, Trudy, and Jamal. They would meet up with Roxie and her van a block from the Underwood estate. Their initial mission was to monitor the front and back exits to the property. We had to know who left the estate, assuming they were going to Lorenzo's party. Jamal was in full homeless gear as he had been the night we'd infiltrated

Gheata's house and would be stationed in the alley near the estate's back exit. Harlow and Trudy, along with Russell, one of the vamps, would be at the end of the alley, monitoring and backing up Jamal.

Roxie had reviewed the manor's security and found three active zones. She would take them down one by one once Sergi gave her a go. Everyone had earbuds, while the humans and each team lead also wore body cameras.

Devon and Sergi jogged down the steps, but before I could follow, Lyra and Colantha stepped out of the front door.

"I was wondering if you would come to see us off." I gave them a hearty smile, jazzed and ready to go.

Lyra's eyes sparkled, which told me she'd probably just come from a dreamwalk with Hamilton. It was weird to see her starry-eyed, but I couldn't fault her. After a hundred years of torment, no one deserved more giddy happiness than her.

"I wish I was going with you." Lyra grabbed my hand.

"No, you don't. Besides, your place is here to defend the castle."

Her tinkling laugh made my grin wider. "Yes, and I'll be monitoring Oasis and the two safe houses while you're gone, with Colantha's help."

"You don't need my help, child. Neither of you do. But I'll be here just in case." Colantha eyed me. "You worry about your team, but are you ready?"

I nodded. "I stopped in the kitchen and drank a glass of your special juice. Are you ever going to tell us what's in it?"

Her smile was annoyingly predatory. "Soon."

Always the cryptic one. "I'll only call on you if things get really hairy."

"If things get hairy, as you say, you'll use your dreamwalker power to correct the situation. Only if you can't hold them will you reach out for me."

I glanced down at the stonework on the front porch and rubbed the toe of my boot back and forth. "Right."

"You've done it before—you can do it tonight. Just make sure you advise your team before the construct, though I think they'll understand what's happening once they see the enemy turn into, what did you call them, zombies? Though true zombies would still be moving. Mannequins might be a better term."

"Mannequins." I shivered. "I suppose that is more accurate. I get it, and I'll follow your advice."

"Of course, you will. I would hate for you to spend more time in remedial training."

I winced. I'd spent two hours that morning working through various constructs with Colantha. The same kind of fast-paced jumps from one construct to another she liked to perform, and then long moments within each one, holding three wary volunteers in a single construct. It was intense, and I needed a half-hour nap and a small glass of juice to refresh before I could join the rest of the team reviewing the plans. I didn't want to have to repeat the exercises.

"Cressa. Let's go." Sergi stood next to the lead SUV, and I noticed everyone else was in the vehicles.

"Wish me luck."

"Luck is for fools who aren't prepared." Colantha smiled, her gaze full of humor. Always with the witty comebacks.

I was halfway down the steps when she called out, "To your success."

I smiled and gave her a wave as I met up with Sergi. "Everything look good?"

He nodded. "Bella reported three SUVs leaving the estate five minutes ago."

I considered it. "So, worst case, if the SUVs were full, there could be up to six vamps per vehicle."

He nodded again. "Yes."

I took a step back and studied him. Vamps did it all the time, and he didn't seem bothered by it. "Thank you for the excellent work you've done so far. I appreciate it."

He gave me that stare that was supposed to make me shake in my boots. "Are you going soft?"

I snorted. "Hardly. I just think teams work better when they get a little praise."

"That's a human trait."

"Maybe. It doesn't make the sentiment any less true." I turned to the opened back door, but before I got in, Sergi had to have the last word.

"Do what you do best, Cressa. Plans are only a guide. Follow your instincts. Be Pandora tonight."

I didn't turn around, but I nodded. His words meant the world to me and were a stark reminder that best-laid plans rarely went without a hitch. We were prepared for that.

Chapter Twenty-Six

THE SUV STOPPED behind Roxie's van, and I scanned the neighborhood from the back seat. Dusk was fading into night, and the street was quiet. Sergi stepped out and knocked on the back door of the van. Roxie, the young, dark-haired hacker, stuck her head out, glanced around, then waved Sergi in, closing the door behind him.

We waited. I checked my watch every minute until Devon put a hand on my leg.

"Take a breath. There's still two minutes to go."

I glanced at Mateo, who sat in the front passenger seat, sure that he was listening while focusing on the right side of the street. The driver's head was turned toward the left.

My earbuds crackled.

"Checkpoint test. Team One." Sergi's voice was calm.

"Team One check," I responded.

"Team Two check." Harlow's voice was all professional. On a typical heist, Harlow maintained his composure, but it wasn't unusual for him to utter a random sexual innuendo or share some inane trivia he'd recently read. When he worked with vamps, all that went away, for the most part.

While the rest of the teams checked in, I went through my utility belt and touched my dagger. When we'd first slid into the SUV, I noticed my short sword was on the floor. Devon must have added it. It would be up to me whether to use it. Maybe for phase two. For now, we were on a seek, find, and remove mission.

Once the last team checked in, I moved forward in my seat, ready to go, my leg bouncing.

"Team One and Team Two. The security net is down. You have a go to the first checkpoint."

Devon and I opened our doors at the same time, quietly shutting them before running down the street toward the main entrance of the estate. We kept low as we approached the double wrought iron gates. I pulled on one, and when it opened, I slid inside. Devon was right behind me, and he pulled it shut.

I kept to the trees as I led Devon to the pool house, which was our first checkpoint. We moved quickly but stayed in the shadows. The estate was lit with landscape lights, but with the thickening clouds, there was more than enough darkness to hide in. We anticipated outside guards, but we didn't run across any as we approached the pool house. Harlow and Russell would be coming through the back gate. I sighed with relief when I spotted two dark shapes leaning against the wall of the pool house.

Harlow nodded with a wide grin. So far, so good.

"Teams One and Two at checkpoint one." I readied for the next command.

A minute went by before Sergi responded, "House security is down. Teams One and Two, you have a go."

The reason I'd selected the pool house for our first checkpoint was two-fold. We would have to run through a portion of the property, allowing us to spot any outside guards. Since Harlow hadn't reported anyone, it was a fair assumption that if there were any outside guards, they would be at the house and not the gates or the perimeter.

The second reason was that the pool house was only twenty-five yards from the manor and was positioned center to the house. I led Devon to the front of the house while Harlow's team worked their way to the utility door at the back of the house.

When we got to the front door, I bypassed it and moved to the garage. If anyone in the house noticed the security was down, the front door would be a dangerous place to enter. And it was the prime location for a camera. They should be down with the security, but I preferred not to risk it.

Roxie would be monitoring the security sensors and the handful of cameras around the house. But just because security was down didn't mean there wasn't a vamp on the other side of a door. That was why I chose to stay away from the two patios with French doors and as many windows as possible.

The side door to the garage was locked, and I pulled out my lock picks. Within a minute, the door popped open, and we moved inside. I moved directly to the door that entered into a long hall. We passed by the laundry room and a second pantry. The hallway continued to other rooms on the first floor, but I turned down a short hall toward the foyer where the main staircase was located. So far, no one was around. The house was deathly silent.

I stopped at the stairs and pointed to the right. Devon nodded and moved on, searching the bottom floor for any signs of humans or vamps. I remained behind the staircase and waited. Harlow would have entered near the kitchen and should be stationed by the back stairs.

While I waited, I hit my earbud. "Team One in position, clearing the first level."

I waited but heard nothing from Harlow. There weren't any sounds, but it was a big house.

"Team Two in position. One vamp down."

That woke me up. But if there was a vamp in the house, it wasn't surprising they might be in the kitchen or the small entertainment room down the hall from it.

Then Devon was back, and he shook his head.

"Team One. First floor cleared. Moving to the second floor."

The earbuds crackled again. "Teams Three and Four, move into position."

They were our backups in case someone came home early, or we found more vamps than we bargained for.

I led the way up the stairs. My heart rate intensified with each step I took. If my mother was being held against her will, I assumed she would be in her bedroom. They could have locked her in any room, but April, mesmerized or not, would want her mother comfortable. The master bedroom had a small entertainment center, a master bath, and a mini fridge.

Harlow's task was to head for Christopher's office on the first floor and search for anything that could link April to Venizi or any other vamp House. I made the assumption that, after Christopher's death, April would continue to use her father's office. That would change over time, but not this soon.

Devon and I cleared the front bedrooms. April's room was next to mine with windows that looked out over the east portion of the estate. When I opened the door to my room, I paused. Nothing had changed since I'd been there. It was like I would come home someday and settle back in. I'd expected Christopher would have demanded the room be redecorated, but he'd always let Mom have her way with the decor, as long as it was tasteful. The only exceptions were his office and his entertainment center. Perhaps he didn't care because he was too busy with his mistresses.

I closed the door and paused. The master bedroom was down the hall on the right and overlooked the pool. There was a room next to it that Mom used as her personal office. It was more of a mini library with a desk and resting chair she used for reading.

With the number of SUVs that left the estate earlier, we suspected that one or two vamps would be left behind. Russell took care of the one downstairs. If there were any others, they would most likely be in Mom's office, and it looked like the door was partially open. If there was someone in there, why didn't they hear us? We'd been quiet, but a vamp should have picked up something—if they were paying attention.

Devon took the lead, but I was right behind him. He stopped short of the door, turned to me, and raised his hand, pointing one finger, two, and then three. He moved quickly as he entered the room, and by the time I followed behind, he was already moving on the vamp, who'd been sitting on the resting chair, wearing a headset, and focused on his laptop. My guess was that he was watching a movie or gaming, but it didn't matter.

He glanced up, probably thinking it was his buddy, then tried to move when Devon, moving like an avenging angel, took two steps, picked the vamp up, and with a single knife thrust to the lower back, hit the kidneys, and the vamp went limp.

I ignored the blood that seeped over the resting chair and the plush carpet. Mom wouldn't care. She wouldn't be returning here any time soon—if at all. I wanted to race to her room, but there could be a third vamp, so I waited for Devon to drop the vamp by the door.

He took a position on one side of the master suite's double doors while I took the other. I sucked in a breath and slowly opened the door as I peeked in.

A single bedside lamp was lit, casting enough light to show someone in the bed. Devon came in behind me, quickly scanning the room, then the walk-in closet, before moving for the bathroom. He walked out and shook his head. We were alone.

It was barely nine o'clock. Mom wasn't a night owl, but this was still too early for her to be in bed. But if she'd been locked in this room for hours or days with nothing to do, her sleep patterns could have changed. Television had never been her thing, but there was a stack of books on the circular table between two comfortable lounging chairs.

I tiptoed to the bed, not wanting to scare her. Once I stopped next to the nightstand, I got my first glimpse of her. Her hair was tousled, but she looked peaceful in sleep. I tapped her shoulder.

"Mom."

Her breathing remained steady. I shook her shoulder and spoke louder, "Mom. Wake up."

It took a heavier shake and two more requests before she slowly rolled onto her back. My breath caught. Without makeup and her hair in a tangled mess, she looked old. All of her vibrancy appeared to have been sucked out of her. I went rigid. Had they been using her as a blood donor?

When her eyes opened, they were glassy. It took her a moment to focus, squinting as she took me in.

"Mom. It's me. Cressa."

When there was no recognition, I panicked. I grabbed her shoulders. "Mom. Wake up. It's me."

I thought she'd been mesmerized, and maybe she had been, but I recognized the signs of sedation. Had she been taking sleeping pills, or had they been slipping them into her food?

I rubbed her hands. "Mom. You need to wake up. We need to go."

Her eyes blinked a few more times. "Cressa?" Her voice was raw as if she hadn't spoken for days.

"Yes, Mom. We're going for a ride. Can you stand?"

She glanced around the room then her gaze stopped on Devon. After a long stare, she said, "I know you from somewhere."

He stepped closer. "Yes. We met a few months ago at La Sedona."

She wrinkled her nose. "Good wine, but horrible people go there."

"I remember." He squatted so he wasn't towering over her. "Cressa and I want to take you someplace safe. Your escape plan, remember?"

She put a hand to her mouth and tapped a finger against her lips. "Yes. I have money hidden in the craft room." She laughed, but it didn't sound right. "I hate crafts, but Christopher never knew that. It was a perfect place to hide stuff."

"We can come back for that later." Devon ran a hand through his hair and glanced at me. "Right now, I want to take you to where Cressa and I live. You'll have your own place where you can recover."

Her eyes, still unfocused, skittered around the room like she didn't remember where she was. Then she looked up at me. "Cressa? What are you doing here?"

I turned to Devon. "I think she's been drugged."

"Probably easier than mesmerizing." He moved toward the walk-in closet while I tried to pull Mom up.

It was harder than I thought. She had no motivation, and while she didn't resist, it was like moving dead weight.

Devon came out with a long raincoat and slip-on shoes. "This will be enough to get her out of the house."

I took advantage of her refusal to stand and slipped the shoes on. Then Devon helped get her to her feet, and we each took an arm to slide the coat on. Then Devon picked her up.

Mom let out a small cry before leaning her head against his chest. "I'm just so sleepy. Where's April?"

"She's at a party right now, but she'll be coming, too."

We moved out of the bedroom, striding back the way we'd come. I stopped where the vamp was slowly coming around, pulled out my dagger, and stabbed him in his other kidney.

I tapped my earbud. "Team Two, what's your status?"

"Almost done." Harlow's response was quick and professional.

"We need a pickup in the second-floor hall."

A minute went by. "He's on his way."

Russell showed up in seconds and picked up the vamp. "I'll leave him with the other one I zip-tied and gagged in a back closet."

Devon nodded, and we moved. Our exit strategy was to meet at Team Two's point of entry. We waited for Harlow, who came from a different direction than I'd expected.

"I thought I'd check the other rooms while we had time. There were other files in the entertainment room, so I grabbed them, too. You'll need to determine if they're important."

I studied his face and his wide grin. "Did you take his baseball card collection?" Christopher had a framed collection of six baseball cards on his desk that was worth a lot of money—or so he always said.

"He won't miss it."

I shook my head. Harlow was a thief. What did I expect? Since it belonged to Christopher, Harlow was correct. Dead men didn't take their possessions with them, and Mom wouldn't care.

When I closed the back door, I hit the earbuds again. "Teams One and Two headed for the back exit. The package has been obtained."

We'd barely reached the back gate when an SUV pulled up. Jacques jumped out and opened the back door. Devon laid Mom on the back seat, and she curled up.

"She's probably been drugged, but we're not sure," I said. "Keep an eye on her."

Jacques nodded then jumped back in, and Bella took off. They would park a block away and wait for their second delivery, assuming we could grab April.

Harlow leaned against the back wall and pulled several folders from under his vest. "What do you want me to do with these?"

"Get them to Trudy, then return to base position." Devon nodded to Russell, and the vamp followed Harlow to where Trudy had parked at the end of the alley. Effectively, Harlow, Trudy, and Jamal were done for the evening. However, they would stay in position with Russell as watchers should anyone try to exit the back gate. There would be two two-man teams positioned close for any cleanup required.

I hit the earbud. "Teams One and Two clear. Phase one complete."

Chapter Twenty-Seven

ONCE THE WORD was given that phase one was complete, Sergi's calm voice came through the earbuds. "All teams, prepare for phase two. Teams Three and Four move to your next position. Teams Five and Six you have a go. Team one, move to your next position."

Devon and I returned to the house, meeting up with Teams Three and Four. Once we were all inside, I ensured the lock I'd opened coming in from the garage was re-engaged. Devon locked the utility door leading to the backyard.

Teams Three and Four each had four vampires, including Simone, who was the lead for Team Three. We grouped together in the foyer, and I reported in. "Teams One, Three, and Four are in place and secure."

A minute later, Sergi responded. "House security is back on."

"Check."

"Team Five is in place." Decker was the lead for a team of eight who would secure the front of the property. It included three shifters—him, Elijah, and Rachel, and five vamps. They would stay in the shadows and behind trees and shrubs. Decker and Rachel would be positioned near the garage, while Elijah and a vamp would be positioned close to the front door but well hidden behind a hedge that ran along the path to the pool. The other four would spread out between the house and front gate.

"Team Six is in place." Lucas led another team of eight—seven vamps and Ginger. Lucas and Ginger would be positioned near the back door, with another two between them and the back gate to the alley. The other four would break into two teams and cover the sides of the house, including the pool area and patio doors, for anyone attempting to flank them.

Sergi responded to the check-in. "All teams be aware the security net for the perimeter has been reactivated. Radio silence is in effect until the party arrives." It must have killed him to say the last part, and to be honest, I didn't think he would. My reference to the mission as being a party had annoyed him. Maybe Roxie had something to do with it. Her high energy and irreverence to rules would grate against the steadfast Sergi. I couldn't imagine what the next few hours would be like in the van.

There was no telling how long April would stay on Shadow Island, but we assumed it might be closer to dawn before they returned. Either way, Roxie was tapped into the security cameras so she could advise when cars arrived at the front gate. She could also monitor where the vamps were located, either entering the house or moving to perimeter positions around the property.

Regardless of where the vamps ended up, they'd have no idea that twenty-six skilled commandos waited for them, all with kill orders for everyone but April and Jasper Hunnicutt. Devon wanted that vamp alive. He'd wrestled with his kill order for the others, not knowing exactly which House they belonged to. We'd been concerned that the SUV caravan that left the estate might not be going to Shadow Island, so Decker had asked Remus to watch who was boarding the ferries to the island. We received confirmation that April had arrived with her caravan. And that was when Devon issued the kill order.

With hours to wait, I wanted to check in with Bella to see how Mom was doing, but radio silence prevented me from doing that.

If there were a problem, Sergi would contact me. The no news is good news adage would have to be my only comfort. Devon and I waited with Teams Three and Four in the main living room. It had exits to all the different parts of the house, including the stairs, so once we got the word April's caravan had left Shadow Island, we'd move into place. Worst case, if the shifters missed her exit, since it might be difficult to pinpoint her if the ferry from the island was filled with guests, we'd know the minute they pulled up to the front gate. That still provided more than enough time for us to get into position within the house.

"I think I'll go up and pack a bag for Mom and April."

Devon nodded as he flipped through one of the several magazines Mom liked to keep on the enormous coffee table. The room was used mostly for business guests, and Christopher always liked to show off his wealth.

Simone stood. "I'll help."

I didn't argue. The two of us hadn't spoken much since Colantha arrived, so I didn't mind the human and vamp time.

We didn't speak as we climbed the stairs, and I took the lead, heading for the master bedroom first.

"There should be a suitcase in the closet." I went to a dresser and began removing a handful of panties, bras, and two nightgowns.

Simone returned with one and laid it on the bed, opening it. "Only one, or do you want a second one for April? Until we know their condition, they will need to be separated for a while."

I nodded. "April should have a suitcase in her closet." I dropped the undergarments and nighties on the bed. Simone followed me to the closet. "Are you going to hide away at Oasis until Colantha leaves?" I walked past the racks of clothing, pulling things down at random—slacks, blouses, a couple of jackets.

"I'm not hiding. I'm overseeing repairs and upgrades to the security system."

"I get it, but Devon mentioned all that was completed a couple of days ago." I shoved the clothes to Simone. If she was going to follow me around, she might as well be useful.

She repositioned the clothes in her arms. "I have other matters to attend to."

I picked up a pair of flats and two pairs of short-heeled pumps my mother favored before turning to assess Simone. She had recently taken blood, mostly likely for tonight's mission. I handed her the shoes that she piled on top of the clothes.

"Devon mentioned you were trying to reach an old friend." When the tips of her fangs dropped, I ignored them. If we were in a training room, I'd immediately drop into a fighting stance, but Simone sometimes released her fangs when she was emotional. That didn't mean I wouldn't keep on eye on her. Simone could be unpredictable, though this time, she was warning me I was heading into personal matters.

I waved a hand as I grabbed a sweater and a robe, which I draped over my arm. "I'm not prying, but after trying to reach my family, I understand what it's like to get nothing but dead air."

I pulled out a couple scarves, then went back to the bed, where I dumped everything. Simone, being a fashion diva, was more respectful of the clothing. Once she laid everything down, she began folding the items and placing them in the suitcase.

"It's frustrating." Simone startled me by sharing her emotions. "We haven't spoken in centuries until I was gathering information on Gheata. We parted on good terms." She chuckled, and I gave her a quick glance. Chuckles or any form of laughter were rare for the vamp, even with her wicked sense of humor.

"Did you try calling?"

"I only have an email. It's his preferred method of communication."

I nodded as I went through drawers, not looking for anything in particular, just seeing if there was anything she might want. I found a drawer of bathing suits and pulled one out. "That makes sense if he wants to reduce the ability for anyone to track him. I know Devon uses phones with the GPS tracking removed, but not everyone trusts technology. Email is safe, considering he could be accessing it from anywhere in the world."

My last stop was the nightstand. There were three books but no phone or tablet. I grabbed the books and tossed them on the bed, then searched for her purse. It was in the closet. That was odd, but it told me something. Mom hadn't left the house in some time and apparently wasn't going to anytime soon. I took out her wallet and personal phone book. She was old school when keeping track of her friends and contacts, but there wasn't any phone. April or Jasper most likely had it.

Simone had the suitcase packed, and I added the wallet and address book on top before she zipped it up.

"What's next?" Simone picked up the bag.

"April's room."

I was in for a shock. April had always been ultra feminine. Lots of pink and lavender. Not anymore.

She'd gone goth and it was heavily reflected by the decor. Black and deep purple seemed to be her new colors. She hadn't lost her fashion sense, but the dark colors made me wonder if this reflected a more angsty April after Christopher's death—because there was no way he would have approved of this—or whether it was influenced by Jasper. Goth would have been more my style, if I had one.

Simone grimaced when she walked into the room. "This is different."

"It's not the April I knew." I went to her closet to see if her clothes were different as well.

Simone followed me in, and we simply stared. On one side of the small walk-in closet were the clothes I'd always seen April wear —bright colors, a little preppy, and fitting for someone who went to a private school. The other half was the new April—all black with the occasional deep violet or red.

I sighed. "I wish I knew if this was a personal choice to change, a change because of her new boyfriend, or because she was mesmerized."

"Mesmerizing could force a change if she was being directed to follow someone else's preferences. But this wouldn't come from Venizi." Simone found the suitcase and picked it up.

"Based on the wardrobe he hand-selected for me, I agree. Maybe that's why she's kept her older clothes."

"Maybe. Let's get her packed."

I went through the same ritual as I had for Mom, selecting undergarments before making a decision on the rest. Unsure which to choose from, I selected a couple outfits from the old-April side and some from the new. I couldn't care less which she preferred. I'd gone through my own goth period, though it had been to irritate Christopher more than anything else. Wasn't that what a rebellious teen was supposed to do? April wasn't a teen, but she was still in her early twenties. Maybe she was all business-woman by day and turned goth on her off hours. I wasn't sure how things would go with April, and it depended on whether she was mesmerized or simply pissed at the world. Either way, she might as well wear what made her comfortable. It wasn't like we couldn't buy her something else if she was unhappy with my selection.

We dropped the luggage in the closet by the front door. It would be easy to grab on our way out.

Once that was done, it was a waiting game. Devon had someone check on the two vamps tied up in the hall closet every hour, and Sergi checked in every half-hour. All was quiet, and so far, no ferries had returned from the island.

"What if they're staying overnight?" I asked.

"They'll be leaving soon." Devon had moved on from the magazines and was flipping through channels on the LCD panel. "I don't remember there being housing for a large number of overnight guests."

Simone had turned to meditation while the other vamps had found a deck of cards and switched between playing gin and poker.

I was tempted to ask Sergi to check on Mom but had to remind myself that he'd have advised me if there were a problem. It was still irritating not knowing.

At two thirty in the morning, Devon ran us through the plan, finishing moments before my earbud crackled. Sometimes, I truly believed Devon was psychic.

"To all teams, the first ferry has arrived, and the target has been spotted. Anticipate twenty minutes for arrival."

The television was turned off. The cards were returned to the drawer and the furniture restored to order, down to how the magazines had been arranged. Teams Three and Four moved into position, and Devon and I went upstairs to the room across from April's.

Twenty minutes later, as Sergi predicted, we received the anticipated update.

"All teams. Three SUVs have arrived, and the gates are opening. Teams Five and Six, stay alert. Teams One, Three, and Four get in position.

"Team One is in position." I glanced at Devon, who leaned against the wall, alert and relaxed at the same time.

"Team Three is in position."

"Team Four is in position."

"Team Six is in position."

"Team Five. The target vehicles have cleared the gate and are approaching the manor."

At this point, Roxie should be changing the security codes on the gates. We didn't want anyone leaving by vehicle. It didn't mean someone couldn't escape on foot, but they'd have to scale the walls. And we were ready for that.

"Team Five is in position." Now that the targets were at the manor, Team Five would spread out, forming a secure perimeter around the front of the mansion, including the garage, the front door, and the path leading to the pool.

"This is Team Five. We count four from the first vehicle. April,

Jasper, one other vampire, plus the driver, who's moving the vehicle toward the garage. The second vehicle also has three plus the driver. They also appear to be vampires. The last vehicle is moving toward the garage, the number inside unknown. Everyone has cleared the front door."

Teams Three and Four remained on the first floor. This was the tricky part. The house was huge, with a lot of rooms and hallways on both floors. The issue with the first floor was the front rooms. They were the largest in the house and built with an open floor plan and, with the current decor, left no good places to hide.

The other rooms were smaller, and if Mom and April kept things like Christopher always wanted, several of the doors were always open while a few others were kept closed. Finding spots to hide eight vampires on the first floor and still be effective would require craftiness.

Our goal was April and Jasper. The plan was for Teams Three and Four to remain hidden until Devon gave the order to go. April would want to change into something more comfortable and would likely head to her bedroom first. If she was close with Jasper, it was a fifty-fifty chance he'd follow her up. They might also want to confirm that Mom was still where they'd put her.

At the same time, they'd want to check on the two vamps they'd left to watch her. One had been in the room down the hall from where Devon and I currently hid, and we'd made the assumption Jasper would check. The problem was the one on the first floor. It came down to whether our teams could remain hidden until April got to her room.

It didn't take long to hear voices, even with my human hearing. Devon took point at the door while I stood on the opposite side, watching his face, ready for any signal.

Voices grew nearer. Someone was coming up the stairs, but they were too far away to make out the words or whether they were male or female. Devon nodded. At least one of them was April, and it was quickly confirmed when she reached the hallway.

"I've got to get out of these shoes." April's voice sent a shiver of memories through me. The good April, the one who tried to make my life easier.

"I'd like to help you get out of other things," said some unknown I assumed to be Jasper.

I rolled my eyes, and Devon shook his head. He was all business, but honestly, couldn't the vamp come up with a better line?

It didn't seem to matter to April, who just giggled. Hells bells, was she mesmerized or really into this dude?

Their progress slowed, and now it was Devon's turn to be annoyed. He didn't roll his eyes, but he closed them. He was making a decision, and I wasn't sure why.

Then I heard someone bump into a wall. They were close.

Then April groaned.

I rolled my eyes again. I couldn't help it. They'd stopped to make out. They wouldn't get to her room before someone downstairs was discovered. Devon opened his eyes, and he nodded.

We weren't going to wait for them. We would use their making out to our advantage. The plan was for him to take Jasper while I restrained April. For a split second, I took the time to quickly run through how Simone showed me to take someone out without hurting them. I'd practiced the routine dozens of times. Now was the real deal.

Devon held up a finger. On the third count, he'd give the go command, followed instantly by us rushing out to take them.

When he reached the second count, a violent crash came from downstairs.

"Team Three engaged." It wasn't Simone's voice, but Devon didn't care.

Devon yelled, "All teams go."

Chapter Twenty-Eight

SIMONE MADE the decision to hide in the pantry. She knew vampires. They didn't need to eat often, but when they were stationed at a particular place over an extended period of time, they got bored and lazy. Over the centuries, she'd come to the conclusion that having the same vampire with the exact same job for more than two days was problematic.

It wasn't their fault. It was vampire nature. The fact a vampire was at the bottom rung of a security hierarchy didn't mean they lacked intelligence. Someone had to be at the bottom, and they held that position for one of several factors. They could be new to the security detail, they lacked experience or skill for that particular job, or there were just more senior vampires on that particular detail.

And it was the vampire's superior intellect that created the boredom. Yes, vampires could remain in a single position for hours without moving. That didn't mean their mind stopped working. At some point, vampires required stimulation. From what Devon told her, humans had similar traits, the only problem was that their attention span was much shorter, and she thanked her maker that she only had to deal with Cressa and Ginger on security details.

The problem in this particular instance was that the vampires had returned from a vampire party. They would be overstimulated and ready for action of any kind. That included wandering the house, and, just like humans, they would either gravitate toward the bar or the kitchen. If it were one of her details, they would have immediately searched the house upon their return. Team Four reported that someone was coming down the hall on the other side of the house, most likely searching for the vampire currently hidden in a closet.

That had been a minute ago.

"Hey, get me one of those seltzer waters."

She'd counted two vamps based on their footsteps and heard the refrigerator door open.

"There aren't any in here. What about a soda?"

"Check the pantry. I like them warm."

And just like that, Simone's expectations came to fruition. Bored and uncaring about their missing vampire. If she radioed that she had to move, they would hear her, and that wasn't the protocol for tonight's mission.

The minute the pantry door began to swing open, she waited until it was almost fully open before slamming it shut. It hit the vampire in the face, then, just as swiftly, she pulled the door open and yanked the vampire inside. She slit his throat, stabbed him in the kidneys, and pushed him back so she could get out of the pantry before the other vampire noticed.

The vampire slammed against the shelving harder than she'd intended, and the entire wall of shelves crashed down. The noise rang in her ears. She ignored it and ran, rolling as she exited out the door and into the kitchen. She heard two things simultaneously— Devon's voice yelling go and a gun being fired.

Lucas, Ginger, and the other six vampires spread out along the back of the property. Lucas remained halfway between the back gate and the back of the house. Ginger was to his right, standing behind a fir tree where he could see her. Two of the vampires were positioned at the back gate in case anyone slipped by Lucas and Ginger. The other four had split, with two moving to the right of the house while the other two disappeared toward the pool house. Though he couldn't see them from his position, he didn't question they were where they were supposed to be.

Their job wasn't to move in unless Sergi countermanded their mission. They were to hold the perimeter and would only make radio contact if they engaged the enemy.

As much as he hated his father, he appreciated the military tactics he'd been taught that had come in handy through the decades. In this type of scenario, where a perimeter had to be maintained, some leaders considered it a position for their weakest fighters. The ones who wouldn't have to face the enemy head-on.

They were so wrong.

It didn't matter the type of battle or how well-trained a vampire was, everyone had an instinct for survival. Most would keep fighting, even when all seemed lost. That was a critical moment for an army. When it appeared the battle couldn't be won, the last thing a leader wanted was for soldiers to give up hope. It was the moment each warrior discovered how much faith they'd placed in their leader to persevere. If there was the slightest doubt, fear for one's life over the mission could shatter an army.

If only one or two ran, it didn't mean the end of the battle. But if more followed, then doom was only a matter of time. Lucas knew someone would run. If these were Venizi's vampires, he guessed that two might run. If these vampires were from a lower House aligned with Lorenzo, they could all scatter.

It was imperative their team held the line.

When the gunshot, muffled as it was, came from within the house, it was unexpected. Although everyone wore armored vests, vampires didn't typically rely on firearms, and they rarely stopped another vampire. It might have been April who fired it. Either way, he immediately knew who would respond poorly to the sound.

He glanced over at Ginger as Devon's command came through. Lucas followed it with a stern, "Team Six, hold your position."

Ginger had taken two steps from her hiding spot and turned to look at Lucas. He shook his head, and she turned hers toward the house.

Come on, Ginger, don't do it. Don't make me come after you.

He was ready to give the command to hold again, but she stepped back to her position. He blew out a breath just before two vamps raced out the back of the house, both heading for the alley exit.

DECKER HAD a bad feeling no matter how well this plan looked on paper. It was difficult to judge someone's actions until they were put in a tough position. He might be a shifter, but he'd been around vampires his whole life. Devon and the cadre aside, his dealings with vampires came mostly from The Den, a fight club he owned in the Hollows.

Some of the vampires, especially the fighters, were rogues with loyalties to no one but themselves, but most of his vampire customers belonged to a House. What most of the vampire and shifter communities didn't understand was that the two species weren't that different from each other. And one of those truths came down to the strength of the House or the pack.

When it came down to a struggle between life and death, loyalty or survival, a vampire or shifter would give up their life for their leader. But only if they were strong leaders, fair leaders, leaders who wouldn't put their Family or pack into unnecessarily dangerous positions.

This particular mission might be considered unnecessary by some. The likelihood of it impacting the fight against Venizi and a corrupt Council was minuscule at best. But Cressa was Family and a strong ally to Remus. She was a burgeoning dreamwalker who could solidify a strong alliance between vampires and shifters. And that meant that saving her human family from what appeared to be another ploy by Venizi to lure Cressa out in the open made this a critical mission. One that everyone here, whether from Devon's House or Remus's pack, was willing to lay down their life for if needed.

Decker glanced at the manor and then scanned the landscape, searching for anything out of place. All was quiet since the vampires had returned with Cressa's half-sister. There were still an estimated six vampires in the garage unless they entered the house through the utility door. He couldn't tell from his current position, but he hadn't seen anyone head out for perimeter duty. That meant that without knowing where these six were, they had to be considered a high risk. It was also the reason he put two vampires outside the garage, in case someone tried to use an SUV to run.

Team Five's mission was to monitor the front of the property, including the front gate and this side of the pool area, to ensure no one escaped. The three wolves on the team were assigned the closest to the house. They'd come armed, but they were at their best once they shifted to their wolves.

Some inner instinct scratched at him to shift. He never ignored his gut.

He pulled his shirt over his head and unzipped his pants, stripping down in less than a minute. They were supposed to remain radio silent, but this was too important. He whispered into his headset, "Going wolf."

He could see Rachel from his position but not Elijah. When he saw Rachel had already begun stripping before his words were out of his mouth, he knew Elijah had probably already turned. The instincts of an Alpha were too strong for anyone close to ignore the call.

The transition typically took ten minutes, but Elijah, as a powerful Alpha, could force a faster change. And that had to be what was happening because the shift was intensely painful, and Decker sucked in a deep breath to stop from howling.

The timing couldn't have been better. When the first vampire ran from the house, Decker thought one of Devon's vampires would have to take care of him. The vampire was a good distance down the driveway, racing for the gate, before the solid gray wolf known as Rachel dragged him down.

Decker howled into the night, pleased when another vampire, who'd been in the garage, raced past his reddish-brown wolf. The hunt was on.

~

DEVON THREW the door open and leaped out. April was standing in the middle of the hall, staring at Jasper's back as he raced toward the stairs.

"Stay with your mother and lock the door," Jasper yelled as he ran.

Devon grabbed April and shoved her back toward her room. Confident that Cressa would deal with it, he raced after Jasper.

"Jasper!" April called out.

If Jasper heard, he didn't turn around, and he had a good head start on Devon. There were more crashes from the first floor, and when he reached the stairs, Jasper was taking the last few steps to where two vampires were fighting.

Jasper reached into his jacket and pulled out a dagger, the lights of the chandelier flashing off the silver as he raised it toward one of Devon's vampires. He wouldn't make it down the stairs in time. Devon was still at the top of the stairs, but he didn't take more than a second to change his trajectory. He grabbed the railing and leaped over it, pulling out his own dagger as he hit the floor.

If nothing else, it surprised Jasper before he could take a swing at one of Devon's team members. But Devon shouldn't have worried. His security details never fought without keeping an eye on their surroundings, but that didn't always protect them from someone coming up from behind. In this case, the team member caught Devon's leap, and he kicked out at his opponent while dropping and rolling.

Jasper wasn't anticipating the move, and though his swing only hit air, he didn't stop. Instead, he changed tactics, but he had a problem. It was two on two, and it appeared the first vampire, while only taking a glancing blow from Devon's team member, hadn't been faring well in the fight.

Devon ignored the team member and his opponent, his entire focus on Jasper.

When Jasper turned and caught Devon racing for him, his eyes widened with recognition, and then he grinned before he ran. He took a right at the hallway, which would take him toward the back of the house.

Devon took a moment to glance to his left, where several vampires were fully engaged. He spotted one of the opposing forces heading for the front door and let him go, directing his energy to follow Jasper. The moment to survey his team cost him a few seconds, and when he turned down the hall, Jasper was gone.

He slowed and blasted open doors with a forceful kick as he passed them, peering in for a quick scan of each one. Most of the rooms didn't provide any place to hide, but two of them required him to check closets.

While he continued down the hallway, he performed a mental review of the floor plan. All the rooms at this end of the house only had one door, with the exception of two that were more like salons exiting into another hallway.

He put his trust in his outdoor teams, allowing him to

continue his methodical search. A crash from upstairs didn't alarm him at first, as he assumed Cressa would be dealing with April.

When he came to the first room that had a second exit, he took a different approach. If Jasper had been paying attention, and if he was in there, he'd expect Devon to kick the door down. Devon hadn't forgotten the sound of the gun and suspected Jasper was carrying a firearm as well. He reached for the door handle and slowly opened the door. Once it was clear of the door-jamb, he shoved it open, but before he could jump aside, Jasper fired.

The bullet hit his left shoulder, and the burn of silver registered as the pain gripped him. His beast instantly flared to life, his gaze reflecting its icy blue glow. All he saw was the flap of Jasper's jacket as he raced out the other door. He ignored the bullet as he felt his body forcing it out while his blood mended the damage.

All the vampires had taken blood donations before the mission. No exceptions. It wouldn't stop them from losing their heads, but any other injury would heal faster. He didn't know why Jasper didn't just empty his gun, but he'd have to reload, and Jasper had no idea how many intruders were in the house. Or maybe Jasper was still regrouping and trying to figure out what the hell was happening.

When he reached the other door, he glanced left then right. There was an exit to the backyard to his left, but the door was closed. Why hadn't Jasper gone that way? More crashing came from above, and now his fear grew.

He started toward the right, his gut telling him Jasper was returning to the second floor, but after a few steps, he stopped to listen. There was fighting somewhere toward the living room and maybe the kitchen or dining room.

He turned back and raced for the back stairs. The only ones on the second floor should be Cressa and April. Would Cressa anticipate Jasper returning? He was halfway up the stairs when a gunshot from above filled his veins with terror.

∾

SIMONE HEARD the shot as she rolled out of the pantry. She was halfway to standing when she was knocked backward. Her feet went out from under her, and she dropped like a stone weight. She glanced up. A vampire was rising to his feet while two others struggled behind him.

He had a gun in his hand, and he looked down at it, then back at her.

She tried to stand, but her legs wouldn't move. Her vision was blurred, and she wiped at her eyes, surprised when she noticed her hands. They were covered with blood. She glanced back up at the vampire.

The asshole had shot her.

She still couldn't move her legs, and it was fairly obvious she was in trouble. The vampires struggling behind this tableau were using varied martial arts and appeared evenly matched. Her team member had his hands full.

She grabbed her side as if she might have another injury. At least her arms moved, but the odds weren't in her favor.

The vampire set the gun on the counter and pulled out a short blade.

Her body froze, but not from her injury. She didn't want to give away her only move. Without her legs, she was at a severe disadvantage.

She'd taken donor blood before the mission; however, her legs weren't healing. They were numb. The bullet must have done more than graze her head. She didn't feel any pain, but the blood continued to drip down her face and into her eyes, making it almost impossible to make out the vampire who crept toward her.

This was not the way she planned on dying. Not on a simple mission to grab a couple humans. Venizi must consider them important because these vampires were more skilled than what he'd thrown at them before.

Had they somehow known an enemy would be waiting? She didn't see how, but her thoughts weren't coming as fast as normal. A sharp pain slammed into her, making her double over. She pushed past it, not wanting to give the approaching vampire easy access to her neck.

She didn't understand why her injury suddenly hurt, but then she felt the burn of silver. The asshole shot her with silver bullets. Her body would automatically purge the silver. The pain must be coming from the bullet being expelled from her body. Her legs were still numb. If her body was doing any healing, it wasn't helping her legs.

When she straightened, she tightened her grip on her short blade and immediately swung upward. The steel edge glided off the other vampire's blade. He brought the blade around again, and she managed to block it.

In a standing position, he had all his weight to bear as he swung, but she was strong. And though her arm shook from the exertion, she didn't give an inch.

"Well, aren't you a strong one?" The vampire pulled back and paced in front of her, keeping his eye on her. "I normally don't play with my prey, but I don't get the opportunities like I used to. You know. Back when we weren't so civilized."

His swing came fast, but she was ready for it and blocked it easily. Then he spun around, and when the blade came again, he held it with both hands as he brought it down with a sickly grin.

Her blade fell from her hand before the swing came, and when it struck, she held up her arm in defense.

The slice came fast, and she felt it to the bone. The only reason it didn't go all the way through was that the vampire hadn't kept his blade sharp. It didn't matter. The intense pain surpassed the growing one in her head.

Her vision went dark, and she didn't think it was from the loss of blood. She was defenseless, and before she hit the floor, she heard the unmistakable thud of a head hitting the floor.

Then the voices came.

"Simone is down. We need a healer and donor. Now."

She would have laughed if she could. A healer couldn't put her head back on her neck.

"We have to clear the scene first."

"There's no time."

She sighed. There was never enough time. She'd been so close to having her own House. An image of a dark-haired man came to her. Gaius. No time to make amends. Maybe he was dead, too.

"Simone. Simone. Oh god, Simone."

<h1 style="text-align:center">Chapter Twenty-Nine</h1>

DECKER'S WOLF chased the vampire, slamming into his back and dragging him down. The wolf immediately went for the neck. He was taking a chunk out of it when he heard the gunshot. The vamp struggled to toss the wolf off when Decker stopped and turned to scan the area.

A wolf lay on its side. It was impossible in the darkness of the driveway to see who it was. A vampire stalked toward it, the gun still in his hand as he raised it for another shot. Decker was too far away to get to him in time.

Out of nowhere, another wolf flew out from the shadows and took the vampire down. There was no mistaking this wolf. Full black, blending with the night—Elijah. That meant the downed wolf was Rachel.

Elijah ripped into the vampire's throat, chomping at muscle and tendons until the body went limp. He lifted his blood-soaked muzzle and glanced around until he spotted Decker. His lips lifted in an angry snarl before he lifted his head and howled.

The musical notes sent shivers over Decker. It was a call that couldn't be ignored. His wolf instincts took over, and much like the beast inside a vampire, Decker no longer had control.

It was war.

The red wolf glanced around in search of other prey. He sighted in on another vampire. The wolf, even in a manic rage, could identify friend from foe. He ignored this particular vampire, recognizing him as one of his temporary pack and, not seeing another immediate threat, glanced down at the vampire who was building strength beneath him.

The wolf nudged him with his muzzle. Then he sniffed at the vampire's neck, licked it, and let the taste of blood fill him with centuries-old hatred of those who'd kept them down. Treating them no better than dogs in chains.

He howled in return, pleased as the sound echoed through the night. When the vampire beneath him squirmed, the wolf bore his teeth before tearing into the bloody neck, ignoring the screams that finally quieted as the head separated from the body and rolled away.

He didn't stop there. His ears pricked.

Another vampire shot out into the night. Then another one after that.

One of Decker's vampire team members chased after them, but the red wolf was faster. He raced past the vampire and met up with the black wolf. Even though Decker had been the team leader before the shift, his wolf slowed, allowing the black wolf, as Alpha, the first kill.

The two wolves took the vampires down in what their team members would later say was an amazing synchronous attack. And while the swiftness of their kill was a bit unnerving to the vampires, they understood why their House leader had partnered with the shifters. And if nothing else came of that night, a stronger bond had formed between the two species.

Decker, taking control of his wolf but remaining in its form, laid down next to Rachel. He was still keyed up. Elijah, who'd taken the time to shift back to human, knelt naked next to him and ran a hand down his back, ruffling his fur.

"Be calm. The enemy has been vanquished." Elijah gave him two more strokes before turning his attention to the vampire kneeling over Rachel. "I could hear her heartbeat before I shifted to human."

The vampire nodded. "She's alive. It's a leg wound. My concern is the loss of blood. We just cleared the scene with Sergi. The healer is on her way."

His words were barely out of his mouth before a car pulled up. Soon, Madame Saldano and another healer dropped next to Rachel.

"Can you make her shift?" Madame Saldano asked.

Elijah nodded and bent low. "Rachel, you need to shift."

The wolf whined and began to struggle, but nothing happened.

"Rachel, I command you to shift. Now."

Elijah's fierce command rolled over Decker but kept him alert for danger. All the others took a step back as the gray wolf, whimpering in obvious pain, gave a short yip and morphed into a naked woman with blood soaking her legs.

The healer went to work, but Decker refused to change. Not until he knew Rachel was alright. Not until he was comfortable there were no more enemies.

His ears pricked when the vampires became agitated. When he shifted to wolf form, he'd lost his earbud, so he had to wait for someone to share the information that had rattled the team.

"What is it?" Elijah asked.

"It's Simone. She's near death."

"Send in the healer. Rachel can wait." Although Elijah said the words, Decker didn't believe the Alpha meant them but understood this was the vampires' mission. Their packmate would have to wait.

But the vampire and healer both shook their heads.

"The house hasn't been cleared to send anyone in," the vampire said.

"Besides, I need to get this bullet out before she can shift again," Madame Saldano replied. "It's silver. I'm impressed you actually got her to shift. It helped bring the bullet closer to the surface. Once I get it out, you'll need to make her shift again."

"But Simone—" Elijah didn't get any more words out before the vampire spoke.

"Devon and the cadre's orders. Treat who we can once the target area has been secured. Most grievous injuries first, regardless of species."

Decker whined and howled. He understood Devon's wishes, but Simone was his friend. He laid his head down and put a paw over his muzzle as Elijah rested a hand on his back. Madame Saldano would never defy Devon's orders.

Blood donors stood ten feet away. Unable to do anything but wait.

THE TWO VAMPIRES exited the house together and raced toward Lucas. Not that they could see him. When they got closer, Lucas drew out a throwing star and was ready to let it fly when he saw the gun rise in the lead vampire's hand.

He'd heard shots coming from the house and knew they were carrying, but what a cowardly action. Though he'd been aiming at the first vampire, he changed direction and threw the star. It flew by the vampire with the gun with less than an inch to spare, and though the whirling blade had bypassed him, he stopped to rub his cheek, discovering the throwing star had missed him.

Behind him, however, the second vampire stumbled and fell forward, face-first into the lawn. He wouldn't be down for long.

The first vampire refocused on his exit strategy and lifted his arm, the weapon once again trained on Lucas. Before he could get a shot off, a blur raced in from the right.

He had no idea Ginger could move that fast, but she'd taken

some of his blood before the mission. It must have hyped up her metabolism. At first, he assumed it was one of the other team members, but there was no mistaking the ponytail.

The second vampire was rising, but another team member raced out of the darkness and, with a single swing of her blade, removed his head.

Lucas went after Ginger, who must have wrestled the gun away from the vamp because it went flying into the night. The vamp pushed her off, but she was getting up, and as soon as she was on her legs, she gave him a roundhouse kick to his head before he could get off his knees. He went down.

Lucas grabbed her, but it was like pulling a wild cat from a fresh kill. She wasn't done. He clamped his arms around hers and dragged her away as the vampire attempted to rise. He never made it to a knee before his head slid off his shoulders.

Lucas nodded at Roberta. Blood dripped from her sword, and she grinned at them as Ginger stopped fighting. He let her go, and they stared down at the headless vamp.

"We should get the gun," Ginger suggested.

Then, the voice came through the earpiece. "Simone is down."

They listened for another thirty seconds before Ginger started to run, but Lucas tugged her back.

"We're not done with our assignment."

"It's Simone." Ginger pulled away.

"What can we do?" Lucas wanted to go to Simone, but they weren't healers.

"I'm a donor."

That stopped him. Sometimes, he forgot she was human, especially when she fought like she did.

"Go. We've got this." Roberta nodded to the other five on their team, who had gathered but were still monitoring the house for movement.

Ginger didn't hesitate. She was flying across the yard with

Lucas right behind her, catching up and passing her before she made it to the back door.

He stopped before opening it. "The house hasn't been cleared. I go first."

She opened her mouth, must have recognized his own stubbornness, and nodded.

He wasn't sure where Simone was, but he found two downed vampires on his way toward the foyer. Neither of them were team members. Doors along the way had been smashed open or ripped from their hinges, giving him a clear view to confirm they were empty.

The first team member he ran across was holding his arm, probably waiting for it to heal based on the blood dripping on the floor.

"Where's Simone?" Lucas asked.

"The kitchen." His eyes glowed with the beast. "It doesn't look good."

Ginger must have had enough of the stalling because she pushed past him before he could stop her. They'd all memorized the floor plan, and she didn't hesitate as she cut through a room with a second exit that led directly to the kitchen.

Neither of them could have anticipated what they found. Four team members were in the kitchen. Levi, the vampire from the city safe house, was holding Simone's head in his lap while the others stood at the door perimeters, moving aside as Ginger barreled her way through.

There was blood everywhere. It wasn't all Simone's. Three other vamps lay headless on the floor. But glancing at Levi, his pants were soaked in what must have been her blood.

"The house was just cleared, but the healer has been delayed. One of the wolves was shot, and she went to them first since she couldn't get in the house." He stopped and listened to something coming through his earpiece. Sergi must be giving information to specific team leaders since Lucas wasn't hearing anything.

"It will be another five minutes."

Lucas nodded and turned in time to see Ginger pull her dagger and slice her wrist. When she knelt next to Levi, he opened Simone's mouth. Blood dripped into her mouth, and Ginger pushed down on her forearm, forcing the blood out faster.

"Is she hurt anywhere else besides her head?" Ginger asked.

It was obvious she had a head injury based on the blood-soaked kitchen towel wrapped around it.

"Her arm took a good slice. It's healing but not quickly."

"Show me."

Another towel had been lying over Simone's right arm, but Lucas had assumed it was to replace the head bandage, which clearly needed to be changed. When the towel lifted, Simone's shirt had been cut away from the wound. It was a long cut, but he couldn't tell how deep from where he stood.

Ginger dripped her blood over it until Levi nodded. He grabbed a fresh towel from behind him and covered the arm. Ginger then placed her wrist on Simone's mouth.

"Drink, Simone. Drink."

Lucas knelt next to Ginger, helpless to do anything. Everything they could do was being done. All he could do was watch Ginger's tears fall as she tried to save her friend.

Chapter Thirty

I ONLY SPARED a second to watch Devon race down the hall after Jasper. Then I turned my attention to April, who had been a bit shell-shocked, but she recovered quickly and stared at me with venom.

"What are you doing here?" April spat and moved into a standard martial arts pose. Was she kidding?

"I came for Mom." I could have asked if she'd been the one sending texts about my father, but we didn't have all night, so I went with the simplest answer.

She risked a quick glance down the hall to the master suite.

"Oh, don't bother. Mom's not there anymore."

"How dare you come in here and kidnap her. I knew you were nuts, but you won't get away with this."

"How dare you prevent her from leaving the house. And from all appearances, she looks drugged." When April didn't respond, I added, "Or has she been mesmerized?"

April laughed. "Please. That's not a real thing."

"Really? And how would you know?"

"Because Jasper told me."

I laughed. I couldn't help it.

"You don't know anything, Cressa. Mom has been depressed since you had Dad killed. Completely despondent."

"That's a lie, and you know it. First, I didn't have Christopher killed. Lorenzo Venizi had him killed, and Jasper should know that. Second, Mom had an escape plan to leave Christopher because of the dangerous people he did business with and his constant cheating."

"He never."

"I don't have time for this. We're leaving, and you're going with us."

She attacked. Her kick came faster than I expected since I wasn't expecting it at all. It was simple enough to block. Most of my defensive moves came automatically now. Daily training will do that for a person.

April didn't stop. She apparently had her own set of offensive moves, most likely taught by Jasper or the local dojo. I was more curious about when she began her training. After Christopher's death or when Jasper began grooming her for whatever he had in mind?

I had to admit, she had game, but she had nothing on my skills. I didn't want to hurt her. Not if I didn't have to, so all I did was block her strikes and kicks, waiting for her to tire herself out. But that could take more time than they had.

I was deciding on which defensive move would be the least damaging when she stopped and slowly moved to find a better position to come at me. The hallway was wider than most homes but still too narrow to offer many options.

Her eyes flashed as she looked past me and smiled. Hell. Why not just tell me there's someone behind me without saying it? I moved in quick as a snake and kicked her in her midsection, which launched her several feet backward where she landed on the soft carpeting.

I twisted around to see Jasper racing toward us, a gun in his hand. I'd heard several gunshots, but if there was any chatter from Sergi, he was keeping it localized to the various team leaders. Had we lost anyone to a gunshot? Probably not. We were wearing armored vests, and the vamps had recently fed. They'd heal quickly.

Time slowed as I stared at the barrel of the gun. The asshole was going to shoot me. Had that been their plan the whole time?

Jasper pulled the trigger.

I blinked.

I was in the coffee house in San Francisco. Why did I always end up here? Well, to be honest, I usually ended up here when Colantha was in control of the construct.

Devon had once told me that Colantha always took him to a classy pub in a Dublin hotel. She never took me there, but I was going to make it a point to request it the next time I had the opportunity.

I picked up my latte and stared at my guests over the rim of the cup. After taking a quick sip—it was too hot to drink—I set the cup down and observed their expressions. They'd spent the first minute twisting their heads around as they took in the coffee shop. Then, after April screamed for another minute, only stopping when Jasper yelled at her to shut up, they stared at each other and rather comically turned their heads as one to stare at me.

"What the hell was that?" Jasper bellowed. He wanted to be in control, and he played the game to pretend he was, but the shadow of fear in the back of his eyes, or maybe it was the dull glow of his beast, told me he was scared shitless.

Then he tried to move. He couldn't. Not even his arms. "What are you doing? What kind of magic is this?"

I chuckled then April screamed again in a vain attempt to attract someone's attention.

"Help us. We've been kidnapped."

The coffee house was busy, and most of the tables were taken, but they couldn't see us or hear us.

When no one looked at her, her eyes grew larger, and she began to cry. "What are you doing to us?"

"Hells bells, you two are the whiniest people I've ever been around. We're on a dreamwalk. I didn't want to show you this because we're not ready to reveal ourselves, but Jasper, who decided to take the coward's way out by bringing a gun to a vamp fight, gave me no other choice. Besides, I don't think Jasper will be returning to his House.

"As for you, April. Well, I don't know what we're going to do with you. I'll see if Mom has a suggestion after she comes down from whatever drugs you've been pumping into her."

"What is it with you and Mom? You haven't even been in her life since you walked away after graduation."

"Shut up, April. For fuck's sake, this isn't about your mother." Jasper stared at me. "He said dreamwalkers were real, but I didn't believe him."

"Was that Lorenzo?"

He nodded.

"I have to say, after spending a few rather unpleasant days with him, I wouldn't believe much of what he said, either, but on this, he wasn't lying." I narrowed my eyes. "Was he the one who put you up to luring me out with some crap about my father needing help?"

His expression went blank. "I don't know what you're talking about."

"I see." I sipped my latte. I didn't bother giving them something to drink. It seemed cruel since they couldn't move their arms.

"How does this work? How are we here?"

"You have the wrong idea. You don't ask the questions. You are my hostages." I shrugged. "I'm just having a little pick me up—" I lifted the cup and took a longer swallow of the cooling drink "—until someone comes along and ties up your bodies."

"Our bodies." April glanced at Jasper. "What's she talking about?"

"I don't know."

"Then let me clarify that one point. I know you feel like you're in your own body." I moved my arms around and then slammed my fist on the table, making my cup jostle in the saucer. Both of my guests jumped. "But we're not really here. Our bodies are lying in the hallway, completely defenseless."

"So if my vampires find us first?" Jasper asked.

I lifted a shoulder. "It's doubtful. But should that happen, we'll appear asleep. I imagine they'll drag us off and probably tie me up as a prize for Venizi." The thought made me shudder, but that wasn't going to happen, not even if they were playing with guns.

Before he could respond, Jasper disappeared.

April startled. "Where'd he go?"

I smiled. "I think the cavalry arrived."

April yelped before disappearing.

I finished my latte, wiped my lips, and returned to the hallway.

When I opened my eyes, Devon was staring down at me, a grim grin on his face. He pulled me up.

"I'd tell you how impressed I am by your solution to Jasper with a gun, but Simone is in trouble."

That dropped my smile and plunged me into dread. I glanced around and saw two members of Team Four walking April and Jasper out, both with their hands zip-tied behind them.

I raced with Devon down the hall, then the stairs, and through the house to the kitchen.

All of Team Three was there, in addition to Lucas, Ginger, Madame Saldano, and one of the blood donors. The kitchen was painted in blood, and as I followed Devon as he pushed his way through, I noted the two dead vamps. No. Make that three dead vamps that had been piled next to the stove.

Simone was deathly pale. Blood smeared the side of her head, and she lay in a pool of congealing crimson. It was difficult to get anything more than glimpses because Madame Saldano kept moving between her medical bag, a tray of what appeared to be surgical instruments, and Simone.

"What's her status?" Devon moved Lucas out of the way and grabbed Simone's hand. I didn't see her grip back.

Then Ginger was next to me, her arm around my waist and her head on my shoulder.

"She's alive." Madame Saldano shook her head. "You have Ginger to thank for that, but she's unresponsive."

I glanced down at Ginger and noticed the blood smear on her arm. Lucas was focused on Simone, but I understood what had happened. Ginger must have fed Simone, and Lucas healed her cut. I put my arm around Ginger, and we hugged each other, neither of us able to tear our gaze away from Simone.

"The problem is the bullet. It was silver. Her body, as you know, instinctively pushed to expel it. If it had been any other organ, the damage wouldn't be a problem, but in the brain? The bullet could have created more harm exiting than entering." She shrugged. "I believe she will recover, and with the right medication and time, her brain should repair itself."

"What aren't you saying?" Devon demanded.

"The brain is a strange thing, even for vampires. I don't know if there will be lasting side effects from this. Memories, knowledge, motor skills, anything and everything the brain controls could repair itself differently. If it had been a lead bullet, the body would have expelled it more slowly. I'm not saying she wouldn't still be in a critical condition, but vampire bodies push silver out faster as a defense mechanism. In the brain, that tends to do more harm than good."

She's alive. She's alive. My mantra was the only thing keeping me from screaming.

"Does she require more donor blood?" Devon asked.

"Not yet. She received enough that her arm is almost healed.

The brain takes longer to recover. I'd prefer a few medications before attempting more blood. But Michael will stay with us for when the time comes." She stood with Devon's help. "We need to move her to a place where she can remain until she heals."

"Of course." Devon nodded to Lucas. "We'll take her to her room at the manor." He glanced at the human standing next to the kitchen island. "Michael, you'll stay at the manor for now, if that's alright."

Michael bowed his head. "Yes, absolutely."

Devon picked Simone up as if she weighed nothing, and Team Three made a path for them. I stayed to help Madame Saldano pack up, but she shook her head. "I have two others to see to first."

Ginger and I held onto each other as we followed Lucas out of the house to an even wilder scene in the front yard.

All the SUVs had been brought into the driveway. Devon was laying Simone in the back of one, and one of the Team Three members climbed in after her before the door was shut. Devon hit his fist on the back of the SUV, and it took off just as Roxie's van pulled up. One other car followed, which would be Harlow with Trudy, Jamal, and Russell.

Sergi jumped out of the van and ran to Devon. "How's Simone?"

"She's alive but unresponsive. We won't know more until she wakes. What do you have to report?"

By then, the leads from all the teams arrived except for Decker, and a vamp appeared to be standing in for him. When I surveyed what at first appeared to be a chaotic scene, it wasn't as disorganized as I first thought.

To my far left was a stack of bodies. I assumed dead enemy vamps. Not far from them were two vamps from Team Five, who monitored three enemy survivors in zip ties—April, Jasper, and another vamp I didn't recognize. To the far right was another small group of a shirtless Elijah, a naked Rachel sitting on the ground with a jacket around her shoulders, and a red wolf. That would be

Decker. Why was he still in wolf form? I couldn't tell from where I stood, but his fur appeared matted. Two other vamps from Team Six remained close.

"All teams have reported in," Sergi responded to Devon's question. "We have four injured, including one of the shifters. All of the enemy combatants have been accounted for, the best we can tell. Three remain alive."

"What do you mean the best you can tell?" Devon's fear for Simone had been pushed aside, and he was growing irritated. I would have gone to him, but Ginger was still clinging to me, and Devon didn't need his girlfriend to help him with the aftermath, even if I'd been the mission leader.

"The wolves were chasing down two vampires when one shot Rachel. Elijah and Decker didn't take that well. Let's just say it would take too much time to put the body parts back together, so we're doing a head count." Sergi couldn't help but grin at his macabre joke.

I took a closer look at the front yard and turned my head away. There were definitely body parts in the yard, and while I wasn't sure I'd eat anytime soon, I had to give the wolves credit. I hadn't been sure how well they'd work in a real battle when lives were on the line. The skirmish at Oasis hadn't been the best testing ground. Now I knew.

"Get a clean-up crew here. I want it to look like Willa and April simply left."

Sergi nodded. "Bella and Jacques took Willa back to the manor. She woke up and was disoriented and combative." He glanced to where I stood, then turned back to Devon. "Bella gave her a sleeping aid, and they're watching her. What do you want to do with the three we kept alive?"

"Take Jasper and the other vampire to the coastal safe house." He gave it another minute thought, then added, "Take April there for now. Keep them separate and in chains, except for April. Make sure she's comfortable and has food, but she needs to remain confined. I'll decide what to do with her after I speak with Cressa and Willa. I also want all cell phones, tablets, and computers you can find brought to the manor. Let's see if they're the ones who've been texting Cressa. We'll also retain Roxie's security codes on the house and gates. No one comes or goes without your knowledge and approval."

Sergi nodded and strode away, issuing orders to the team leads.

Devon waved for me. Ginger and Lucas followed.

"Get in the lead SUV. I want to do a quick check on the injured, and then we'll be on our way." He strode toward Elijah, and I waited as they shook hands. Devon squatted next to Rachel and placed a hand on her shoulder.

She nodded and gave him a weak smile before Devon nodded at the red wolf who sat on its haunches, his tongue hanging out. Decker wasn't going to leave her side anytime soon.

Lucas helped Ginger into the back seat of the SUV while I climbed into the passenger seat.

This whole night had been a fiasco. My plans were a sham, and Simone might never be the same. I didn't realize I was crying until Devon got in the driver's seat and wiped a tear from my cheek.

"Simone will be fine. We didn't lose anyone. We have your mother, sister, Jasper, and data to sift through. This was a successful mission."

I wiped my eyes. "This was a cluster fuck."

He shook his head. "All the teams performed as they should have. From what little Team Three was able to tell me, the bullet Simone took was a freak accident. We'll know more once we get a few hours sleep. Don't beat yourself up. It might appear messier than we expected, but it worked as planned."

When I didn't respond, he turned my face to meet his icy blue gaze. "If they were guarding April and Willa with guns, they have something they're hiding. It's just a matter of time before we know what it is. I know you're worried about Simone. So am I. But she'd be the first to say this was a success. The same goes for Sergi."

I snorted. "I didn't hear him say that."

He laughed as he started the vehicle. "After hundreds of campaign battles, I know a thing or two about Sergi. He might be what you call OCD, and I agree he's always been a tidy man, but when it comes to battles, he likes them messy. If he's irritated, it's only because he had to watch from the sidelines."

Chapter Thirty-One

I HADN'T REALIZED I'd fallen asleep until Devon opened the door, and I fell into his arms. "I don't know why I'm so sleepy."

"The dream construct must have sapped your strength. Maybe you should drink a glass of Colantha's juice the next time we go on a mission."

"I did."

His lips skimmed my ear, his voice too low for anyone else to hear. "Perhaps the emotions of the evening have simply caught up. You're not invincible, you know."

"Says you." I could have stayed in his arms until he carried me to bed, but that wasn't going to happen. Not tonight. "Put me down. I'm not returning home from a mission with you carrying me."

He chuckled as he released my legs, but he kept his arm around me. "You know, just because you're coming home without being drenched in blood or sporting a physical injury, you risked a lot by dreamwalking in an unsecured environment. You were lucky I was the first one in that hallway rather than one of Jasper's vampires. I would hate to think what I would have found."

I turned to him, understanding his concern and his fear. After the evening we'd had, he didn't deserve one of my platitudes. "All I saw was that gun. He was going to shoot me, and I wasn't sure if the armored vest would be enough. I could have returned us sooner than I did, but I knew you'd be there. I didn't question it."

He leaned his forehead against mine. "I'll always be there."

"Are you going to continue to make dove eyes at each other or come in and update me on the mission?" The Wolf stared down at us, his arms crossed in front of his chest.

"Not that it isn't good to see you, but why are you here?" Devon asked. "I know you're concerned about your wolves, but they're fine, and they'll be here soon."

"I've already heard from Elijah. Thanks to your healer, Rachel's injury to her leg is almost healed. She'll have full motion once she returns to training." He ran a hand over the back of his neck, his expression turning rueful. "I'm sorry for the mess they left behind. The wolves, well, once they're in wolf form and one of their own is attacked in such a cowardly fashion, they tend to hunt on instinct."

Devon shook his head. "What happened to the days of swords and hand-to-hand combat? When you looked your enemy in the eye? When you knew you were taking a life? Now we kill people with drones, never seeing their faces."

"We have made war more civilized." He paused, seeming to lament how easy war had become. Then he clapped his hands. "Enough of that for now. I have much to show you, but I realize this might not be the best time. Though, I'm not sure how long it can wait."

Devon turned to watch another SUV drive up. "We'll need a few hours rest. Can I offer you a room until then?"

"He's already been given a room, brother." Lyra stepped out with Colantha behind her.

Colantha was holding a glass of juice and handed it to me after I dragged myself up the steps. "Drink it all, and don't ask questions."

"How did you know I'd need this?"

She rolled her eyes. "I just said don't ask questions, and it's the first words out of your mouth. Drink, and we'll talk after you've slept at least four hours." Then she turned and touched Remus's arm. "We have more to discuss while they rest."

Remus nodded. "I'll be in as soon as I see to my wolves."

I drank the juice as we entered the manor and turned for the hall to return the glass to the kitchen when Devon took it from my hand and gave it to Lyra.

"Do you mind?"

Lyra laughed and took the empty glass. "Not at all. I need to talk to Cook about a late breakfast. We've been up all night waiting to hear about the mission. I think a hearty meal will be in order once we've all rested."

I almost made it to the second floor but missed the last step. Devon instantly lifted me into his arms and turned for my room. I wrapped my arms around his neck and laid my head against his shoulder, unable to keep my eyes open. The juice should have restored my energy.

I lifted my head, but it fell back. "Damn her. She drugged me." My eyes, apparently with a mind of their own, refused to stay open.

His breath was warm against my forehead. "You should have known better. She knew you dreamwalked."

"Yeah." My voice was sleepy. "She must have been checking on me."

Devon sat me on the bed, and I fell back as he removed my shoes and clothing. He repositioned me on the bed so my head hit the pillow. His kiss was soft against my lips before he threw a blanket over me.

"We need to talk," I managed to slur. We needed to settle things between us.

"Soon."

Devon shut down his computer and swiveled his chair to stare out at the early dawn, the sun's rays barely touching the tips of the sycamore tree. He leaned back and closed his eyes. A blood donation had revitalized him, but there was still so much to do.

Once he'd put Cressa to bed, he checked on Simone, who was still unresponsive. He stopped by Rachel's room next, where he found Elijah.

"I just wanted to check on her."

Elijah rubbed his face, and his eyes were shadowed. "She was overly feisty and refused to settle down." If Devon had to guess—and based on his own experience with the vampires in his Family—Elijah was probably as irritated as he was proud of his beta. "I had to call in Remus. Then I asked the healer to give her a sleeping potion."

Devon chuckled. "She's not one to typically give a sleeping potion to someone who simply refuses to rest."

Elijah's smile was slow. "She changed her mind after Rachel scratched her."

"That would do it. Let me know if you need anything. And thank you again for your help."

"I'll remember that if my pack ever needs a hand."

Devon shook his hand. "Any time."

When he returned to his office and met with the blood donor, he checked on other Family business. After finding nothing that couldn't wait, he took a moment for himself. He must have nodded off because the knock startled him.

"Do you need more time?" Sergi asked.

"No. Just resting." Devon turned back to the office.

Sergi dropped into his usual chair and shuffled through the folder of paperwork. "I've taken a quick glance over the files Harlow pulled from Underwood's mansion. I need to read them more thoroughly, and I haven't opened the computer or tablets we confiscated, but I think we'll have enough to tie Underwood, April, and Jasper to Venizi." He lifted his gaze to Devon's. "I did check the phones, one of which was a burner. We have the Rasmussen texts that were sent to Cressa."

"As we expected. At least that's one issue resolved."

"I'm curious why they delayed so long between responses." Sergi sat back and rubbed his chin. "The best I can come up with was that they were running Cressa's responses through Venizi."

Devon walked to the espresso machine. "That makes sense. Do you want one?"

"Please."

A knock on the door brought the rest of the cadre. Once Devon returned to his chair and took a sip of the espresso, he nodded to Lucas to begin the reports.

"Everyone on the mission has received another blood donation." Lucas opened his tablet and reviewed it. "We only have a handful of donors who can donate in an emergency until the others have rested."

"What about for Simone?" he asked.

Lucas shook his head. "Michael gave her some blood, and Madame Saldano said that was sufficient for now. She wants to see how her potions do before any more blood is given."

"I'm not expecting any more raids unless Venizi has another surprise for us. I doubt anyone had time to contact him once the fighting started, but either way, he'll need to regroup. If we need blood, we can ask our human staff for small donations. See that Madame Saldano provides elixirs for the donors to help rebuild their blood. And no work for them, even if they feel up to it."

Lucas nodded.

"I'll also need you at Oasis to monitor security and see if there's anything pressing. And take Ginger with you. I'd like her to work with the human staff and extend their training. Let's make sure the shifters, especially the new ones, are introduced to the entire Family. After tonight's experience with the wolves, let's make sure our rogues know who they're guarding."

He turned to Bella. "Where's Willa?"

"She's in the room next to Cressa's. According to the healer, who, by the way, could use some rest of her own, Willa has been heavily medicated rather than mesmerized. But she won't know for sure until the drugs are out of her system. We also don't know what kind of drugs were used, but we could go back to the mansion and look for them."

"Duly noted on the healer needing rest," Devon replied. "Let's hold off going to the mansion. The cleaners are finishing up. Let's see if they find anything. Did Madame Saldano give any indication of when Willa might wake?"

Bella shook her head. "She gave her a potion that should help ease her out of the medication." She leaned against the coffee bar. "Time will tell. I can monitor her until Cressa wakes."

Devon nodded. "In case anyone asks—especially Cressa—April, Jasper, and the other surviving vampire were taken to the coastal safe house. Interrogations on the vampires have already started. Sergi and I will go over later this afternoon. I was informed April has undergone an initial examination by the healer and then sedated. It's been confirmed that she'd been mesmerized and probably over a long period. It will be a difficult recovery. Madame Saldano has an interesting idea on a path to recovery, but we'll wait for Cressa and Willa before we discuss it. Anything else?"

With nothing left to report, the group left. Devon finished his notes from the meeting then turned to stare at the sycamore. It was time to see what Remus brought him.

DEVON FOUND Remus in the library, and he closed the doors behind him. Locks weren't required in the manor. If doors that were usually kept open were closed, it was for a reason, and no one intruded—except for cadre in cases of an emergency.

Remus sat in a far corner in one of Devon's mother's favorite wing-backed chairs. A stack of papers Devon knew to be the *De første dage* translations sat on the cherrywood table positioned between the chairs. Remus reviewed a page before turning to the next. A manila folder sat next to the stack, which was most likely the lab results. Next to that was a decanter of an amber liquid with two accompanying glasses, one of which was partially filled.

"How many times have you read it?" Devon took a seat opposite him at the table.

"This is the fourth, not counting my review of the original text." Remus sat back, refilled his glass and poured another one that he slid to Devon.

"A bit early for scotch, isn't it?"

"After reading this and what I've seen of the lab results, it's never too early." Remus slid the folder toward Devon.

He let it sit. "What do you make of Colantha's thoughts on the two languages and the Blood Poppy?"

Remus savored a sip as he considered the question. "I've tried reading the translation from a number of views, but it all comes down to the same thing. The exchange between vampiric to Drakrotian is smooth, as if someone picked up a pen and simply carried on with the information, just in their own language. I assume the two languages were a built-in safety mechanism to ensure both sides understood it was both species who wrote and agreed to this. I would have preferred signed signatures so we had the names of the authors."

"Or a House or Tribal symbol."

"Perhaps they're in the original book and no one understood the importance."

"I'll have Lucas reach out to Philipe or Fiona and have them take a look. We could only hope. I agree it would give more credence to the text."

"As far as the Blood Poppy, I'd agree with her assessment."

Devon wasn't surprised, but it still created a mix of emotions —fear and hope. Then, anger pushed everything else away. He pulled the folder close and flipped it open. He spent the next fifteen minutes reviewing graphs and the researcher's summations.

"I don't understand. This shows that the marker that was in Cressa's blood, the marker we associated with the dreamwalker species, matches one of the markers in the three samples Aramburu supplied." He scanned the graphs again. "How is this possible? It also appears similar to the results from the Blood Poppy. So is this marker dreamwalker or Blood Poppy?" He also noted but didn't mention, that the Magic Poppy results reflected a mere blip of the same marker.

"My researcher was beside himself with ecstatic enthusiasm. I don't see that often in vampires." Remus chuckled as he stacked the translation into a neat stack. "He was already comparing the results of the blood work with his work on the decline of vampire fertility rates. He can't be sure, but at first glance, he's seeing a correlation. But whether that has to do with dreamwalker blood or the Blood Poppy, without deeper analysis of this particular marker, he can't make a final determination."

Devon wanted to punch something. How much of this did Venizi know? He, like Sergi and the cadre, believed Lorenzo was behind the Magic Poppy, but considering the other revelations, further investigation on that could wait.

"Have you spoken to Colantha about this? I know you've spent time with her on your visits here."

Remus finished his drink. "No. We've mostly discussed the translations and what she knew of shifters during those times. And before you ask, she has little knowledge of shifters. She believes the dreamwalkers didn't condone what the vampires were doing, keeping us enslaved, but her species were fighting for their own survival."

"Cressa mentioned that an orange potion she received from

the healer at Aramburu's compound tasted similar to Colantha's juice. I think it's time to understand why that is."

"If we could get some of that juice, we could test it." Though Remus's comments were conciliatory, the yellow glaze of wolf shone through.

"But if we're all truly partners in this?"

"Then she would simply reveal the truth."

Devon nodded. "She's been cagey from the start. I understand why. Their species is more threatened than either of ours."

"Then, perhaps it's time to ask her."

RATHER THAN HAVE someone search the manor for where Colantha might be, Devon led Remus to Lyra's room. Lyra had taken a liking to Colantha, and perhaps she could provide a balance between the parties. He didn't think Colantha was fearful of him or Remus, but it wouldn't take her long to pull them into a construct if she felt threatened. Besides, it felt right to include Lyra.

Devon knocked on the door and waited.

"Come in, brother. And Remus is also welcome."

Remus lifted a brow, and Devon shook his head. "Don't ask. I don't know how she knows."

Remus grinned and nodded as he followed Devon in. Devon wasn't surprised to find his sister on the divan facing the western windows as the sun lit the ocean. Nor was he surprised to find Colantha sitting next to her.

Frederick was placing a pot of tea and two cups on the low table in front of them. Jamison stood against the eastern window, hands behind his back. Colantha's guards were on duty as usual.

"Were either of you surprised by our visit?" Devon asked as he took a chair next to the sofa while Remus took the one across from him.

Colantha chuckled. "I'm not a mind reader. I was here to facilitate a dreamwalk with Hamilton. But this is the next logical step."

"I thought Hamilton was able to create his own constructs." Devon eyed Lyra, but she didn't seem upset. In fact, she had that dreamy look whenever she thought of Hamilton.

"He can, but he wanted to try without his medallion. A test, if you will, of his growing powers as he heals."

"And?"

"He's able to call us into his construct, but he's not capable of controlling those he brings in."

Remus shifted in his seat, crossing a leg over his knee, appearing comfortable, but Devon sensed he wasn't anywhere near settled. "And this is something you're striving for?"

Colantha chuckled. "Not normally, no. But we're preparing for war, are we not? From what I've been told, Cressa created a construct during last night's raid to save herself from a bullet. And, no, I haven't spoken with her—she's still sleeping—but I felt her presence in the Nexus. I didn't know why until I read Sergi's preliminary report, which he shared with me."

She sipped her tea and appeared to be formulating her next words. "What if Cressa hadn't been wearing her medallion? Would she have been able to call forth a construct to save herself? I don't think so. She has the power but not the training."

Devon considered this, and while he agreed and understood the need, something wasn't connecting. "When Cressa was in Spain, she said she was able to override the dreamwalkers who'd created the construct."

"To a point, yes." Colantha leaned forward, her gaze bright. "And that's the perfect first step. But she didn't create the construct. Someone else was holding it together. She used her power, and I imagine her anger, which we know is a powerful stimulus, to take over. That only happened because the dreamwalkers were weak. She'd mentioned she'd felt several dreamwalkers holding the construct together.

"It happens at my training compound all the time. Most dreamwalkers only have the power for a simple construct, typically with a location they're already familiar with, and only bring one or two other dreamwalkers to it. In order to build something more complex or have more people included, the dreamwalkers must pool together. If one weakens, so does the construct.

"This is something I need Hamilton and Cressa to practice together. Both must be able to defend themselves should they not have their medallion or if it's taken from them. Hamilton's life would have been quite different if he'd had that skill when Venizi took him from this House."

Devon sat back, absorbing her words. It tracked with what he'd learned before from Cressa and Colantha.

"But that's not what you came here for," she continued. "I suspect Remus has lab results to share."

That broke Devon out of his musings, and he smiled. "You have an uncanny ability for someone who doesn't read minds."

"You're both logical men. Nothing more is required."

Remus chuckled and leaned over to hand her the folder. Lyra scooted closer to Colantha to read over her shoulder. Devon was surprised when Frederick handed him and then Remus an espresso. He'd been so enthralled with Colantha's additional explanations into dreamwalker psyche he hadn't heard the espresso machine.

Fifteen minutes went by before she handed the folder to Lyra to peruse. "I suspect you want to know about the similar markers between Cressa's blood, the Aramburu samples, and the Blood Poppy."

"It does seem some explanation is in order." Remus sipped his espresso, looking all the more like a college professor than the leader of the shifters. "Especially since Devon's blood only reflected the marker after taking Cressa's blood to put the beast to rest."

She nodded as she considered his words. "You have questions regarding the juice."

Devon was no longer surprised by her ability to know where the conversation was headed. And now that she stated the summation rather succinctly, it was apparent the juice must play some part in everything.

She refilled her teacup and added a sugar cube she hadn't added before. When she noticed Remus and him watching, she shrugged. "I'm diabetic. My vampires monitor what food I eat, what I drink, and how often I consume the juice." She slid her bodyguards a glance with a sweet smile. "Worse than mother hens, but they only have my best interest at heart. I believe this discussion allows me some discretion."

She stirred the tea and leaned back. "I'm not a scientist, but based on the lab results, I would say the marker you're seeing is definitely the Blood Poppy. And yes, the juice has Blood Poppy in it. Not in a large amount, but in combination with other herbs meant to strengthen the mind and focus our natural mental energy."

It was beginning to make sense, but Remus spoke first.

"This is what you explained about the Blood Poppy being the bringer of life. It's the missing piece to the vampire's fertility."

She nodded. "And dreamwalkers as well, as it turns out. However, we didn't know for sure until the vampires destroyed most of the poppy fields. Our own birth rates dropped except for those Tribes who still had access to the Blood Poppy. Isn't it strange that the vampire and dreamwalker species both require the Blood Poppy for its survival as a race, yet the shifters don't?"

"It seems that makes the shifters more kin to humans," Remus offered.

"Or another species without the dependencies," Colantha agreed.

"You said the juice was addictive." Devon sat forward, remembering the taste of it and Cressa's withdrawal symptoms.

"It's quite addictive. That's why I only use the bare minimum of Blood Poppy and why the juice can't be drunk for long intervals."

"I've suspected that Magic Poppy was derived from the Blood Poppy, yet there doesn't seem to be much evidence to support that theory based on the lab results."

"I noticed that." Colantha set down her teacup. "I agree the two are linked, but we need a sample of the Magic Poppy to validate those assumptions. Something else would have to have been added to the Blood Poppy. That alone, regardless of the amount, wouldn't create madness in a vampire or force the beast to take control. There must be other chemicals involved."

Remus ran a hand through this hair. "There were other unidentifiable markers in the blood sample of Devon's beast. They could be anything. I agree we need a sample of the Magic Poppy to determine any connection to the Blood Poppy."

"We need to find Venizi's lab." Devon was positive all the answers were there.

"That was something I wanted to share with you," Remus said. "We have a strong lead regarding the lab, and I've sent a team to investigate."

Chapter Thirty-Two

I SLIPPED ON MY JEANS, a sleeveless blouse, and sneakers and ran out the door, surprised it was almost time for lunch. It wasn't that I didn't need the sleep, but there was too much going on to sleep half the day away, even if we hadn't returned to the manor until almost dawn.

I found Letty coming out of the room next door. It had been empty since I first came to the manor.

"Oh, Miss Cressa, I was just dropping off some food for Jacques. Your mother is still asleep."

My mother. Devon must have put her there so I could be close to her. "Thank you, Letty. I just woke up and wasn't sure where she was."

Letty nodded and moved down the hall with a spring in her step. The house was crowded with vampires, humans, and shifters. Cook must have the kitchen staff hopping. It wasn't often they got to show off their skills.

I was shaking my head when I gave the door a light tap and then entered.

Jacques wiped his mouth from what looked like a bite of a

roast beef sandwich. "Sorry, I hope you don't mind. I haven't eaten since yesterday's lunch."

"Don't you eat more often, or did the blood donation curb your appetite? I've always wondered and never seem to remember to ask Devon. He always ensures Cook provides three meals a day."

Jacques wiped his hands and picked up a baked potato chip. Baked chips were the only kind Cook allowed in the manor. "The three meals are more a way to bring us together as a Family. I haven't decided whether Cook is happy with that or not."

"Why's that?" I glanced at Mom, who appeared to be sleeping peacefully. It was an improved condition from how we'd originally found her.

"We never know who will be around for the meals, so Cook has to make meals based on who he thinks might be there. He could plan his own menus, then everyone either eats what's served or not. But you know how he is. He wants to please everyone and surprise them with their favorites."

I laughed. "Like my blueberry scones."

He grinned and bit off the end of a pickle. "Exactly."

"Has she stirred at all?"

"I've only been here an hour. We're taking four-hour shifts. Bella said she's been in the same position as when they put her in the bed. Madame Saldano gave her one of her potions that should calm her mind, even in sleep. Now it's just a matter of waiting for the drugs to leave her system."

That explained her peaceful appearance.

"I want to check on Simone and April, then I'll relieve you."

He shrugged. "No worries."

I stepped closer and took Mom's hand. It was warm, and though she didn't squeeze back, it was enough to see her so serene. She hadn't had much tranquility over the years, and while Christopher had caused most of her grief, I hadn't been the best daughter. That was going to change. Starting now.

I was out the door but didn't know where to go. I stuck my

head in the room. "I guess I should ask where Simone and April are."

"Simone's on the third floor. Second door on the right."

"A room without a view?"

"She likes her room dark. I think it's a holdover from her youth. She won't say it, but I think the darkness comforts her." He gave me a steady look before continuing. "April is at the safe house under guard. You'll need to speak to Devon before going over. It's for everyone's safety until they determine how deep the mesmerizing is."

I frowned. I'd expected as much, but it felt worse when it was confirmed.

"Sorry, I guess you didn't know."

"I suspected. I was hoping I was wrong. If I remember correctly from when Lorenzo was mesmerizing me, at some point, the mesmerizing can't be reversed." When Jacques appeared to be preparing his statement, I got angry. "Just spit it out. No one needs to tiptoe around me. I can't prepare myself if people aren't honest with me."

He raised in hands in defense. "That doesn't mean it can't be phrased gently."

I ran a hand over my face. "Of course not. I'm sorry."

"Not a problem. In most cases, it's extremely difficult to erase long-term mesmerizing. But we don't know how long or often she's been mesmerized. Madame Saldano is convinced she's had some mesmerizing. However, if your sister believed she was doing the right thing, perhaps something her father had convinced her of, it's possible not much mesmerizing was required. We also don't know the depth of feelings she has for Jasper, which could explain some of her actions."

"Affections for Jasper?" I'd assumed it was all mesmerizing.

Jacques laughed. "You're not judging her for dating a vampire, are you?"

I gave him an exaggerated look with an added eye roll for good measure. "Haha. While my stepfather might have been sleeping around with vamps, somehow, I don't think he'd approve of April dating one." A hysterical laugh slipped out. "I can't imagine what he would have said, or my mother for that matter, with both daughters dating vamps."

"I know what my father would have said had his sons been dating humans."

We both chuckled. "Thank you, Jacques. Not just for now, but for taking care of Mom during the mission."

"We always protect mothers, even vampires."

I winked before closing the door and racing up the stairs to the third floor.

I WASN'T EXPECTING to see two guards at Simone's door.

"Mateo." I nodded to the other guard who I didn't know. "Is it okay if I go in?"

"Yes. Madame Saldano is with her, but as far as I know, she hasn't woken yet."

I nodded solemnly and took a deep breath before entering. The room was as dark as Jacques claimed. The walls were a deep burgundy. That part was easy to tell from the dozens of lit candles scattered around the room. With the mirrors adorning the walls, it seemed more like hundreds. A desk lamp was lit where the healer had laid out her array of colorful potions. Some I recognized, most I didn't have a clue.

"Am I disturbing you?" I glanced at Madame Saldano, who was lighting more candles. While I was afraid to look at Simone, I couldn't help it. I became as distraught as I thought I would, unable to pull my gaze away from the vampire in the bed.

It was a queen-sized bed, and though Simone was tall, she appeared diminished. A single silk sheet that matched the color of the walls covered her to her shoulders. A white bandage, thankfully blood-free, had been wrapped around the top of her head.

"No, child. I'm told Simone likes her candles lit while she meditates. I thought it couldn't hurt."

"That's nice. She always told me to select one candle." I dragged my eyes away from Simone's still form and took a longer perusal of the room. It wasn't as stark as I'd expected. There was a table with two chairs, a resting couch against one wall where a floor lamp with a mosaic shade stood behind it, a single dresser, a small walk-in closet, and a bathroom. A couple of wall paintings and several art pieces completed the room.

It was strange to see so many rooms with bathrooms, like some vintage hotel, but the manor had been built by Devon's father more than a century earlier and was planned to house dozens of vamps. A shared bathroom down the hall wouldn't have cut it.

Two chairs had been pulled next to the bed, and I took the one on the far side. As I had with my mother, I picked up Simone's hand, surprised by its warmth.

"What's the prognosis?" I asked, almost afraid of the answer.

The healer sat in the opposite chair and stared down at her patient. "It's difficult to tell. From what the vampire who'd raced into the kitchen first told me, her legs seemed to go out as soon as she was shot. It might have been from hitting a cabinet wrong when she fell backward. That could mean a spinal problem easily remedied with fresh blood. Or it might be some damage to the brain that impacted her motor skills. However, it seemed to have only affected her lower extremities.

"The bullet pushed out on its own as her body rejected it, so I don't know if further damage occurred. We were able to get more blood into her than what Ginger donated, so she's well-hydrated. I've given her two different potions to help with the healing and one to make her sleep. It's the best way to allow her brain to heal itself."

I nodded, understanding but not liking it. This was the first mission I'd planned where team members had been injured. At least I'd seen Rachel enter the mansion on her own two legs, scowling at the attention she was getting.

"Is there anything we can do?"

"No, child. I'm mixing a couple more potions, and I'll leave instructions with Mateo. I'll return later this evening to check on her and your mother." She turned her attention to me. "There's nothing I can do for your sister at this time. She's still excitable. I've given Rafael a potion to add to her food that should calm her anxiety. My only suggestion is to prepare for a long road." Her gaze softened and her voice filled with compassion. "She might never believe you didn't have something to do with her father's death."

I nodded. I'd expected that, hadn't I? It sounded so wrong when someone else said it. I gave Simone a last glance, suddenly sorry I'd left my room.

MY ORIGINAL PLAN was to search for Devon after my visit with Simone, but now, I wasn't fit to be with anybody. Besides, he'd either be busy wrapping up the mission, planning the next one, or resting. Yep. Lame excuse, but it was what it was.

I'd reached the stairs to rush down to my room when Ginger blocked my path. She stood at the landing, her hands filled with a tray of silver-domed dishes.

Crap. I'd never get past her. I ran through various options to avoid being dragged into Lyra's room. When she noticed me, her grin was wide, then it faltered. Shit.

"Don't even try to get past me. Turn right around."

I didn't move.

"This tray is heavy, and I'd hate to drop it, ruin Cook's food, and waste the effort he put in."

"I have things to do." Yeah, the lameness continued.

"The only thing you have to do is walk to Lyra's room. Colantha's been looking for you, and I'm not joking about how heavy this is."

I sighed and, with my head down, trudged to Lyra's room like some errant child. I knocked lightly, then opened the door to find Jamison blocking my entrance. He moved aside and immediately took the tray from Ginger. He probably heard our entire conversation with those vamp ears.

Once Ginger was tray-free, she pushed me into the room, and I was surprised to see Remus walking the room. He took his time viewing the multitude of Lyra's paintings either hanging from or stacked against the walls.

"I have one over here you might like." Lyra went to a corner and moved a painting aside to pull out one I'd never seen before. There were two wolves—a black one and a gray one. The setting was familiar, but that was as far as my memory went.

"Cressa told me the story of the two wolves that helped her at the paper mill when she went to save Devon from his beast. I wasn't there, of course, so I never saw the wolves. I discovered later it was Elijah and Rachel who helped that day. When Cressa was being held at Shadow Island, Colantha came to assist with the rescue plan. Part of that activity included bringing Cressa to dream constructs to break Lorenzo's mesmerizing. At one point, Cressa took us through several constructs from her returning memories, and that moment at the papermill was one of them. I instantly knew who these wolves were."

Lyra turned around and smiled at me. "I got it right, no?"

I nodded, my tongue suddenly thick. "Yes."

Remus gave me a quick assessment before turning back to Lyra. "Are these for sale?"

She smiled. "I once sold my art at a gallery a very long time ago. Perhaps someday, I'll try again. For now, my paintings are only to be gifted. I would like you to have this one."

Remus appeared truly touched as he ran a hand over the edges of the canvas. "It would be my honor if I could gift this to Elijah's pack."

Lyra nodded at Frederick, who picked up the painting. "It will be waiting for you in the foyer. Now, let's see what Cook sent us."

Colantha patted the couch. "Come, Cressa, sit by me."

This was everything I knew it would be which was why I'd wanted to avoid it.

"Stop moping, it's not a good look."

I couldn't help but chuckle and dropped onto the couch next to her. At some point, I'd stopped expecting her soft side since she rarely showed it. In an attempt to ignore her, I glanced at Remus.

"I'm sorry about Rachel."

"For what?" Remus sat across from me and perused Cook's offerings, selecting a slice of pork sandwich. "She was shot by a vampire with a gun. I believe they used guns in the attack at Oasis. We'll need to be more prepared next time. At least these particular vampires won't be a problem anymore." He popped the sandwich in his mouth.

Ginger snorted. "Not based on the number of body parts left behind." She shivered, then picked up a deviled egg. "God, I just love these."

"I was particularly interested in how Cressa found a way out of being shot herself." Colantha picked up her glass of iced tea, though her eyes grazed the food offerings.

"It was a spur-of-the-moment decision." I heard the hollowness of my words, and while the others glanced at each other, I stared at my hands.

"Exactly. That's why I found it exceptional work." Colantha sipped her tea before setting it down in favor of a strawberry tart. "As a dreamwalker, the instant reflexive action to call upon your powers is exactly what I've been training you and Hamilton for. It's not meant to prevent you from choosing another method of defense, whether it's your martial arts or a dagger, but to give you something else in your arsenal. Martial arts or a dagger won't always help you out of a situation, but your dreamwalking will, assuming you're brave enough and quick enough to create a construct while binding others to it."

I shrugged. "It kind of felt like cheating."

Remus barked out a laugh, brushing his hands from the second slice of sandwich. "In battle, the key is to take down the enemy while staying alive. There are no rules, especially if you find yourself at a disadvantage. Your actions gave your team the time to capture the two people required to complete a successful mission." He didn't appreciate my second shrug and leaned toward me with the fierceness of The Wolf. "I've seen this many times before through the decades, usually from a new Alpha after their first mission, where wolves were injured or killed. No mission is ever safe from injury or death. From what Devon tells me, all your missions before this one have been to steal something. This time, you were in charge of planning a mission. Not to steal some artifact or evidence, but hostage recovery and an enemy capture. You knew there would be fighting, and regardless of how well the teams train for it, no one can plan for every variable. Quite frankly, with the close-quarter fighting in a house where one side had guns, I'm surprised there weren't more injured. No one from House Trelane died. Injured, yes, but not dead. The team retrieved the hostages and captured three enemy combatants. That, my dear Cressa, is a successful mission."

Everything he and Colantha said made sense, but I wasn't ready to release the guilt. Remus seemed to sense it and changed the topic by pulling out a folder. He handed it to Colantha, who passed it to me.

"Those are the results of the blood tests from my lab." He gave me time to review them before explaining the discussion he had with Colantha and Devon.

"Let me make sure I understand." I rubbed my forehead. "You're saying these markers wouldn't have shown up in my blood if I hadn't been drinking Colantha's juice?"

Colantha shrugged. "I'm not aware of any dreamwalker having their blood tested, and it will be difficult to find one who hasn't drunk the juice to know if that's true."

"Perhaps if someone refrained from drinking it for a period of time, we could test the theory," Remus replied. "After the war, we can perform further studies. In the meantime, these lab results will be important when Devon files his case with the Council. But we also need to know what Venizi is doing in his lab."

"He's been studying the declining fertility rate in vampires, right?" I asked.

Remus sipped the iced tea, frowned, and set it down. "He's been studying it for decades. His lab is either inept, or he's hiding the information. Better yet, a look at his labs might expose more than fertility testing."

"You're thinking Magic Poppy," I said.

Jamison handed Remus another glass of iced tea he brought from Lyra's mini kitchen.

Remus tasted it and smiled. "Thank you. Much better. I'm not a fan of peppermint. And yes, that's exactly what we're thinking. I'm hoping to have confirmation of where his lab is located in the next couple of weeks. We're taking it slow, so no one knows we've located it."

"Now, that we got that over with, let's turn to something more exciting." Ginger sat straighter and glanced around. "I think a dinner party is in order. First, for the success of our mission." She picked at the end of her silk scarf, and her excitement faded a bit. "The second reason is somewhat bittersweet. An opportunity came up." She glanced around at the expectant faces. "While Simone is recovering, Devon asked Lucas to fill in for her at Oasis. We'll be leaving in the morning."

"Oh," was all I could say.

Ginger rushed to my side and held my hand. "I know this will be difficult with the lockdown. It's not like we can just drive back and forth to see each other. But Devon can arrange for you to visit once your mom is feeling better."

"Sure." I forced a smile. "That might be good for her." There wasn't a chance in hell he'd let me do that. "Speaking of Devon, where is he?"

Remus stood. "He went to the safe house with Sergi to speak with Jasper and check on April." He nodded at the folder. "That's Devon's copy."

"Are you leaving so soon?" Lyra asked.

Remus chuckled. "I think it's best I move on before I become part of the furniture."

She smiled and placed a hand on his arm. "You know you'll always have a place here. And don't forget your painting."

"Come down and give it to Elijah yourself. It would be better coming from you. He and Rachel will be leaving with me."

Everyone left the room except for Ginger, who grabbed my hand. "Let's make this a movie night."

It took me a moment for her words to sink in. "I told Devon we needed to talk."

"I think that conversation should wait until everything with the mission has settled. And if you don't want to wait that long, you can at least wait until after I'm gone." She tapped the side of my head. "Where I'll be gone for who knows how long." When I didn't respond, she squeezed my hand till it hurt. "It won't be for long. Simone will be up and back to work in no time. Come on, let's go do a little sparring and clear your head. I'll see if Cook can make his famous popcorn medley, and I'll blend up a pitcher or two of margaritas."

She pulled me up and dragged me out the door. And for once, I followed rather than trying to lead.

Chapter Thirty-Three

GINGER and I were on the second floor returning to our rooms when the door to Mom's room popped open.

Jacques stepped out. "I thought I heard you. You saved me a trip to find you. Your mother is waking."

Ginger threw her arm around my shoulders. "That's so good." She stepped back. "But don't forget. Let's grab a light meal on the patio, and then it's off to the bar for margaritas before the movies."

"I won't forget." I blew past Jacques but stopped before entering. Was she still drugged? Would she be mad at being taken from her home? I took a deep breath and stepped across the threshold.

Jacques closed the door, remaining outside.

Mom was sitting up, flipping through a magazine.

"How long have you been awake?" I asked. Jacques made it sound like she'd just opened her eyes.

"Only a few minutes." Her voice was a little hoarse. Maybe from the drugs or from disuse. "That young man was going to get you immediately, but I demanded he tell me where I was before I allowed him to go."

"So, you know you're at Devon Trelane's home?"

She nodded. "And from what I can tell, yours as well."

I nodded in return, then took the chair next to the bed. "I've been living here for almost a year now. Devon and I have—" Have what? That's what we were supposed to be discussing that evening.

Mom finished for me. "An intimate relationship?" She laughed, and it was so good to hear her do that. "Did you think I thought you'd been celibate all this time? I know you don't want to hear it, but your father wasn't the only one I'd slept with before Christopher." She played with the edge of the magazine, dog-earring the page. "I don't know why I said that. I should be drowsy, but this is the most cleared-headed I've been in days."

"The healer, Madame Saldano, gave you something to help calm your mind while the drugs worked their way out."

"Well, that explains it. Though I'm not sure I'm a hundred percent yet." She glanced at the drapes.

"Do you want me to open them?"

"Not yet. I feel a bit of a headache. Where's April?"

"She's at Devon's safe house. She needs more time to acclimate."

That sounded lame to my ears, but Mom nodded.

"Yes. I believe that vampire mesmerized her. That's what you call it, right?"

I nodded. "It might be a long and difficult road for her, but Devon will make sure you're both cared for."

"Oh, honey. I'm so sorry." Mom threw her arms around me. "By the time I figured out what was going on, it was too late. They started drugging me, and when they caught me on the phone with you, they must have given me a heavier dose because I don't remember much after that before now."

I hugged her tight. "There's nothing to be sorry for."

"It's been awful."

"It's over now. It's all behind you."

"I'm not talking about the last few weeks. I mean since I married Christopher."

Her statement confused me for a second, then all the history between us instantly faded. My life had been tough, but hers had to be worse when she finally saw Christopher for who he was. I locked eyes with her, so she'd know I was being truthful. "That's behind us, too."

She gripped me tight enough to squeeze the air out of me. I sucked it up and let her cry. When she was done, she wiped her eyes and looked around.

"Let me get you a tissue." I ran to the bathroom, grabbed the box, and dropped it next to her. After she dried her nose, she asked, "Now what?"

"It will depend on April. Devon wants to wait to see how much of the mesmerizing will fade on its own. Until then, you stay here with me. April isn't that far away. I'll ask Devon when we can see her."

Before she could say anymore, the door opened, and Madame Saldano marched in. Jacques followed and shrugged an apology. All I could do was smile. No one stopped the healer when she was seeing patients.

"Well, good afternoon. I see our patient is awake." She set down her bag, removed several vials, then turned her sights on my mother. "I'm Madame Saldano, and I'm your healer. You look rather spunky for someone who's been drugged for the last few weeks."

Mom placed a hand to her throat. "Has it been that long?"

"From what Devon tells me." The healer glanced at me. "I just came from the safe house. He said April only seemed willing to share the information so we could properly treat your mother."

At least April still cared about Mom. I nodded.

"I'd like the room now. I want to examine your mother so I can determine the next steps. Then she needs to rest." She raised her hand as if ready to defend her position, though no one seemed ready to argue. "I know you feel good, Willa, but your body has been through quite a lot. I've asked Cook to make a broth for you, then you can have something more substantial this evening. You still need bed rest." She glanced at the magazine Mom held and then at the stack of books and tablet on the table. "It appears you have enough entertainment to keep you busy until tomorrow, and then I'll reassess your activity level." She turned to me. "Out. Now. You can visit her in a couple of hours."

I backed away, not daring to question her.

"Cressa, do you have my phone by any chance? I'd like to call the girls and then check in with the salon and spa."

"I'll have to see if Devon recovered it. If not, you can use mine." I glanced around and found her travel bag on a chair. I opened the side pocket. "Here's your phone book." I laid it on top of the tablet.

She nodded.

I went to the door, but before I left, I asked, "What are you going to tell the girls?"

"That I've been suffering from a horrible migraine attack and stomach flu and that I'm irritated with April for not telling them." She gave me a grin I rarely ever saw. One of those mischievous, she's going to do something completely out of character smiles. "At least it has a spark of truth. Right now, I could wring April's neck."

I left her room, feeling lighter than I had in days. When I heard the light steps behind me, I sighed. Something told me I was about to be derailed from good old-fashioned alone time.

Sergi's tone was light and his expression unreadable, which doused my good mood with dread. "Devon would like to see you in his office."

I FOLLOWED Sergi to Devon's office. When he turned down the hall that led to his office, I stopped and stared after him. He'd said Devon's office, hadn't he?

"Devon's office," he called back as if he heard me.

So, Sergi was just the messenger. Curious, I increased my pace to Devon's office and tapped on his door. I'd barely opened it when Devon said, "Come in."

He was at his desk, writing with his fountain pen on what looked like his more expensive linen stationery. "I'll be with you in a minute."

I stood patiently, arms crossed over my chest. One hip might have been stuck out as if I was in a mood, but my grin was wide. He had no idea who'd walked into his office. For such an observant vamp, he had one huge blind spot. I was convinced it had to do with his fountain pen. As forward-thinking as he was, he loved the tactile feel of years gone by. His primary mode of communication was either email or text with the occasional phone call. But to impart important events or to correspond with certain people, he hand-wrote letters. I'd seen him write dozens without a single blemish or blotch of ink. And while he wrote, he seemed momentarily transported to a different time, as if he lived inside a snow globe. If he'd been typing out an email or text, he would have glanced up the moment the door opened. I found it endearing.

He signed his name then set the letter aside before capping the fountain pen and returning it to its special holder made of cherrywood and brass. Then he finally looked up.

"Cressa! Why didn't you say something?" He noted my grin and smiled.

"You know I love watching you write."

He pushed the chair away from the desk and turned it sideways, waving me over. It was going to be that kind of meeting. Suddenly, I didn't mind losing out on my alone time.

I walked around the desk, and my grin turned wicked when he patted his lap. "Should I lock the door?"

"I wish there was time for that."

I sat on his lap, my back against his chest, and he twirled the chair so we could look out the window. I laid my head on his shoulder and stared at the branches of the sycamore tree.

"I'm sorry to send Sergi to find you. I had a few letters that need to be sent immediately and have several more emails to write before going back to the safe house."

"You're having success?"

"Not really, but I've discovered over the centuries that intense pressure the first few days goes a long way to loosen lips. It doesn't always work. Jasper will be tough, but I'm sure his friend will break, and that might be enough. But it doesn't leave much time between our sessions." When I shivered, he added, "It's not torture. At least, not yet. It's more annoyance than anything."

"But you need to cancel our evening plans."

"I heard your mother is awake and feeling better than we expected."

I hadn't been prepared for the change of subject. "Yes. I just came from there. She looks much better, but still tired."

"Did Ginger tell you about Oasis?" Again with the subject change.

"Yes." The word was drawn out, and he squeezed me before shifting topics again.

"Sergi has high hopes for Kirk. That's the other vampire."

I laughed. "Kirk. He sounds like a kid with a skateboard."

"He looks about the same age. He tries to be tough, but he's terrified."

"Enough you might be able to flip him to our side?"

I felt his shrug. "Sergi believes so."

So that meant he did, too. "But you need to spend a lot of time with him."

"Yes." He kissed my temple. "Always the smart one. April has calmed slightly, but she's not very forthcoming. She's eaten and was sleeping when we left."

"From the drugs Madame Saldano gave her."

"She told you?"

"Jacques."

"Aah. We didn't think she'd eat so quickly, but they did more drinking than eating at Venizi's party. And being human, she can't go long before hunger sets in."

"She didn't fight drunk." I rubbed my upper leg where she'd clipped me with one of her kicks.

"It was her survival instinct after being ambushed. Anyway, with Ginger going to Oasis and with the lockdown still in effect, I thought you might want to go with her. You can take your mom and April. It would give everyone time to get to know each other. There's plenty of space to relax and provide some much-needed family time. Lucas could also use your help with security, but the rest of the time is your own."

I twisted around on his lap so I could look at him. "Is it safe for April to travel and be on her own?"

"Not at first. She'll travel under a security detail and will be housed in the security office until Madame Saldano's potion has time to take effect."

"What does that mean?"

"It's not like mesmerizing, but she'll become more pliable and less aggressive. It's nothing permanent and will naturally work its way out of her system when she stops taking the potion. It won't change her anger toward you, but it will tone it down. She also won't have the energy to escape or fight, but she'll be able to listen to conversations and join in if she chooses. The healer at Oasis will monitor her and modify the dosage as required. It's not the answer, but it's a start."

I nodded. "How long will we be there?"

"Until Simone is ready to return. But we'll assess April's condition before making any plans for her and Willa."

I bit my lip. "I wanted to be here for Simone."

"I know. But you know how she'll be once she wakes. And if the injury has left any weakness—"

"Say no more. My presence, or anyone who's not a vamp, will make her work too hard."

"And spending time with your family will take your mind off

her." He pushed a lock of hair behind my ear, then caressed my cheek. "It's not like we won't talk a couple of times a day."

"Only a couple?" I ran a finger along his stubbled jawline. Then I kissed him. It was filled with a hungry passion, and he met it with his own before slowly lifting his head.

"I know the timing interferes with our own discussion."

"It will wait." I sighed and laid my head on his shoulder. "I'll miss you."

<h1 style="text-align:center">Chapter Thirty-Four</h1>

THE SUV MOTORCADE pulled up to the coastal manor, and I jumped out, excited to be home. It's not that I didn't enjoy the two weeks at Oasis with my family and Ginger. My mother could put away more alcohol than I thought possible and added a secret ingredient to Ginger's margaritas that made us tipsy on too many nights.

The positive side of being drunk was that April relaxed more. She openly despised me, but once we were drinking, I'd catch her smiling at something funny I said. It was a start.

Lucas, doing his best to fill Simone's shoes, all but begged me to review the security upgrades and weekly rotation changes. I could have hugged him. A real project. It was exhausting between the project and socializing with the family, but I loved every minute of it.

The only downside was the calls to Devon. Each one was heart-warming. He made me laugh, and I missed him terribly. And I hated to admit that his suggestion to take some time away to think about the two of us and the cancellation of my debt had been a good one. I did think about it as I relished the time with my family and Ginger. We might be securing Oasis for an attack, but other than living among vamps and shifters, their world seemed planets away.

While I wanted nothing more than to see Devon, he wouldn't be at the manor. He was inspecting the city safe house and, on a recommendation from Levi, the safe house's security chief, had scheduled a meeting with the Lobos gang. Levi wanted to make sure the gang leader understood that their relationship with the vampires was for the security of the neighborhood and not approval of their business models. Devon wasn't expecting trouble, it was a simple meeting to show respect and maintain the alliance. He promised to be home in time for dinner.

"Hey, Mateo." I walked through the opened door and dropped my duffel on the floor. "Where is she?"

"In the training room. Would you like me to have your bag sent to your room?"

"I can grab it later." I stalked down the hall, knowing full well that while Mateo asked the question, my answer didn't matter. He'd have someone take it up.

I stopped in the kitchen to give Cook a hug and kiss on the cheek. He blushed as he always did before handing me a mug of coffee. It was like I never left. I sipped the coffee as I strolled toward the training room. I wasn't necessarily sneaking up on it, but I slowed, thankful the door was partially open.

The first thing I heard was a grunt and a garbled curse. I couldn't decipher the word, but the tone was clear enough. I leaned in, just enough to catch a glimpse. My feet were firmly planted so I could spring back if anyone glanced at the door.

Simone stood in her Wonder Woman stance as she stared at the climbing wall. She paced the length of it, never taking her eyes from it as she turned and stalked back to her starting point before repeating her steps.

Something was off. Her posture was the same, but she didn't have the fluid grace of a panther I'd come to expect. She stopped in the center of the wall and took five paces backward. She shifted a step to the left, realizing she hadn't backed up in a straight line.

That wasn't normal.

She took off without warning and leaped for the wall. Her hands grabbed solid holds, but she ran into trouble when she tried to place her feet. Her left foot caught the rock, but her right foot slipped, and try as she might, she couldn't get it to stick.

She attempted the climb anyway, which required an amazing amount of arm and hand strength to pull her body up without the support of her legs. Her left foot hit its mark, but her right leg missed again and threw her off balance.

Her fingers slipped, and she fell. Rather than land on her legs, which went out from under her, she landed on her back. Another grunt and a curse.

I stepped back. Devon had said her coordination wasn't back. He wasn't kidding. I gave some thought to the best way to play it and decided on the safer approach. Let her tell me—if she wanted to.

I backed up until I was twenty feet from the door and yelled, "Hey, Simone, are you in there?" I pushed through the door, took a swig of coffee, and grinned. "Did ya miss me?"

She rolled her eyes, something she'd never done before meeting me and Ginger. "Back so soon? We were hoping for another week."

"Good to see your sense of humor is still as lame as ever."

She gave me a once-over. "You're not training?"

"I trained with Ginger this morning."

She picked up a towel and a bottle of water, which she opened and drained half of.

"You done for the day?"

"Yes, you caught me at a good time. I'm headed for the hot tub."

"I'll follow."

Once she was in the tub, I pulled over a lounge chair and laid back. I sipped from my mug, waiting to see if I would have to start the conversation. She surprised me.

"How's your mother and April?"

"Mom seems back to her old self, but I don't think she's sleeping well."

"She's been through a trauma. It won't last long. Is she still seeing a healer?"

"Yes. The one at Oasis is more personable than Madame Saldano."

"Who isn't?"

I laughed because my first thought was of Simone.

"April is another story." I took a long sip of the coffee, ignoring Simone's gaze but knowing her truth meter was fully engaged. "I think she's better, or at least communicative. She hates my guts but is pleasant with everyone else. She occasionally asks about Jasper. I think she really had feelings for him. Or maybe it's remnants of the mesmerizing."

"Until she's brought out of that control, assuming she can be, you'll never know for sure. Neither will she." Simone shrugged. "Perhaps that's alright. If she considers it a lost love, that might be easier than the truth."

"I hadn't thought of it that way. Maybe so."

"So, why are you back? I'm not scheduled to return to Oasis for another week. Devon insists I wait for Madame Saldano to release me."

"Maybe that's for the best." When she lifted her brow, I continued, "Devon tried to rush past his mental fugue, ignoring Madame Saldano's assessment that it would go away once his brain was fully healed. She seems to know something about head injuries, and she did bring me out of my psychic coma."

Simone eyed me for a long moment before turning away.

I bit my lower lip, unsure if I should take the next step since

Simone seemed fine with ignoring her injury. "I was thinking of starting Tai chi again with a build-up to kung fu. I could use a partner since Ginger isn't here."

"I knew it."

"What?" There hadn't been an easy way to broach it, so I should have known I wouldn't have slipped anything by her. But I decided to play dumb for as long as I could.

"Devon told you about my coordination issues. Do you think I didn't hear you sneak up to look in on me? An elephant would have been more quiet."

I bristled. Yeah, I suspected she might have heard me. But I was quieter than an elephant. I went with retaliation.

"I was planning on bursting in and forcing you to run laps for every fall you took. If I remember right, that was your solution when I had difficulties with the wall."

"Then why didn't you?"

I refused to look away and held her stare. "Because I know how difficult it was for Devon to admit to the fugue. And I know how I'd feel if I was in your shoes with no control over my body."

We stared at each other for a full minute before she turned away.

"I don't think I can do Tai chi. My left leg is better, but my right leg..." She moved her hand back and forth over the water, creating a ripple and not finishing the sentence.

"That's the reason for Tai chi. It will be difficult at first. So what if it takes time to get past the first couple of forms. The point isn't quantity but the quality of each movement."

"I don't know who's worst—you or Sergi."

"Oh, it's Sergi. It's always Sergi."

Simone rolled her head back and laughed out loud. "If you tell anyone I said it, I'll deny it, but it's good to have you back."

~

I LEFT Simone in the hot tub and stepped into my bedroom, stopping at the threshold to take a deep breath of the floral arrangement on the dresser. Roses with a variety of annuals. Greta's little welcome. It was so good to be home. As expected, my duffel was next to the dresser. I ignored it and began stripping as I shuffled to the bed.

I kicked off my shoes and slid my pants off. In tank top and panties, I crawled across the bed to the pillow and crashed. I missed this bed. At Oasis, Lucas had my old room prepared, but when I spoke to Devon that evening, he insisted I stay in his room. At first, I balked, but after the first night, with his scent lingering in the room, I wouldn't stay anywhere else. And each night, I stared down at the garden where so many of our shared dreams took place.

I smelled him now. A scent that reminded me of fall nights in front of a fire—cinnamon and cloves. It was so strong I could almost reach out and touch him.

"Cressa."

"Mmm." I snuggled into the bed and reached out but couldn't find the covers. Then my hand hit something solid.

"Wake up, sleepy head." A warm breath tickled over my skin.

I grinned. "I'm cold."

A soft chuckle. "You're a tease." The weight of his body slid over me, and it felt good. Safe. Protected. Wanted.

I turned my head, and though I couldn't see the windows, the shadows told me it was late afternoon. "What are you doing home early? I thought it would be later."

"Were you maybe expecting someone else?" He barely hid his humor.

"I just needed a warm blanket."

"So that's all I am now?" His hands slid down my sides, forcing me to curl up with giggles. My one funny spot wasn't the bottom of my feet. It ran along my sides from pits to hips. When in the heat of passion, his slow, deep caresses elicited sensual shivers.

When we were hanging out in bed, and he traced his fingertips over the same area, it drove me wild with giggles.

He turned me over and then his lips were on mine. Sweet Jesus, what a homecoming. I drank him in like fine brandy. It seemed much longer than two weeks. Before I knew what was happening, he pulled back and rolled off me, coming to stand next to the bed. Goosebumps immediately erupted at the loss of his warmth.

"Hey. That was fast." I sat up.

"I don't want to be late for your surprise."

I rubbed my eyes and watched him go through my dresser. He pulled out sweats and a sweatshirt, tossing each one as he found them.

"Come on, get dressed."

"Really?"

"Yes. Hurry."

I picked up the sweats and pulled them on, a bit wobbly on my feet. I'd been in a deep sleep when he woke me, but his strange excitement made me smile, and after two attempts to get the sweatshirt over my head, I tugged it into place.

He handed me my big furry socks, the ones I use during the coldest part of winter.

"I need shoes."

He looked me over. "You're fine as you are."

I gave him a long perusal, noticing for the first time he wore sweats, too. How did I not notice that? Oh yeah. He'd covered me with his warm body, and nothing else mattered.

He grabbed my hand and pulled me out the door, raced down the stairs, then through the halls until he reached the stairs that led to the widow's walk. Our special place. But what was the rush? Maybe he had something to tell me and didn't want prying ears. A difficult feat with a house full of vamps.

When he flung the door open to the outer walk, my breath caught.

It was sunset. The sky was filled with a kaleidoscope of oranges, pinks, and yellows. Sparse blue-gray clouds hung in the sky in anticipation of the setting sun, which was only minutes away.

"Wow."

"Quick. There's still time."

My eyes were on the sky as he tugged me forward, and then I was falling. My heart dropped to my belly until I made a soft landing. I looked around as Devon laughed. Then I glanced down. We were lying on a down sleeping bag. Make that two down sleeping bags, both fully opened. One acted as a bottom sheet and the other the cover. I pushed on them as I struggled to sit. There was an air mattress beneath them.

"What is this?"

He tugged me higher on the mattress to where six huge pillows had been stacked. He leaned against them and pulled me into his arms. I snuggled into him as we watched the best view anyone could have from bed.

"How long have you been planning this?" I asked, somewhat wistful as the sun sunk below the horizon.

"Since the day you left for Oasis."

I found his hand and squeezed, bringing it up to place feather-light kisses across his knuckles. "You are such a planner."

"You know me well. How's your mother and April?"

I gave him the same information I'd given Simone, then asked, "Were you the one responsible for suggesting the bread and breakfast in Colorado?"

Remus had called after the first week we'd been at Oasis, asking if Decker could meet with my mother and me to discuss the next step in April's recovery. He offered up a six-month getaway for Mom and April at a posh but private B&B in a tiny resort community run by a couple of shifters. It wasn't a widely known resort area, but it was located in a shifter stronghold and catered to the wealthy with lots of shopping, recreation, and places to work.

There were two healers in town, and the shifters sent their troubled souls to the B&B for rest and repair, as they called it.

"I might have mentioned something to Remus. What did your mother think?"

"At first, she wasn't sure, but April loved the idea. She still asks about Jasper, but she seems to understand what happened to her. I think she wants to get better—to know what's real and what isn't. They're willing to give it a try."

"They'll be safe there."

"What happened with Jasper and the other vampire?"

"Kirk is being sent to a House back east where he can start over. It's a small House with ties to House Beall. He seemed happy with the assignment, and one of the security detail he's grown close to will be going with him. He'll be watched for the first year to ensure he doesn't stray." He sighed. "Jasper is a different issue. Maybe we should have killed him rather than save him, but he wavers in his responses. There are days when he screams that Venizi will come for him. Other days, he's open to listening to Rafael and Roberta discuss the future of the vampire race. He's conflicted. So, he'll remain where he is for now. We moved him to a secure room that provides more creature comforts. Rafael brings him books to read, some written by vampire philosophers, and Lucas set him up with a gaming station."

"Wait, vampires have philosophers?"

Devon shook his head. "Hard as that might be to believe, yes."

I grinned. "Sorry. It just seemed an odd statement."

His grin was wicked. "Sergi reads quite a few vampire philosophers. You should discuss it with him."

"That's just mean."

He pulled me to him. "The two of you are too much alike."

"That's enough of that." I tried to get out of his grip, but he played dirty, tickling me until I screamed, "Uncle." It didn't help that he had no idea what that meant and only stopped when I laughingly told him I couldn't breathe anymore.

We finished watching the sunset, both of us satisfied to be in each other's arms. Then he leaned over and kissed me. It was heated and it was like we never left my bed. I pulled him closer and reveled in his passion. His lips traveled down my neck, his fangs grazing a path across my collarbone, and suddenly I was too hot.

He must have guessed it because he pulled back and ripped off his sweatshirt and then mine. We pushed our sweatpants off and removed everything else until the soft, cool ocean breeze caressed our naked bodies.

When he kissed my breasts and nipped at my nipples, I arched into him while he continued his journey south until he was between my legs. I gripped his hair as his tongue worked me into a frenzy. Two weeks had seemed like forever without him, and it didn't take long for him to rip a scream out of me that was whisked away with the ocean breeze.

Then he rolled over, yanking me with him until I straddled him. He was ready for me, and I wasted no time settling myself over him. Once I was fully seated, his whole body relaxed beneath me.

Neither of us had to say a word to know we'd come home. Though I'd known it deep down, this was the reason Devon wanted me to take time away. So we'd both experience what life would be like without the other. It was something neither of us wanted.

He had to know that.

And I did everything I could to make him see how much I understood as I gently rocked until he gripped my hips to move me faster as he settled deeper within me. My head fell back as I released all my thoughts, choosing to live in the moment as the orange-hued sky turned to dusk and the first stars appeared.

The rocking moved faster as one hand moved to pinch my nipple while his other hand squeezed my hip harder. I barely noticed as shivers ran through me. The intense pleasure of our joining built until I couldn't hold back. Didn't want to hold it back as ripples of delight rolled through me.

Another scream tore out of me, but I didn't stop. When his body tensed, I kept the pace of our rhythm. The icy blue glow of his gaze heightened my pleasure before a scream that turned into a howl ripped out of him. I instinctively knew that it was more than Devon who was with us. That howl had come from his beast, and it was also satisfied.

We were one.

I collapsed on his chest, and he held me tight, kissing my temple. We lay still with nothing more than heavy breathing between us. He caressed my hair as I slowly ran my hands up and down the muscled angles of his chest, loving the feel of his skin under my fingertips.

After several moments, when our thumping hearts had calmed to matching steady beats, I breathed out a long sigh. It was time to put our own personal house in order.

"I wasn't prepared for when you released me from my debt." His body tensed a fraction. "Maybe because I was still half asleep when you told me, or maybe it was the way you rushed from the room." I chuckled. "It took me a while to understand that you wanted me to make my own choice without the strings. You were right. The two weeks at Oasis with my family were exactly what I needed. It gave me time to step back and analyze my life with a clear perspective. What I hoped for my future.

"I walked into this manor on that first day with only one expectation—work off my debt. I can't determine the point where I forgot about my debt. I was drawn deeper into your world, to you, and some might say it was just a different type of manipulation. But you didn't just open a new world to me. You helped me discover my own truth. I found my history. You gave me back my human family while allowing me to explore who I am as a dreamwalker.

"I could walk away, find a home with the dreamwalkers, and

stand by Colantha and Hamilton's side. But that's not what you're fighting for, and it's not who I want to be. Your fight isn't to stand with your species, but with all the species who have a common goal."

I rolled off him and sat up. He did the same until we sat cross-legged, our knees touching. I placed a hand on his cheek. "I love you, Devon Trelane. This war isn't just yours. It belongs to the shifters and the dreamwalkers. It's about balance and how we survive in a world run by humans. I choose to walk beside you for only one reason. I love you. This is where I belong. It's always been where I belonged."

He kissed me. Light and sweet, but he couldn't hide his growing passion, the heat beneath the kiss.

"I love you, Cressa Langtry. I've told you that a number of times, but I can't seem to remember if I said it in a construct or in the real world. But it doesn't matter. The truth follows us in our dreams. I've had time to do some soul-searching of my own, and I've come to a single conclusive fact."

Did I want to hear it? By the icy blue glow of the beast, I absolutely wanted to hear it.

"Whatever comes in this war and after, my place is at your side. You might be consort to the leader of House Trelane, but I have an equal role in being yours. We are one."

We fell back on our bed and stared at the night sky. The stars were quickly taking over, but the moon had yet to rise.

"Now what?" I asked.

"We sleep and make love under the stars. This is a new dawning for us. We're at the brink of war, and we grow stronger every day."

Before I could ask about his plans, my stomach issued a low growl.

Devon chuckled. "Luckily for you, I'm a forward-thinking vampire who ensured we had a cooler with food and drink."

I sat up and glanced around. Sure enough. A lantern sat on the table with a thermos and a bottle of wine. A cooler sat next to the table filled with who knew what magical wonders from Cook.

I leaned over and kissed Devon. I ran my fingers over his lips, his stubbled chin, and down his neck. "Food is good, but it can wait. I'm hungry for something else."

He cupped my face, his eyes sparkling with love, and behind it, his beast glowed for me. His fangs dropped. "I have a few ideas."

Thank You For Reading!

BUT DON'T GO! Keep reading for more of House Trelane.

Sergi
Of Blood and Dreams - Book Seven

A FAILED MISSION. A vampire on his own—until the beast comes out.

SERGI, cadre of House Trelane, takes on a dangerous mission to locate the secret lab of Lorenzo Venizi where it's believed Magic Poppy is being created. Everything the Vampire Council had hoped to keep hidden is slowly being unraveled, but Trelane needs proof.

When the mission goes wrong, Sergi must hold on in hopes a rescue can be mounted. But will it be in time? The lab is running horrific experiments, and Sergi is a prime candidate.

Shifter 473 was captured months ago and through sheer will and plenty of luck, she has somehow survived the dark and unimaginable horrors of shifter experimentations. But how long before they come for her? When she discovers a vampire being held prisoner, she has one decision to make. Is he the salvation the shifters need to break free of their captors or will he be their damnation?

AND NOW A GLIMPSE...

Sergi

DROPS of tepid water slapped against hard stone, the sound echoing through the dark, dank tunnels. The wider tunnels led to a maze of narrower ones, lined with lanterns that dimly reflected the aged wooden doors, barely bright enough to ward off the lurking shadows. Behind the doors, small barren rooms carved from granite like the tunnels themselves were mostly empty.

Except for one.

In one cell, third from the end of this particular passage, the latent sound of dripping water slowly pierced the peacefulness of sleep and woke the beast. It took a moment for its eyes to adjust to the darkness. It was weak. Hungry. Thirsty. The tremors clutched its gut and sparked every nerve ending. The bone-chilling air was the only comfort as it numbed most of the excruciating pain.

But nothing tortured it more than its hunger. Its ravenous need to feed.

Sometime later, he lifted his chin from his chest and glanced through the dim light, confirming he was still alone. And he was grateful.

He let his head drop back down. A four-inch steel band, bolted to the wall on either side, stretched across his chest and was the only thing preventing him from falling to the ground. His arms were spread wide, held in place by his manacled wrists that were strapped to the wall by more steel.

Even the beast wished for the hard surface to lay on.

He wasn't sure if he'd fallen asleep again, but his eyes popped open at the clatter of the lock on the door being released. His body tensed, preparing for the next round of torture—or worse—the tainted blood.

The door scraped along the stone floor as it was pushed open. The torchlight from the hallway cast a long shadow of the lone figure. It scurried in, quick as a rat, and closed the door.

The beast howled.

~

THREE WEEKS earlier

I UNROLLED from my fetal position and slowly stretched my aching muscles, stiff from the cold air. Eleven months, and the chill still bothered me. Though not nearly as much as the hard surface of the stone floor, barely tolerable beneath the thin, lumpy pad.

I pushed back my unwashed hair, still expecting to feel the long, dark strands that had been sheared off when I'd first arrived. It had grown to frame my face, but even this short, it was dull and tangled. At some point, they'd chop it off again.

Accustomed to the darkness, I made my way to the bucket in the corner, lifting my knees in a highly exaggerated manner, a macabre march to start the blood flowing, grimacing as the pins and needles sensation worked its way through me. After relieving myself, I continued with my morning ritual, shuffling to a different corner to run my fingers over the scratched markings on the rock wall. I bent and picked up the small stone tucked away in an easy-to-find spot and spent several minutes scratching another mark. I ran my fingers over them as I counted and breathed a sigh, pushing back the tears I thought I'd spent months ago.

Day twenty. Bath day.

Thank god. I didn't think I could take another day of my own stink.

After running through my exercises, I ran a filthy finger over my teeth. It was the only way to remove the film from the evening until the daily ration of water arrived with the porridge. If I was lucky, they'd include a hardboiled egg.

Even better if they assigned me to a work detail. I hadn't been given one since my last bath day. Not after I stuck Tallon, my guard, in the neck with a fork. He didn't die—unfortunately. But he was the floor leader, and no one questioned his right to take whatever female he wanted.

Until I said no.

I'd take the twenty days locked alone in my cell to rape any day. The fear had dissipated months ago, but I wouldn't give up my hope or my humanity. Not yet.

The dull whack of the billy club on wooden doors brought me around to face mine, placing myself in the middle of the room, ready to defend myself. Or grab the tray the guard slipped through the slit in the bottom of the door.

The next few moments were a fifty-fifty chance of going either way.

When the bolt securing the door slid to the side, I braced myself. They didn't come to take me for my bath until midday. Maybe I was being assigned to a work detail.

I squinted against the glare of the light as the door burst open. When the shifter came at me, I moved as quickly as I could, but there was nowhere to run in my ten-by-ten cell. It was more my well-honed instinct not to make it easy on anyone meant to harm me.

It was useless to fight, and most of the time, I played the game and appeared weak—but not with this guard. Tallon quickly caught me and slammed me against the hard stone wall. His hand gripped my neck, holding me in place, and I tugged at his fingers as he slowly choked me, my feet dangling an inch from the floor.

His breath stank as he slowly sniffed me, his body leaning into mine. "I should throw you on your mat and take what I want. I should have done it months ago. But the Master has forbidden it. Even after you stuck me in the neck." He squeezed my breast before running his hand between my legs.

"They think they know you. That you've tamed down to a willing slave. That you only acted out because I wanted a taste of you." His lips hovered over mine, then he continued his sniffing like the good hound he was. He whispered in my ear, "But I know better. They'll have problems with you. Remember one thing, girl. The Master might have a say during the day, but he's not here during the long, cold evenings. There are ways to hurt you that will never leave a mark."

He let go. I dropped to the floor and clutched my aching throat, grateful for the chilled air I slowly sucked in as it numbed the pain.

"The Master has an assignment for you." He chuckled. "And I can't think of anyone better for the job. Now get up. You're to eat your breakfast in the common room today."

I scurried to my feet, unwilling to give him any excuse to hit me. Not that he needed one, but I wouldn't lose the opportunity to get out of my cell, even for a day.

I didn't like the sound of this new assignment, but if it kept me away from this bastard, it was enough. How simple life became when you only had one thing to worry about.

Survival.

~

TALLON LEFT me with the women attendants who stripped the ragged shift from me before they pushed me into a wooden tub of cold water. I shivered as they soaped and scrubbed me with harsh brushes until my skin turned red. At least they washed my hair.

A clean shift made of rough fabric wasn't new. It would have been scoured and bleached many times over. Old stains marred the brown fabric, giving it a mottled appearance. I gave up wondering where the stains came from long ago. Just like I'd stopped wondering if anyone would come for me, or whether they thought me dead.

The first few weeks after my capture, I'd pace my cell over and over again, fighting the claustrophobia and fear that I would never leave this hell hole. Not until I was dead. One year. Five. Longer.

Would I be the same person or forever changed? Would the self-preservation blanket I wrapped myself in morph from the terror of living in this place to fear of everything outside these barren walls? Was it possible I might escape, only to live alone, afraid of my own shadow?

I smiled as the attendants handed me the worn rubber-soled slippers. The icy air forced goosebumps to rise over my skin, and I shivered, almost laughing as they sneered at me as if I were a raging beast.

My thoughts wandered to my uncle and his words of comfort so freely given. He would stare down at me with his deep brown gaze, searching into the depths of my soul before leaning in until our foreheads touched. "You are wolf. Let no one take that away from you. She will protect you."

So, every morning when I woke, I spoke to my wolf. It was against the rules to shift, punishable in ways I didn't want to know. I'd heard enough as the screams echoed through the tunnels.

But sometimes, on nights when my uncle's words couldn't comfort me, I let the wolf come out. If nothing else, I slept warmly, until I heard the first slam of a wooden billy club hit the door at the end of the hall, and I shifted back.

"Come on, girl." Tallon stuck his head through the open doorway. "You're late if you want any breakfast."

I trailed behind him as we traversed the passageways that were no longer made of rock but of drywall and painted a stark white. My slippers shuffled over pristine tile floors rather than rough stone. Cool filtered air streamed through vents and smelled of disinfectant rather than unwashed bodies, feces, and blood.

The cafeteria, where some of the prisoners were allowed to eat, was the dividing point between the cells and the labs. A thick wall of impenetrable frosted glass separated the paid lab staff from the rest of us. It wouldn't be proper to force the privileged to look upon the slaves while they ate.

It was bad enough they might have to look upon those who were deemed safe enough to work in the labs. Not that we'd ever be entrusted with anything important, but someone had to clean the rooms or, and the thought made me shiver, become a subject for the scientists' experiments.

Breakfast was a thick porridge, what I would usually get in my cell, in addition to scrambled eggs and a few slices of banana. I savored the coffee, which was surprisingly strong, and it warmed my bones.

I ate quietly at a table with six other prisoners. Talking amongst ourselves wasn't permitted. The only sound was the scraping of spoons as we finished our meal.

"Shifter 473." The woman's voice was monotone as she studied a tablet. After a moment, when no one responded, she lifted her head. "Shifter 473." This time her words were spoken slowly and loudly as she gazed around the room, her eyes stern and her jaw clenched.

We didn't have names—just numbers. And it took a moment to realize she was calling out the one I'd been assigned. It had been some time since I'd heard anyone use it. I was usually called girl, or dog, or some other unpleasant curse.

I raised my hand, and two male attendants grabbed my arms

and pulled me from the table. I didn't struggle as they led me to the door where the woman stood. She looked me over, her face a mask of indifference, then nodded.

"She'll do."

I didn't like the sound of that, and when I was led down a corridor with more white tile flooring, white walls, and white ceiling tiles, I wanted to squirm. Was I someone's next experiment?

The attendants released my arms but stayed two steps behind me as I followed the woman, panic seizing my throat with the more rooms we passed until we came to a set of double doors. The woman waved her badge over a pad, and the doors slid open.

I took a step back when I saw the carnage inside, a hand flying to my mouth in a reflexive movement to keep my breakfast from returning. The attendants pushed me forward.

Blood was everywhere, mixed with lumps. A quick glance was all that was needed to know it was bits of flesh, some with short strands of hair still clinging to it.

The gore was on the floor, on the walls, and dripped from the ceiling. It had splashed over the stainless steel tables and counters. The scent was easy to recognize. Shifter flesh. The heat of the lamps and overhead lighting warmed the blood and intensified the stench.

Humans wouldn't smell the decaying flesh as intensely as a vampire or shifter, but it would still activate the gag reflexes, as was evidenced by the woman who began breathing through her mouth.

"We need this lab spotless by tomorrow. Shifter 272 will show you where the cleaning supplies are stored. You'll be returned to your cell once the lab is ready for the next experiment." She glanced at her tablet then nodded at the attendants, who stepped back.

If I weren't so sick at the sight of the lab, I would have smiled at how pale the attendants had become.

"272, come here." The woman tapped the tablet against her leg.

A sound of scraping came from a far corner, and an older male shifter lifted his head and glanced around. Seeing the woman, he nodded and moved out from around a counter. He wasn't very tall and was as thin as the rest of us. He walked with an exaggerated limp, but if it caused him any pain, he didn't show it. So, an old wound.

"Yes, mistress." His tone was submissive as he bowed his head. A good little shifter slave greeting his master.

"This is 473. She'll be assisting you today." The woman gave me a side glance, and I lowered my head. "If she works to your satisfaction, I'll consider her for your assistant. We've been ordered to increase the experiments."

I gave the woman a quick peek. Did she notice the twitch in his shoulders, the tension now riding along his back? I didn't think so, but, as a shifter, it was possible I was the only one who would notice. For the moment, I would hold my judgment on 272 until I spent time with him. But I would have to tread carefully.

While most of the imprisoned shifters would fight if given half the chance, some had been enslaved for too long and would defend their masters—human or vampire.

272 took a moment to look me over with a detached glance. "Yes, mistress."

"I know she doesn't look like much, but according to her chart, she listens and does what is asked of her. We'll see if she can appropriately handle the benefit of working outside the cells."

"Yes, mistress." He continued to nod like a bobblehead.

"I'll send someone to check your progress in two hours."

The doors slid shut and the lock engaged.

272 turned to me, his blank expression never changing, but I saw a spark of interest in his gaze before he dropped his head. "Follow me."

Thank You For Reading

Sergi
Of Blood and Dreams - Book 7
Coming March 2025

Make sure you never miss a new release!

Join my FB Readers Group - Kim Allred's Heart Racing Romance

Join my newsletter...I'm pretty much unobtrusive.

Follow me at Amazon, Goodreads, or Bookbub

If you can't wait and want to check out my other series, visit my website.

As a special treat, if you haven't already taken advantage of this FREE prequel to the Of Blood and Dreams series, this is the time.

This novella is set one hundred years before the start of the series.

THE CATALYST. The victim. The bridge.

THE ROARING TWENTIES. The time of flappers and Prohibition.

For Lyra, a young vampire and aspiring painter, the world is her canvas.

When she meets Hamilton, a sculptor and her family's gardener, time stops. He understands her like no one else.

But he's a human. And he's not the only one drawn to her. An ancient and powerful vampire has declared his desire to seduce her.

A perfect storm that sets the stage for all that is to come.

Download your copy of Lyra today.

Kim Allred lives in an old timber town in the Pacific Northwest where she raises alpacas, llamas and an undetermined number of free-range chickens. Just like most of her characters, she loves sharing stories while sipping a glass of fine wine or slurping a strong cup of brew.

Her spirit of adventure has taken her on many journeys including a ten-day dogsledding trip in northern Alaska and sleeping under the stars on the savannas of eastern Africa.

Kim is currently working on **The Swan Syndicate**, a follow-on series in the world of **Mórdha Stone Chronicles** and the next books in her paranormal romance series — **Of Blood and Dreams**. Her new time travel series, **Time Renegades**, is on the horizon.